F

Praise for Valerie Hansen

"Consistently excellent characters. Kudos to Valerie Hansen for writing an exceptional story with a puzzle that's nearly impossible to solve."
—*RT Book Reviews* on *Hidden in the Wall*

"*Wilderness Courtship* is a sweet story, with just the right amount of intrigue and mystery to keep readers turning the pages."
—*RT Book Reviews*

"A quick, evenly paced book that gets even better as tension builds…. A delightful story."
—*RT Book Reviews* on *A Treasure of the Heart*

Praise for Janet Dean

"A delightful and entertaining read about forgiveness and the restoration of faith."
—*RT Book Reviews* on
The Bounty Hunter's Redemption

"A wonderfully sweet love story."
—*RT Book Reviews* on *Courting Miss Adelaide*, 4.5 stars

"Dean writes from her heart, and her characters are deep and touching. A tender love story."
—*RT Book Reviews* on *Courting the Doctor's Daughter*

Valerie Hansen
and
Janet Dean

Wilderness Courtship
&
Courting Miss Adelaide

HARLEQUIN® LOVE INSPIRED®CLASSICS

LOVE INSPIRED BOOKS

Recycling programs for this product may not exist in your area.

ISBN-13: 978-1-335-00758-2

Wilderness Courtship & Courting Miss Adelaide

Copyright © 2018 by Harlequin Books S.A.

The publisher acknowledges the copyright holders of the individual works as follows:

Wilderness Courtship
Copyright © 2008 by Valerie Whisenand

Courting Miss Adelaide
Copyright © 2008 by Janet Dean

CONTENTS

Valerie Hansen was thirty when she awoke to the presence of the Lord in her life and turned to Jesus. She now lives in a renovated farmhouse in the breathtakingly beautiful Ozark Mountains of Arkansas and is privileged to share her personal faith by telling the stories of her heart for Love Inspired. Life doesn't get much better than that!

Books by Valerie Hansen

Love Inspired Suspense

Military K-9 Unit

Bound by Duty

Classified K-9 Unit

Special Agent

Rookie K-9 Unit

Search and Rescue
Rookie K-9 Unit Christmas
"Surviving Christmas"

The Defenders

Nightwatch
Threat of Darkness
Standing Guard
A Trace of Memory
Small Town Justice
Dangerous Legacy

WILDERNESS COURTSHIP

Valerie Hansen

Assuredly, I say to you, inasmuch as you did it to one of the least of these my brethren, you did it to me.
—*Matthew* 25:40

To all the parents who continue struggling
to do the best they can, and to those extraordinary
individuals who take in other people's children
and make them their own. It is truly a gift.

Prologue

New York, 1853

The wooden deck of the three-masted freighter *Gray Feather* rose and fell, rocked by the building swells. Thorne Blackwell knew a storm was imminent, he could smell its approach in the salty air, hear the anxiety in the calls of the soaring gulls and feel the changing weather in his bones. Pacing nervously, he awaited the arrival of his half brother, Aaron, and Aaron's family. Once they were safely aboard he'd relax. At least he hoped he would.

It had been over two years since Thorne had heard from Aaron, or any of the other Ashtons for that matter, and he wasn't quite sure what to expect. Would Aaron have contacted him if he hadn't been desperate? It was doubtful. Then again, Aaron had good reason for whatever misgivings he still harbored.

Thorne braced his feet apart on the pitching deck, pushed his hat down more tightly over his shoulder-length dark hair and drew up the collar of his woolen frock coat against the impending gale. Of all the nights for anyone to decide he needed immediate passage to San Francisco, this had to be the worst. Then again, Aaron's note had contained such evident panic, perhaps the risk was warranted. Thorne hoped so, since Naomi and the child would also be boarding.

Lying at anchor in the crowded New York harbor, the *Gray Feather* was fully loaded and awaiting final orders to embark on her third voyage around the horn. They'd hoist sail at dawn and be on their way, providing the storm didn't thwart their plans. Thorne had fought nature before. But for the grace of a benevolent God, he would have been a resident of Davy Jones's locker instead of the owner of the finest full-modeled vessel ever built in Eastport.

Why God had chosen to spare him from drowning at sea when so many of his comrades had lost their lives he didn't know. The only thing of which he was certain was his current role as his only sibling's protector.

Peering into the fog he spied a bobbing lantern in the prow of a small boat off the starboard. Shouting orders, he assembled members of the crew and affected a safe, though treacherous, boarding.

Aaron handed the sleepy two-year-old he was carrying to his wife, then shook Thorne's hand with vigor and obvious relief. "Thank you. I was afraid you might not want to help us. Not after the way we last parted."

Touched, Thorne hid his emotion behind a brusque facade. "Nonsense. Let's get you all inside before the rain begins in earnest. Then you can tell me everything."

He winced as his brother placed a protective arm around Naomi's shoulders. Her head was bowed over the blanket-wrapped child in her arms, her face hidden by the brim of her burgundy velvet bonnet, yet Thorne could see her golden hair as clearly as if they were once again walking hand in hand through a meadow and dreaming of an idyllic life together.

He set his jaw. Whatever else happened on this voyage, he was not going to resurrect a love better left dead. He and Naomi had had their chance at happiness, or so Thorne had thought, and she had chosen to wed Aaron, instead. That was all there was to it and all there ever would be. He had long ago concluded that romantic love was highly overrated and nothing had happened since to change his mind.

Guiding his guests into the captain's cabin he explained, "I've arranged for you to occupy these quarters until we can prepare a suitable suite elsewhere. It's not the quality you're used to, of course, but it's the best I could do on such short notice."

"It's fine," Aaron was quick to say as he ducked to guide his wife to a chair beneath a swaying lantern suspended from a beam. "I don't know how to thank you."

"All I ask is an explanation," Thorne replied. He leaned against the inside of the cabin's narrow door and crossed his arms. "What has happened to make you so insistent on leaving New York?"

Aaron's gaze darted to his wife, then rested lovingly on the small boy asleep in her lap. "It's mostly because of Jacob," he said sadly. "Father has grown more and more irrational as the years have passed. We think he may be going insane, although no doctors will agree to it and chance losing the exorbitant retainers he pays them. He's turned against us just the way he turned against you."

Thorne gave a deep-throated laugh. "I doubt that

very much. At least he doesn't keep reminding you you're not really his son—or refuse to allow you to call yourself an Ashton."

"He may as well do so," his brother said. "He's made up his mind that my family is evil and has ordered me to divorce my wife and abandon my child."

"What?" Thorne's dark eyes narrowed. Unfolding his crossed arms, he removed his hat and raked his fingers through his thick, almost-black hair. "Why would he do that?"

"It's evident that his mind is unhinged. Some of the threats he's made lately are dire, indeed. There is no way I would consent to remain under his roof one more day, let alone subject my family to his lunatic ravings."

"I can understand that," Thorne said. "But why leave the city?"

"Because," Aaron said with a shaky voice, "if I won't agree to a divorce he has threatened to free me by having Naomi and my son killed."

Chapter One

San Francisco, 1854

Charity Beal stood on the board walkway outside the hotel, pulled a paisley shawl around her shoulders and raised her face to bask in the sun's warming rays. A mild breeze off the ocean ruffled wisps of pale blond curls that had escaped her neatly upswept hair and her blue eyes sparkled in the brightness of the day.

Smiling, she did her best to ignore the noise of the passing horses and wagons as she sighed and breathed deeply, enjoying the sweet, salt air. Thankfully, a recent shower had washed away most of the dust and dirt, yet hadn't left the streets too muddy for normal travel.

Spring days in the city by the bay were more often foggy than clear and Charity was loath to retreat back inside even though it was now her duty to assist Mrs. Montgomery in the kitchen. Perhaps stealing a few more precious moments of sunshine would be all right, she told herself, appreciating the balmy weather yet cognizant of her place as part of the hotel staff.

The Montgomery House Hotel had been rebuilt of

brick after its damage in the earthquakes and fires of 1850 and 1851, as had many of the other commercial buildings, including the Jenny Lind Theater. Few of the thousands of immigrants who crowded the city could afford to board at Montgomery House but those folks who did were usually well satisfied, especially since the rooms now contained real beds with feather ticking instead of the narrow, hanging cots of the previous structure.

Charity and her father, Emory Beal, had begun as tenants and had quickly decided to stay on. At least Emory had. As far as Charity was concerned she knew she could be happy anywhere as long as she remained a widow.

Remembrances of her cruel husband made her shiver in spite of the warmth of the day, and she drew her shawl more tightly against the inner chill. She knew it must be a terrible sin to celebrate anyone's death but she couldn't help being grateful that the Lord had seen fit to liberate her from her degrading marriage to Ramsey Tucker. Just the thought of that vile man touching her again made gall rise in her throat.

Shaking off the unpleasant memories and turning to reenter the hotel, Charity noticed a small group of people trudging up the hill from the direction of the wharf. Travelers of that class weren't often seen, yet it was the imposing gentleman in the lead who immediately caught and held her attention.

He reminded her of someone going to the gallows—or perhaps the hangman, himself—such was his aura. A short, black cape furled from the shoulders of his coat as he walked and he carried a silver-tipped cane. His Eastern-style felt hat had a narrow enough brim that she could easily discern his scowl and square jaw.

Trailing him were a man and woman holding the hands of a small child who struggled to keep up while walking between them. Their clothing was elegant and obviously expensively tailored but their countenance was as downtrodden as that of the poorest immigrant.

Charity hurriedly ducked through the doorway and had almost reached the visiting parlor when a deep, male voice behind her commanded, "Wait."

She whirled to face the dark-haired traveler she'd been surreptitiously studying. "Yes?"

Instead of approaching the desk where a young clerk awaited, the stranger removed his hat, bowed slightly and addressed her. "We require rooms. Can you vouch for the character of this establishment?"

She nodded. "Yes, sir. I certainly can."

"Have you stayed here often?"

"My father and I live here," she said. "If you choose to join us in the dining room for supper, you'll meet him. The evening meal is served at seven. Dinner is at one but as you can see—" she gestured toward the grandfather clock at the far end of the room "—you've missed it." She peered past him to smile at the weary child. "I can probably find a few cookies and a glass of cold milk if the little one is hungry."

"Jacob always enjoys a cookie," the pale, light-haired woman replied. "We would be obliged." She bent down to the boy's level and added, "Wouldn't we, son?"

He merely nodded, his eyes as wide and expressive as a frightened doe's.

Charity approached and offered the woman her hand. "I'm Miss Beal, please call me Charity. And you are…?"

"Naomi. This is my husband, Mr. Ashton." She shyly glanced toward the taller man who had proceeded to the clerk's station and was signing the register. "And that gentleman is his half brother, Mr. Thorne Blackwell."

Charity lowered her voice to ask, "Does he always order strangers around?"

Naomi's cheeks reddened. "A bit, I'm afraid. But his heart is in the right place. We've just come from a long sea voyage around the horn and we desperately need our rest."

"Then don't let me keep you," Charity said. "As soon as you're settled in your rooms, I'll bring young Master Jacob his cookies and milk."

She was taken aback when Naomi's husband clamped a hand on his wife's shoulder, shook his head and gave her a wordless look of warning.

Startled, Naomi immediately took Charity's hand and held it as if clasping a lifeline. "I spoke foolishly just now. Please, if anyone asks, you must swear you've not seen us. Promise me?"

"Of course, but…"

"I'll explain later."

"All right. I won't breathe a word."

The men hoisted their belongings and started up the stairs while Naomi balanced the child on her hip. Waiting until they were out of sight, Charity crossed to the desk clerk. "What names did that gentleman sign?"

The young man smirked as he spun the register book for her perusal. "Mr. Smith and Mr. Jones and family, if you choose to believe such tales."

"I see."

She checked their respective room numbers, then headed for the kitchen. So what if their new boarders were traveling incognito? That was often the case west of the Rockies. Here, a person could begin again without having to explain past sins. She should know. That was exactly what she'd been doing ever since her fateful journey from Ohio by wagon train with her sister, Faith.

Those had been the worst months of Charity's life, and although her loved ones had survived the ordeal, they all bore scars of some sort. Connell McClain, Faith's new husband, was scarred from encounters with the Cheyenne, and poor Faith had nursed broken ribs during the latter part of the arduous trek.

Charity's scars didn't manifest themselves physically. They were deeper, in her heart and soul, and the ache of her personal tribulation and loss remained so vivid the remembrances still gave her nightmares.

Nevertheless, she didn't want those memories to fade. She wanted to remember precisely how foolish she'd once been so that she would never, ever, be tempted to make the same mistakes again.

Thorne closed the door to his brother's room and stood with his back to it as he faced Naomi. "What did you say to that woman downstairs?" he demanded.

Tears softened her already pale blue eyes. "I'm so sorry. I know you cautioned us to use fictitious names but I haven't spoken to another lady in months and the truth just slipped out. Charity won't betray us. She promised she wouldn't."

He muttered under his breath. "What good is all the trouble we've gone to if you don't remember to hide your real identities?"

Placing a sheltering arm around his wife's slim shoulders Aaron stood firm. "She said she was sorry, Thorne. What's done is done. I'm sure a simple hotel maid isn't smart enough to engage in subterfuge."

"Hah! Any fool could see that that woman is no simpleton. Nor is she a maid. She said she and her father are hotel guests, not staff, so don't discount her capabilities or count on her loyalty."

Weeping, Naomi knelt to draw the boy into her embrace while Aaron began to pace the floor of the small, sparsely furnished bedroom.

"Don't worry," Thorne said firmly. "I'll take care of it. If the woman can't be reasoned with, she can probably be bribed or threatened."

"You sound just like Father!" Aaron blurted.

Thorne's eyes narrowed and his countenance darkened with barely repressed anger. "Never say that again, do you hear? I won't be compared with that man. He's *your* father, not mine."

"But you've obviously learned from him," the younger man countered.

"No. I've learned from years on my own and from the writings of my *real* father." Noting the shock on Aaron's face, he went on. "Are you surprised? I was. Shortly before I left home, Mother told me all about her brief marriage to my late father and where I might locate the rest of the Blackwell family."

"Did you?"

"Yes, eventually. I didn't seek out my grandfather until I'd spent a few years at sea and felt I'd proved myself." *And had faced death more than once.* "Grandfather and I didn't have much time together before he died but we got along very well. He gave me my father's journal, as well as willing me enough money to buy into a partnership on my first freighter."

"So that's how you became successful."

"No," Thorne countered, "I could have squandered

my inheritance in any number of ways. The investments I made, instead, were based on my experience at sea, not on mere wishful thinking. I knew exactly what I was doing and lived frugally. That's what I was trying to explain when I returned to New York three years ago. But no one would listen to me, not even you."

Thorne noted Aaron's pained expression. It was during that short visit that Thorne had met and fallen in love with Naomi but she had chosen to wed the younger brother, presumably because Aaron was in line to inherit the Ashton fortune.

Squaring his shoulders, Thorne faced him. "Forget the past. It's your future that counts. Leave the details to me. We've come this far together and I'll see to it that your foolish mistakes don't sink our ship, so to speak."

Naomi raised her reddened face to him, tears glistening on her cheeks, and whispered, "Thank you."

It was all Thorne could do to keep from tempering his harsh expression as he gazed at her. She was suffering for her poor choices and for that he was sorry, but, as he had finally realized when he'd encountered her again, any tender feelings he had once harbored were long gone and he was therefore loath to display any tenderness that might mislead her.

If anything good came out of this fiasco, perhaps it was that it had finally freed his heart from the fetters of unrequited love and had given him a chance to make amends with his brother over almost stealing his betrothed.

Charity was climbing the stairs, one hand raising the hem of her calico frock and apron as she stepped, the other balancing a glass of milk on a plate with two freshly baked cookies. As she neared the landing, a shadow fell over her.

Her head snapped up. The mysteriously intriguing stranger blocked her path. "Oh! You startled me."

Thorne didn't give way.

"Excuse me, please," Charity said politely. "I have some treats to deliver."

"I'll take that for you."

As he reached for the small plate she held it away. "No need. I can manage nicely."

"But you're a guest here. You shouldn't be doing chores."

That brought a smile. "Actually, I started out as a guest about a year ago when my father decided to move to San Francisco. Since then, I've taken a part-time position helping the proprietress, Mrs. Montgomery, to pay for Papa's and my room and board."

One dark eyebrow arched as he said, "Really? I would have thought, considering the dearth of eligible women in these parts, you'd have found yourself a suitably rich husband by now."

She could feel the warmth rising to redden her cheeks. "You assume a lot, sir."

"My apologies if I've offended you," Thorne said as he stepped aside and gestured. "After you."

Spine stiff, steps measured, Charity led the way to the room the family occupied. Behind her she could sense the imposing presence of the man Naomi had called Thorne. He was well named, Charity decided, since he was definitely a thorn in her side—probably to everyone he met. Clearly he was used to getting his own way. Equally as clearly, he was not used to being challenged by anyone, let alone a woman.

He placed his hand on the knob of the door she sought and stood very still.

"May I?" she asked boldly.

"In a moment. First, I must ask for your discretion, particularly regarding my brother's family. We're traveling in secret and must therefore guard our true identities judiciously."

Charity's chin jutted out, her head held high. "And your point is?"

"Simply that we require your silence. Since you're a working woman, perhaps a generous gift would help you forget you ever saw us."

She drew herself up to her full height of five and a half feet, noting that the top of her head, even piled high with her blond curls, barely came to the man's shoulder. Nevertheless, she was determined to give him a piece of her mind. How *dare* he try to bribe her!

"Sir," she said fervently, "I have promised Naomi that I would keep her secret and so I will, but it is because *she* asked me for my silence, not because your money interests me in the slightest. Is that clear?"

Thorne bowed from the waist as he said, "Perfectly."

"Good. Because there is a hungry, tired little boy waiting for this food and no bully in a fancy brocade vest is going to stop me from delivering it to him. Am I making myself understood?"

A slight smile started to twitch at the corners of his mouth and Charity couldn't decide whether or not he was about to laugh at her. Since she didn't want to spill the milk, she sincerely hoped she was not going to have to balance it and slap his face at the same time for unseemly behavior.

His dark eyes glistened as the smile developed. To

Charity's dismay she found him quite handsome when he wasn't frowning or trying to appear so menacing.

Averting her gaze she nodded toward the closed door. "May I go in?"

"Of course." He rapped twice, then paused a moment before opening the door for her and standing back to let her pass.

The child had already fallen asleep on the bed. Aaron stood facing the only window, staring into the street below. Naomi was the only one who looked happy to see Charity. She smiled. "Oh, thank you!"

"It's my pleasure. I'll leave this plate on the dresser for your son when he wakes," Charity said, speaking quietly. "There's fresh water in the ewer on the washstand. Is there anything else I can do for you?"

She noted Naomi's nervous glance toward Thorne and sought to ease her fears. "The gentleman and I have come to an understanding, so there's nothing to fret about."

Naomi looked as if she were about to weep with relief.

"Rest well," Charity continued. "I see the men have pocket watches but we also ring a gong for supper so you'll know when to join us, regardless. Please do." She eyed the woman's tailored traveling outfit. "And there's no need to dress. What you're wearing is most appropriate."

"Thank you." Naomi sniffled. "For everything."

"It was my pleasure to be able to assist you," Charity said formally. Stepping closer so she could speak without being easily overheard, she added, "And don't give that thorny brother-in-law of yours another thought. He doesn't scare me one bit."

From behind her a deep voice said, "I heard that."

Charity whirled and found him grinning at her.

"Good," she said, hands fisted on her hips. "Because the sooner you and I understand each other, the better I'll like it."

"I wasn't trying to intimidate or insult you, madam. I guess I'm too used to dealing with rough seamen."

"Apparently." Charity boldly stood her ground. "Listen, Mr. whatever-your-name-is-today, you may be used to having your own way but you can't hold a candle to some of the folks I've dealt with since leaving Ohio."

Like my late husband, she added to herself. After living through that dreadful marriage and the abuses she had suffered during the journey to California, there wasn't much that frightened her. Not anymore.

She started past Thorne toward the open door, then paused to add, "You may be a tad overbearing but I can tell you're not evil. Believe me, I know *exactly* what that kind of man looks like."

The flabbergasted expression on Thorne's face was fleeting and he quickly regained his usual staid composure as she swept past and left the room.

Although Charity couldn't begin to guess the plight of the little family, she vowed to add them to her daily prayers. Clearly, they were embroiled in some kind of trouble, perhaps dire, and her kind heart insisted she help in some way. If they wouldn't allow her to render physical assistance she'd simply bring them before her Heavenly Father and let Him do what He would.

A benevolent God had carried her and her sister through many terrible trials and she knew He wouldn't abandon an innocent little boy and his sweet mother.

The stranger stood outside on the walkway and lit up a cigar. Now that he'd spotted his quarry and knew where they were staying, there was no rush. On the contrary. Given the pleasures of San Francisco's wilder side he was going to enjoy this part of his assignment. He'd simply post a guard to make sure the Ashtons didn't leave without his knowledge and stop by to check on their status from time to time. Then, if it looked as if they were going to travel on, he'd be able to follow without being recognized. If not, there would be plenty of opportunity to rent a room at the Montgomery House and take care of business from the inside.

Either way, he and his cohorts couldn't fail.

Chapter Two

Fashions of the time dictated that both boys and girls wore dresses until the former reached the age of about six. Since Naomi had also chosen to keep her son's curly dark hair long, it occurred to Thorne that it might be safer to try to pass him off as a girl. Aaron would probably object, of course, but the more Thorne considered the idea, the more it appealed.

He broached the subject as he joined Aaron and the others to go downstairs to supper. "Jacob is awfully pretty for a boy," he said, smiling and patting the top of the child's head. "I think it would be safer if we called him Jane, for a while, don't you?"

As expected, his brother bristled with indignation. "I disagree completely. Think of how confusing that would be, especially for him. We can call him anything you want as long as he remains all boy."

Thorne shrugged. "Very well. Have it your way. I was just trying to protect you. Jacob is a common enough name so we may as well continue to use it."

"Don't worry. We'll be fine as soon as we reach

Naomi's parents in Oregon Territory. They'll take care of him—and of us."

"Missionaries? How much protection can you expect from pacifists?"

"Just because Mr. and Mrs. White practice what they preach doesn't mean they'd allow any harm to come to us. Besides, they're well acquainted with the natives and settlers on both sides of the border. No strangers will be able to sneak up on their mission without arousing suspicion."

"I hope you're right," Thorne said soberly. "I heard there was an Indian uprising near there."

"I assume you're referring to the Whitman massacre?"

"Yes."

"That occurred seven or eight years ago. Things have settled down considerably since that unfortunate misunderstanding. You can't blame the Indians. They were fed erroneous information about Dr. Whitman and acted on it because they didn't understand how measles was spread. Besides, those were the Cayuse and Umatilla. The tribes Naomi's parents minister to are farther north, around Puget Sound. I understand they're quite accommodating."

Naomi chimed in. "That's right. The Nisqually and Puyallup leaders have actually helped my father in his dealings with less civilized tribes. Mama told us in her letters."

"If you say so." Thorne wasn't about to argue with her and give her more reason to worry. Whatever she and Aaron decided to do next was no concern of his. He'd gotten them safely as far as San Francisco and that was all they had asked of him. Still, he had grown attached to their winsome child during the long, tedious voyage and he could tell the boy liked him, too. It was Jacob's future that concerned him most.

He felt a tiny hand grasp one of his fingers as he started down the stairs. He smiled at the boy in response. Of all his relatives, Jacob was the one to whom he felt closest. Theirs was a strangely intuitive bond that had begun almost as soon as Aaron and Naomi had boarded the *Gray Feather* and had deepened as time had passed. Jacob had seemed unusually bright for a two-year-old, as well as curious almost to a fault and Thorne had taught him a lot about the workings of the ship during the long sea voyage. To his chagrin, he had to admit he was really going to miss the youngster when they parted.

Looking up, he noticed that their approach had drawn the attention of the young woman he had infuriated earlier. He greeted her politely as he and the boy reached the bottom of the stairs. "Good evening, ma'am."

"Good evening." She offered her right hand, then smiled and withdrew it when she noticed that his was being firmly controlled by his diminutive nephew. "Looks as if the nap helped."

"Resting has certainly improved *my* outlook," Thorne said. "Again, I must apologize for unintentionally offending you."

"No apology is necessary," Charity said. As the man and boy passed her, Jacob reached for her hand, grabbed her index finger tightly, and kept them together by tugging her along, too.

Charity laughed softly. "I see someone in your family likes me."

"Apparently. If you'll forgive my saying so, the boy has excellent taste. You look lovely this evening."

"Thank you, sir."

Noting the soft blush on her already rosy cheeks and the shy way she smiled, then averted her gaze, Thorne was confused. He had pictured this woman as a stiff, bossy matron, yet now she was acting more like an ingenue. Truth to tell, he didn't imagine she was more than nineteen or twenty years old. Still, by the time he was that age he had sailed around the horn more than once and had considered himself any man's equal.

Leading them to the table, Charity made brief introductions without citing all the travelers' names. "Those gentlemen over there are new guests, too," she said. "They're from Virginia and Pennsylvania, I believe. And this is my father, Emory Beal." She indicated a thin, gray-haired man at the far end of the rectangular dining table. "Next to him is Mrs. Montgomery. She owns this hotel and several other buildings along Montgomery Street."

The round-faced, portly woman grinned and patted her upswept, salt-and-pepper hair. "Land sakes, girl. You make me sound like a land baron. I'd of had more to brag on if the storm last November hadn't carried off sixty feet of the wharf at Clark's Point. That was pitiful."

"I'd heard about that damage," Thorne said. "I'm sorry the losses were yours."

"Well, these things happen," the proprietress said with a shrug. "Lately I've been concentrating on improvements to this here property. I reckon we'll have coal gas lamps to brag on soon, just like the Oriental Hotel and the Metropolitan Theater. Can't let the competition get ahead of me. No, sirree."

Thorne agreed. "Exactly the reason I've chosen the

most modern sailing ships. We've already seen steam travel on a single vessel as far as the Isthmus of Panama. Someday I hope to be sending my own steamers all the way around the horn."

"My, my, you don't say."

"Yes, ma'am, I do."

Thorne stepped aside to shake hands with Emory while he waited for Aaron to seat his little family. That left Thorne with only one available chair, which happened to place him next to Jacob. Charity was already seated on the boy's left.

The other guests, all men, nodded brief greetings but were clearly more concerned with dishing up their share from the bowls and platters already on the table than they were with making polite conversation.

Thorne was about to reach for a nearby plate of sliced beef when he saw Charity clasp her hands, bow her head and apparently begin to pray. Since the hotel proprietress had not led any blessing on the food, he saw no reason to join in until he noticed that Jacob had folded his little hands in his lap and closed his eyes, too.

All right, Thorne decided. He was a big enough man to let a woman and child lead him, at least in this instance. Following suit he sat quietly and watched the young woman out of the corner of his eye until she stopped whispering and raised her head. He was about to reach over and tuck a napkin into Jacob's collar to serve as a bib when Charity did just that.

"I can manage him," Thorne said.

"It's no bother. He's a sweet child. So well mannered. He reminds me of my own nephew."

"You have family here?" Thorne asked as he plopped a dollop of mashed potatoes onto the boy's plate.

"My sister and her family live over near Sacramento City," she answered. "It was just chosen as the official state capitol to take the place of Benicia, you know." She looked to the child seated next to her. "Would you like some gravy?"

Thorne answered, "Yes, thanks."

That brought a demure laugh from Charity. "I was talking to my short friend here. I'll gladly ladle some over your potatoes, too, if you'd like."

"I think I can handle it myself," Thorne said with a lopsided grin. "But thank you for offering."

"You're quite welcome." She began to cut the slab of roast beef on her plate, then paused. "This piece is very tender. May I give him a little of it?"

"Of course. He doesn't like much, though. And cut it into very small bites."

"Believe it or not, I know how to feed a child."

"We should be doing that," Naomi said from across the table. "If you want to send him over, he can sit on my lap and eat from my plate."

Judging by the firm way the boy was grasping his fork and leaning his chin on the edge of the table, Thorne knew that Naomi's suggestion was not to his liking. "He's fine where he is. A little variety is good for him. And I promise we won't spoil him too badly."

"Speak for yourself, sir," Charity gibed. "I plan to enjoy my supper companion to the utmost."

When she smiled at the child, Thorne was astounded at how young and lovely she appeared. Her hair glistened like sunbeams on fine, golden silk and her eyes were as blue as a cloudless, equatorial, summer sky. It was as if the presence of the boy had lightened her usual burdens and given her a new lease on life. And Jacob had taken to her, as well, he noted. The two were acting as if they had always known each other.

Pensive, Thorne glanced at his brother and Naomi. Their countenance was anything but joyful by contrast. Aaron was eyeing the strangers at the table, looking ready to leap upon the first one who might pose a threat, while Naomi appeared near tears, as she had been during most of their sea journey. The one time Thorne had tried to discuss her concerns with her she had merely said that she feared for the lives of her dear ones.

He couldn't argue with that grim conclusion. Not if Aaron's words were to be believed. Louis Ashton had never been much of a father to either of them, nor had he been a kind, loving husband to the dear mother they shared. For that, alone, Thorne had grown to detest the man.

When Louis's last beating had raised welts on Thorne's sixteen-year-old shoulders, he had gone to his mother and begged her to leave the Ashton estate with him. Of course she had refused. But that was the night she had opened her heart and explained her painful past, including revealing her fears regarding the untimely demise of her first husband and her growing suspicion that Louis Ashton might have somehow been responsible.

Rather than be too specific, she had likened the tale to the biblical saga of King David and Bathsheba with Thorne's real father playing the part of the hapless Uriah. From there on, however, the basic facts of the story had diverged. Louis had rushed the new widow Blackwell into marriage and had gotten more than he'd bargained for a mere six months later. He'd gotten

Thorne, another man's son, and he'd never forgiven the boy for being born.

At sixteen, Thorne had wanted to take Aaron with him and run away to sea but Mother had convinced him otherwise. Once he had entered that occupation and realized what a hard life he was facing as a young seaman, he was glad he had listened to her wisdom, at least in regard to his baby brother.

Yet look at him now, Thorne thought. Everything Aaron had hoped and planned for was ruined. He had no home, no source of income and no plans for the future other than to elude any assassins Louis might send in pursuit. It was a terrible, dangerous existence that faced the little family.

Thorne had known in his heart that he could not simply abandon Aaron in San Francisco and hope that he and his loved ones eventually managed to reach Naomi's parents in the Northern territories. Now that he thought about it in detail he knew what he had to do. Like it or not, he must accompany them. And in order to do that he had to transfer some of his business duties to underlings or risk financial disaster before he could return.

Having decided, he addressed his brother. "I know you're in a hurry to be on your way but I will need several more days to arrange my affairs before I can travel. The telegraph only connects to a few cities close by so I shall have to handle my business mostly with personal dispatches. Nevertheless, I think I can have everything settled by next Friday. How does that sound?"

Aaron's mouth gaped. "You're going with us?"

"Yes. If you have no objection."

"No, I..." He looked to his wife. "If it's all right with Naomi."

She merely nodded, her eyes misting.

"Good," Thorne said. "We'll need to keep our rooms a little longer than planned, Mrs. Montgomery. I trust that won't be a problem?"

"Not at all," the proprietress said cheerfully as she pushed back her chair and arose. "Save room for dessert. Our Charity baked two delicious apple pies this afternoon and I think they're almost cool enough to serve. I'll run and fetch 'em."

Watching the matron scurry away, Thorne wondered how such delicate hands as Charity Beal's could have spent much time in the kitchen, let alone have fashioned a pie worth eating. When he was served his portion and tasted it, however, he almost purred.

"Mmm, this is delicious. Are you sure Miss Beal really made it?"

The young woman bristled. "I beg your pardon? Are you insinuating that I would lie?"

Thorne couldn't help chuckling in response. "No, ma'am. I wouldn't dream of suggesting such a thing. I was just so impressed with your culinary prowess I was momentarily at a loss for words."

"Ha! That will be the day," she said. "It has been my experience that you have plenty of words for every occasion, sir, whether they are warranted or not."

Across the table, Emory Beal broke into cackles. "Atta girl, Charity. You tell him."

Thorne was laughing so heartily he covered his mouth with his napkin and nearly choked on his bite of pie.

When he glanced around at his fellow diners, however, he was struck by the taciturn expressions on some of the other guests' faces. It appeared that several of the younger men were particularly upset with him, perhaps because they had their sights set on wooing Charity Beal. Not that he blamed them. If he were seeking a wife, she would certainly be worth a second look.

Later, when Emory cornered him and thanked him privately for lifting the girl's spirits and helping to restore her gumption, he was so surprised he truly was at a loss for words. According to her father's insinuations, Charity had been through some unspeakable experiences which had caused her to become withdrawn and often to brood.

Thorne had no idea how his presence had elevated her mood but he was nevertheless glad to hear of the improvement. He liked her. And so did Jacob, which was even more important. The poor boy had been through plenty already and their arduous journey was far from over. A little sunshine in his short life was certainly welcome and the woman who had cheerfully provided it ranked high on Thorne's list of admirable people.

In the street outside the hotel, a small group of men had gathered to discuss the situation.

"They're leaving in a few more days," the tallest, youngest one said. "That means we have a little more time to plan."

There was a murmur of agreement before their portly, red-haired leader spoke. "We won't need much. We'll move tonight."

"What do you want me to do?"

"Slip this note under Ashton's door, then leave the rest to us." He handed a folded slip of paper to his wiry cohort and glanced at the other two burly men who were standing by waiting for their orders. "Just make sure you're not seen when you do it."

"I have the room just down the hall from them. Nobody will catch me. Is that all?"

"Yes." He started away. "And if you see any of us on the street afterward, you don't know us. Is that clear?"

"Perfectly."

"Good. Now go back inside and try to act natural. The hardest part will be over by morning."

Charity couldn't sleep. After tossing and turning for what seemed like hours, she arose, pulled on a lawn wrapper and tied the sash before she peeked out the door of her room to be sure no one else was up and about. The hallway was deserted.

She quickly lit a small oil lamp and tiptoed to the stairs, intending to help herself to one of the leftover cookies in the kitchen. She paused to listen intently. There were no sounds coming from any of the rooms except for Mrs. Montgomery's familiar, loud snoring at the far end of the hotel.

Proceeding, Charity was halfway down the staircase when she overheard muffled voices and stopped in her tracks. It sounded as if the parties involved were in the sitting room, which meant that her path to the kitchen was blocked unless she chose to dart around the newel post at the ground floor and hope her passage down the side hallway went unseen.

That idea didn't please her one iota. Dressed in a floor-length white wrapper and carrying a lit lamp, there was no way she wouldn't be noticed.

She was still standing there, trying to decide what to do, when one of the parties below raised his voice.

"I'm not going back with you," he said.

A response that sounded like a growl followed.

"No," the initial speaker replied. "It's not open to discussion. You won't harm me. You don't dare. Now get out of here."

This time, the growling voice was intelligible. "I have my orders and I aim to carry them out."

Charity wished she were back in her room, blissfully sleeping, but curiosity held her rooted to the spot. She did have the presence of mind to dim her lamp and cup her hand loosely around the glass chimney, however.

Soon there was the reverberation of a smack, followed by a heavy thud. Her heart began to hammer. It sounded as if someone—or something—had fallen.

Furniture scraped across the bare floors. Glass broke, or perhaps it was crockery, she couldn't tell which. There was more stomping and crashing around just before the rear door slammed.

Afraid to move, she waited and listened. All she could hear was the rapid pounding of her heart and the shallow rasping of her breath.

Above her, a second door opened and closed. Footfalls echoed hollowly on the wooden floor. She sensed another presence on the stairs.

Someone grabbed her arm before she could turn and look. She started to scream. A hand clamped over her mouth and a male voice, a familiar voice, ordered, "Hush."

Recognizing that it was Thorne, Charity nodded and he eased his hold. Instead of trying to explain what was going on she merely pointed in the direction of the parlor.

"Shush," Thorne hissed in her ear. "Stay here."

Grasping the banister she watched him descend as gracefully and quietly as a cat. He crouched, then whipped around the corner and disappeared.

In moments he returned. He had tucked the tails of his nightshirt into his trousers and was pulling his braces over his shoulders. "There's no one there now," he assured her. "I'm sorry if I frightened you. What's going on?"

"I don't know." She was trembling like a silly child, but couldn't seem to hold the lamp still even by using two hands. "I was hungry so I came down to get a cookie. The ground floor was dark. I heard voices. It sounded like an argument."

"*Men* arguing?" Thorne asked.

"Yes. Two of them, I think. There was something rather familiar about one and the other was almost too faint to hear. I thought he sounded very menacing, though. I suppose I was just nervous because I expected to be alone."

"What did they say?"

"Nothing much. One was talking about having a job to do and the other told him he wouldn't dare, or some such nonsense. They sounded like two school-yard bullies."

"Then what?"

She shrugged. "I don't know. I couldn't see a thing from up here on the stairway. I guess there was a fight but it was over so quickly I'm not certain. I did think I heard dishes breaking just before the door slammed."

"There is some damage in the kitchen but the place is deserted, now." His dark eyes suddenly widened and he dashed past her to continue climbing, taking the steps two at a time.

Charity followed him straight to his brother's room where he began to pound on the door.

"Aaron! Open up. Now."

"Hush. You'll wake every guest in the hotel," Charity warned.

Instead of heeding her admonition Thorne grabbed her lamp, then kicked the door and broke the lock away from the jamb. He held the light high, illuminating a circle that encompassed most of the small room.

In the center of the glow, Charity saw Naomi sitting in bed and clutching covers that were drawn up to her neck. Beside her, the exhausted toddler barely stirred in spite of the ruckus.

"Where's Aaron?" Thorne demanded.

"I don't know. Someone slipped a note under our door. Aaron read it and said he had to go out." Naomi began to sniffle. "I begged him to stay here with me but he insisted."

"What note. Where is it?"

"I—I think he put it in his coat pocket and took it with him. Why? What's happened?" Her breath caught. "Is, is he…"

"Dead?" Thorne muttered under his breath. "I doubt it. But I don't think he's in the hotel anymore, either. I strongly suspect he's been kidnapped."

Naomi gasped. "Are you sure?"

"Relatively. I explored the whole ground floor and he wasn't down there. Nobody was."

"I'll wake Papa and send him to fetch the sheriff," Charity said from the hallway. "We'll search everywhere. We'll find him."

In her heart of hearts she hoped and prayed she was right. If Aaron remained on land there was a fair chance they would be able to locate him, especially since San Francisco was rather isolated by the surrounding hills. If he had been taken aboard one of the many vessels coming and going by sea, however, he could already be out of their reach.

It was a frightening realization. It was also the most logical escape route for anyone wanting to effect a successful kidnapping!

Chapter Three

Thorne finished dressing, pulled on his coat and joined Emory Beal as he hurried from the hotel.

"I don't know where to start looking for the law, do you?" Thorne asked the older man.

"I've got a sneakin' suspicion where the sheriff'll be," Emory replied. "Follow me."

They made their way up Sacramento Street and located the lawman holding court with the mayor and half the city council in the What Cheer House saloon. A large crowd was toasting the previous day's groundbreaking ceremonies at Presidio Hill for the soon-to-be-built municipal water system and everyone seemed to be having a wonderful time drinking and eating the free food offered at the bar. A pall of smoke hung low in the stuffy room.

Thorne was glad that Emory was with him because the older man was well-known and was therefore able to readily convince the celebrants to form a vigilance committee and join in the search for Aaron.

Leaving the saloon in the company of dozens of inebriated, raucous men, Thorne jumped up on the edge of a watering trough and grabbed a porch support post for balance while he waved and shouted to command everyone's attention.

"There will be a large reward for my brother's return," he yelled, pleased to hear a responsive rumbling of excitement in the crowd. "He's a city fellow from New York so you should be able to pick him out from amongst the prospectors and immigrants. He was wearing a brown suit and vest. His hair is lighter than mine and he's a little shorter. He has no beard or mustache. If any of you spot him, I can be reached through the Montgomery House Hotel or the freighter *Gray Feather*. She's moored close to the main pier. Let's go, men. Time is of the essence."

Stepping down, he started off with the others. He would have preferred to head a sober search party but under the present circumstances he figured he was fortunate to have found a group of able-bodied men awake and willing to help at this time of night.

"It's all Chinese down that way," Emory told him, pointing. "Your brother'd stick out like a sore thumb in that neighborhood. The sheriff said he wants us to check the wharf while he and some of the others look in the gambling and fandango houses we still have. Come the first of April, bawdy houses'll be banned on Dupont, Jackson and Pacific. Don't know what this city's comin' to."

"All right," Thorne said. "I probably know the waterfront as well as most of the folks who live here."

"Been a sailor all your life?"

"In a matter of speaking." Thorne didn't think this was an appropriate time to mention that he had long since graduated from employee to employer. Nor was it a good idea to flaunt his wealth in a town with a reputation for lawlessness and greed, mainly thanks to the gold rush. San Francisco had come a long way from the canvas and board shacks he remembered from 1850 but it still hadn't managed to attain anything resembling the degree of civility Aaron and Naomi were used to back in New York.

Although Thorne's clothing bespoke a full purse, his actual worth far exceeded the external evidence. And that was the way he wanted it. He'd found out the hard way that if a man had money there was always someone eager and willing to separate him from it, one way or another. That much, he *had* learned from Louis Ashton.

The difference was what lay in a man's heart, not what lined his pockets, Thorne reminded himself. He would gladly pay whatever it took to get his brother back and not miss a penny of that money. Unfortunately, if Louis's hired thugs were responsible for the abduction, he feared that Aaron's freedom was not going to be for sale at any price.

Although Charity had wanted to join in the search, she knew better than to venture out onto the streets unescorted, especially after dark, so she had stayed behind to try to comfort Naomi.

By dawn the poor woman had sobbed herself into exhaustion and had finally fallen asleep. Although Charity was weary, too, she took pity on Jacob and kept him beside her while she did her morning chores and helped prepare breakfast for the remaining hotel guests.

Fortunately, the current Montgomery Hotel didn't house as many souls as it had before being rebuilt. Now that they were able to offer private rooms, the income from the establishment had improved while the work-load had lessened. For that, Charity was doubly thank-ful. She didn't begrudge her father his ease but she sometimes did wish he'd contribute more to their daily necessities.

She shook off the negative feelings and reminded herself that she was blessed to have a roof over her head and to be in the company of a papa who loved and for-gave her in spite of her folly as a younger woman. That she had survived at all was a wonderment. That she and Faith had both managed to locate their father and work together for the common good was almost miraculous, given the hardships and dangers they had faced.

Jacob had been gripping a handful of Charity's skirt ever since she had awakened and dressed him and she had allowed it because he seemed so determined, so needy. She felt him give her apron a light tug. Smiling, she looked down and asked, "Are you hungry, dear?"

The little boy nodded and her smile grew. What a darling. The depths of his chocolate-brown eyes spar-kled and his thick, dark lashes would have been the envy of any girl.

Leading him to a table in the kitchen she lifted him onto a chair and said, "My, what a big boy you are. You sit here and I'll fetch your breakfast before we serve the others so you can eat first. Would you like that?"

Again he nodded and grinned, showing even, white teeth and dimples.

"You're spoiling that child," Annabelle Montgomery said as she kneaded dough on the opposite end of the table. "Not that I blame you. He's a cute one, all right. And such a little man. So brave, what with his…" She broke off and glanced at the ceiling.

"Yes, I know," Charity answered. "I've explained that his mama is ailing. Jacob is going to stay with me today so she can rest."

"Good idea. I don't suppose he'd like some flapjacks and homemade jam."

The little boy's head nodded so hard his dark curls bounced.

"My, my," the proprietress said, "looks like he just might. While this dough rises a bit I'll run out to the spring house and fetch some cool milk."

"I should do that for you," Charity said.

"Not this morning. You're needed here." Annabelle's gentle gaze rested on the child and she shook her head slowly, sadly. "Perhaps we'll hear from our Emory soon and we can all relax. I've been prayin' hard ever since he left."

"So have I." Laying her hand atop the boy's head Charity stroked his silky hair. "I meant for Papa to find the sheriff and then come home but I should have known he'd want to stay and help in the search. I just worry about him, that's all."

"So do I," the portly proprietress said.

To Charity's amazement she thought she glimpsed moisture in Annabelle Montgomery's eyes as the other woman wheeled and left the room.

Thorne returned with Emory several hours later. Charity had set aside biscuits, as well as extra servings of ham and a bowl of red-eye gravy, assuming they'd be famished when they finally came home.

She was seated in a rocker in the hotel parlor, Jacob asleep in her arms, when the two men walked in.

Thorne approached her while Emory headed upstairs.

"Did you find your brother?" she asked.

"No. The sheriff is still keeping an eye open but there was no sign of him in any of the usual places."

"I'm so sorry."

"Yeah. Me, too."

"There are plates of food waiting for you and Papa in the warming oven over the stove," she said, continuing her slow, steady rocking. "I'd get up and serve you but as you can see, I'm otherwise occupied."

Thorne's overall expression was weary, yet a slight smile lifted the corners of his mouth. "Poor Jacob's probably as tired as the rest of us," he said, gazing fondly at the child. "I don't know what we're going to tell him about all this."

"I wouldn't say anything, for now," Charity suggested. "He's too young to understand the details and I don't see any reason to upset him needlessly."

"How's Naomi?"

"The last time I looked in on her she was sleeping. She wore herself out last night."

"Little wonder." He had already removed his hat and he raked his fingers through his wavy, uncombed hair as he paced the sitting room. "I wish I knew what to do next."

"Eat," Charity said sensibly. "You have to keep up your strength for whatever trials are to come. Seems to me you're the only member of your family capable of making wise decisions or taking any useful action."

"I'm afraid you're right, Miss Beal. Thank you for everything. I don't know what Naomi or Jacob would have done without you."

"You're most welcome."

Watching him leave the room she smiled knowingly. She hadn't expected Thorne to include himself in the gracious compliment but she could tell that he was as in need of her assistance as the rest of his party. His self-confident nature wouldn't let him admit as much, of course, but she was content with knowing it was true.

The child in her lap stirred, blinked up through sleepy eyes and snuggled closer.

Charity hugged him to her and began to pray silently for his future. The way things looked now he was going to have a rough road ahead and she wished mightily that she could do more than merely comfort and care for him for the time being.

She laid her cheek against the top of his head and whispered, "He's yours, Father. Please bless and guide and watch over him."

A solitary tear slid from her eye and dropped onto the boy's hair. So young. *So innocent. Oh, dear God, help him.*

The ensuing days seemed to pass in a blur. Men of all kinds and all classes, including several of the hotel guests whom Thorne had originally deemed unfriendly, kept popping in to update him on the search. He had set up an office of sorts on the end of the counter behind which the desk clerk also stood so he could keep all the reports straight. It was his goal to speak personally with each and every searcher and thereby leave no stone unturned.

Upstairs, Naomi had taken to her bed and the doctor had diagnosed her condition as lingering hysteria. Thorne wasn't sure that was all there was to it. He'd seen plenty of people overcome by grief and disaster but he'd never known one to lapse into a state of near helplessness the way his sister-in-law had.

Thorne thanked God that Charity Beal had so readily assumed the role of his nephew's caretaker because he didn't know how he'd have adequately looked after everyone else and managed to coordinate a systematic search for Aaron at the same time.

A week had passed and they'd fallen into a routine that varied little from hour to hour, day to day. That was why Thorne was so astonished to suddenly see Naomi descending the stairs. She was dressed to go out and acting as if nothing unusual had happened.

Wearing her favorite traveling dress, a matching, ostrich-plumed hat and white lace, fingerless gloves, she carried only her reticule. Instead of approaching and greeting Thorne as he'd expected, she headed straight for the front door.

"Naomi!" he called. "Where are you going?"

She turned a blank stare toward him, said nothing, then continued out onto the boarded walkway.

As Thorne prepared to follow her he was detained by one of the regular hotel residents. He made short work of the tall, thin man's inane questions but by the time he reached the front door of the hotel, Naomi was already strolling away on another man's arm as if nothing was amiss.

Thorne raced after them and shouted, "Hey! Where do you think you're going?" He was nearly upon the pair before he recognized Naomi's beefy, reddish haired escort as one of the most recently arrived hotel guests.

The man paused and turned with a cynical expression. "The lady wanted to take a walk and I'm looking after her. What's wrong with that?"

"Nothing, under normal circumstances," Thorne replied. "But in this case I must insist we all return to the hotel. Immediately."

"No. I'm going home," Naomi said as if in a fog.

Thorne had touched her free arm to stop her from proceeding and was glaring at the other man when Charity joined them, toting Jacob on one hip.

The boy's enthusiastic squeal brought no visible reaction from his mother.

"What's the matter with her?" Charity asked Thorne.

"I don't know." He continued to gently restrain Naomi and she made no effort to escape. She also didn't seem to recognize her own son.

Ignoring the two men who appeared about to come to blows, Charity concentrated on Naomi and spoke gently. "Where are you going, dear?"

"To see my mama and papa." She sounded as if she, herself, were a child.

"Why don't we go inside and sit down to talk about it," Charity said. "You'd like to tell me about your trip, wouldn't you? I'd love to hear all about your parents. I know they're wonderful people. Aren't they missionaries to the Indians?"

"Yes," Naomi said. Her determination seemed to be wavering, so Thorne exerted a gentle pressure on her arm, guiding her away from the other man and back the way they'd all come.

Following, Charity whispered to Jacob. "Mama's still sick, dear. I know she loves you very much but she isn't herself right now."

In response, the confused child wrapped his pudgy

arms around Charity's neck and laid his head on her shoulder. Her heart ached for him. In the space of a few brief days and nights she had grown to love the little darling as if he were her own and it pained her to see him so rejected and forlorn.

Leaving the portly, confused-looking man behind, Thorne led Naomi to the settee in the parlor where she perched primly on the edge of the velvet-covered cushions as if she were visiting strangers.

"I can't stay long," she said, removing her gloves and tucking them into her reticule. "Mama is waiting for me and she doesn't like it when I'm late for supper."

"Where is your mother?" Charity asked.

"Just up the road, I think." Naomi frowned momentarily. "I'm not really sure. I seem to be lost. But I know Mama will take care of me as soon as I can get home. She loves me, you know."

"I'm sure she does," Charity answered. Looking to Thorne she saw that he, too, was at a loss as to how best to respond.

"Why don't you stay a bit longer and have dinner with us," Charity said. "I'm sure your mama would want you to."

"Do you think so?"

"Yes, dear, I do. Mrs. Montgomery is roasting a brace of California quail that one of our guests brought us." She raised her head to sniff and added, "They smell delicious, don't they? And you must be famished."

Naomi nodded, still seeming befuddled. "Yes, I guess I am hungry. I don't know why I should be, though. Mama made me a wonderful breakfast this morning."

Eyeing Thorne to make sure he understood that she

expected him to stay close by and observe, Charity said, "Actually, I need to go help in the kitchen and set the table. Would you two mind watching Jacob for me while I do that? He's a good little boy so I know you won't have any problems with him."

When Naomi didn't answer, Thorne held out his arms and took the child from Charity. "We'll be glad to, ma'am. Let us know if we can be of any other assistance."

Seeing the subdued two-year-old clinging to his uncle's neck while Thorne gently patted his back gave Charity a surprising pang of longing and blurred her vision enough that she turned and hurried away to hide her emotional reaction. That was what love should be like, she concluded. Simple and pure and safe, the way the child trusted that hardheaded yet tenderhearted man.

Too bad adult love couldn't be like that, she added, recalling her horrid marital experience. If she'd learned anything from her frightful days as Ramsey Tucker's wife it was that she wanted no part of the intimacy that marriage demanded. All she could recall of the few nights when he had accosted her was her own sobs and the way he had beaten her into silence. The only good thing about that was the oblivion of semiconsciousness that had spared her from feeling or hearing most of his disgusting advances.

Biting back tears, Charity busied herself by spreading a fresh linen cloth on the long, rectangular dining table and beginning to place the dishes and silverware. It had been a long time since she had questioned her current life or had entertained the slightest notion that there might be a different kind of happiness waiting for her just over the horizon. That notion was staggering. And frightening.

Rejecting it outright, she reminded herself that she was perfectly content to look after her dear papa and tend to the chores of the hotel. That was her lot in life and she was comfortable with it.

So why did she suddenly feel such a stirring of dissatisfaction? The Good Lord had rescued her from servitude to an evil, disreputable man and had reunited her with her loved ones. Why wasn't she the happiest woman in San Francisco—or in the whole country, for that matter?

"I am happy. And I love it here," she murmured.

Mrs. Montgomery chuckled from across the room as she used a corner of her apron to blot perspiration from her forehead. "I'm right glad to hear that," she said. "I don't know what I'd do without you, girl."

"You don't have to fret about that," Charity said. "I'm never going to leave Papa. I promised him that long ago and I aim to keep my word."

Thorne held the child close and continued to stroke his back while Naomi prattled on about her life as a little girl. There was no doubt in Thorne's mind that his sister-in-law was a very sick woman. What he could hope to do about that without Aaron to help him was a different question.

The searchers had narrowed down the possibilities of Aaron's disappearance to one of two packet boats that had left the harbor with the mail soon after his abduction. That, or he had been spirited away overland, which was an unlikely scenario given the inherent difficulties in getting all the way back to New York via that route. Thorne had to assume that delivering Aaron to Louis was the kidnapper's assignment, else why take him at all?

No, Thorne had reasoned, they had to have left the city by sea. Since there was no use trying to catch up to the individual boats at this late date he had telegraphed ahead and already had dozens of men working on the puzzle. Until one of them wired back that he had located Aaron, there was nothing for Thorne to do but keep his vigil at the hotel.

He was relieved when Mrs. Montgomery summoned everyone for dinner. As soon as his gaze met Charity's he shook his head slightly in answer to her unspoken query.

She relieved Naomi of her hat, gloves and reticule, then guided her to the same chair she had occupied the last time she and Aaron had eaten at that table, hoping it might trigger her memory. It didn't.

Thorne took a seat opposite his sister-in-law and gave Jacob the chair beside him, as usual. Many of the guests they had met during their stay had moved on. At present there was only Charity and her father, the proprietress and the young desk clerk, Thorne, Jacob, Naomi and two single men sharing the table. To Thorne's disgust, one of them resembled the fool who had tried to take Naomi out for a stroll and the other was the prattling idiot who had delayed him so long that she had almost escaped.

Thorne tried to make polite conversation with Charity while tolerating the other men for the sake of propriety. He was running out of things to say when a gangly, hatless youth with black elastic bands holding up his shirtsleeves burst into the hotel. His boots clomped on the wooden floor as he made straight for the dining room.

"Mr. Blackwell. I'm plumb glad I found you," he said, panting and looking extremely agitated.

Thorne's breath caught when he recognized the telegrapher. He pushed back his chair and stood. "What is it? Do you have news?"

"Yes, sir." The younger man handed him a slip of paper.

Reading it, Thorne tried to hide his distress. One quick glance at Charity's concerned expression told him he had failed.

She arose and circled her chair to join him. Gently laying her hand on his coat sleeve she urged him to share the message. "What have you learned?"

"They're absolutely certain that they traced Aaron and two other men to the port of Los Angeles, where they all boarded a ship bound for New York, as I had suspected they might."

"Then that's good news, isn't it?"

He shook his head. His heart was pounding and the hand that held the paper was trembling. "No. Not if he actually was aboard the *El Dorado,* as they believe. That ship just sank in a hurricane off the coast of Mexico with all hands reported lost."

Feeling Charity's fingers tighten on his forearm and seeing the compassion in her blue eyes, he covered her hand with his before he said, "It appears Jacob has no one left to look after him and his mother but me."

"What are you going to do?" Charity asked softly.

"I don't know."

From across the table, Naomi spoke as if she hadn't understood a thing they'd just said. "I must be going home to *my* mama soon. She'll be worried."

Thorne's gaze traveled from Naomi to Charity and then to the wide-eyed child. "You're right. You should go to your mother. We'll pack tonight and leave as soon as I can book passage on a packet boat headed north toward Puget Sound."

His fingers closed around Charity's. "I know this is sudden, Miss Beal, but will you come with us? Jacob needs care and Naomi should have a gentlewoman like you as a traveling companion."

She pulled away. "I'm sorry. I can't."

"Why not? I'll pay you well for your trouble and treat you as if you were part of my family. I know it may be an arduous journey but surely, if you won't do it for Naomi, you'll take pity on the child."

"That's not fair," Charity said. "You know I care for him but my papa needs me and I promised I'd never leave him. I assure you, I take that vow quite seriously."

Emory cleared his throat, drawing everyone's attention. "I suspect this is a good time to make an announcement that I've been savin' for just the right moment." He reached for Annabelle Montgomery's hand and clasped it for all to see. "Mrs. Montgomery has consented to become my wife."

"Papa!" Charity was thunderstruck.

"Don't look so shocked, girl."

"But, what about Mama?"

He sobered and shook his head. "Your mama's gone to Glory but I'm still down here. And I'm not dead yet."

"I know, but…"

Emory was adamant as he beamed at his intended bride. "This is a fine, upstanding, Christian widow woman and I'm proud she fancies me. She'll make you a wonderful stepmother." He kissed his future wife's hand before he continued, "I release you from whatever promise you think you made, Charity, even though I don't recall any such nonsense. Your sister would already be upstairs packin' her duds if somebody had offered her an adventure like that. What're you waitin' for?"

Thorne could see that Charity was deeply hurt. He reached for her hand once again, hoping she wouldn't pull away. "Please? At least promise me you'll consider my offer?"

When she nodded, then turned and fled up the stairs to hide her tears, his heartfelt sympathy went with her. He knew *exactly* how it hurt to be treated as an outsider in one's own family. He'd dealt with that kind of unfair pain all his life. And he wasn't done doing so.

The two so-called gentlemen who had shared the communal meal in the Montgomery hotel stood in the shadows outside and spoke in whispers while they lit up after-dinner cigars. "Do you think it's true? Could the others all be dead?" the taller, thinner one asked.

His balding, stocky companion shrugged. "I don't know. Blackwell looked pretty upset when he heard the bad news but the wife didn't make a peep. It might be a ruse to throw us off the trail."

"And it might not. Now that there's maybe only two of us left, what do you think we should do?"

"Split up," the second man said, hooking a thumb in his vest pocket and leaning his head back to blow a succession of smoke rings. "You go back East by sea, explain this new development and tell the old man what we know so far."

"I don't much cotton to that idea. He's gonna be fightin' mad if it's true."

"Still, he's paid us plenty. He has to be informed, even if the news is bad."

"Oh, sure. And what're you gonna be doin' while he takes it out on me for bein' the messenger?"

"Getting even for our lost friends. Ashton's wife trusts me now. I'll stay close to her and her kin, wherever they go, and finish what we came for, one way or another."

"You sure you don't need my help?"

He shook his head, his thick jowls jiggling. "No. I can handle it. Even if I don't get another chance till they're on the trail, it'll be fine. All I'll have to do then is hang back and pick them off one at a time, starting with the brat."

The taller man winced. "I never did like that part of the job. Doesn't seem fair to kill him when we could just snatch him and maybe sell him, instead."

"That kind of thinking is clear stupid. Which is why I'm sending you home and handling things here by myself. When you talk to our boss, make sure you tell him straight out that I'm the one with the stomach for this job or you'll have to answer to me when I get back."

"*If* you get back."

His laugh was derisive. "Oh, I'll be back. And I'll expect to find a big bonus waiting for me when I show up in New York with the proof that I was successful."

"Proof? How're you gonna do that?"

The laugh deepened and took on a more sinister tone. "Same way the Indians do. I'll bring Ashton their scalps."

Chapter Four

Charity didn't know what to do. On the one hand she wanted to stay safely at home in San Francisco with her beloved papa. On the other hand, he had as much as told her she was no longer needed or wanted.

And what about poor little Jacob? He did need her and she did care about him. Why, oh why, did life have to be so complicated?

Standing in the middle of her sparsely furnished room she pivoted slowly as she took in the accommodations. There was a bed with a feather mattress atop tightly stretched ropes, a dressing table and mirror, a washstand with a pitcher and ewer, a small trunk containing most of her clothing, and pegs on the wall next to it where she could hang her few dresses and petticoats. The place wasn't lavish by any stretch of the imagination, yet it suited her. She didn't need much, nor did she deserve luxuries, although she had once thought otherwise.

Looking back, it was painful to envision how spoiled and selfish she had once been, not to mention the difficulties she'd caused her long-suffering sister, Faith, while they were crossing the prairie together.

Charity shivered and wrapped her arms around herself. Would she never be able to banish those horrible memories?

In the past, she had clung to them as if their presence was necessary to keep her humble. Now that she was being offered a chance to do something extraordinary for the benefit of an innocent child, perhaps that would be enough to cleanse her soul and give her the peace she had lost.

Verbal prayer was impossible with her mind whirling and her heart so torn and broken, but her unspoken thoughts reached out to God just the same. Was this what He wanted her to do? Was He giving her the second chance she'd so often prayed for? Or was she about to listen to her own confused feelings and become a victim of emotion and foolishness once again?

She pressed her fingertips to her lips and sank onto the edge of her bed. The tears she had begun to shed when her father had announced his forthcoming marriage were gone, leaving only a sense of emptiness. Of loss. Everyone she loved had left her; first Mama when the tornado had taken her life, then Faith when she'd married Connell and now Papa. It wasn't fair. She had given them as much devotion as she could muster, yet they were all gone now. Even Papa.

Bereft, she tilted her head back, closed her eyes and spoke to her Heavenly Father from the depths of her soul. "Please, tell me what to do? Please?"

She felt a soft tug on her skirt and opened her eyes. There at her feet stood the little boy whose well-being was at the heart of her concerns. She blinked. Smiled. Opened her arms, leaned forward and embraced him.

As she lifted Jacob onto her lap she sensed another presence and glanced toward the open door. Thorne was watching, silent and grave, clearly expecting her to speak.

Charity cleared her throat and smiled slightly before she said, "You really know how to influence me, don't you?"

"I hope so. Will you come with us?"

Sighing, she nodded and did the only thing that seemed right. She capitulated. "Yes."

Thorne was astonished that the slightly built young woman had agreed so easily. Now that she had, he was having second thoughts. Was he doing the right thing by including her in their traveling party? He knew having a female companion was best for Naomi and the boy but he wondered how much more trouble it was going to be looking after an extra woman, especially if the journey was as arduous as he feared it might be.

Then again, anyone who had crossed the great plains in a wagon and was now tolerating the constant earth tremors in San Francisco had to be made of sterner stuff than the average person. He didn't think he'd ever get used to all the shaking in that city, although its citizens seemed to take it in stride.

He huffed as he turned and headed back downstairs. They'd be safe enough in a hotel this substantial unless another big shake started more fires like the ones the citizenry had experienced several years back. Volunteer fire companies had been organized to handle small blazes but it was easy for fires in multiple locations to get away from them no matter how often they trained or how diligently they worked to douse the flames.

Once the city water system was completed that would help. So would rebuilding in brick as many had lately, he told himself, but there was still plenty of flammable material around, especially in the poorer sections of town.

Suddenly uneasy, Thorne paused at the base of the stairs and stood stock-still, his hand on the newel post. It hadn't been his imagination. The ground was trembling. Again. He could tolerate the pitching of a ship's deck in a storm at sea much easier than he could the unsteady shore. At least on board his ships he could predict oncoming swells and brace to ride them out. Here on land the shaking always took him by surprise.

He was still standing at the base of the stairs, waiting for further tremors, when Charity joined him.

He glanced past her. "Where's Jacob?"

"He fell asleep on my bed so I covered him, shut the door and left him there. He's exhausted, as well you can imagine."

"We all are," Thorne said with a sigh. "I must apologize for putting you in such an untenable position. If you don't wish to accompany my party, you don't have to."

"Yes, I do," she replied. "I knew that as soon as I looked into that poor little boy's eyes."

"You're very kind."

"No, I'm not. I have a lot of mistakes to make up for and helping you fulfill your obligation to your brother will start to pay that debt."

"I can't imagine what you could possibly have done that would call for such penance."

"It's not only what I did, it's what I didn't do when

my sister needed me. It's only by the grace of God that she survived and we were reunited."

"Then you and I have even more in common than I thought," Thorne said with empathy. "I have often wondered why God continually spared my life during my years at sea."

"Really? Perhaps we were destined to work together for the common good."

His eyebrows arched. "Perhaps."

"Where's Naomi?" Charity asked. "Not gone off again, I hope."

"No. Mrs. Montgomery and your father are looking after her for the present."

"Good." Charity stepped down and led the way to the parlor as she continued to speak. "My life began on a small farm in Trumbull County, Ohio. I thought I understood what hard work and deprivation were but until I crossed the prairie in a wagon train I had no true picture. That was the worst experience I have ever had."

Thorne stood until she had seated herself on the settee, then chose a nearby armchair. "Then you shouldn't go with us to the territories. It will be much more primitive up there than it is here."

"It wasn't the lack of amenities that bothered me. It was being married to evil personified, himself."

"You were *married?*"

"Yes. I thought my father had told you."

Thorne hoped he was successfully hiding his initial shock. "No. All he said was that you had undergone some terrible experiences during your journey. He never mentioned marriage."

"Hmm. I see." Lacing her fingers together in her lap, she paused for a moment before she went on. "I suppose you should know more particulars about my past before you actually hire me."

"That's not necessary."

"I think it is," she said, stiffening her spine, raising her chin and staring at the opposite side of the room as if she were gazing into the past. "I was very young. Just sixteen. We were halfway to California when my sister, Faith, was kidnapped by men we thought were Indians. I feared I'd never see her again."

"I'm so sorry."

"Oh, there's more," she said with resignation as her eyes met Thorne's. "I didn't know it at the time but the wagon boss, Ramsey Tucker, was not only responsible for Faith's disappearance, he got rid of her because he had designs on my father's gold-mining claim and she was too smart for him. She saw his true character while I was blind to it."

Thorne waited patiently for her to continue, aware that she was struggling to find the proper words and assuming she was trying to explain without exceeding the bounds of propriety.

Finally, Charity said, "Without my sister I was all alone, single and unescorted, and therefore in a terrible predicament, as you can imagine. I was so overwrought and afraid that I took the easy way out. I misjudged that horrid man and let him talk me into marrying him in order to continue the journey and find Papa again."

"Are you still married?" Thorne asked quietly.

Charity's eyes widened. "No! Nor was I legally wed in the first place, as it turned out, which makes every-thing even worse. Before he was killed, my so-called husband confessed that he was already married and had therefore led me, and countless other women, astray for his own disreputable gains."

She lowered her gaze to her clasped hands and Thorne noted that her knuckles were white from the pressure of her tight grasp.

"Surely, none of that was your fault," he said kindly.

"Wasn't it? I try to think about those awful days as little as possible. No one here knows much about my past. Not even Mrs. Montgomery."

"Yet you just told me. Why?"

"Because I could be considered a loose woman, especially if we were to encounter any of the other folks who crossed the plains on the same wagon train or were present in the gold camp when my…husband…was killed."

Thorne had to smile. He leaned forward and rested his elbows on his knees, clasping his own hands. "Perhaps it will help if you know how I came to be called Blackwell while my brother is an Ashton."

"That isn't necessary," Charity said.

"Still, I think hearing this will make you feel less alone and help you understand why we all fear and loathe my stepfather the way we do. My mother began married life as Pearl Blackwell, then…"

As he concluded an abbreviated version his mother's tale he noted the concern in Charity's blue eyes. "Do you think Louis Ashton actually got rid of your real father so he could marry your mother, the way King David did to Uriah the Hittite in the Bible?"

"That was the way Mother told the story. She has come to that conclusion by piecing together the facts over the course of many years. As you did with your husband, she misjudged the kind of man Louis Ashton was and has been paying for her mistake ever since."

"Oh, poor Pearl. Can't you free her somehow?"

"Not as long as she chooses to remain in his house as Louis's wife. I've offered to support her for the rest of her days if she will leave him but she always tells me she considers her marriage vows sacred and won't break them. Not even now."

"How awful." Charity paled. "I suppose I should be more thankful that Ramsey Tucker is dead and gone."

"We have no control over things like that," Thorne said with resignation. "At least we shouldn't. For your sake, I'm glad he's no longer around to menace you."

To Thorne's relief he saw a slight smile beginning to lift the corners of Charity's lips.

"*Menace* is the *perfect* word to describe that man's behavior," she said. "I wasn't joking a bit when I referred to him as evil personified."

"I think I prefer to reserve that term for my stepfather."

"There really are a lot of evil people in this world, aren't there?"

"Yes. But you've been delivered from one of them and now it's time for the two of us to rescue Naomi and Jacob from another. Are you up to it?"

"Oh, yes," Charity said. "I'll be packed and ready to travel as soon as you say the word."

"You're sure? You're not afraid?"

She laughed lightly, her pink cheeks revealing a touch of embarrassment. "What does fear have to do with making this trip? As long as I believe—and I certainly do—that the Good Lord wants me to help you, why would I hesitate just because I happen to be scared witless?"

Thorne stood. "Good for you, Miss Beal. Forgive me

for being so bold but I think you are one of the stron-
gest, most worthy women I have ever had the pleasure
to know."

"Let's hope your opinion has not changed by the time
we reach Naomi's parents."

Nodding and politely taking his leave, Thorne kept
his negative thoughts to himself. He was familiar with
the upcoming sea voyage as far as the part of Poverty
Bay now called Puget Sound. He'd even been to Ad-
miralty Inlet, north of there, but that was as far as he'd
traveled. Once they left the coast and started inland
he'd be as lost as a sailor adrift in a lifeboat without
compass or sextant.

Was this a fool's errand? he wondered. Perhaps. But
he knew he must undertake it all the same. Even if his
brother had not survived the sinking of the *El Dorado*
there was still danger looming over Naomi and little
Jacob.

Thorne could not, would not, abandon them to Louis's perfidy.

Pearl Ashton, red-eyed and clutching a lace-edged
handkerchief, heard her husband opening the front door
of their uptown mansion. She had been pacing the foyer
and waiting for what seemed like hours.

Although her earlier tears had dried, the sight of
Louis, so pompous and so handsomely clad in a gray
cutaway coat, perfectly tailored pants and embroidered
pearl satin vest brought fresh moisture to her eyes.

She dabbed the sparse tears away as she hurried toward him, the train from her bustle silently brushing the
polished marble floor. "Where have you been?"

"I told you we were having another meeting of the

Merchants' Society about that greensward we've been planning. We're going to call it Central Park if I have my way, and I believe I shall."

He scowled and peered past her as he removed his hat. "What is the matter with you, woman? And where in blazes are all the servants?"

"I sent them away."

Louis slapped his kid gloves into his overturned bowler. "What? Why on earth did you do that? I don't pay them to lollygag, you know."

"I wanted to be alone with you when I showed you this," Pearl said, reaching into the pocket of her skirt and producing a crumpled piece of yellow paper. Her hand was shaking as she thrust it at Louis.

Instead of accepting the paper, he strode past her toward the parlor as if she were far less important than the absent servants. "Just tell me what it says and be done with it, woman. I don't have time for your childish games."

"Childish?" Pearl's voice was strident enough that her husband hesitated. She knew she was already overstepping the limits of his volatile temper but at that moment she didn't care. She waved the paper. "What have you done?"

"I have no idea what you mean."

"No, of course you don't," Pearl said, nearly screaming at him. "First you drive away my eldest son and now this! How can you be so cruel?"

"What are you babbling about?" Louis grabbed the yellow telegram from her. As he scanned it, Pearl saw the color rise in his bearded cheeks.

"Is it true?" she demanded.

"What if it is? It's certainly no concern of yours."

"You've killed him!" she wailed. "You've killed my baby!"

"Don't be ridiculous. You're getting hysterical for no reason. All this says is that Aaron and some of my acquaintances are on their way back from Los Angeles."

"On the *El Dorado*." Pearl was sobbing as she raced to her favorite chair near the hearth, grabbed up the *New York Gazette* and returned to shove it in her husband's face. "Look, Louis. See for yourself."

She watched as the high color left him. He staggered back against the divan, his face pasty, his usually hawk-like eyes growing rheumy.

"It sank!" Pearl screeched, beginning to beat on his chest and shoulders with her fists. "You couldn't let him go and now he's dead. I hate you. I hate you, do you hear? Of all the things you've done to ruin my life, this is the worst."

Louis regained enough self-control to grab her thin wrists and stop her assault. "What do you mean, all the things I've done? What have I done except give you a life of luxury and treat you like a queen."

"A queen in a dungeon," Pearl countered. "You've deprived me of the love of both my sons."

"I've lost, too," Louis reminded her, thrusting her aside. "I loved Aaron as much as you did."

"But not Thorne. Never Thorne."

"Of course not. He wasn't my son."

Pearl crumpled on the velvet cushions of the divan and sobbed uncontrollably. Her heart was so badly broken she no longer feared for her own safety. If Louis chose to beat her for her outburst, or for what she was about to add, she believed she would welcome the pain, the eventual oblivion. Without her dear boys, life was not worth living.

After a few moments, sniffling and wiping her eyes, she got to her feet and faced the man to whom she had pledged her troth so many years before. As soon as he looked at her she demanded, "Tell me. How did you kill my beloved Samuel? Did you do it yourself or did you hire it done?"

Louis's eyes narrowed. "Don't be ridiculous. Samuel Blackwell was hit by a runaway dray after the driver lost control of his team. It was an accident."

"Was it?" Her chin jutted out, her lips pressed into a thin line. "Can you prove it?"

"Of course not. No more than you can prove it wasn't. There is something I *can* do, however. I can check with my friend James Bennett at the *Herald* instead of taking the word of the *Gazette*. If Bennett says he got the same news about the *El Dorado*'s sinking then I'll send men to Mexico to investigate and make certain the reports are accurate."

Pearl clasped her damp handkerchief in both hands and drew them to her chest over her cameo brooch. "Do you think they might be wrong? Could Aaron be alive after all?"

"If he is, I'll find him," Louis vowed. "And if you want to learn whatever facts I do manage to garner, I suggest you get control of your wild imagination and go back to being the well-behaved wife I expect you to be."

He had her. Pearl knew she would capitulate, as had always been her practice, and Louis would win again.

Drawing a hesitant, shaky breath, the enraged matron gritted her teeth and let her already-reeling mind spin out of control. If, in the final analysis, Aaron was really gone forever, perhaps she would join him in heaven. But, she added with surprising malice, she was not going to give up until she had sent Louis to a place where neither she, nor her loved ones, would ever have to see him again.

The cruelty and callousness of her malevolent thoughts shook her to the core. Had her trying years with Louis made her so hard-hearted that she could actually contemplate taking his life? Apparently so.

Weeping, she cried out to God for forgiveness, fell to her knees and begged Him for a return of the hope she had lost.

Chapter Five

Thorne spent the next morning at the docks, arranging passage for his party on the U.S. Mail Packet the *Grand Republic*. She wasn't big but she was a fast side-wheeler with a shallow draft and could therefore put them ashore almost anywhere along the coast if need be, an important advantage as far as Thorne was concerned.

There were plenty of other small packet boats he could have chosen. Steaming up and down the Pacific Coast, hauling mail, freight, passengers and gold dust had become a very lucrative business, especially in the five years since the original discovery of gold on the American River.

Once every fortnight, around the first and fifteenth of the month, larger freighters arrived in San Francisco Bay bringing supplies, as well as the latest news. Representatives of the city's twelve local papers waited at the docks for those dispatches, determined to be the first to disseminate information that may have come all the way from New York City, once the nation's capitol and still an important focal point of world affairs.

Thorne remained at the wharf in the hopes of getting his hands on further news about the ill-fated ship his brother had been aboard. He finally managed to obtain a newly arrived, abbreviated copy of the *New York Herald* and found the article he sought near the bottom of the second page.

It read:

The honorable Aaron Ashton, son of our fair city's esteemed banker, Mr. Louis P. Ashton, was reported to be a passenger aboard the three-masted freighter *El Dorado* when she floundered and sank in a frightful gale off the southern coast of Mexico last month. Local reports indicate that all unfortunate souls aboard were lost. Mr. Louis Ashton, a friend of the *Herald,* has indicated to us that he will sail for Mexico at the first opportunity to ascertain his son's whereabouts and to see to arrangements, if necessary. Our condolences and heartfelt prayers go out to the Ashton family.

Thorne crumpled the paper and threw it into the bay. He watched while the ebbing tide beat the few thin pages against the side of the wooden-hulled freighter until the paper disintegrated. Soaring, screeching gulls dived at the shreds as if they were as incensed and anxious as Thorne.

So, the old man was headed for Mexico, was he? Well, good. At least that quest would keep him busy and out of Thorne's hair for the present. If Aaron had managed to survive after all, Louis would see that he received the best care possible.

And in the meantime? Thorne turned and strode purposefully back toward the Montgomery House Hotel.

In the meantime he would prepare his party as best he could and make ready to depart.

He would have preferred that no one else knew where he was bound or with whom. Unfortunately those plans were already common knowledge, thanks to his public discussion with Miss Beal at the hotel dinner table. He would, however, request that her father and Mrs. Montgomery keep their counsel if other seekers came later. Even with Aaron and his abductors out of the picture it was possible that Louis might send more villains to wreak havoc on what was left of his brother's family.

Instead of going to his room, Thorne went looking for Charity and found her in the kitchen, peeling potatoes for the large, afternoon meal.

"Forgive me for interrupting," he said with a polite nod as he removed his hat. "I wanted you to know I've arranged passage on the *Grand Republic*. We leave tomorrow morning on the outgoing tide."

Charity laid aside her paring knife and dried her hands on her apron. Jacob, who was lurking in the folds of her skirt, giggled and ducked back to hide.

"You're going, too, little man," Charity said. "Won't it be fun! Your mama and Uncle Thorne and I are all going on a wonderful trip with you. We're going to see your grandma and grandpa White, up in Oregon."

"Papa?" the child asked.

"I expect your papa will join us as soon as he's able," she said.

Thorne assumed by her ensuing look of contrition that she was hoping the Good Lord would forgive her attempts to pacify the child by stretching the truth. He smiled benevolently at both her and Jacob, then met her gaze directly and merely said, "Thank you."

"You're quite welcome. I've laundered all of Jacob's things, except what he's wearing, and have done the best I could for Naomi, as well. We'll all be ready to go whenever you give the word."

Thorne reached into his pants pocket, withdrew a twenty-dollar Liberty Head gold piece, and handed it to her. "I should have been as considerate of your needs. Please consider this an advance on your wages and buy whatever you may need for yourself, Miss Beal. I want you to travel comfortably."

Seeming reluctant but smiling nevertheless, Charity accepted the coin and slipped it into her apron pocket. "I don't require much beyond what I already possess but I am obliged. Have you thought about other supplies we might need once we reach land again?"

"I figured to provision our party in Oregon or Washington Territories rather than try to buy everything here and transport it all that way. Since we don't know exactly what we'll face, it makes more sense to wait."

"I suppose so. But it will be much more expensive. My sister, Faith, and I paid dearly to stock up on flour and bacon in Fort Laramie."

"I'm sure you did. One added advantage we'll have is that the Northern Pacific railroad line has recently been completed as far as Puget Sound. Between that supply line on one side and the sea on the other, merchants should be well stocked."

"My, my. That's amazing. I had no idea."

Thorne saw her glance past him and pause. He looked over his shoulder and his curiosity turned to annoyance when he saw who was standing in the doorway. "Can we help you?" he asked the all-too-familiar, portly hotel guest.

The man smiled and nodded. "I couldn't help over-hearin' you talkin' about headin' north. I have business in the territories myself and I was a mite curious, that's all."

"Then I suggest you get yourself down to the docks and find passage on a packet boat. There are plenty to choose from," Thorne said flatly. His stare was plainly meant to intimidate and the other man responded as he had hoped he would—he took his leave.

Thorne gave him plenty of time to have reached the front door, then spoke quietly to Charity. "Was he standing there eavesdropping for very long?"

"I don't know. I can't be certain. Why?"

"I don't like him."

"That's probably because he took Naomi for a walk without your permission. He seems harmless enough to me, pretty full of himself but otherwise not particularly odious."

"When did he first come here? Do you remember?"

"A few days ago. I can check the register if you want me to be more precise. I think his name starts with an S. Maybe it's Smith." She chuckled demurely. "Like yours."

"Very funny. I suppose there must be some genuine Smiths somewhere or it wouldn't be such a common name."

"I suppose so."

Thorne had run out of valid reasons to linger in the kitchen. He reached into his pocket and withdrew a large key, gesturing with it as he said, "I'll go check on Naomi. I trust she was well this morning?"

"As well as can be expected." Charity gently stroked Jacob's hair as she spoke. "Mrs. Montgomery has been brewing motherwort tea for her three times a day, with a touch of lady slipper root and ginger. That seems to be helping settle her nerves. We haven't heard her pounding on the door or raising a ruckus at all lately."

"Good. I've asked the doctor for a bottle of laudanum, too, in case she becomes more unhinged while we're traveling."

"Do you really think that's necessary?"

"I hope not," Thorne said soberly. "I sincerely hope not."

Charity had grown more and more agitated as the day had progressed. She doubted she'd sleep a wink all night, especially since she was now sharing her narrow bed with the wiggly child.

That situation couldn't be helped, she reasoned, gazing fondly at the place atop her mattress where Jacob lay, already napping. Poor little man. He was exhausted, as well he should be, given his trying circumstances.

She had often tried to return him to his mother during the past three or four weeks. Each time, Naomi's unbalanced mind had demonstrated how unwise that would be. Since Jacob's mother had no idea who he was, there was no way Charity was going to leave them alone together. For all she knew, Naomi didn't even remember how to properly care for a young child.

She took a deep breath and released it as a sigh. Looking at her meager pile of belongings she was struck by how cumbersome the small trunk would be, especially if they were forced to travel astride horses or mules instead of employing a wagon on the final leg of their journey. Perhaps Mrs. Montgomery had a large carpetbag she could borrow. If not, she'd ask her to watch over Jacob in case he awoke and she'd make a quick trip to the dry goods store at the corner of Dupont and Washington.

Charity glanced out the window of her second-story room and hoped she hadn't waited too long to make this decision. Dusk was nearly upon the city, the rays of the setting sun reflecting off the waters of the bay and the ocean beyond to bathe the buildings in warm color.

In that muted, golden light it was easy to overlook the muddy streets and the unattractiveness of the poorer sections of town, especially those nearest the wharf. Washington Street was due to be paved in stone soon, from Dupont to Kearney, so Charity knew it was only a short time before those buildings bordering it would also be spruced up. The canvas and tar paper shacks of the gold-rush era were quickly being replaced with real buildings, thanks in part to the new law forbidding frame structures within the densely built sections of the city, and she was often awed by the rapid changes.

Hurrying downstairs, she found Mrs. Montgomery in the parlor, knitting while visiting with Emory. It was still hard for Charity to picture that woman taking her mother's place but she couldn't fault her father for being lonely. She just wished they could all go back to being the close family they had been when she was a girl—before he had headed for California to seek his fortune.

The happy couple were chatting away as if they were the only two people in the world and Charity was struck by the notion that maybe her father had found true riches, after all. He had definitely found another life's mate. Although she was glad for him, she was also quite aware that she was the only member of her family who was still alone, still unsettled.

Forcing a smile she entered the parlor and greeted her future stepmother. "Annabelle, I wonder if you might have a carpetbag I could use? I've decided it will be too much of a bother to tote my trunk."

The older woman returned her smile. "I'm sorry, dear, I don't. You can probably get one at the mercantile."

"I know. That was my second choice. Could you keep an eye on Jacob for me while I run down there? He shouldn't be any bother. He's sound asleep on my bed and I shut the door so outside noises won't wake him."

"Of course. Don't you worry one minute. I'll run up and check on him right soon."

"There's no hurry," Charity said, wrapping a shawl around her shoulders and wishing she'd thought to fetch a bonnet before she'd left her room. Well, that couldn't be helped. If she was going to reach the store before the clerks locked up for the night she'd have to go without one.

"I'll be back in two shakes of a lamb's tail," she called over her shoulder as she headed for the front door.

The heels of her dainty shoes tapped on the boards of the raised walkway, reminding her that it would be a good idea to purchase a sturdy pair of boots, as well as the carpetbag. It hadn't been that long ago that she'd struggled to cross the barren plains and there had been many times during that trek when she had wished mightily for more substantial footwear.

She was almost running when she reached the corner where the dry goods store stood. The shade was pulled and the sign in the window read Closed.

Breathless, she rapped on the glass window in the entrance door and called, "Hello? Are you still there?"

The face of a familiar gentleman appeared. He recognized her, unlocked the door and peered out.

"I'm sorry to call so late," she said. "But I'm sailing tomorrow and…"

He smiled graciously, stepped back and Charity darted inside.

Thorne had been in the What Cheer saloon, making plans to have some of the local men continue to watch for signs of his brother in spite of the probability that he would never return when he'd noticed a young woman in a yellow gingham dress hurrying past on the far side of the thoroughfare. He recognized Charity Beal immediately. Worried, he left his companions to follow her. When he reached the street, however, she was out of sight.

His thoughts immediately turned to Jacob and Naomi. Yes, he believed they would be safe at the hotel because there were so many others present, yet the fact that Charity was away gave him pause. He figured she was merely out seeking something else to take on their trip but that probably meant that there was no one specifically looking after the boy.

The hackles on the back of Thorne's neck prickled a warning. Concerned, he wheeled and headed back toward the hotel at a trot.

Annabelle had been having such a wonderful time making plans for the future with her groom, she waited longer than she had intended before going to check on the sleeping child. Climbing the stairs wasn't as easy for her at sixty as it had once been, nor was it painless. Every change in the weather brought new aches and the harder she labored, the more she hurt, which meant that going from the first to the second floor was neither easy nor enjoyable.

Still, she had promised Charity she'd look in on Jacob, so she would make the extra effort. She was halfway up when Thorne straight-armed the door behind her and strode into the lobby.

Annabelle paused and greeted him. "Oh, good. You're here so you can go check on the boy. I was goin' to but these old bones are achin', and that's a fact."

"He's alone?"

"Sleeping. Miss Charity put him to bed in her room and he hasn't made a peep. I've been listenin'."

Thorne hurried past. She was far enough up the stairway to watch the big man go directly to Charity's door and ease it open.

A few seconds later his shout startled her so badly she nearly lost her balance. Grasping the banister she struggled the rest of the way up and found him on his knees on the rag rug next to Charity's bed. He was hugging Jacob. The child was clinging to his neck and sobbing.

Concerned and winded, Annabelle leaned on the doorjamb for support. "What's wrong? Is he sick?"

The look Thorne shot her in reply was so alarming it made her demand more answers. "What's happened? Tell me."

"I don't know," Thorne said. "When I got here he was sitting on the floor, crying. All I've been able to get out of him was that he was going to see his papa."

"Maybe he was dreaming," the older woman suggested.

Thorne rose with the sobbing youngster in his arms.

"I don't think so. He kept saying he wanted to go with the man."

"To—to see my papa," Jacob stuttered, sniffling.

"What man?" Annabelle asked. "Where is he?"

The boy pointed across the room. "Gone."

"Out the window?" Thorne asked.

Jacob nodded, his dark curls bobbing.

Rather than carry his precious burden to the window and expose him to possible lingering danger, Thorne handed him to Mrs. Montgomery. "Here. And don't let him out of your sight."

She stood there, holding the boy and staring, open-mouthed, as Thorne lifted the sash as high as it would go, bent double and stepped out onto the roof of the porch below.

"Do you see anybody?" she called.

"No. I'm going to climb on up to check the rest of the roof. Take Jacob downstairs and stay with Emory until Charity gets back."

Not about to argue with such a forceful man, especially since he was so upset, the proprietress did as she was told.

She had just reached the parlor, carrying the sniffling child, when she heard a woman's piercing scream echo from the street outside.

Chapter Six

Returning to the hotel with her purchases, Charity wouldn't have noticed the two figures atop the hotel roof if a woman across the way hadn't shrieked and pointed.

Mindful of the horse-and-wagon traffic in the muddy street, Charity nevertheless left the raised walk and quickly maneuvered until she was in a position to view what was going on.

She froze, squinted and shaded her eyes. Was that who she thought it was? Was Thorne Blackwell actually scrambling along the rooftop, *chasing* someone?

Backlit by the setting sun, the two men appeared little more than shifting shadows, yet she instantly recognized Thorne from the way he moved, the shape of his broad shoulders, the cut of his clothes. It was him, all right, and he was gaining on his agile, more slightly built quarry.

Thorne lunged. He grabbed for the other man and managed to catch hold of his ankle. Both figures fell, and the slam of their bodies hitting the metal roof carried all the way to the street below.

As Charity watched, the thinner man used his free

leg to kick at Thorne and caught him in the shoulder. Thorne lost his grip and went skidding toward the edge of the corrugated tin roof as if the surface were greased.

Charity was too stunned to remember to pray. She gasped and held her breath as Thorne rolled onto his back, dug in his heels and slowed his descent. He finally came to a halt mere inches from the edge of the precipice.

Instead of abandoning his pursuit the way Charity had expected him to, he immediately turned and started to climb back to the crest of the roof, moving like one of the hundreds of tiny crabs that crowded the shore at low tide.

As soon as he reached the highest peak, he braced himself and straightened, his hands on his hips. Charity assumed from his stillness that his target must have escaped.

She watched until he had given up, edged safely back down onto the porch roof and was preparing to enter one of the windows. That was when she realized that he was climbing into *her* room! The very room where she had left Jacob.

Frightened beyond imagination, Charity hiked her skirts and raced back across the rutted street toward the hotel. Not even stopping to wipe her feet, she dropped her purchases inside the door, crossed the lobby and bolted up the stairs just in time to confront Thorne as he exited her room.

"What is it?" she asked breathlessly. "Is Jacob all right?"

"Yes." He was scowling. "Why did you leave him alone?"

"I didn't. He was sleeping so I asked Mrs. Montgomery to look in on him while I ran to the store. I never have stayed with him every waking moment." She tried to squeeze past.

Thorne reached out and grasped her arm to stop her. "You're right. I'm sorry. I shouldn't have blamed you."

"For what, exactly? What's happened?"

"Someone tried to take him," he said flatly.

"What?" Frantic, she twisted to free herself. "Let me go. I have to see him."

"Settle down. He's safe now. He's with Mrs. Montgomery and your father."

"Oh, thank the Lord!" Charity said, meaning the praise with every ounce of her being.

Suddenly weak-kneed, she was glad Thorne had not yet released his hold on her. She sagged within his grasp. He stepped to her side to begin guiding her down the stairs toward the parlor.

"I saw you out on the roof just now," Charity said as they descended. "Was that man the one who tried to steal Jacob? Was that why you were chasing him?"

"Yes. Jacob told me he had fled out the window. When I followed, I spotted him running away."

"Did you recognize him?"

"I'm not sure. I think he may have been one of the hotel guests."

"The man who was listening to us talk in the kitchen?" she asked, barely whispering and looking from side to side to make certain they were alone.

"No. A different person. I don't recall his name but I'm fairly certain I've seen him around." His frown deepened and he paused with her before they reached the ground floor. "As a matter of fact, I think he's one of the volunteers who was helping me search for Aaron."

"But, why would he try to take Jacob?"

"Probably because he's working for my stepfather," Thorne said with obvious malice.

His arm tightened around her shoulders and Charity permitted the social faux pas. At that moment she needed Thorne's strong moral and physical support more than she needed to maintain her usually prim demeanor. Jacob had been in mortal danger and she had failed him. She could only thank a benevolent providence for the child's deliverance.

That was a direct answer to her prayers for Jacob and Naomi's safety, she realized with a start. Even though she had temporarily failed in her duty, God had looked after the innocent little boy. *And his mother, also?* she asked herself.

Grasping the banister with her right hand, she swiveled to look back up the stairs. "Wait. Have you checked on Naomi, too?"

Thorne froze. "That's where I was headed when I ran into you. Stay here."

"Not on your life," Charity said. "From now on, where you go, I go."

"No. It might be dangerous."

Charity gave a nervous laugh as she dogged his steps in spite of his sensible admonitions. "Fine," she muttered, speaking as much to herself as to Thorne, "if you get into any more trouble like you did on the roof, I'll be there to clunk the other fellow over the head and rescue you."

Naomi was asleep when Thorne unlocked her door but he thought it best to rouse her and make certain she was unmolested.

"Naomi?" He gently touched her shoulder.

"Oh. Is it morning?" she asked, yawning and blinking rapidly. "Dear me. I seem to have fallen asleep without getting ready for bed. What will Mama say?"

"I'm sure she won't be upset," Charity volunteered. "Are you feeling better after your nap?"

"Fit as a fiddle." The paler woman swung her feet over the side of the bed and looked at her own feet. "My, my, I've left my shoes on, too. How silly of me."

She stood, stretched, then smoothed her fitted jacket over her skirt with a delicate tug at the braid decorating the bottom edge, as well as the collar and cuffs. "Well, I'd best be going."

"I think you should come downstairs with us," Charity said before Thorne could object.

He agreed. "You're right. It will be best if we all stick together until we sail." Looking to Charity he added, "You can sleep with Naomi tonight and I'll keep the boy with me. We'll leave our door open so we'll hear you if you call out."

"Do you really think that's necessary?"

"Vital. Do you have a gun?"

"No. I've never been fond of firearms."

"Well, you'd better get fond of them because you may need to defend yourself. Have you ever learned to shoot?"

"Yes. Faith insisted I practice with Papa's old Colt. It was so heavy I had to use two hands to lift it."

"I'll find you something lighter, something you can safely carry in your apron pocket or your reticule."

"If you insist."

Seeing Charity shiver and pull her lacy shawl closer brought a tightness to his gut. What had he gotten her

involved in? And how was he going to protect all three
of his charges if they were ever separated? Jacob was
dear to his heart and Naomi was kin, but the notion of
having to choose them over Charity Beal gnawed at his
conscience. The only sensible conclusion was to see that
the four of them were together all the time until he had
delivered Naomi to her parents. After that, he'd simply
escort Charity back to San Francisco and everyone's
troubles would be over.

Thorne would have felt a lot better about those logical conclusions if his heart and mind had not immediately countered them with serious misgivings. First, it
would be improper for him to travel with only Charity. Although she was perfect as Naomi's chaperone
and Jacob's caretaker, escorting a lovely, single woman
like her posed an altogether different moral dilemma.

And that wasn't all that was bothering him. There
were clearly forces of evil at work. Try as he might, he
couldn't seem to clear his mind of vivid images of
impending doom. Images that involved Charity Beal.

Naomi had taken Thorne's arm, leaving Charity to
follow them down the stairs. She wasn't offended. After
all, she reminded herself, she was merely the hired help,
not a part of his family, no matter what he had promised about treating her as such. Besides, she had only
accepted the position because she cared about poor little Jacob.

And now look what's happened, she chided. *You left
him alone and he was nearly kidnapped. Or worse!*

That dire conclusion brought unshed tears to her
eyes. She had made a bad mistake and the Lord had
sent Thorne to set things right again. She would not

make any more errors of judgment. From now on she was going to stick closer than that child's shadow. No one was going to harm him. Not while she still had breath in her body.

When they reached the lobby, Charity dodged past the others and made a beeline for Annabelle and the boy. It was clear that Jacob had been crying because his eyes were red and his cheeks streaked by tears.

She held out her arms. He immediately scrambled down from Mrs. Montgomery's ample lap and ran to Charity as fast as his short, pudgy legs would carry him.

She scooped him up and held him tight for a long moment before she smiled and said, "Look at you. We need to wash your face."

"I want my papa," he whined.

"I know you do, dear. But I can't do anything about that right now." Balancing him on one hip she started toward the kitchen. "Let's go get you cleaned up and then maybe we can find you another cookie. How does that sound?"

A glance back toward Thorne told her he wasn't keen on having the child out of his sight for even a few minutes.

"We'll be right here in the kitchen," she said flatly. "If you want to join us, you're most welcome, but it's not necessary. I will not leave him alone again, I promise you. Not for any reason."

"We'll be right here, talking," Thorne said as he formally escorted Naomi to the settee and placed her beside Annabelle. "Don't be long."

"No longer than it takes to wash and find a treat." Charity smiled. "And don't bother telling me I'm spoiling him. I know I am. And I fully intend to continue."

To her relief, Thorne returned her smile, although his was more lopsided and wry than what she was used to seeing. It gave him an impish air that she fancied was more a reflection of the boy he had once been than of the man he had become.

"I'm not at all surprised," he said. "I'd be doing the same thing if I were not otherwise occupied."

"Then I'll give him a cookie on your behalf, too. How does that sound?"

With his eyes glittering suspiciously and his voice hoarse he answered, "Please do."

Charity was so touched by the tenderness she noted in Thorne's response she had to bite her lip to keep from weeping tears of joy and relief. They had had a terrible scare, one that might very well have spelled the end of their proposed rescue mission, and she was so thankful to have the child in her arms, healthy and unharmed, that she would have given him just about anything he had asked for.

The one thing she couldn't give him, of course, was the return of his missing father. It was hard to believe Aaron was actually deceased, although all indications pointed to that heartrending result.

Then again, Charity told herself, the ways of the Lord truly were mysterious. Aaron could still be alive even if he had been shipwrecked.

Thinking that gave her an inkling of peace and she chose to latch on to the possibility that he had survived rather than dwell on his probable death.

She sat Jacob on the edge of the enameled sink while she pumped fresh water to wet a clean cloth. "This is a bit cold," she said, wiping his cheeks, "but your face is really dirty, you know that?"

He nodded and accepted her ministrations stoically. "Uh-huh." Looking past her shoulder at the doorway into the parlor, he asked, "Is Uncle Thorne mad at me?"

"Oh, honey, no," Charity said quickly, kissing his damp forehead. "He was just worried, that's all. You must never go off with strangers, not even ones that seem nice or say they can take you to your papa. Promise?"

His lower lip quivered. "Uh-huh."

"Good." She tried to lift his spirits by pretending she wasn't concerned when what she really wanted to do was clasp the child tightly to her breast for the rest of the day and night. "Now, how about that cookie?"

"Two cookies," the bright child said as she lifted and set him on the floor. "One from you and one from Uncle Thorne."

Charity laughed. "That's right. Hold up your fingers and show me how many that is."

When he struggled to display only two fingers and finally succeeded, she clasped his hand and kissed his extended fingers. "That's right. What a smart boy you are."

"I'm almost three," Jacob said, laboriously adding another digit and displaying the count.

"That's wonderful. When is your birthday?"

He looked puzzled, then brightened. "Mama knows. We can ask her."

Charity had to turn away. She busied herself getting his cookies while she sought to compose herself. What were they going to do if Naomi never regained her memory or even came to her senses about the simplest things? What if she continued to believe that she, too, was a child? What would happen to her little boy then?

The dreadful consequences of such a misfortune were unthinkable.

* * *

"Hey, don't look at me like that. I almost had him," the wiry young man said.

"And nearly got yourself into serious trouble. I told you I'd take care of it."

"Yeah, yeah, I know. You just want all the glory for yourself."

"I deserve it," the heavier man replied, giving his tall companion a look of disdain. "I never would have tried a stunt like you pulled. Not right under their noses. What were you thinking, man? What if you'd gotten caught?"

"But I didn't." He peered from one end of the alleyway to the other, clearly wary and understandably nervous.

"Not yet you haven't. The night is still young." Blowing puffs from his cigar into rings, the heavyset smoker paused for effect before he said, "If I were you, I'd be down at the docks right now, looking for passage out of here on the first boat I could find, like I told you."

"I was goin' to do that come morning."

"No. You'll do it now. I don't want you hanging around here drawing attention to me." He patted his cuff where they both knew he carried a hidden derringer. "The way I see it you have a choice. Either you hightail it for the boats or I'll shoot you where you stand and eliminate any connections between us. It's up to you."

"Okay." He held up his hands in a gesture of compliance. "I'll go." Glancing toward the hotel windows above he added, "What about my clothes?"

"I'll pitch them out the window for you. If you or any sign of you is still in San Francisco in another hour, you're a dead man."

"We were partners," his companion grumbled. "Why should you want to kill me?"

"For sheer stupidity if nothing else. Now, stay put and keep out of sight. I'll go get your things."

"There's a pistol under my pillow. Don't forget that."

The stronger-willed assassin laughed coarsely. "You must think I'm a fool. You'll get it—but without any bullets."

"Awww… What'll happen to me if I ain't armed?"

His eyes narrowed menacingly. "One more word out of you and neither of us will have to worry about what happens to you, gun or no gun. Is that clear?"

"Yeah. I s'pose I can get more black powder, ball and caps down in Chinatown. Just hurry it up, will ya?" His wary gaze darted to the streets at either end of the alley as if expecting imminent attack.

"I'll be shoving your clothes out that window just as soon as I can sneak into your room." He pointed up with his half-smoked cigar. "Be ready."

"What if somebody sees you?"

"Then I'll play it safe, protect myself, and you'll be leaving without your duds. Just remember you're leaving, period. Even if it's feetfirst."

Chapter Seven

❧

Charity packed everyone's clothes except Thorne's and turned in early that night. Naomi caused her no trouble, thanks to another cup of Mrs. Montgomery's special tea, but every creaky board, every quarrelsome gull that perched on the porch roof, every passing carriage or horseman below seemed to startle Charity and keep her from falling asleep. As a consequence, she was exhausted in the morning when Thorne rapped on the door to her room.

She gathered her wrapper around her and tied the sash on her way to the door. "Who is it?"

"It's me," he said. "We should leave within the hour."

Opening the door a crack Charity hid behind it and peeked out. "We'll be ready. Naomi is still sound asleep but I'll have her up and dressed in plenty of time. I promise."

"You look tired," he said gently.

"I am, and that's a fact." She peered past him and scowled. "Where's Jacob?"

"Downstairs with Mrs. Montgomery and your father." He began to smile. "You should see those two working together in the kitchen. She's giving the orders like a ship's captain and he's trying to keep up with her. Looks to me as if she'll be wanting to hire some more help very soon."

"I don't doubt that. Papa never was much of a cook or housekeeper. His miner's cabin at Beal's Bar was pretty rustic."

Loath to shut the door all the way and bid him good-bye, she tarried a moment longer. When Thorne took a step back she assumed she was keeping him. "I don't want to delay you. We'll be down in a jiffy."

It pleased her to see that Thorne seemed as reluctant to depart as she was to have him leave.

Finally, he asked, "Do you want me to wait out here until you're ready?"

"Mercy, no. By the time we dress and do our hair up properly you could be through eating breakfast."

Still, he hesitated. "I don't know that I should leave you."

"We'll be fine. This is a respectable hotel and one of our clerks is on duty all night. I warned him to be on the lookout for the man you caught bothering Jacob, so I know there's nothing to worry about."

Thorne nodded. "All right. I'll stop by the front desk and check with him about it just to be sure. In the meantime, you ladies make ready to travel. And be sure you have your heavy coats. It can get blustery on board those packet boats, even if they do stay closer to shore than my heavier freighters. You'll doubtless need warm clothing the farther north we sail, too."

"Oh, dear. I hadn't thought of that. I'm afraid I don't have anything really heavy."

"Then bring Aaron's overcoat for yourself," Thorne

said. "I was planning to leave his suits and things behind for your father, anyway. Emory won't need that coat nearly as much as you will."

"All right. Perhaps I can take my sewing box and make the necessary alterations while we're traveling." She wasn't pleased when Thorne laughed.

"Do as you wish. Just remember, the less we have to transport, the easier the trip will be," he said.

"I know." Pursing her lips and making a face she nevertheless had to admit he was being sensible. "All right. I'll wear the coat as it is and roll up the sleeves if need be. Will that satisfy you?" Seeing his continuing amusement, she added, "What's so funny?"

"Nothing. I apologize. I was just picturing you floundering around in that big coat."

"I never flounder. Besides, if your brother's coat warms me when I would otherwise be freezing, I certainly won't let pride keep me from wearing it. Now, if you'll excuse me…"

She eased the door closed and left him standing there in the hallway, grinning like a child with his hand in a penny candy jar at the mercantile. She had been honest when she'd insisted she wasn't prideful. Now that she thought more about their upcoming situation she decided it was just as well she wouldn't look very appealing while clad in Aaron's oversize coat.

The last thing she wanted was to make herself attractive to a man—any man—and her burgeoning feelings for Thorne Blackwell and his nephew would be far better denied than expressed.

Yes, he already knew she cared deeply for the boy but that was simply a mother's instincts. All women had those. It was her undeniable affinity for Jacob's taciturn yet intriguing uncle that threatened to be her undoing.

Charity pressed her back against the closed door, looked around and sighed. This was the last time she would see this cozy room for who knew how long, and the thought of leaving San Francisco and all that was familiar tugged at her heart. She knew that sacrifice was necessary. She also knew she was doing the right thing.

Nevertheless, she wished she could change the current circumstances. The notion of making a journey into a wilderness that lay beyond her current experience was unsettling. The idea of doing so in the company of a forceful man like Thorne Blackwell was doubly so.

Thick, damp, bone-chilling fog shrouded the city as Thorne led his little party toward the wharf where the *Grand Republic* awaited. He knew the crew would already have a head of steam built up in preparation for sailing and he was in a hurry to board.

The docks were bustling with activity in spite of the dreariness of the early morning. Bulging cargo nets swung from overhead hoists mounted on the foredeck while dozens of men pushed heavily laden carts across rickety planks that spanned the short distance between the pier and the boat's portside. Over the years, many a hapless man had missed his footing and plunged to his death from such planks. It was a hazardous profession but never lacked for willing workers.

Thorne hired a man to follow with their luggage, then began to escort the adults in his party across the planks one at a time, beginning with Charity so he could safely pass Jacob into her care.

"Take him and wait right here with our bags while I get Naomi," he ordered.

Charity smiled and gave him a mock salute. "Yes, sir."

He understood that she was merely trying to lighten his mood but he couldn't bring himself to respond in kind. Maybe it was because of the foggy morning or maybe he was just unduly jumpy, but he couldn't seem to banish the sense that they were being watched.

His footsteps echoed hollowly on the springy plank as he returned to shore for his sister-in-law. She wasn't where he had left her! For an instant he feared that she had wandered off again. Then, he spotted her about fifteen feet away, standing with her back to the *Grand Republic*.

It wasn't until Thorne drew closer that he realized she was in the company of the same portly man who had tried to take her for a walk near the hotel.

He quickened his approach. "Hey, there. What do you think you're doing?"

The man doffed his hat to reveal thinning, reddish hair and smiled instead of retreating. "I was just telling this dear lady that I was certain you would be right back." He took a step to the side as Thorne grasped Naomi's arm. "I remembered how upset you were the last time we met so I refrained from allowing her to talk me into escorting her anywhere. I trust that suits your pleasure?"

"Yes." Thorne nodded, polite but wary. "Thank you."

Starting to guide Naomi away, he scowled at the other man. "What brings you to the docks so early? Did you find the passage you wanted?"

"I certainly did," the man said. He raised his lit cigar

and blew a smoke ring that disappeared almost instantly in the pea soup air. "I'm sailing aboard this very boat. You?"

"We're on the *Grand Republic,* too."

"Excellent." He extended his hand. "Allow me to introduce myself. Cyrus Satterfield, recently of Philadelphia. I believe I had the pleasure of dining with you several times at the Montgomery House Hotel."

Although Thorne was hesitant, he responded out of habit and shook the other man's hand. "Smith," he said.

"And you're from...?"

"I live at sea," Thorne told him. "Excuse us."

"Of course, of course. I'm sure we'll have plenty of time to get better acquainted while on board."

Thorne had made up his mind long ago that he was going to keep his family from getting acquainted with any other travelers. Now that he knew Cyrus Satterfield was aboard, he was even more determined to sequester them. There was something about the man that bothered Thorne. He recalled that Charity hadn't had the same misgivings, yet he couldn't seem to banish his concern.

Perhaps Satterfield was simply an unctuous fool. Then again, perhaps Thorne's first impression had been the right one. He'd disliked the man from the moment he'd first laid eyes on him.

Charity tried to distract herself, and Jacob, by showing him all the interesting cargo that was piled on the open, lower deck of the steamboat. There was extra wood for the boilers, sack goods such as grain and milled flour, barrels of pickles, crackers and hardtack, enormous bales of what looked like fodder for the sheep penned on the foredeck, a few cages filled with hens and all sorts of other miscellaneous freight.

She smiled as Thorne and Naomi joined them. "Jacob likes these chickens. He wanted to know if he could have one as a pet."

"Maybe your grandma White has chickens where she lives," Thorne replied. He gestured with his free arm. "We should go on up to the passenger deck so we're not in the way while the longshoremen finish loading and the crew prepares to cast off."

Charity, toting Jacob on one hip, led the way. "Oof," she told the child, "you're getting heavy now that you're almost three years old. What a big boy you are."

"His birthday is in June," Naomi said. Then she flushed and looked astonished. "Mercy me. How do you suppose I knew that?"

Charity didn't know what to say in response so she remained silent.

"It's the tenth, if I remember right," Thorne volunteered. "We should be at his grandparents' by then. We'll have to have a birthday party."

"With cake," the child added, clearly delighted. "I like chocolate. Mama always makes it for me."

It tore at Charity's heart to see the little boy look at his mother so lovingly. It was evident he now expected her to begin talking to him the way she used to but the woman had resumed her blank stare. Whatever twist of fate had triggered her sudden recall, the occasion had apparently passed.

"Well, if your grandmother doesn't know how to bake the kind of cake you like, I do," Charity said. "I'll see that somebody makes you one for your birthday. Okay?"

He nodded so hard his curls bobbed. "Okay!" Wrapping his arms around her neck he added a soft, tender, "I love you."

If she hadn't been in such close proximity to the rest of the family she would have buried her face in his curls and allowed herself to weep.

As it was, she simply gave him a hug, forced a smile and said, "I love you, too, sweetheart."

Thorne could tell that Charity was getting far too attached to the child for her own good. He knew exactly how that could happen. He'd done the same thing on their journey around the horn.

At his young age, Jacob was open and loving to a fault. He had not yet realized the extent of the disappointments that life had dealt him, nor would he have to bear them alone, if Thorne had his way. He didn't know how he was going to accomplish that, especially once they delivered Naomi and the boy to the missionaries, but he was certainly going to try. Above all, he was going to keep sending money for their support so they never became a financial liability to anyone.

Louis Ashton had always complained loudly about the terrible burden Thorne's presence had caused. One of the most violent outbursts had occurred shortly before Thorne had left home for good.

"I can do as I please whether you like it or not," Louis had shouted at his wife. "If I choose to beat the no-good boy within an inch of his life, it's my right."

"You have no rights to him," Pearl had sobbed as she'd clung to her husband's sleeve to stay his hand. "No rights!"

"I'm his father, remember? You should. It's your fault I was saddled with raising him."

"He goes by my first husband's name already. What more do you want?"

Louis had laughed maniacally then. "What I want is illegal, my dear, or I would have put him in the ground when he was born."

Though the bruises had long ago healed, the memory of that last bout of physical and verbal abuse was still painful. If Thorne could protect Jacob from ever feeling unaccepted or unloved, for whatever reason, he would.

When Thorne had first learned the truth about his own origins, he had blamed his mother for his troubles. Since Pearl had known she was carrying her late husband's child, why had she kept that news from Louis until after they were married? It was little wonder Louis had been hurt and angry as a result. That much was understandable. The only thing Thorne could not forgive was the way the man had treated him as he was growing up in the Ashton mansion. He had no doubt, if it hadn't been for Pearl's intervention, Louis would have tossed him into the streets at the first opportunity and never thought of him again.

In retrospect, incurring Louis's hatred was actually better than enduring his so-called love, Thorne concluded soberly. The old man's interference had probably caused Aaron's death. Even if his brother was still alive, Louis had gotten what he'd wanted. Aaron's little family had been split asunder.

Thorne clenched his fists. If he ever laid eyes on his stepfather again, he was going to have to struggle to control his temper. He knew what the Good Book said: "Vengeance is Mine, I will repay, saith the Lord," but he wasn't the kind of man to stand back and expect a bolt of lightning to come from heaven and handily eliminate his enemies for him.

If such a strike was to end Louis's miserable life, perhaps it was meant to come from the hand of the man he had so often cursed and screamed at in hatred.

Thorne gritted his teeth. Could he kill in cold blood? He strongly doubted it.

Then again, he added with silent determination, if brutality was necessary to protect the lives of Jacob and Naomi—or Charity—he would not hesitate to act in their behalf. Of that he was positive.

He gazed at Jacob through eyes of love. That boy could have been his son. If Naomi had not chosen to wed his brother, her firstborn *would* have been his child.

Struck by the significance of that thought, he stared. His heart leaped. Why had he not seen it before? The darker hair, the deep brown eyes, the stockier body… the child looked a lot more like him than he did Aaron. Had it happened to his family again? Had the wrong man been called "Father"?

He set his jaw, his anger building. If Naomi were in her normal state of mind, she would know. Even if she lied, he felt he'd be able to discern the truth from her words and expression. But now that she was as incapacitated as a babe herself, he might never find out.

Did he really want to know? *Oh, yes.* If he could prove to all concerned that Jacob was not Aaron's son, perhaps he could then convince Louis to leave the boy alone and let him and his mother escape.

Was such a thing possible? Thorne's remembered guilt was intense. He had not meant to sin. Even though he had not seen it as such at the time, he'd understood that what had happened was morally wrong. That was why he had begged Naomi to break off with Aaron and marry him, instead.

She had stolen into his room late at night, after he and Aaron had been drinking heavily to celebrate Aaron's recent betrothal, and had slipped under the covers beside him before he had realized she was even there.

In the ensuing frenzy, Thorne had lost his self-control. He had rued the mistake almost immediately.

"We—we can make it right," Thorne had told her as she had started to leave his bed. "Marry me, Naomi. I can make you happy."

"On a smelly old boat? At sea? Not in a million years." He remembered the scorn in her expression, in her tone. She'd swept her slim, silk-clad arm in an arc that encompassed the lavishly appointed bedroom suite. "I want all this, Thorne. A mansion, money, the prestige of becoming an Ashton of the New York Ashtons."

"Then why did you…?"

"Because you're a beautiful man and I fancied you," she'd said with a half smile. "You're going away tomorrow and I wanted to say a personal goodbye, one I'd never forget."

Thorne had arisen, gathered his things and left the house hours before the rest of the family had awakened. Aaron, however, had followed him to the dock and had insisted on an explanation of why Naomi was sobbing inconsolably and why he was leaving New York so abruptly.

Although Thorne had not gone into detail about their assignation, he had confessed to asking Naomi for her hand in marriage. When Aaron had struck him in response, he had simply stood stoically and accepted the punishment, knowing he deserved much worse.

Later, when he had nearly drowned at sea and had turned to God for salvation, he had repented and had believed his sin was forgiven.

He still believed that. Now, however, it looked as if the consequences of that sin had come back to change his life even more than he'd dreamed. The question was, what was he going to do about it?

Leaning his elbows on the railing of the upper deck, he clasped his hands and stared into the distance at the lighthouse that marked the deep water entrance to the bay. His thoughts spun and wandered like an oarless rowboat caught in a cyclone.

If what he now imagined was true, he was partly responsible. Not only had his indiscretion possibly hindered his brother's marital bliss, it might have created the very reason for Louis's vendetta. Even if the old man did not suspect what Jacob's origins might be, the boy's looks may have reminded him too much of Thorne as a child and therefore predisposed him to feel hatred.

"So, what do I do now, Father," he prayed in a whisper. "What do I do?"

The answer came immediately, not as a spoken word but as a firm assurance. His course was set. He would follow the plan that most benefited his brother's family. Then, if Aaron returned, he'd be able to tell him he had acted honorably. This time.

Chapter Eight

Charity was enough aware of Thorne's moods to realize that he was tormented by something. What could be bothering him, however, was a puzzlement. If anyone in their party had reason to act sad or upset about leaving San Francisco, it should be *her*.

Bidding her father and his intended bride farewell at the hotel had been a heartrending experience. Softhearted Annabelle had gotten teary-eyed and even Emory had sniffled when Charity had hugged the two of them goodbye. Their wedding was only a few weeks off but she'd had to depart with Thorne's party so she had promised to celebrate with them when she returned. If she returned.

That recent memory caused her to recall equally reluctant goodbyes when she and her sister had packed all their worldly goods and had left Ohio by wagon train. In the ensuing four years, Charity felt as if she had lived a whole lifetime and was now wise far beyond her true age. Maybe she was. She'd certainly lived through more than enough danger and trauma to last her the remainder of her time on earth.

And *now?* she asked herself. It was foolish to worry about the future when she had no control over it, but her active imagination kept suggesting scenarios right out of her worst nightmares. What if they became separated? What if Naomi wandered off and got lost? What if the man who had attempted to steal Jacob tried again—and succeeded?

Charity tightened her hold on the child until he began to squirm.

She smiled at him. "I'm sorry, sweetheart. I didn't mean to squeeze you too hard. I was just giving you a special hug."

"Okay." Putting his arms back around her neck, he ducked inside the brim of her bonnet and planted a wet kiss on her cheek.

Laughing lightly, she stood at the outside railing on the upper deck and pointed. "Look over there? See the new lighthouse on Alcatraz Island? The light in it had to come all the way across the ocean from France. Maybe one of Uncle Thorne's ships brought it."

"He has sails on his ship," the boy said, looking up at the fluted smokestacks of the steamer. "It's big."

"I know. Did you have fun riding on it?"

"Uh-huh. I even got to turn the wheel."

"Good for you. Was it hard to do?"

The dark curls bounced as he shook his head vigorously. "Nope. Uncle Thorne helped."

"I imagine he did." Grinning, Charity was once again amazed at how quickly the child's zest for life was able to lift her sagging spirits. Seeing the world through his eyes gave everything a lovely quality of newness and a sense of discovery that was missing in the jaded views of most adults, including her.

Watching others waving farewell to loved ones on the docks, she wished her father had been free to come down to the shore to see them off. Unfortunately, Emory and Mrs. Montgomery would be up to their elbows in the hotel kitchen by now, preparing to feed the guests. That kind of endless toil was one part of Charity's daily life in San Francisco that she was positive she would not miss.

Beneath her feet the painted wooden deck trembled from the vibrations of the engine. Pale smoke billowed from the *Grand Republic*'s twin stacks. A shrill whistle near the pilothouse suddenly came alive and blew two long blasts, making her jump.

Seeing the boy's equally wide-eyed response, she was quick to speak. "My, my, that was loud, wasn't it? I think that means we're about to cast off. Shall we go over to the other side and watch the paddle wheel turn?"

"Yeah!"

Charity saw Thorne and Naomi standing together at the far railing as she approached. It was clear from Thorne's posture that he was being protective of the other woman. Charity knew that was as it should be, yet she experienced an unexpected twinge of jealousy.

Instead of surprising them, she announced her arrival with a pleasant, "Hello again. Can we see the paddle wheel from over here? I promised to show it to Jacob."

Thorne stepped aside to make room for her and the boy next to an ornately carved, white-painted post supporting the roof above that portion of the passenger deck. "Take my place," he said. "I've seen it all before."

To Charity's astonishment he stepped close behind her as soon as she had joined Naomi. His presence was so strong, so dizzying, she wondered briefly if she should pass him the child for safety's sake.

Instead, she sat the little boy on the railing with his back to her and held on to him tightly so he wouldn't accidentally slip off.

The *Grand Republic* hissed and moaned and creaked while it slowly backed away from its moorings. Brown pelicans, startled by the noise, took flight from the ends of the piers. Flocks of soaring, diving gulls followed the boat's turbulent wake, squawking and vying for the best positions close to the water.

The paddle wheel soon reversed directions, then picked up speed as the packet boat headed out to sea. It began to lightly splash those passengers brave enough to remain too close. Jacob giggled and swatted at the salty drops.

"We'd better move back," Thorne said. With his arm around Naomi's shoulders, he guided her away through the dispersing crowd.

Charity scooped up the child and followed. She couldn't help noticing that Thorne seemed uneasy, as well as morose.

As soon as he had settled Naomi on a white-painted bench beside the pilothouse, Charity touched his sleeve and drew him aside. "What's wrong?"

"Nothing."

"Don't lie to me, mister. I told you I can tell when a person isn't being truthful. You've been acting strangely ever since we boarded."

He nodded as he scanned the crowd milling around on the passenger deck. "All right. One of our friends from the hotel is also aboard."

She gasped. "Not the man you were chasing!"

"No. Not him. The one who was listening to us talk in the kitchen yesterday."

"He did say he was looking for a boat headed north, too."

"Yes, but…"

"I'd meant to ask what you'd found out this morning and didn't have a good opportunity. Had that man you chased across the roof shown up at the hotel again?"

"No. Nobody has seen hide nor hair of him since yesterday. When the clerk went up to check his room, I went with him. The room was empty except for the usual furnishings. Everything personal was gone."

Her brow knit. "How? If he never came back after he tried to steal Jacob, how could he have gotten upstairs to pick up his belongings?"

"I haven't an earthly idea." Thorne removed his hat and raked his fingers through his thick hair. "Did you notice if he seemed overly friendly with any of the other guests?"

"Such as the one who's on board, you mean?"

"Particularly him."

"I'm afraid not. They may have spoken in passing from time to time but many of our lodgers did that. I never saw those two in the same place except at meals."

"Okay. We'll give him the benefit of the doubt, for the present," Thorne said. "I've had our bags taken to the stateroom I reserved. All except mine, that is. I'll be sleeping in a chair in the saloon with some of the other men."

"You don't have a berth?"

"No. I could only find one available room on a boat that was sailing immediately. Since the episode with

Jacob, I thought it was more important to leave quickly than to wait for better accommodations."

"That makes sense." Charity sighed. "All right. I'll need to know where the facility is for our little man pretty soon."

"There'll be a commode in your suite. Use that. I don't want any of you wandering around outside unless it's absolutely necessary." He paused and lowered his voice. "Don't even trust your steward."

She lowered her voice. "Do you still think we're in danger?"

"I don't know. I'd rather assume so and find out I was being overly cautious than be lax and suffer the consequences, wouldn't you?"

"Yes, of course. It's just that I have never seen the coast and I've heard it's beautiful. I thought it might be enjoyable to watch it pass. If you think it's unwise to do so, I won't venture out."

"I can call for you from time to time," Thorne suggested. "If you don't mind *walking out* with me."

Charity blushed at the intimate connotation of his offer. "I wasn't hinting that I wanted to be treated as if you and I were *courting,* I assure you."

"I know you weren't." He smiled wryly. "If I had thought so, I wouldn't have offered to escort you."

Thorne had guided Charity, Naomi and Jacob to their cabin, made sure the women would lock the door, then had proceeded to the saloon to reconnoiter.

Leaving the damp, still-foggy atmosphere on deck, he entered the interior seating and dining area. Smoke from a multitude of tobacco users was drifting in visible layers that rippled and eddied every time a door was opened and closed.

The saloon was clearly designed more for the usual pleasure of gentlemen than of ladies. Yes, there were side chairs upholstered in red velvet and matching swags with gold braid and tassels decorating the windows, yet the room was definitely a masculine bastion, as witnessed by its almost exclusively male occupants. Most of the men were bellied up to the bar or seated around the small, rimmed tables and bending an elbow in a show of camaraderie.

Thorne had not taken another drink of whiskey or any other spirits since the fateful night he and Aaron had gotten drunk together and Naomi had come between them. The only time being a teetotaler bothered him was in instances like this, where he thought it best to try to blend in.

He approached the bar and leaned against it sideways, not ordering until he was pressed to do so. "A shot of whatever you're serving," he said, knowing he wasn't going to actually drink it.

"Yes, sir. Coming up."

Thorne paid the bartender, then nonchalantly fingered his glass while he continued to size up his fellow travelers. Most were citified, as was to be expected on this first-class level of the steamer. Those who had to work for their passage or who had been unable to pay much fare were delegated to the lower decks, in second and third class, with the cargo and livestock.

There were friendly card games already underway at several of the round tables where meals would later be served to those who could afford them. Judging by the appearances of the players, none was professional, although a few seemed to take the games of chance rather seriously.

"Speaking of serious." Thorne muttered to himself. Looking across the room he easily spotted Cyrus Satterfield conversing with another individual. The second man was a shade taller than Satterfield and appeared to be thinner.

Thorne stiffened. Could that be the same man he'd chased over the rooftop? Since both travelers were wearing overcoats it was impossible to tell if the second was as lanky as the scoundrel who had recently tried to abduct Jacob.

Leaving his drink untouched, Thorne strode across the room toward the other men. Now that the *Grand Republic* was underway, there was no avenue of escape, short of jumping overboard and swimming to shore. If this fellow was the one he sought, the one who had bothered his helpless nephew, Thorne was more than prepared to help him leap over the side.

Without introduction or even a polite hello, he grabbed the thinner man by the shoulder and spun him around, much to the astonishment of those passengers standing close by.

Thorne immediately knew he'd made a mistake. This fellow was tall and wiry, all right, but he had a thick, well-waxed mustache that must have taken a year or more to grow and shape so elegantly.

"I'm sorry," Thorne said quickly. "I thought you were someone else."

Giving him the once-over and frowning, the man he had accosted simply walked away. That left Thorne facing only Cyrus Satterfield.

"Do you always come on so strong?" Satterfield asked.

"If I think I need to."

"Well," he said, chuckling wryly, "in that case, remind me to stay out of your way."

"Leave my sister-in-law alone and we'll have no more trouble," Thorne told him.

"My error." The thickset man gave a slight bow and arched an eyebrow. "I had understood that the lady was a widow or I never would have offered her my arm."

"*If* my brother is dead, and I'm not saying that he is, his widow is my concern, not yours."

"Not a very friendly attitude," Satterfield said, tipping his head back to blow smoke into the already-thick atmosphere. "But have it your way. The widow is all yours."

The last was spoken with a sneer that was almost insulting enough to prompt Thorne to take a swing at the pompous fool. He refrained. No sense getting into a melee and drawing attention to himself or his party. If Satterfield was a man of his word and did keep his distance, no further action would be necessary.

If he broke his promise to leave Naomi alone, however, Thorne was more than ready to impress him with his folly, to whatever degree the situation demanded.

Charity was still tense and jumpy and the closeness of the tiny cabin did nothing to soothe her nerves. Neither did the restless little boy. The projected journey of six or seven days and nights promised to be most trying. Although she was able to catch glimpses of the passing terrain as the sun rose and eventually burned off the coastal fog, she couldn't see nearly enough to satisfy her curiosity. Or Jacob's.

Finally she decided to don her shawl, open the cabin

door and stand there with him in her arms so they could both safely observe the changing landscape.

Beams of the rising sun bathed the coastal hills in golden-green light. Mighty live oaks stood in groves like sentinels over the vast ocean beyond their shores.

There was raw beauty in the ruggedness of the coast with very little evidence that man had altered God's handiwork. Here and there, Charity caught a glimpse of what could have been signs of settlers or Indians but by and large the landscape was unsullied.

She was still marveling at the passing scenery when Thorne appeared on deck and approached her.

"I thought you promised to stay in your cabin," he said gruffly.

"I'm sort of in it," Charity countered with a sheepish grin. "At least my heels are inside."

"I meant with the door locked, and you know it."

"Yes, I know. It's just so stuffy in there and so beautiful out here." Shifting Jacob to her other hip she pointed. "Look at those rocks. And that cliff! It's so steep. Every couple of miles the terrain seems to change to something altogether new."

"Those are the famous redwoods of California you see up there," Thorne said, swinging his arm and pointing. "They don't grow anywhere else in the world, that I know of."

"I've seen the wood, of course, but I've never had the pleasure of seeing a live tree still standing. I've heard they're very impressive."

"They are. Maybe someday you'll have the chance to view them more closely."

"Maybe." She grew subdued. "Who knows what the future holds?"

"God does," Thorne said with conviction.

"You really believe that?"

"Yes, I do." He held out his arms to relieve her of Jacob. "You look tired. Let me hold him for a while."

"Thank you."

Thinking of all the trauma and tribulations she'd faced while crossing the plains, Charity was moved to speak her mind. "Why do you feel that God even cares?" she asked. "I mean, with all the evil in the world, how can you possibly say that?"

"I don't know. I'm no theologian. I can't explain it to myself so I'm pretty sure I can't make it clear to you, either. All I do know is that when I was shipwrecked and positive I was about to draw my last breath, I called out to God in desperation and He gave me peace for whatever happened. I wasn't even sure I was going to be rescued. I simply knew I was safely in the Lord's hands, no matter what."

"Is that why you're still holding out hope that your brother survived? Because *you* did?"

"Partly, I suppose." He smiled wistfully. "It is my fondest wish that Aaron and his family will find happiness again."

Empathetic, Charity lightly touched his sleeve on the arm that was supporting the child. "The Good Book does mention children as being special. If you're right about God looking after all of us, I imagine He's even more tenderhearted toward these innocent little ones."

"As are you," Thorne told her. "I don't know what we'd do, how we'd manage without you, Miss Beal."

"It is fortunate that you chose to stop at the Montgomery House."

"Fortunate?" Raising one eyebrow, he began to

smile. "I would much rather consider it providential, although that may be a gross understatement. Now that I've given the matter more thought, I would say that you're definitely part of the Lord's plan for me."

His words took Charity's breath away for an instant, until he added, "And my family."

Chapter Nine

Jacob had fallen asleep in his uncle's arms so Thorne had carried him inside and laid him tenderly on an empty berth, then had bid the women a polite good-afternoon.

Charity hadn't expected to see hide nor hair of him again until morning so she was surprised when someone rapped loudly and insistently on her cabin door a few hours later. She laid aside her daily journal and pencil and went to answer the knock.

Cautious and more than a little tremulous, she grasped the knob, leaned against the thin wooden door and called, "Who is it?"

"Me."

Her relief at hearing the familiar rumble of Thorne's voice was so great it left her a bit giddy. "I beg your pardon, sir. I don't know anyone by that name."

Giggling, she listened to his masculine mutterings for a few seconds before she unlocked the door and peeked out. "Oh, it's you. Why didn't you say so?"

"I thought I did."

She swung the door wide and studied his face. "So, you did. What's the matter? You look concerned."

"Not overly so. We're putting in at a cove for the night and I thought I should explain what was going on. The weather promises to worsen and the coast is getting pretty rugged up this way. Our captain doesn't want to chance running aground on the rocks or getting the wheel or rudder fouled on the kelp that breaks loose during rough weather. I happen to agree with his assessment."

"Will we be safe?" Charity asked.

"Safer than we'd be on the open sea in this small craft." He smiled at her. "How are you all doing?"

She huffed. "Well, since you've asked, Naomi insists she's seasick and has taken to her bed. Jacob only dozed for a few minutes after you left us and refuses to nap anymore, so he's grumpier than a hibernating bear in January. And I have a pounding headache, all of which I have duly recorded in my daily journal. Therefore, I'd have to say we're coping, as usual."

He wouldn't have laughed in response if Charity hadn't been grinning wryly. "Glad to hear everything is normal."

"I knew you would be. Any more sign of the man you were worried about?"

"No. He hasn't shown up in the saloon since I confronted him and I haven't been able to locate him anywhere else on the boat."

"Then that's good, right?"

"In a manner of speaking. I'd almost rather have him underfoot than have to wonder what else he may be up to."

"You are a hard man to please."

Thorne's smile grew. "You're just now figuring that out? Tsk-tsk. I thought you were smarter than that."

"Smart enough to try to stay on your good side," she

quipped. "Listen, is there any chance we could get a light meal? It doesn't have to be fancy. Jacob has eaten all the food I brought along and I'm starving."

"Sorry. I should have explained. I've already arranged with the galley for your meals to be served in your suite. Would you like me to dine with you or would you prefer your privacy?"

Charity chuckled. "Privacy? In here? It feels more like solitary confinement. I—we—would love to have you eat with us."

"In that case, I'll be back in a jiffy." He paused and stared pointedly at her. "Lock the door again and keep it locked until I get back."

"You worry too much."

Thorne's brow furrowed and his eyes narrowed. "It's not unreasonable to worry if someone is really after you," he said flatly. "Lock that door. Now."

As he turned to go he heard the click of the lock. She might think he was overreacting but he knew better. Any of Louis Ashton's prior reprehensible deeds would have been enough to convince Thorne that nothing short of death would stop the old man from carrying out his plans to eliminate Aaron's family.

The way Thorne saw it, he was the only deterrent standing between that family and an untimely death. He, and Charity Beal.

He knew he couldn't have asked for a more dedicated, loyal ally.

Charity was perplexed. She stood in the center of the cabin and tried to figure out where they should spread their repast. The closer the boat drew to the shore the choppier the water became and although she and Jacob seemed fine, poor Naomi lay in her narrow berth, moaning.

Finally, Charity decided it would be wiser to relocate the small wooden writing desk and use it for a table than to leave it where it was in the cramped cabin. If she dragged it out onto the deck, she reasoned, they could breathe fresh air as they supped and no one would have to listen to Naomi's laments.

She had nearly finished relocating the makeshift dining table and two armless side chairs when Thorne reappeared. She could tell by his expression of disgust that he wasn't pleased by her choice of arrangements.

"Don't look at me like that." Charity faced him with her hands fisted on her hips. "I imagine it won't bother an old salt like you but there is a very ill woman in my cabin and I don't relish the notion of having to try to eat while in the same room with her. It wouldn't be good for Jacob, either."

Thorne nodded and acquiesced. "You're right. Naomi is definitely not a sailor. She hardly ate a bite during our entire voyage around the horn. Aaron plied her with sugar cubes dosed in peppermint oil but she remained ill in spite of it."

"Poor thing. No wonder she seems so frail," Charity said. "I'll see if I can coax her into eating a sop of bread or chewing on some gingerroot, later. We should be better off once we've stopped, right?"

"As a matter of fact, we're already at anchor."

"But how can we be? I still hear the engine."

"The captain is keeping the boilers fired up to counter the tide when it turns. That way, we can also be underway as soon as he deems it safe. It's a wise decision."

"I see. There's certainly a lot to know about running a boat, isn't there?"

"Or a sailing ship," Thorne said. He carefully placed a basket of food on the deck. "You might want to bring a blanket outside and we'll make this a picnic. Keeping everything on the top of that little desk in this weather will be nigh impossible. Dishes were sliding off the tables in the saloon just now, even though those are made with rimmed edges."

"Well, why didn't you say so before? It took me ages to drag that cumbersome thing outside."

"Then stay put and watch the boy. I'll put it back for you."

"Nonsense. I can handle it."

"I know you can, but…" He bent over and reached for the edges of the desk at the same time Charity did.

Their heads bumped and their hands overlapped, his atop hers. His touch was firm and reassuring.

Instead of giving ground or jumping away, she froze and tilted her head to look at him. At the same instant Thorne's gaze met hers. His face was mere inches from hers and she could feel his warm breath on her cheeks, on her lips.

Looking into his dark brown eyes, she was struck by their unexpected intensity, their emotional impact on her very being. Charity imagined it would be easy to drown in the all-encompassing depths of his gaze.

Finally, after what had seemed like aeons, she came to her senses, slipped her hands free, straightened and stepped back. Thorne made no comment.

Instead of following him into the cabin while he replaced the desk and chairs, Charity called, "There's an extra blanket folded at the foot of my berth. Bring that one for us to sit on? Please?"

Remaining silent, he did as she asked, handed her the blanket, then stood aside while she spread it on the deck.

Except for cautious peeks at him through lowered lashes, Charity kept her gaze averted. She wondered if Thorne's emotions had been as affected by their accidental proximity as hers were. She doubted it. After all, he was a man of the world, a successful ship owner and veteran traveler. He had seen faraway places and had certainly met many women much prettier, more educated and more interesting than a simple farm girl from Ohio.

No, her heart corrected, *not a girl, a woman.* A woman who was once married, sullied by cruelty, and therefore ruined for any good, normal man who might someday come along and wish to become her husband.

Thorne knew all about that part of her history, she reminded herself. Little wonder he had said he wasn't going to take her walking the way a suitor might and was now acting reluctant to even look at her again, let alone purposely take her hand, which was just as well. Thanks to the painful memories of Ramsey Tucker's abuse, she normally recoiled from any grown man's touch, except perhaps that of her own father.

Now, however, Charity was puzzled. Something very troubling had just occurred and she wasn't prepared to deal with it. Although she realized that Thorne had merely covered her hands with his by accident rather than purposefully, she had not been repulsed by the contact. Not in the slightest.

Admitting that startling fact, even to herself, was almost as frightening as their continued flight from would-be assassins.

* * *

The simple meal of cold meat, bread, cheese and canned peaches had been quickly completed. Since the weather was worsening and rain had begun to dot the deck beyond the sheltering overhang, Thorne had bid them good-night, picked up the basket and politely taken his leave.

Bone weary, Charity had seen to Jacob's personal needs, then had done as much as she could for Naomi, including making her a weak ginger tea out of tepid water to settle her stomach. Adding a drop of laudanum to the tea had helped Naomi relax and sleep.

Although no one had actually dressed for bed due to the dangers inherent in the inclement weather, Charity had loosened her clothing and slipped off her shoes and stockings before lying down.

She forced herself to close her eyes as she listened to the creaking of the wooden craft and the drum of activity belowdecks. Every so often there was also a long, drawn-out hiss which she attributed to the venting of excess steam.

Recalling Jacob's bedtime antics, Charity smiled to herself. Due to the narrowness of the berths she had said, "I'll make you your very own bed and we'll slide it under mine. That way you'll still be close by and your mother and I won't step on you if we have to get up during the night. How does that sound?"

When he'd answered, "No," and started to whine she'd realized she should not have posed the idea as a question.

"I want to sleep with you, in a real bed," he had insisted, sniffling and rubbing his eyes with his fists.

"Okay, if that's what you want." Charity chose her

words more carefully this time. "But these berths are awfully narrow for two. I thought you'd like making your very own cabin. We could have fun pretending it's a fort or a cave—and you could even be a bear."

"Really?" Pout forgotten, his dark eyes had sparkled. "A bear? A big bear?"

"Yes. Of course, if you don't want to..."

"I do, I do." He'd dropped to his hands and knees to peer into the narrow space. "Make me a cave."

As soon as she had prepared his pallet, he had gladly shinnied onto it and had quickly discovered an added bonus to his make-believe den. Roaring as if he were a real bear, he'd begun kicking at the bottom side of her thin mattress and giggling when she'd pretended to be scared.

They had laughed and teased for a few minutes until she had dimmed the lamp and he had dozed off. So had Naomi. Charity was heartened to hear the other woman's soft sighs in the nearly dark cabin. At least the poor dear was no longer moaning and tossing about. That was certainly something to be thankful for.

With both her charges finally in repose, Charity was free to begin to unwind. She began by saying her prayers, then let her mind drift beyond the confines of the cabin and imagined herself standing on the shore amid the towering trees Thorne had pointed out.

Unfortunately, once she fell asleep and began to dream, her lovely visions became tortured and filled with her late husband's threats and cruelty. Her heart pounded. Beads of perspiration dotted her forehead and neck. She saw herself running blindly in the midst of a whirling, punishing tornado like the one that had leveled their Ohio farm and killed her mother.

In the nightmare, Charity was fleeing from an ugliness too foul, too indescribable to even have a face, yet she knew who it was. Who it had to be. Though Ramsey Tucker was dead, the memory of him continued to haunt her.

She called out to God in her terror. Suddenly her eyes popped open. She blinked rapidly. Torrential rain was beating against a small window with such alarming ferocity it seemed sure to break through the fragile glass at any moment.

For a few seconds Charity didn't remember where she was or with whom. It was the rocking and pitching of the room that reminded her. She threw aside her blanket and swung her feet to the floor while she fought to calm down and regain her sensibilities.

"I'm on a steamboat," she whispered, rubbing her eyes. "I'm safe. We're safe. This cabin is secure and everyone is fine."

She strained to listen, to reassure herself. All she could hear was the rapid beating of her own pulse, the creaking of the wooden hull, and the incessant hammering of the deluge against the walls and tin roof.

Her lamp had apparently gone out while she slept. She reached for the place she was certain she had left it and touched thin air, instead.

Lightning flashed. Thunder shook the cabin.

Charity blinked and tried to focus, wishing the burst of light had lasted longer so she could get her bearings. Whatever had she done with that lamp? It couldn't have fallen to the floor or she'd smell spilled coal oil.

Standing, she extended her arms and groped across the short distance to Naomi's berth. Her knees bumped against the railing along the side.

She bent cautiously, wary of losing her balance and falling against the other women. Her hands touched the blankets. They were warm. Rumpled.

Charity patted the surface of the berth, then slapped it more vigorously.

Her breath caught as she realized there was no doubt. The bed was empty. Naomi was gone!

Thorne was dozing with his feet propped on one of the red velvet chairs, his torso half reclining in another, when he felt icy drops of water hitting his face. Someone was shaking his shoulders. Someone very wet.

He opened his eyes, ready to snap at whoever had disturbed him. It was Charity. Her hair was plastered to her cheeks and neck and her clothing was soaked. One look at her wild-eyed expression brought him to immediate alertness.

"What is it? What's happened?"

"Naomi's gone!"

"When? How?"

"I don't know." She shivered and wrapped her arms around herself to fend off the chill. "I didn't hear a thing. I just woke up and she was gone."

"What about the boy?" When she didn't immediately respond, Thorne was sorely tempted to give her a shake.

"He's—he's fine. I think," she finally said.

"You locked the door when you left him, right? *Right?*"

Her expression of utter terror and confusion was all the answer Thorne needed. He was out the saloon door and running along the deck before he'd made a conscious decision to do so. One quick glance over his shoulder told him that Charity was following.

He jerked open the cabin door and fumbled to strike a match. His heart fell. All the berths were empty.

Whirling, he pulled Charity inside and demanded, "What happened? Tell me exactly what you remember?"

"Nothing."

Thorne could tell she was fighting tears but he didn't have time to coddle her. "There must be something. Think. What woke you?"

"A—a nightmare. I dreamed I was running away and it was raining. There was terrible wind, like a tornado."

"Your mind may have been prompted to think that when the door was opened and you felt the storm blowing in on you from outside. Did you rise immediately?"

"Yes. I couldn't find the lamp. I thought I knew where I had left it but it wasn't there, so I felt my way across the room to check on Naomi. She was gone."

Thorne could hear the catch in Charity's voice, sense the pathos she was feeling. "All right," he said. "You can't go running around out on deck like that or you'll have the ague by morning. Put on your heavy coat to keep warm and we'll rouse the crew to help us look. Naomi must have taken Jacob with her. Chances are we'll find them together."

"No. Wait," Charity shouted. She fell to her knees and reached beneath her berth. "He's here! Praise, God, Jacob's still here."

Thorne joined her as she eased the sleepy child out from his hiding place and enfolded him in her embrace. More lightning revealed that tears were sliding down her cheeks. He could understand her emotional response. His was similar.

He swallowed hard past the lump in his throat before he asked, "What was he doing under there?"

"Pretending to be a—a bear," she stuttered. "I didn't want him to get stepped on if I had to get up in the night to see to Naomi so I talked him into sleeping out of the way. I—I was just trying to be practical. I never dreamed it would keep him safe the way it did."

The little boy had wrapped his arms around Charity's damp neck, as if clinging to a life preserver. Thorne wanted to hold him, too, but decided to leave him right were he was, safe and secure in the tenderhearted woman's embrace.

Instead, he leaned closer and asked, "Are you all right, Jacob?"

"Uh-huh." The child seemed to be looking over Charity's shoulder and searching the darkness. "Is he gone?"

"Is *who* gone?" Thorne asked.

"The man. The bad man. I saw him but I was scared to holler." He began to sniffle. "I'm sorry, Uncle Thorne."

"There's nothing to be sorry about," he answered, taking care to temper his tone so the child wouldn't become more frightened. "Did you see what happened? Did he take your mama away?"

The tousled head nodded vigorously.

"What did he look like?"

"I don't know. He had on a real shiny coat."

"Black, like the captain and crew wear?"

"I think so." Jacob yawned. "Will you go get Mama, Uncle Thorne? She shouldn't be out in the rain."

"No, she certainly shouldn't." He looked to Charity. "You stay here with him and lock the door after me."

"What good will that do? I had it locked and someone got in anyway."

"Humor me." Reaching into his pocket, he withdrew a tiny pistol barely as big as his palm. "Here. It only has two shots, one in each barrel, but it's better than nothing."

Cautious, he held it out and waited until she accepted it. "Don't be afraid, just be careful," Thorne said. "It won't fire unless you cock it first, so it's safe enough. Make sure you don't point it at anything or anybody unless you intend to shoot."

"I don't think I could purposely hurt anyone."

"Could you if they were threatening the boy?" Watching her expression change to one of resolution and seeing her nod, he was satisfied she'd be capable of defending his nephew if need be.

"That's what I thought," Thorne said. "All right. I'll go do what I can to find Naomi."

Charity grabbed his sleeve as he turned to leave. "How can I help?"

"Pray," Thorne said without hesitation. "Pray harder than you ever have before. I'm going to need divine intervention. And so is Naomi."

Chapter Ten

W**ind** pushed wave after wave of rain in blinding sheets, driving it nearly parallel to the decks of the pitching steamer.

The man struggling across the slippery starboard deck with an unwilling, groggy woman in tow was having trouble keeping his feet. It galled him that he hadn't been able to locate the child, too, and make short work of them both. Oh, well. As soon as he managed to drag his burden farther aft and hurl her over that railing, he'd be half done. That was enough to crow about.

He had taken the only lamp from the Ashton woman's cabin, then had decided it was too much bother and had tried to toss it into the ocean. When he'd heard its glass breaking against a lower deck he'd realized he'd have to drag his victim to the rear of the craft to make sure she dropped directly into the icy water. After all, in a storm like this, accidents were bound to happen.

A shout echoed above the sound of thunder and the crashing of waves. Another followed. He could hear the clomp of several pairs of boots running along the deck. Although the rain masked much of the sound, he suspected his deed had been discovered and he was being pursued.

Pausing, he hit the woman in the jaw to stun her more, then released his hold and let her fall to the deck. If he was lucky, maybe she'd slip when she tried to get up and the rolling of the waves would cause her to plummet overboard without his help. If not, he'd simply try again. It wasn't as if Louis Ashton would ever know he'd failed. Nor would he reveal his inability to locate the boy in the darkened cabin.

Lightning flashed. He saw shadowy forms racing toward him. Ducking around the port side below the pilothouse, he shed his long, black slicker just as he darted through a narrow doorway leading to a back passage into the saloon.

"The fools have underestimated me," he muttered, satisfied that his ruse had worked and pleased that he'd had the foresight to scout out an alternate way to reach the cabin he had chosen to occupy.

He laughed softly at his wit as he reminded himself that the cabin's previous owner had been far too dead to object when he had tossed his carcass over the side earlier.

Straightening his clothing, Cyrus Satterfield brushed off his coat sleeves, then smoothed what was left of his reddish hair over his partially balding head. There were times, like now, when he was glad he didn't have a thick head of hair to deal with or try to keep dry. As it was, any slickness of his pate would be taken for pomade, not water, and nobody would be the wiser.

He sidled into the ship's saloon, intending to merely pass through. Unfortunately, all the ruckus on deck had awakened others. Rather than appear furtive, he decided to simply join the group as if equally concerned.

Nodding politely, he approached a crewman at the bar. "What's going on? I thought I heard shouts. We aren't sinking, are we?"

"Naw," the man drawled. "Some fool woman got herself lost and the cap'n was hollerin' for volunteers." He guffawed. "You won't see me riskin' my neck out on deck in this storm if I don't have to. No sirree."

"I see. Has there been any word of her yet?"

"Not directly. I suppose they found her 'cause the yellin's stopped. Stupid woman. Never should allow the likes of them on board if you ask me. I'll be plumb glad when she gets off at Astoria."

Satterfield perked up. "Astoria? I thought they…"

"Beg pardon?"

"Nothing. Are you sure she's getting off?" He forced a nonchalant air and a smile. "I mean, the sooner the better if she's such a poor sailor, right?"

"Yeah. Cap'n Nash said the folks in her party was headed up the Columbia a ways, so I suppose they'll go ashore when we dock there. We're bound for Puget, up north."

"I know. I had thought to sail all the way with you. How long does that leg of the journey usually take?"

"A lot longer than it should, once we leave the mouth of the Columbia River. Lots of rocks and little islands out there, not to mention the bar. Real tricky to navigate. But don't you worry. We don't draw much more'n five or six feet of draft fully loaded and our captain's a wonder with the charts. Never seen him make a mistake."

Before Satterfield could comment the door burst

open and another crewman entered, bringing news of the rescue.

Pretending to listen and feigning shock at word of the heinous crime, Cyrus smiled to himself. There would be another day soon. Another chance. As long as he never gave up, he *would* be successful.

Thorne had been the first to come upon Naomi. He'd found her lying on the deck and curled into a fetal position.

He'd lifted her gently and supported her by the shoulders. When she had opened her eyes and taken one look at him, she had fainted dead away.

Scooping her up in his arms, he had assured the other searchers that she was in good hands and had headed for her cabin. Not able to knock easily, he gave the door a swift kick and shouted, "Miss Beal. Open the door."

The instant she did, he shouldered through.

Charity gasped. "Is she all right?"

"I think so. She's swooned but she's breathing well."

"Put her on the bed." She turned to reassure the worried little boy. "Mama's fine, honey. She's just a little woozy right now."

Thorne stepped back. If the man who had tried to abduct Naomi had been dressed like one of the packet boat's crew, did that mean a crewman was also on Louis's payroll? The possibility was strong.

"She's coming around," Charity said as she vigorously rubbed Naomi's hands and forearms and patted her cheeks.

"Good. I'm going to go talk to the captain and see if he can shed any light on who might have access to rain gear besides his men. Will you two be all right alone?"

"We aren't alone." Charity smiled at Jacob. "We have each other and now that his mama is back with us, we'll be just fine. As soon as you leave I'll get her wet clothes off her and make sure she's good and warm."

"Lock the door after me," Thorne ordered.

"Don't you ever get tired of telling me that?" she asked, rolling her eyes.

All he said was, "No."

Disgusted with herself for failing to watch Naomi well enough and mad at Thorne for being so brusque about the whole situation, Charity made a droll face at his departing figure.

To her surprise, Jacob mirrored her comical expression. She couldn't help but laugh. "It's okay to do that this time, honey, but I don't think you should make funny faces at Uncle Thorne again."

"Why?"

Charity giggled, carrying on the conversation with him while she also undressed his shivering, uncommunicative mother. "Because it's really not polite. Besides, he might ask you where you learned to do it and you'd have to tell him the truth. I don't want him to be angry with me for teaching you something bad. Understand?"

"Uh-huh. Can I go back under the bed and be a bear again?"

"I think that's a wonderful idea," Charity said with a tender smile. "And if you see that bad man again, I want you to tell me or your uncle right away. All right?"

"I could roar and scare him away," the child said, demonstrating by forming his pudgy fingers into claws and giving his best growl.

"Why don't we just let Uncle Thorne do that for us? He might feel bad if we took his job."

"What job?"

"Why, the one as our brave protector," Charity said, realizing that she meant every word. "Uncle Thorne is doing his best to take good care of all of us."

"Even you?"

"Yes, even me." She tucked the covers around the still-dazed woman and straightened.

"Good. 'Cause I love you, Miss Charity."

She leaned down and placed a kiss on the top of Jacob's head. "I know you do, dear. And I love you, too."

"How 'bout Uncle Thorne?"

"I'm sure he loves you, too, Jacob."

"I mean, you. Does he love you?"

Blushing, Charity searched her heart for the right words before she spoke. "I just work for him, taking care of you and your mama while we travel. That's why he wants to keep me safe, too."

"I think he likes you," Jacob said with a grin, before he whirled and skipped back to his pretend cave. He stuck his head out from under the bed to add, "You're real pretty."

"Thank you, dear."

The child's innocent praise made her doubly aware of the sorry state of her damp hair and clothing. She had no doubt Thorne Blackwell had been unimpressed by her so-called beauty when she'd raced out into the downpour to fetch him. On the contrary, some of the soggy chickens penned on the cargo deck probably looked far more presentable than she did at the moment.

That comparison made her chuckle to herself. There was a time, long ago, when her appearance had been all she'd thought about. Her hair had to be curled and arranged just so, her dresses had to be spotless and crisply ironed, and the lace hems on her petticoats had to be as white as a summer cloud. Until her trip across the plains with her older sister, she had never gone out in the sun without a hat or a bonnet, either, yet by the time she had reached California she was sporting the freckles that still dusted her nose and rosy cheeks.

It no longer mattered to her whether or not her complexion was flawless or her hair a silky gold. As long as she was clean and did the best she could with what she had, she didn't obsess about her looks.

The state of disorder she was currently displaying was another matter, however. She owed it to her employer, and to his family, to make herself as presentable as possible.

She sighed. It was difficult to tell the time without a watch but she felt as if dawn must surely be approaching. Assuming that to be so, she would don dry clothing and do what she could with her own hair before trying to rouse Naomi and helping her do the same.

In the back of Charity's mind was the niggling doubt that she was not polishing her public image totally because of her job. Like it or not, she wanted to look more than respectable.

She wanted to look pretty.

For Thorne Blackwell.

There were plenty of men still milling around in the saloon by the time Thorne joined them. He immediately noted that Cyrus Satterfield was present. So was the boat's captain and some of the crew.

Ignoring the inquiring looks of others, Thorne went

straight to the captain. "I'm glad I caught you, Captain Nash. I was on my way to the pilothouse to ask if any of your men was missing a slicker. I just found this one lying on the deck." He held up the shiny coat and watched water drip off it. "Can you tell whose it is?"

Nash shook his head. "Standard issue, I'm afraid, sir. Why?"

"Because my nephew says the man who took his mother was wearing one like it. I thought he'd still have it on but apparently he shed it outside."

"I'm sure none of my men was responsible. They're all totally trustworthy."

"I'm sure they are. Would you mind asking if any of them are missing this coat?"

"I could ask," the captain said, "but I'm not going to. Your party has been reunited and all is well. I don't want my crew all riled up for nothing."

"For nothing?" Thorne didn't try to hide his displeasure. He shook the coat for emphasis and more drops scattered. "I hardly consider this nothing."

"Nevertheless…" Turning, the captain walked away and left the saloon, ending the discussion.

Thorne held up the coat again and queried the crowd. "Do any of you know anything about this? There'll be a reward for information on who was wearing this slicker tonight."

To Thorne's disgust and dismay, the only man who paid attention to his offer was Cyrus Satterfield.

Edging his way along the bar, Satterfield raised an eyebrow and smiled. "I guess they're not that interested in earning a reward," he said. "I, however, might be. What sum did you have in mind?"

Thorne was hesitant to name a figure so he hedged. "Are you saying you know something about this?"

"No. But I'm willing to ask around and see what I can come up with if you'll make it worth my while."

"Forget it," Thorne told him. "I can do that myself."

"Have it your way. Well, I guess I'll be getting back to my cabin since all the excitement is over."

That simple declaration raised the hackles on the back of Thorne's neck. He scowled. "Hold on. How did you get a cabin? I booked passage before you did and I was only able to reserve one."

"Perhaps I'm luckier than you are," the heavyset man said with a snide expression and a wave. "Good night."

Watching him leave the saloon, Thorne remained puzzled. He supposed he could query the captain about Satterfield's cabin. If he disclosed his own background at sea and encouraged camaraderie, he might get better cooperation. Unfortunately, since he didn't want to reveal his true identity, even to Captain Nash, that wasn't feasible. Nor was it wise.

Given his working knowledge of shipboard politics and loyalties, Thorne knew who else to ask. There wasn't a ship's cook on the high seas who didn't know everything that went on belowdecks. Hopefully, the same would be true on the smaller packet boat.

Thorne toted the slicker with him as he headed for the galley. As expected, he found members of the crew already hard at work preparing upcoming meals. The overheated room was heavy with the pleasant aroma of cooking and the less appealing odor of the provisions that had been spilled and wasted during the storm and were now being trod underfoot through the wooden grating. If he had been captain of the *Grand Republic* he'd have insisted the galley crew clean the place before doing anything else.

He'd met the chief cook for the first time when he'd picked up the evening meal for Charity and Jacob so he made straight for him.

"Food's not ready yet," the cook said, wiping his brow with his soiled muslin apron. "Be another hour, at least."

"I wasn't looking for something to eat," Thorne said. "You have lists of all the passengers in the cabins and what meals they've requested, don't you?"

"Yeah. You wanna make a change?"

"No, no. I was just wondering if I could take a peek at the list and make sure it's right." He forced a grin. "Wouldn't want the little woman to miss her tea or something and fuss at me for it."

"Long as she don't fuss at me," the cook said with a huff. He pointed. "Book's over there in that drawer. Have a look-see. Just make it snappy and be sure you put it back like it was when you're through."

"Certainly."

Thorne draped the slicker over his shoulders as if it were his and retrieved the ledger. Large lamps swung from the rafters, just as they had on his ship. He braced his feet on the still-pitching deck and oriented himself to the light to read.

He scanned the list twice. Nowhere did it mention anyone named Cyrus Satterfield occupying a cabin. Either the man was lying about his accommodations or he'd been lying about his name. Or both.

Chapter Eleven

The *Grand Republic* had hoisted anchor and headed back out to sea that morning as the weather had cleared and the sun had begun to peek over the hills to the east.

Although the paddle wheeler had continued to skirt the coast as before, she'd occasionally had to pull farther from shore for safety's sake, or so Thorne had explained.

Charity didn't care what the boat did as long as it continued to steam steadily northward. She knew they'd make stops along the way to pick up and deliver more mail and freight but she didn't want to delay any longer than was absolutely necessary.

Now that Naomi had recovered from her seasickness during the storm and was acting healthier, the poor woman had resumed her previous state of befuddlement, much to Charity's dismay.

Jacob had gotten to the point where he seldom tried to converse with his mother, preferring to bring his needs and interests to Charity's attention, instead. She understood why. She just wished he could relate better to his own mama.

Keeping the restless, curious child occupied was far more difficult aboard the steamer than it had been on land. Finally, in desperation, Charity had insisted they take regular turns around the passenger deck as a group, weather permitting.

To her surprise and delight, Thorne had chosen to join them. It was a true relief to have an extra pair of eyes watching the rambunctious little boy. Jacob seldom met a stranger and he got into more than his share of mischief. He also delighted in finding older adults to talk to and had to be reined in quite often. It seemed as if he never tired, never slowed down except to sleep.

The farther north the *Grand Republic* took them, the more rainy and cloudy the weather became. Because Charity was used to the moderate temperatures in San Francisco, this part of the country chilled her to the bone. If she had not had the exuberant child and her other chores to occupy her mind, she feared the dank weather would have seriously dampened her spirits, as well.

Sitting on deck with Naomi and watching Thorne and Jacob play tag like two children, Charity couldn't help smiling. In her mind's eye she could see that Thorne would make a fine father some day. He was firm but patient, never too busy to explain anything the little boy asked about.

When Jacob dashed up to her, grabbed her hand and tried to tug her to the railing, she laughed. "What's so important, dear?"

"The big river! Come look. We're almost there!"

Charity stood, wrapped the too-large overcoat more tightly around her and urged Naomi to come along. "It must be the mouth of the Columbia," she told the other woman. "That means our journey at sea is nearly over. Aren't you excited? Let's go see."

Although Naomi rose, Charity could tell she wasn't totally comprehending. What a pity. All Charity could hope for at this point was that the presence of Naomi's mother and father would help restore her to the whole person she had been before Aaron's abduction.

Charity sighed. Even if Naomi didn't recover, at least dear little Jacob would be with grandparents who would love him. If she had thought otherwise, she would have wept for him constantly.

Taking a place beside Thorne at the starboard railing, Charity smiled. He had scooped up the child and was pointing to a broad expanse of water in the distance.

"Over there," Thorne said. "See how the color is different? That's where the fresh water and saltwater come together."

Charity shaded her eyes against the sun's glare. "It's so wide. I never would have imagined anything so large being a river. It looks more like an extension of the ocean."

"Parts of it are saltwater, depending on the tide," he said. "Larger ships have to wait for high tides to sail across the bar or they may go aground on the shifting sand. It can be treacherous."

"Once they get across are they safe?"

"Yes, except for the storms that arise so often up here."

"I can see that sailing is a terribly dangerous occupation," Charity said with concern. "I shall worry about you from now on."

Speaking from the heart without censoring her

thoughts, she realized belatedly that he was staring at her. She met his compelling gaze.

"Will you? Truly?" he asked quietly.

"Of course."

"I believe you mean that."

Totally absorbed in the tenderness of his expression, she was unable to make herself look away. She had to pause for several heartbeats to gather her wits before she said, "Of course I do."

"As I will also worry about you. This has been the easy part of our journey," Thorne said soberly. "From now on it may be even more hazardous. I wish…"

Charity could only imagine what he had been going to say. "What?" she asked. "What do you wish?"

Her slim hand was resting on the railing. Thorne shifted Jacob to the opposite side, then placed his hand over Charity's as he said, "I wish I had not urged you to come with us."

Startled, she stared. "Because you think me incompetent?"

"No." His brow furrowed, his dark gaze growing even more enthralling. "Because you have become so important to me, Miss Beal."

Before she could form a coherent reply he'd released her hand and stepped back.

"Forgive me," he said formally. "I had no right to speak to you that way. It was unseemly."

But lovely, she added to herself. *So lovely.* She would not encourage him by expressing that thought, of course. To do so would be unfair. She was never going to allow herself to remarry and accepting anything less was unthinkable.

Still, she told herself, turning away to gaze at the entrance to the mighty Columbia River gorge, if she ever were to consider giving another man a special place in her heart, that man would have to be a lot like Thorne Blackwell.

It had been easy to befriend him, she admitted. And to trust him as an ally. But there was far more to marriage than standing at the railing of a steamboat and having a pleasant conversation. It wasn't the overt parts of a relationship she feared, it was the hidden parts, the intimacies she knew she could never again bear, no matter how tender her husband's touch might be.

The mere thought of being under a man's control gave her the shivers and made her stomach turn. Four years ago, she had sworn she would never again allow herself to become anyone else's possession. Anyone's chattel. There was much in life which confused her but about *that,* she was adamant.

"I'll take Jacob back to your cabin. Will you see to Naomi?" Thorne asked.

Charity nodded. She wouldn't look at him, couldn't look at him, because she was certain her anguish and abhorrence would show and he was not deserving of resentment. If anything, knowing him had given her a glimmer of hope that she might someday overcome the reservations which continued to govern her.

Unshed tears gathered in her eyes and blurred the image of the wooded coastline. What kind of a Christian was she when it was her fondest wish that Ramsey Tucker was presently burning in Hades? God might have removed him from her life but He had not provided the strength to forgive. Without divine help, Charity knew she would always hate her late husband with a vengeance that made her literally ill.

Did she *want* to forgive him? she asked herself. Or was she purposely dwelling on the sordid memories of him to reinforce her loathing and keep from having to go on with life in a normal manner?

She scowled. For the first time in years she was starting to question her motives, her abject hatred. The conviction that that doubt brought with it was hard to accept.

It was far easier to continue to hate, she realized, than it was to consider putting her sad past behind her. Assuming she actually wanted to, was it possible? Did she want to try? Surely not.

Charity closed her eyes and thought of parts of the prayer her mother had taught her so long ago. "And forgive us our trespasses as we forgive those who trespass against us," she whispered. That was the key, wasn't it? And that was exactly what she was *not* doing.

"But he hurt me so," she murmured, her words lost on the sea wind, tears beginning to slide down her cheeks.

Still standing next to her, Naomi reached out and gently patted Charity's hand. The gesture was fleeting and without explanation, yet Charity felt as if it were a sign from God, as if He were saying to her, "Now you see. Now you can begin to heal."

The sensation of peace and tranquility was so unexpected Charity's knees nearly buckled. She grabbed the railing and held on tightly. A peek at Naomi showed no change in her blank expression, yet apparently the Lord had used her to convey His support.

Awed and ashamed, Charity stopped trying to contain her tears and let them flow freely. As they fell, she felt as if they were cleansing her all the way to her soul.

She was sniffling, regaining control of her raw emotions and preparing to escort Naomi inside when the other woman turned, embraced her tenderly and began to pat her on the back the way a mother would comfort a distressed child.

"Don't be sad," Naomi said. "God loves you. My mama says so."

If Charity could have found her voice to answer at that moment she would not have known what else to add.

The enormous mouth of the Columbia was crowded with ships and boats of all sizes and shapes, including rustic dugout canoes, some large enough to transport dozens of blanket-wrapped Indians all at once.

Charity had heard of Indian canoes, of course, but had never dreamed any were so large and imposing. To her surprise and relief, the canoe riders seemed more interested in selling or trading fish, fowl and baskets full of fresh oysters than in causing mayhem or injury. Their shouts for attention were mostly in an unfamiliar tongue but judging by the way they were gesturing and displaying their wares, Charity had no doubt of their aims.

Beside her, Thorne pointed to the shoreline. "There's Astoria. See it? We'll change boats and proceed up the Columbia River to the Cowlitz before we start out overland."

"I understand your wish for haste," she said, "but wouldn't it be easier to continue on this steamer and take the coastal route all the way to Puget Sound?"

"Easier, perhaps," Thorne said soberly. "Not necessarily wise. We already know we have at least one enemy on board, maybe more. The sooner we thin the crowd and start to travel alone, the safer we'll be."

"That is a valid point," Charity said with a nod. "I was talking with one of the other women passengers, a Mrs. Yantis, whose husband owns a sawmill up in Olympia. She told me how much more tedious the journey by sea can be."

"You didn't reveal anything about us or our plans, did you?"

"Of course not." Charity gave him her best scowl. "I had to physically drag Naomi away from the conversation because she kept wanting to tell the woman about her missionary parents, though. I assume that's the kind of careless talk you were referring to?"

"Among other things. Once we reach land we may as well resume the use of our real names." A wry smile began to lift one corner of his mouth as he said, "I keep forgetting whether I'm supposed to be a Smith or a Jones, anyway."

Charity laughed lightly. "I know what you mean. I haven't concealed my last name but it is hard to remember how to address you and the rest of your family."

She sobered. "I suppose we're only fooling ourselves, since someone obviously already knows who you, Jacob and Naomi really are."

"Or they wouldn't have tried to harm her? You're right. Subterfuge seems pretty useless at this point."

"You know," Charity said, pursing her lips and striking the pose of a thinker, "it seems to me that our trouble has followed us from San Francisco. Therefore, I have to also assume that whoever is causing the grief must have come from there, too."

"Only if you also assume that our nemesis followed

me and Aaron's family from New York harbor, and that's impossible. The *Gray Feather* carried no other passengers and was already fully manned. I would have known immediately if there were strangers on board."

"Oh. I hadn't thought of that."

Thorne nodded slowly, pensively, and drew his thumb and fingers along his jaw to the point of his chin as if smoothing a nonexistent beard. "There is no place on earth that Louis Ashton's influence and wealth cannot reach to cause harm. No city or territory that's too far or too remote. That's the main reason I want to start overland as soon as it's feasible."

"It seems odd that a seaman such as you would be so eager to start walking."

Thorne smiled at her. "I have no plans to walk. We'll ride horses when we have to and employ small boats as much as possible, including hiring Indian canoes, if you and Naomi have no objections."

Her eyes widened and her hand went to her throat in a natural gesture of self-protection. "Oh, dear. Are you sure that's safe?"

"I won't do it if I'm not assured so by local people. Captain Nash is convinced these Indians on the Columbia are friendly but I want more than one man's word on it. I'll go ashore in Astoria and see about immediate passage up the river as far as Rainier. From there we'll follow the Cowlitz, as I said."

"What about provisions. If I need to start cooking I shall need proper equipment and foodstuffs." She glanced at the Indian canoes, reluctant to buy from them when there was such a serious language barrier.

"There's supposed to be a good merchant at Rainier. We'll either get what we need from him or from the store up the river at Cowlitz landing. Don't worry. I told you I have this all planned out."

"So, I see." She had to smile to herself at Thorne's overconfident attitude. Although he was cautious and thoughtful to a fault, she knew that the slightest change of circumstance could upset his well-laid plans like a bushel of apples in the bed of a runaway wagon. She had been through enough trials, experienced enough surprises, good and bad, to know that man's plans in the face of nature and providence were often laughable.

They had already weathered storms at sea and had coped with Naomi's continuing illness. Whatever was to come was unknown and might easily negate any sensible choices they made at present.

Charity looked to Thorne, smiled and said, "I am in your hands, sir. Whatever you feel is best for us, I shall endeavor to accept with grace."

He laughed. "I'll be holding you to that vow, Miss Beal. I sincerely hope you don't come to regret it."

Returning his grin she said, "So, do I, Mr. Blackwell. So, do I."

Chapter Twelve

Thorne found, to his relief, that the captains of the steamers plying the Columbia were a close-knit fraternity, prone to good-natured rivalry. Thus, he was able to procure passage for his party at a more than fair rate with immediate departure promised.

In reality, the *Multnomah,* another side-wheeler, remained in port at Astoria hours longer than he had been told it would and Thorne was getting more and more testy.

"This boat is bound for Portland but we'll disembark long before then," he told Charity and the others as he paced the small private space they had been assigned.

"Good." Charity eyed the pouting child seated on the floor. "Jacob is as restless as you are. I was hoping for a little time ashore. Are you sure we can't do just a tiny bit of exploring?"

"I'm afraid not. I was watching the dock area a few minutes ago and I saw Cyrus Satterfield climbing the hill toward Astoria. It's a very small settlement. I see no reason to tempt fate by joining him. Now that he's gone, our troubles may be over."

"You must be joking."

"No. Not at all. Satterfield is not continuing upriver with us so I see no more problems."

"Not from him, maybe," Charity countered. "That's assuming he was responsible for sneaking into our cabin, as you initially thought. We have no proof of his guilt one way or the other."

"Meaning, I may have been wrong? I doubt it. My skills for judging people are well-honed. Satterfield was up to no good. I'm certain of it." He could tell by the dubious look on Charity's face that she remained unconvinced.

"I suspect you may have been a tiny bit jealous of his interest in Naomi," she ventured with a wry smile.

"What? Don't be ridiculous."

Although she looked away rather than rebut his declaration of innocence, Thorne remained bothered by her suggestion. Surely, that could not be the case. Yes, he cared what happened to his brother's family but that was simply because he owed such an emotional debt to Aaron, alive or dead.

Examining his innermost heart, Thorne found no trace of lingering affection for Naomi. On the contrary. He wasn't deliberately placing blame for her presently unstable condition, but he did suspect that her own guilt over her prior maltreatment of her husband was at least partially responsible.

What he wanted most to do was continue the present discussion with Charity and explain exactly how he felt about the other woman. Since all of them were together in the cramped cabin that would be impossible, of course.

Further considering the constraint, he began to

view it as advantageous. There were things—personal things—he was tempted to say to Charity that *must* remain unvoiced, at least until they had reached their destination in Washington Territory.

After that, perhaps he would consider speaking of his serious intentions. It had been years since he had entertained such notions toward any woman and he knew he should proceed with caution, especially in Charity's case. There had been times, when they had inadvertently touched, that he had glimpsed something akin to fear in her eyes and it had cut him to the quick.

Above all, he would strive to make sure she trusted him fully and was assured he would never cause her harm or pain of any kind. The best way to do that, he reasoned, was by example. He didn't know where his opportunities might lie but he was certain they would arise as they followed the trail north. And when they did, he would be ready to take advantage of them.

He just hoped and prayed that Miss Charity Beal would be open to accepting his sincere efforts to win her confidence and then, perhaps, her heart.

And if he failed? What then?

Thorne gritted his teeth and squared his shoulders as he pictured having to bid her a final farewell. He didn't even want to contemplate such an utterly intolerable event.

Gazing at her as she played with Jacob, he realized that bidding either of them goodbye was going to tear his heart out.

Cyrus Satterfield had walked slowly away from the dock to make sure his entrance into Astoria was plainly visible. He wasn't going to try to follow Blackwell and his party too closely from here on out. He'd had his fill of encountering the taciturn seaman and trying to keep from laughing in his face. Besides, it wasn't brawn that would win the day, it was brains.

The first order of business was refilling his pockets with enough coin to buy his way through whatever snags he might encounter in the wilderness. Ashton had already supplied him with a generous stake and would have added to it in a heartbeat, he knew, if he'd had access to quick communication. As things stood, however, Cyrus figured he'd be lucky to keep up with his quarry even if he didn't wait around for more traveling money to arrive.

He sauntered into the first saloon he came to and bellied up to the bar. "Whiskey. And none of that rotgut you palm off on the Indians. Understand?"

"Yes, sir."

Purposely paying the bartender more than the drink was worth he gave him a conspiratorial smile and leaned closer to say, "I'm looking for a high-stakes game of chance. Any idea where I might find one?"

The man cocked his head toward a doorway in the rear. It was covered by a dirty, tattered, gray blanket nailed to the top of the frame rather than having an actual wooden door.

"In there?" Satterfield asked, incredulous.

"If you're up to it. They don't take no guff off'n strangers. You'd best have the wherewithal to play or they'll run you out of town. Or worse, if you get my drift."

"I fully understand," Satterfield said, picking up his drink and starting to turn away. "This shouldn't take long."

"Don't underestimate those fellas," the bartender warned. "They take their game very serious."

"I take everything seriously," the assassin replied with a snide smile. He paused. "Tell me, how much would it cost for you to get somebody to go down to the docks and delay the departure of a certain riverboat for an hour or two?"

Charity had managed to keep her small charge busy by sitting on the floor with him and teaching him to tie knots in the fringe on a lap robe she'd found in their new quarters. He was becoming very accomplished at the knots and she was kept well-occupied untying them so he could try again and again.

Thorne had gone out on deck long ago. She was beginning to wonder what had become of him when he reappeared to announce, "They're casting off. Finally."

"Good. No more sign of that man you were worried about?"

"No. None. Thank God." As he spoke he looked heavenward and Charity knew his thanks were being properly delivered.

"Then we can relax." She could tell by the look on Thorne's face that he didn't agree so she asked, "Well, why not? Surely we're safe on this little boat."

"From my stepfather's perfidy, perhaps," Thorne said. "But there are other dangers ahead."

"I thought you trusted God to look out for you. You once said you believed He knew our future. Have you changed your mind?"

"No." He offered his hand as she attempted to gracefully rise.

Since the boat was now in motion, Charity accepted

his assistance rather than chance tripping on her skirt or voluminous petticoats. There were times, like now, when she envied the ease of men's movements, unhindered by all the cloth that fashionable women carried about on their persons. Her sister, Faith, still had the buckskin dress a Cheyenne woman had given her and was forever praising its comfort and simplicity.

"Thank you," Charity said, using both hands to smooth her skirt as soon as she got her balance. "How long do you expect this leg of our journey to take?"

"Probably several days, particularly because we'll be fighting the current. In this case I highly recommend that you do take in the sights. The gorge is quite amazing, especially if you haven't seen it before."

"Oh, that's wonderful news! I do so prefer to be outdoors." She noted that he was beginning to smile at her and supposed he was amused by her childish enthusiasm. Well, that couldn't be helped. She'd been a virtual prisoner on the *Grand Republic* for over a week and had lived a terribly sheltered life at the hotel before that. Standing on deck to enjoy the unspoiled beauty of the wild lands on both sides of the immense river would be akin to being released from jail and transported straight to the Garden of Eden.

"I would have thought that a lady like you would have preferred a drawing room to the windy deck of a riverboat."

"Then you do not know me nearly as well as you think you do," Charity countered, also smiling. "I may once have been a delicate, shrinking violet but life has made me far more sturdy than that."

"Are you saying that some of your experiences were good for you?"

She laughed. "I wouldn't go quite that far. Suffice it to say that I have learned how to appreciate that which I do have and to waste less time coveting that which I do not."

"Such as?"

"I think this conversation has gone far enough, sir," she said, continuing to smile demurely. "Would you be so kind as to watch Jacob so I may take a turn around the deck?"

"Alone? Shouldn't I accompany you?"

"If you feel you must," Charity said honestly, hoping he would understand her need for time to contemplate, to soak up the wonders of the scenery without distraction. "Truth to tell, I covet a bit of peace and quiet." Eyeing the child she felt a pang of motherly love. "I do enjoy our little man but there are times…"

"Say no more." Thorne lifted the child in his arms and carried him to the door so he could open it for Charity. "You'd best wear the heavy coat. It's always windy here and as soon as we sail into the depths of the gorge the sunlight will be blocked by the high cliffs. You'll be easily chilled."

Although she took his advice before heading outside, she made no comment. It was comforting to have someone looking after her but she had been the caregiver for others for so long the shift in responsibilities was a tad hard to accept.

The man means well, she decided as she drew the heavy overcoat more tightly around her slim figure and leaned against the carved, white-painted, wooden railing at the leading edge of the uppermost deck. Thorne Blackwell had obviously appointed himself everyone's caretaker and took that job very seriously. There was nothing wrong with that. She was simply unwilling to surrender totally to his will. He wasn't a bit like her late husband had been, yet the notion of giving up her personage by subjecting it to his, went against the grain.

Charity stood facing into the wind to let the loose curls blow back from her forehead and cheeks, mindless of the damage to her carefully coiffed, upswept hair. She knew she should return to the cabin and fetch her bonnet but she couldn't tear herself away from the wonders before her.

Cliffs adorned with stately pines rose high on both side of the gorge, painting the rocky cliffs with patches of verdant green. Where there were narrow rifts she could often glimpse slim, towering waterfalls that looked as if they had turned to mist by the time they finally reached the base of the cliffs. From there they added their icy drops to the multitude of creeks and rivulets flowing into the mighty Columbia.

Seabirds mingled with eagles and other soaring, diving denizens of the canyon, sharing the air and the forest while calling to each other above the steady march of boats plying the waterway. Deer occasionally peeked out from the greenery, as did smaller creatures indigenous to the woodlands that had so recently been divided into Oregon and Washington territories by the American congress.

Unlike her, the wild animals clearly knew where they belonged, Charity mused. What was it the Bible said? *Don't worry about anything. If God takes care of the birds of the air and the lilies of the fields, you must see that He will also take care of you.*

Oh, how much easier life would be if only she believed that the way Thorne did. She wanted to. Really, she did. Continuing to watch the passing scene, she grew melancholy. Perhaps someday she would find her place in the world, a place where she *knew* she belonged. A place where there was peace and love and acceptance. Home.

Thoughtful, pensive, she happened to glance at the shoreline on her left. At least five Indian dugout canoes were beached there and riders on horses and mules had formed into a group as they trailed their way up from the water on a narrow path that looked as if it followed the course of the river for a short way.

She stiffened. Frowned. Shaded her eyes and strained to see more clearly. Could her imagination be playing tricks on her or did one of those men on horseback closely resemble the man from the hotel whose presence had so vexed Thorne? She had only seen Cyrus Satterfield briefly since they'd left San Francisco, and then only from a distance, but this rider's clothing matched the details stored in her memory. Moreover, he stood out from the others because he wasn't dressed like a settler or an Indian.

There was only one way to find out. Lifting her hem and racing for the cabin, she went to fetch Thorne.

Charity's abrupt arrival startled Thorne and brought him to his feet. "What is it? What's wrong?"

"I—I think I saw him. That man. The one you were watching," she blurted breathlessly.

"Where?" He immediately usurped her position at the door, blocked the entrance with his body and scanned the nearby deck area. "Did he bother you?"

"No, no," she explained. "It was on shore. I think I saw him on the riverbank with some Indians."

"Which shore? North or south?"

"I don't know." She glanced at the sky. "It's too near noon to tell."

Thorne did his best to temper his consternation. "We're headed almost due east. From the bow, north is to the left and south is…"

"North," she nearly shouted. "He was on the north shore."

"Stay here with Naomi and the boy. I'll go have a look," he called over his shoulder, already hurrying away.

In the seconds it took him to round the pilothouse and reach the port deck he prayed he'd be in time to see for himself.

He wasn't. The breath whooshed out of him in disgust. The riders Charity had spotted were still on the hillside but they were already too far away to be seen clearly, let alone identified.

Racking his brain, it suddenly occurred to Thorne to duck into the pilothouse and see if the captain had a spyglass handy.

He knocked but didn't pause before opening the door. "Excuse me," he said, quickly scanning the small room. "I was wondering if…"

The copper, cylindrical device Thorne sought hung in its leather case, just to the right of the doorway. He snatched it and was already back at the railing by the time shouts followed him.

Someone grabbed his shoulder, tried to wrest the spyglass from his grasp. He twisted away with a strong, "Wait! Just one more second."

"You can't go takin' the cap'n's property," the crew member said.

"I know. I'm sorry. I didn't have time to ask his permission. I needed to use it right away."

"Well, you've used it," the man countered. "Now, give it back or I'll have to place you in irons for the rest of the trip."

Thorne knew there was no use arguing further. He'd seen enough through the telescopic device to know that the riders were too far away for anyone to discern their features, even magnified.

He handed over the instrument and walked away without any comment other than a murmured, "Sorry." And sorry he was. If Charity had been right in her assumption that Cyrus Satterfield or others of his ilk were headed in the same direction as his party, they'd better be more vigilant than ever.

And if he wasn't? If Charity had been mistaken? That didn't change anything. As he had already told her, there could still be new dangers around every bend of the river and lurking behind every tree. Whether or not they were in real peril didn't matter. Thorne intended to proceed as if they were still centered in the sights of an invisible rifle and Louis Ashton's finger was poised on the trigger.

Chapter Thirteen

The steamer *Multnomah* put ashore near Rainier, a meager assemblage of rough-hewn buildings at the confluence of the Columbia and the Cowlitz. From there, Charity had been told, they would go as far as possible on the smaller river before undertaking a short, overland trek, passing through Olympia and proceeding to the American Fort Steilacoom.

It sounded too easy, which was partly why she was worried. The trip across the great plains by wagon had been described as simple, too, and it had cost many thousands of pioneers their lives. If accident or Indian attack didn't kill you, cholera or smallpox might, providing you didn't get run over by a wagon or a buffalo stampede or die of starvation and thirst, first.

And speaking of Indians. Charity shivered. Thorne had been talking with four long-haired, buckskin-clad natives while she and Naomi stood aside with Jacob. From the satisfied look on Thorne's face as he returned to them, she feared he had struck a bargain for their transport upriver.

"All's well," Thorne said. "One of their party is an

important leader of the peaceful Nisquallies, so we're in good company. He tells me there are halfway houses all the way to Cowlitz landing where we'll be able to buy horses and supplies for the last leg of our journey."

Grinning, he gestured toward the waiting Indians. "Smile, ladies. We don't want Leschi and his friends to think you're unhappy. They've kindly offered to let us ride along on their trip home. We'll be departing as soon as they're through trading at the mercantile."

Naomi pressed a lace-edged handkerchief to her face below her nose, peered at the canoes and grimaced. "Those boats smell."

"That, they do," Thorne said. "And so do our friends if you judge them by our standards. I'm sure we smell very strange to them, too, and probably just as distasteful."

Charity nodded. "That's what my sister said after she and her husband had spent some time with the Cheyenne and Arapaho. She got so used to the aromas in camp she missed them after she left."

"I feel the same about the ocean," Thorne said, looking a bit wistful. "There is something about breathing sea air that invigorates and blesses me."

"Me, too," Jacob piped up, bringing chuckles from Charity and his uncle.

"Well, I guess we know where our little sailor's loyalties lie," Charity said. "I was pleasantly surprised by how well he handled the bad weather that put his mama to bed. Thankfully, he seems to take after your side of the family."

Thorne's response was perplexing. She had thought, since he seemed so taken with the little boy, he would be flattered by the comparison. Instead, he was acting as if that was the last thing he'd wanted to hear.

He was probably still grieving over the possible loss of his brother, she reasoned. That excused his rigid posture and closed expression. It had been insensitive of her to bring up the subject and although she was sorry to have done so, she felt it best to let the matter drop rather than apologize and draw more attention to her innocent faux pas.

"Will we all be able to fit into one canoe with our baggage?" she asked.

Thorne shook his head. "No. We'll ride with Leschi and one of his companions. The others will transport our bags in the second canoe. The Nisquallies came downriver together and that's the way they plan on going home." He gave her a lopsided smile. "Consider it your own private fleet."

"I think I'd prefer something a bit larger for my armada," Charity said, relieved to have distracted him so easily. "But I imagine it will be safer with more guides. I don't suppose there's any chance they might get lost, since they live here."

"Not likely," Thorne replied. "They don't use compass and sextant like ships at sea but they always seem just as sure of directions as the finest trained navigator."

"Undoubtedly a useful talent," she said with a shy smile. "I, on the other hand, used to get lost as soon as I stepped off Montgomery Street near the hotel. Papa loved to tease me about it."

"You will see him again," Thorne said soberly. "I promise."

She sighed. "They should be married by now." Looking into the distant forest, she let her mind's eye wander. "I know Annabelle wanted the wedding to be held at Mission Dolores because that's where Lola Montez was married to Mr. Hull last year. Papa wanted to use Trinity Church, instead. It will be interesting to see who won out."

"I doubt it matters in the eyes of God," Thorne ventured.

"I hope you're right. I haven't been able to bring myself to attend worship services in a church since I left Ohio. I know I should have, especially when Papa asked me to go with him, but it just didn't seem right without Mama."

"What about your own wedding? Where did that take place?"

Charity shook her head slowly, sadly. "In the middle of a desolate prairie just west of Fort Laramie. It's not a day I particularly take pleasure in remembering."

"Then forgive me for bringing it up."

She looked into his eyes and replied, "If you, too, will forgive me."

"For what? You've done nothing needful of forgiveness."

"Yes, I have. I reminded you of your brother when I mentioned Jacob's sailing abilities a few moments ago. I should have been more sensitive. I'm truly sorry."

"Ah, that," Thorne said with an audible sigh. "You mustn't blame yourself if I seemed out of sorts, Miss Beal. The error in judgment was not yours. It was mine."

Thorne helped both women into the first canoe, then handed Jacob to Charity. With a buckskin-clad Nisqually at either end of the narrow craft and the center space taken up by the ladies and the boy, he could quickly see it would be best if he followed in the second boat instead of climbing in with them.

"I'll ride with the luggage," Thorne said. "It makes no sense for all of us to cram in together when it's not necessary."

"But..."

Although Charity didn't finish her sentence, Thorne saw her eyeing the regal-looking Indian seated in the prow of the canoe. Leschi was taller than his companions and apparently spoke several languages, English among them, which was a definite plus. Yet Thorne could tell she didn't relish being separated from him and his rifle.

"I'll be right behind you," he said to reassure her. "It will be much easier for me to watch out for you if we're not so crowded." He smiled wryly. "You said you'd trust me. Remember?"

She gave him a contrite look. "I did, didn't I? My error."

That made Thorne laugh. The Indians joined in, thereby lifting everyone's spirits. They pushed off with Charity's canoe in the lead and Thorne jumped into the second narrow boat.

He didn't like sending the women on ahead and was adamant that his canoe keep pace with Leschi's. It took an extra payment to the owner of the second canoe, after departure, to ensure that that occurred.

Smiling to himself, Thorne appreciated the crafty way his Indian guide had arranged to squeeze another coin out of him. These Oregon and Washington natives might be uneducated by city standards but they were clearly far from foolish. They had learned to trade from the British of the Hudson's Bay Company and had quickly adapted to the advent of Americans, nicknaming them "Bostons," apparently in the mistaken belief that all such settlers hailed from Massachusetts.

The Nisqually knowledge of world geography might be lacking but the Indians' overall skill at plying the rivers and lakes was quite impressive, especially to a man like him who had made a good living from the sea. He was not only awed with the way each guide handled the small dugouts, he was amazed at how well the canoes balanced as they slid through the water with barely a ripple.

Concentrating mostly on the boat bearing the women and the child, Thorne nevertheless found time to ready a rifle he had purchased on the docks in Rainier. It was a muzzle-loader and had seen lots of hard action, judging by the looks of its scarred stock. It, and the derringer he had given Charity, would have to serve until he found something better and added to their armament.

His guides barely glanced at him as he poured a measure of powder down the barrel, added a wad and ball, and rammed it all home, waiting to place a cap below the hammer until he was ready to test fire it. Not wanting to discharge the rifle for nothing and perhaps startle the others, he laid it carefully aside.

Ahead, Charity had slipped off her bonnet and he could see sunlight glistening off her golden hair. Although she resembled Naomi in coloring and height, there was a warmth and vivacity to her personage that set her apart from the other woman the way a sunset highlighted an otherwise cloudy horizon. She was sunshine to Naomi's shade; roses in full, glorious bloom to the other woman's spent blossoms.

Thorne could tell by watching their Nisqually guides

that the Indians were growing wary of something. They kept to the center of the Cowlitz and alternately scanned both banks. He knew they would spot any danger long before he did. What they would do to counter it, however, was another question.

Peering into the shadowy vegetation along the riverbanks, Thorne imagined a multitude of threats. Every crack of a twig, every splash of water, every cloud that passed across the sun and left dappled patterns on the ground, made him see adversaries where there were none.

Suddenly, a horse whinnied close by. Another answered. Thorne spun around just as a rifle fired from shore. The sharp sound echoed up the canyon on both sides of the river, masking its origin all too well.

A woman screamed.

To Thorne's horror, he knew the shriek came from Charity.

The moment she had realized what was happening, Charity had thrown herself over the child to protect him.

The Indian called Leschi shouted something to her but he spoke so rapidly she couldn't understand what he was saying. She did know, however, that he and his companion were paddling their canoe much faster and had veered sharply left.

She dared not raise her head for fear of another shot but did manage a quick peek over her shoulder. Naomi had apparently not been hit or even frightened because she was still sitting bolt upright.

Appalled, Charity commanded, "Get down!"

Naomi ignored her.

Charity reached for the other woman's coat and

yanked, toppling her over and pulling her down so they were all lying bunched up below the thick, wooden sides of the dugout.

There was no way to tell if that would be enough protection but Charity figured it was better than letting Naomi just sit there, frozen like a frightened deer waiting for slaughter.

Jacob began to whimper.

"It's okay, honey. We're okay," she crooned. "I'm sure Uncle Thorne will shoot back as soon as he can."

Whining, the little boy displayed his hand. There was blood on it!

Charity took one look, raised high enough to be sure their protector's canoe was following closely, and yelled, "Help!"

She returned to her prone position and cradled the child in her arms to cushion him. "Where is it. Where do you hurt?" she asked.

He pointed. To her.

"You have a owie."

"I do?" Charity touched her forehead and her fingertips came away smeared with crimson. She hadn't felt a thing at first but now that Jacob had called her attention to it, her forehead did smart a little.

The sensation of being shot was nothing at all like she had imagined it would be. She had thought she had merely banged her head on the canoe when she'd ducked, never dreaming that her scalp had actually been grazed by a bullet!

Relieved that Jacob was not injured, she smiled at him. "It's just a scratch. I'm sorry I got blood all over you, sweetheart."

Naomi raised her own head enough to glance at the others, took one look at the gory mess and fainted.

Leschi had his canoe beached and had herded its occupants into the forest for cover by the time Thorne caught up to them.

He made straight for Charity, dropped to one knee and grasped her free hand while she used the other to press a scrap of cloth to her forehead just above the hairline.

He was beside himself, almost afraid to articulate his feelings for fear of revealing the pain he felt at seeing her thus. Finally, he asked, "Are you badly hurt?"

"No. I'm sure it's just a scratch. I'm afraid I frightened Naomi and Jacob terribly, though."

Blinking back tears of relief he heaved a sigh. "You scared me enough for both of them. Who shot at you?"

"I don't know. I never saw a thing."

Thorne didn't want to leave her but there were details he had to know. He arose and turned to the Indians. "Did you see anything?"

"Boston men," Leschi answered. "And Snoqualmies. Patkanim. He bad medicine. Want war."

"Are you sure it was Bostons with him?"

The taciturn Indian nodded. "All King George men tillicums, like Dr. Tolmie. They not shoot at Leschi."

"Friends?" Thorne guessed. "You say they're your friends?"

"Yes. Friends. Boston men not tillicum." He frowned. "Except Charlie Eaton. He marry my daughter, Kalakala."

"Then surely they are your friends, too," Thorne said, hoping to be considered among them.

Leschi snorted derisively and turned to point at Charity. "Why shoot klootchman?"

"What? Oh, the woman? I don't know for sure but I have a good idea. I just don't understand what the Snoqualmies would have to do with all this."

Chuckling, Leschi looked at him as if he thought him daft. "Patkanim's men no need reason. They love to fight. Any Boston man with gun is enemy."

"Then why would they join forces with one?"

"For enough blankets or powder and ball, they will fight for any man. Even a Boston."

Mulling over what the wise Indian had said, Thorne fetched his things from the second canoe and returned to care for Charity. Her beautiful hair was matted and her frock probably ruined but that was of little consequence as long as she recovered.

He again knelt at her feet as he poured water from a canteen onto one of his clean shirts.

She resisted his ministrations. "You are not going to use that lovely shirt to clean my wound. It's a ridiculous waste. I won't permit it."

"Do you have a better idea?"

"Yes. I can take care of myself." Starting to rise she swayed slightly.

Thorne was immediately at her elbow to steady her. "So, you say. It looks otherwise to me, Miss Beal."

Still, she objected to his efforts. "I can dip water from the river and use this scrap of my petticoat to stem the bleeding just as I have been."

"And be shot again for your trouble?" He raised an eyebrow. "I thought you were smarter than that."

"I'm smart enough to know that whoever took a potshot at us is probably long gone by now."

"I have to agree with that. However, I'd prefer to remain in hiding until our guides have checked to make sure."

"I couldn't help overhearing you talking to them. Is it true that it may have been hostile Indians who shot me?"

"Unfortunately. According to Leschi, they were in the company of Americans. They could have been after anything, including our supplies."

Or you women, he added to himself. There was plenty of intermarriage between the settlers of the Pacific Northwest and local women, such as Leschi's daughter. It was the pale, European-featured women that the country lacked and Thorne imagined that they'd be very valuable trade items if they were captured.

The concept gave him a sick feeling in the pit of his stomach. He had brought innocents to this wild territory and it was his sole responsibility to see to their welfare. No one was going to get past him to harm those women and that child as long as he had breath in his body.

And what if something happened to him?

Thunderstruck at the realization of his party's vulnerability, he left the canteen with Charity so she could finish washing up, then took the Nisqually leader aside to speak privately to him.

"I know I only paid you to take us as far as Olympia but I can see I should have asked for more. If something was to happen to me, how much more money would it take for you to promise to care for the women and get them as far as Puget Sound?"

"Hudson's Bay Company or Fort Steilacoom?"

"Preferably Steilacoom but either is fine as long as they're safe there."

"They be safe. I do."

Thorne started to reach into his pocket but Leschi stayed his hand. "No. You tell Bostons at fort that Leschi help you. Give big talk. Make them listen."

"All right." Thorne offered his hand and the two men shook on the bargain. "Why do you want to make such an impression on them? Surely, they know you're a leader of your tribe."

"They know. They make me swear in court against three of Patkanim's braves. Boston's hang them. Say murder."

"And you want me to assure them that you're a good friend to all sides. I see. You have my word."

In his sea travels Thorne had often noted the rivalry between the two factions of settlers in the Northwest. Those British who had founded the colonies for the fur trade were understandably upset about the change of legal boundaries and the necessity to vacate properties they had once laid claim to. But they had no choice. Their government had made a binding agreement. Oregon had been split off from Washington and was now a separate territory to the south, while part of the northern edge of Washington that encompassed the sound also fell within the aegis of the United States.

And, apparently, the local tribes had chosen up sides just as they had during the Revolutionary War seventy-five years before. While the British King George men and the Americans called Bostons quarreled about who owned what, the natives were the real losers. They had probably already ceded too much power to the interlopers and judging by past history they were going to someday find themselves treated as strangers, unwelcome in their own country, the land of their ancestors.

Thorne watched as Leschi spoke to his men, gesturing as he gave them orders. Two of them left immediately and faded into the forest as silently and easily if they were no more than puffs of smoke from a dying campfire.

Those Indians were a part of this wild land just as he was a part of the sea, Thorne reasoned. They belonged here. The territory was their mother and father, their home and their partner in life, providing all they needed for health and happiness. It was little wonder that they resisted the intruders, who were not only plundering their natural treasures but also destroying the good quality of life they had once enjoyed.

The Whitman massacre after the measles epidemic, which Aaron had cited, was but the tip of the iceberg. Disease, against which the Indians had no defenses, had already decimated many tribes and would do so over and over again until they either attained immunity or were wiped off the face of the earth.

Thorne feared it would be the latter. Watching Leschi dispatching his men, he wondered if his new ally had any idea of the long-term danger his whole tribe faced. He strongly doubted it.

And speaking of danger… He set his jaw as he looked over at Charity. She was taking her injury well but that didn't negate its possible seriousness. He'd have to watch her closely for fever or other signs of related illness as a result of the cut, yet he had to thank God that she had not been hit squarely. An inch or two, either way, and the bullet would have entered her brain. Then, instead of arguing over the misuse of his shirt they'd be digging her grave alongside the river.

Nearly overcome at the thought of losing her, Thorne had to fight the burgeoning desire to take Charity in his arms and assure her that he would always care for her. Always love and cherish her.

Although he knew that doing so would be foolish and unseemly, he was right on the verge of acting on the impulse. Then the fat would be in the fire for sure, wouldn't it?

He sighed deeply, thoughtfully, and mustered his self-control. Was it fair for him to ask to court her? Was there a chance she might allow such a thing? Or was she still determined to remain single, as she had stated so forcefully in the past?

He didn't know. Nor was the question relevant at present. They had miles yet to travel and no one but God could guarantee that any of them would survive the trek.

Thorne briefly closed his eyes and prayed that his Heavenly Father would watch out for all his loved ones. Especially Charity Beal.

Chapter Fourteen

By day's end, Charity had developed a throbbing head-ache. Although she was resistant to doing so, she finally resorted to taking a few drops of the laudanum they had brought along to quiet Naomi.

When they put ashore at a landing where a halfway house awaited with meals and lodging, she was feeling a tad better but was nevertheless glad to leave the confining canoe and stretch her legs.

Thorne was already ashore and offered his hand as she prepared to step across. "Careful. The bank is slippery," he cautioned as she passed Jacob to him first.

"I shall have to remember to wear my heavy boots tomorrow," she said. She took his free hand and allowed him to assist her while he held the child in his other arm.

"How is your head?"

"Larger than it was this morning, I fear, but it will do. Leschi tells me his men found fresh prints of unshod horses but no sign of whoever shot at me."

Thorne scowled. "I cannot imagine who would do such a thing to you. Naomi, yes, if the scoundrel was one of Louis's hired killers, but not to you."

"I've been giving that some thought," Charity told him as the friendly Indians assisted Naomi ashore. "I had removed my bonnet but your sister-in-law had not. Perhaps the shooter mistook me for her. We are somewhat alike, same hair color, same size, and I was caring for Jacob. From a distance it would be a natural mistake."

Judging by the look of consternation on Thorne's face she was convinced he had not considered the similarity before now. Truthfully, if she had not had so much time to sit quietly and ponder during the trip upriver she might not have drawn that conclusion, either.

She saw him glancing around at the forest, the river and the lodge built of logs they were about to enter. It was as if he were seeing danger lurking behind every rock and tree and she felt sorry for him. It wasn't Thorne's fault that his brother had disappeared or that his stepfather was deranged, any more than it was his fault that Naomi had become mentally unbalanced recently.

Thorne was clearly assuming responsibility for all the tragedy that had befallen his family. It seemed so unjust. Necessary, under the circumstances, but nevertheless an unfair burden.

She took Jacob from him as he herded everyone toward the place the Indians had called, "Hardbread's", presumably because their meals were rumored to consist of mostly boiled salmon and hardtack. The medicinal, dulling effects of the laudanum were beginning to wear off and she was starting to realize how hungry she was.

Welcoming aromas of cooked food greeted her, wafting on the air from the open doors and windows of the cabin. If it hadn't been for the clouds of mosquitoes and biting gnats that also heralded their arrival she would have felt as comfortable there as in the dining room back at the Montgomery House Hotel.

Off to one side, Leschi and his men were pulling leaves from a fringe-leafed bush, crushing the foliage in their hands and rubbing it over their faces and exposed arms.

Charity smiled at the Nisqually leader and gestured with an unspoken query. To her delight he brought her a handful of the bruised leaves, which reminded her of tansy, and she was able to cover Jacob's face and hands with the juice before also using it on herself. The effect was marvelous. Not a single insect crossed the fragrant, spicy-smelling barrier.

"Thank you," Charity said, smiling.

The Indian bowed slightly, smiled, also, and backed away.

"Aren't they coming in to eat?" she asked Thorne.

"I don't imagine they're welcome," he said.

"Well, I never."

She passed the child back to Thorne and preceded him into the lodge. There were large bowls of steamed, pinkish fish and boiled potatoes on the plank tables. At the end of each stood an open wooden barrel filled with hardtack from which the travelers could apparently help themselves at will.

Without so much as a "by your leave," Charity hefted one of the bowls of cooked salmon, added a handful of hardtack and marched out the door with it.

She didn't look back, nor would she have stopped if anyone had commanded her to do so. Instead, she went straight to the Indians and presented the bowl to Leschi.

He tried to refuse but she persisted. "Are you hungry?"

He nodded.

"Is this food you like?"

Again, a nod.

"Then please take it, with our compliments," Charity said. "Mr. Blackwell will pay the innkeeper for it and you won't get in trouble. I promise."

"You are tillicum klootchman," Leschi said, formally accepting the bowl and holding it as if it were a precious gift. "When we reach Nisqually, I will give you a horse. You choose."

"No, no," she said, "I don't want to trade. This is no more than I would do if you were a guest in my home."

"And I would give you a horse or some other gift," he explained. "It is our way."

Astonished, Charity thanked him and rejoined her party. Thorne had obviously been hovering in the lodge doorway and had already made peace with their landlord over the purloined bowl of fish because no one looked askance at her as she reentered.

Just the same, she felt the need to explain. "I was simply trying to do the Christian thing and feed everyone fairly. However, it seems that is not the way things are done in this part of the country and I am now to become the proud owner of one of Leschi's horses when we reach his home. I sincerely hope we'll need one because I'm afraid it would be an insult to him if we turned it down."

The surprised expression on Thorne's face made her giggle. "I know what you're thinking. I was flabbergasted when he told me, too. But since he had already accepted the food, I didn't know what else to say."

The landlord, a squarish man with enough hair on his exposed forearms to make up for what his head lacked, spoke up. "You did good, lady. Real good. These here Indians don't take kindly to some of our ways and it would of been downright dangerous to refuse that there horse." He guffawed. "Wanna go take him some taters and see if you can git another one from him?"

"I did not feed those poor men for personal gain," Charity insisted. "I did it because it was right."

"Well, right or wrong," the landlord said, "Your instincts pro'bly saved your neck. If you're smart, you'll pick a nice horse when you get the chance, too. It'd be rude to choose an old, weak or lame one. Leschi and his tribe take special pride in their livestock. He'd be shamed in front of his people if you took a poor gift."

It struck Charity that the man was putting other words to the old saying, *Never look a gift horse in the mouth.* She said as much, bringing more laughter.

"That's right smart, ma'am. Besides, you don't need to check his teeth if'n you know horseflesh. Those Indian ponies can be tricky, though. Some old ones look about as good and strong as the younger ones do." He laughed again. "Kinda like them Indians out there."

"They're hardly animals," Charity said, taking no pains to hide her disgust at the man's inferences.

"Wait till you've lived around 'em some longer," he said. "They'll surprise you."

"The thing that surprises me," she began, before catching the look of warning in Thorne's eyes. There was no mistaking his admonition to quell her righteous temper.

She did the best she could to smooth over the situation by adding, "Forgive me for bothering you with my personal problems, sir. I'm weary and hungry and my head is throbbing." Giving the landlord a demure smile she asked, "May we sit down and eat?"

"Be my guest."

As they took their places on the narrow benches that bordered the longest sides of each table, Thorne leaned closer to whisper in her ear, "Thank you. I know that took considerable constraint."

"About all I could muster," she told him aside. "I fear I may have lived amongst city dwellers for too long."

Thorne shook his head. "Things are no different back in San Francisco."

"Of course they are."

"Oh, really?" He held the bowl of potatoes and helped her dish some out for herself and Jacob before he asked, "Then tell me. How many Chinese were lodged at the Montgomery House Hotel?"

Sleeping on the hard, wooden floor of the halfway house would not have been Charity's first choice of accommodations but under the circumstances she wasn't going to quibble.

The night had grown chilly as soon as the sun had sunk behind the surrounding hills and her place next to the hearth not only warmed her achy bones, it also helped keep more bugs away. Outside, the sounds of a forest twilight kept a steady cadence of chirping insects and frogs and the occasional hoot of an owl.

She curled her body around Jacob and cuddled him close so she could cover him with her heavy coat while he used her arm for a pillow.

It was easy to relax because she knew Thorne was

sitting up, watching over them all. His presence was more than a comfort. It was a true blessing.

She wanted to thank him, to let him know how much she appreciated his evident concern over her injury and his efforts to care for her, but she didn't know how to do so without making her praise sound too intimate. If she were to reveal her feelings for him, she was certain he would be either astounded, offended or amused. Perhaps all of those.

In retrospect, she wondered if her initial decision to make this trip had been made for the wrong reasons. She had held Thorne Blackwell in high regard long before they had left San Francisco. And now? Now, her attachment to him was far stronger than simple friendship or admiration.

She lay quietly and listened to some of the men talking softly in the background. It was easy to pick out the familiar rumble of Thorne's voice, to know without peeking that he was vigilantly looking out for her. His concern was beyond any she had ever experienced and she wondered if he was that diligent and devoted to everyone.

Beginning to drift off to sleep, Charity smiled. It was pleasant to think that Thorne's allegiance was aimed toward her, as a person, rather than at the family as a whole.

Family? Yes, she answered, sensing a newfound inner peace. Somehow, she had begun to see herself as a real member of Thorne's immediate family and that view gave her great contentment.

She heard the muted clomp of boots approaching and opened her eyes. Thorne towered above her.

"I'm sorry to wake you," he said quietly.

"I wasn't asleep yet," she answered, drinking in the sight of his dear face. "Is anything wrong?"

"No. I just wanted to make sure you were feeling all right. No fever?"

"I don't think so." Charity yearned for him to bend down and touch her forehead. Before she could reason away her inappropriate desires she blurted, "Maybe you'd better see for yourself."

Thorne hesitated only seconds, then crouched and laid his hand on her brow. She closed her eyes, relishing the caress of his callused hand. All too soon he withdrew and stood.

"I think you're cool enough."

No thanks to your lovely, warm hand, she thought, blushing. What was wrong with her? She had never, as long as she could remember, felt anything like the longing she felt for this man. Had she drifted so far away from church that she'd become immoral?

No, Charity answered without hesitation. It wasn't wrong to dream of the kind of marital bliss her sister had found, nor was it a sin to fall in love.

That thought was enough to make her catch her breath. Was this what love felt like? Could she have been wrong to plan to lead a celibate life after she was widowed? Such a decision had seemed perfectly sensible at the time. Only now was it coming into question.

Her eyes searched the depths of Thorne's dark gaze. Was she imagining it simply because she wanted it to be so, or was there a new tenderness, a growing affinity in the way he was looking at her?

She was afraid to ask, afraid he would deny such emotions. Instead, she smiled and said, "Thank you for looking after me."

"I—I would like to…"

"Yes?" Her eyes widened. For the first time since she had known him, the commanding Mr. Blackwell seemed to be struggling to express himself.

"Nothing," he said flatly. "Go to sleep. We'll be rising early tomorrow so we can reach Cowlitz landing in one more day."

"Sleep well," she said tenderly, sweetly, willing him to know her innermost thoughts and sense her growing fondness for him.

Although he merely nodded, then turned away, Charity was positive she saw telltale moisture glistening in his eyes. In her heart of hearts she took that as an indication that he was becoming aware of her affection. That was a good sign. A very good sign.

She snaked her fingers out from under the heavy coat and gingerly touched her temple in secret as soon as Thorne had walked away. It smarted. A lot. And the skin beyond her hairline felt unusually warm. Speaking of signs, that one was *not* good.

Tomorrow, she would privately ask Leschi to recommend other medicinal plants to help her heal. She was not going to succumb to this wound—or to any other. Not when she was beginning to suspect she had so much to live for.

Their arrival the following evening at Cowlitz landing created quite a stir. It was only after the canoes had docked that Charity realized the furor was not because of her party, it was due to the presence of Leschi. Clearly, he was not only an important person among his people, he was revered.

She watched myriad blanket-wrapped Nisqually men

and women gather around him as he made his way to a clearing located amidst a collection of square log houses which stood apart from the rest of the town's buildings. Every cabin in the group where Leschi had gone was exactly the same size and shape, leading her to conclude that this was the way the local Indians constructed their homes.

That was a surprise. She had listened raptly to Faith's vivid descriptions of the Arapaho and Cheyenne villages and their buffalo-hide-covered teepees so she had expected to see the same here. Obviously, the Nisqually stayed in one place long enough to build log houses.

As soon as Thorne had helped her and the others disembark, Charity asked, "Is this Leschi's home village?"

"I don't think so," he answered, speaking quietly. "But they do seem to respect him here so he's probably related. The Indians often intermarry to join their tribes in permanent alliances."

"Like the royal families of Europe?"

"Yes, now that you mention it. Exactly like that."

Thorne had lifted Jacob into his arms and seemed to be waiting for something so she stood quietly beside him until she ran out of patience. "Why are we just standing here? Can't we go into town and find a hotel?" She pointed. "I think I see several possibilities."

"You do. Our guides tell me a proprietor named Goodell offers excellent food and real beds. We'll spend one night at his hotel before we head for Olympia. But first I want to buy horses from our Indian friends."

"Is this where I'll be choosing the one Leschi promised me?"

"I'm not sure. All I know is, one will not be nearly

sufficient." He glanced at her, then at Naomi. "I assume you can ride astride?"

"Of course. Faith and I used to hop on Father's favorite old mule, Ben, and trot him around the pasture all the time." She felt a blush rising to warm her already-flushed cheeks even more. "Of course, Mother didn't know we were doing it or she'd have pitched a fit."

"I hope Naomi is equally nimble because I'm not sure where I'd find a proper sidesaddle for her in an outpost as remote as this one."

"I'll be glad to teach her how to ride like a man," Charity said with a shy smile and a giggle. "We may not be graceful or totally modest, considering our long skirts, but we'll do. I promise."

"You are truly a marvel, Miss Beal," he said, grinning at her.

"In that case, I think you should begin calling me by my given name."

"That's not proper."

"If we were seated in a drawing room in San Francisco and sipping tea out of china cups I might agree with you. Out here in this wilderness, such formality seems a bit stiff and unnecessary, don't you think?"

"Will you call me Thorne?" He arched an eyebrow and gazed at her quizzically.

"If that is your wish."

He bowed slightly, clearly mindful of the child he was still holding. "It is, Miss Charity. And may I say it will please me greatly to hear my name on your lips."

That comment, along with his obvious good humor and the twinkle in his dark eyes, added even more color to her cheeks and she could feel the warmth spreading to her very soul.

"Then it shall be my pleasure." She hesitated, wondering how it would feel to actually speak his name aloud rather than merely think it. All she said in addition was, "Thorne," but she knew her tone bespoke a fondness for him that was unmistakable.

He sobered, nodded and whispered, "Charity."

The timbre of his voice gave her shivers and sent a tingle zinging along her spine. Never, in all her twenty years, had she heard anything that had thrilled and pleased her more.

"Did you get a look at her?" Cyrus Satterfield asked his Snoqualmie cohort.

"Ai. She is here. I see her with the man and the boy."

"A big man? Dressed in black?"

"Ai."

"All right. That's all I'll need you for. I'll finish this myself."

"No. I go with you."

Satterfield shook his head and gestured with his lit cigar. "You'll do nothing of the kind. If you hadn't shot at that canoe, they wouldn't even know anybody was after them."

"You say kill pale woman. I do."

"No," Satterfield countered with evident rancor. "You didn't kill her. All you did was graze her with your musket ball or she wouldn't be walking around town this very minute."

"I kill next time," the brave insisted. "Put poison on ball like we do arrows."

That got Satterfield's attention. "Poison? You have such a thing?"

"Ai. Kill deer fast."

He noted the Snoqualmie brave's taciturn expression and didn't doubt that his own life would be in danger if he made an enemy of these Indians. "All right. You can stay with me. But only because I may need some of your poison and instruction on how to handle it. I don't want to accidentally hurt myself."

Nodding, the Indian turned and walked away, leaving him standing alone outside the saloon.

Satterfield muttered a few choice curses that referred to both the Snoqualmie's rotten attitude and a questionable parentage, then shrugged off the unspoken threat he'd glimpsed in the brave's eyes and entered the building. There was more money to be made before morning, before he would have to mount up and give chase once again.

In the meantime, he intended to enjoy himself to the utmost, even if the only whiskey he could get was rotgut and the only woman he could find to warm his bed was from a local tribe. He would have preferred one of the willowy blondes Blackwell had with him, but the short, squat Indian squaws would have to do. If he could find one that had not had her head bound as a baby, so much the better. Those sloping foreheads and elongated heads might be the Indians' idea of beauty but they turned his stomach.

Chapter Fifteen

The lodging he'd been able to obtain in Cowlitz landing was not as luxurious as Thorne would have liked for Charity and the others but it had sufficed. He had not been able to purchase everything they would need for the final leg of their journey, either, though he had been assured that one of the stores in Olympia would be able to furnish the rest of his gear.

Thanks to the needs of the lumbering operations nearby and the brisk fur trade, Olympia had sprung up on the banks of the upper Cowlitz between the river and a snaking finger of Puget Sound. All manner of freighting was being carried on there, both by river and via the sound. To his surprise, there was even a newly founded mail service operating by horseback and canoe between the town and the mouth of the Columbia, far to the south.

Thorne would have preferred to keep to the water as they had so far, but from here on it wasn't practical. According to information from the men who ran the mercantile, Rev. and Mrs. White had built their mission farm on the part of the prairie called Nisqually Flats, near Fort Steilacoom. Therefore, the fastest, best access to them was on horseback.

Leschi had wanted to tarry with his kinsmen at Cowlitz landing so Thorne and his party had proceeded without a guide. As they traveled in single file along the well-worn trail north toward Olympia and then Steilacoom, he kept a sharp eye out. He wished Leschi had seen fit to come along but he was thankful that the amiable Indian had at least explained the shortest, best route.

In spite of occasionally having to wade through swampland as deep as the bellies of their horses, Thorne and his party were making good time. They had encountered a startling number of cabins and small farms along the trail, many of which were occupied by American settlers. If they had stopped to visit with everyone who had invited them in, it could have taken weeks to finish the daylong ride.

Spotting a ramshackle, apparently abandoned dwelling just off the trail in a grove of trees, Thorne finally suggested they pause to rest and eat some of the food they had brought. If he had been making the journey alone, he would have pressed on but he could tell the women were tiring. Even Charity was starting to look unusually pale. Besides, the sky had darkened as if a storm were imminent and he didn't want them to be caught in the open if it started to pour.

"Oh, I'd love to get down," Charity said with a sigh of relief. "Jacob has been napping for the last hour or so and my arms are so tired they're tingling."

Thorne dismounted first, tied his horse's reins and the ropes from the pack animals' halters to nearby saplings, then laid his rifle and ammunition aside before he reached up to relieve her of the child. The weary boy barely stirred in his uncle's arms.

"Take him inside and see if you can find a good place for his nap," Charity said. "I can manage myself and Naomi."

"Are you certain?"

"Perfectly. These horses are small but I would still rather you did not watch us climbing down. We may not be as modest as we wish to be."

"All right. Just remember what Leschi told us about Indian ponies and get off on the right-hand side instead of the left. I'll only be a few steps away. As soon as I get Jacob settled I'll come back and see to the horses so you won't have to bother with them."

The land around the old cabin was overgrown and the place looked deserted. Nevertheless, Thorne knocked before entering.

The door swung open with a squeak, revealing a broken latch, as well as rusty hinges. Stepping inside, he noted a tinge of green moss on the flat surfaces of the rough-sawn furniture. Only the sagging and frayed ropes remained on the bed frames. Chipped, stained dishes were stacked on shelves against one wall. Pots and pans sat empty atop a small, black, wood-burning stove. The place looked as if its former occupants had simply given up homesteading and had walked away, leaving most of their belongings behind.

He shrugged out of his coat, spread it on the hard-packed dirt floor, then laid the sleepy child on it before starting back to assist the women and hurry them along. The sooner he got everyone to their final destination, the sooner the knots of nervousness in his stomach would ease.

Spotting another rifle standing in one corner of the single-room cabin, he delayed a moment longer to have a closer look at it.

Charity was loath to admit she was feeling worse by the hour. Hoping she could continue to mask her feverishness, she sat astride the brown-and-white-spotted mare Leschi had given her and watched Thorne until he was out of sight in the cabin.

Thunder rumbled in the distance. To her dismay, her mare and the other horses seemed to be becoming unduly nervous. Since she wasn't familiar with these small, compact, Indian ponies, she assumed it was their nature to be a bit high-strung and the impending storm probably didn't help their temperament.

She mustered her remaining resolve, ignored the throbbing of her head and started to dismount. Just as she swung her leg over the saddle, the horse sidestepped, almost causing her to fall. She kicked her right foot free, jumped and landed squarely on the mossy ground. The jarring of the landing made her already-pounding head feel as if it was about to explode.

"Easy, girl," she crooned, not letting go of the bridle for fear the mare would bolt. "Easy. It's just me. I know you're not used to all these petticoats flapping around but I can't help that."

With the reins looped around her hand, she grasped Naomi's horse's bridle and forced a smile. "Time to get down, dear. Do you remember how I taught you to do it?"

Naomi nodded but Charity could see that the woman was unsure.

"Just swing your left leg over and…"

Suddenly, a whooshing, snorting sound emanated from the forest behind them. It reminded her of the noise a startled deer made when it sensed danger.

Both horses reared back and rolled their eyes, whickering and blowing through flared nostrils. Charity held fast and tried to dig in her heels, but to no avail. She was being dragged along by the wiry animals as if she were as weightless as a feather.

"Naomi! Jump down. Now," she commanded. "Do as I say."

To her relief, that authoritative tone did the trick. Naomi alit with surprising grace and speed but to Charity's chagrin, that action spooked the horses even more.

Naomi's black-and-white mount pulled free first, wheeled, and headed for the wilds with its ears back and its tail held high. Both packhorses immediately jerked their lead ropes loose from the sapling they'd been tied to and gave chase amid more lightning and crashes of thunder.

Charity hung on to her little mare in spite of its determination to follow the others. Where was Thorne? Hadn't he heard the furor? She supposed not or he would have come running by now.

She was continuing to try to calm her mare when a war whoop echoed across the glade and made the hair on the back of her neck prickle.

Another more distant whoop answered from the opposite direction. She thought she glimpsed slight movement through the trees and brambles. Here and there she could catch glimpses of brown color similar to that of the Indian clothing she'd noted in Cowlitz and beyond.

No matter which tribe members had made that chilling noise, Charity knew that she and the others were going to be afoot if she didn't retain at least one horse. She was also convinced that standing out in the open was the worst place to be, especially because any friendly natives would surely have shown themselves by now.

"Naomi! Come on. Never mind the other horses. Help me get this one inside."

Tugging, cajoling and backing away, Charity managed to urge the mare all the way to the cabin door. What she wasn't able to do was convince the horse to step foot into the darker interior.

"Thorne," she shouted over her shoulder. "Help us!"

He wheeled in response to Charity's cry and saw her trying to coax one of the fractious, half-wild Indian ponies through the doorway.

It would have been laughable if she had not had such a distressed look on her face. "What in the world are you doing?"

"Indians," she blurted. "Outside. I'm sure I saw them sneaking through the woods and I was afraid they'd steal my horse."

"Where's Naomi?"

"Right behind me."

The mare had its head lowered, its ears laid back, its neck bowed and its feet set, giving Thorne plenty of room to peer over its back. He caught his breath. "Where?"

"Right out there. The other horses ran off but she's helping me get this one through the door."

Thorne was already shoving the balky animal out of the way, much to Charity's obvious consternation. He didn't care if he made her angry. He had more pressing concerns. He could see most of the clearing and there was not even a hint of his sister-in-law.

About to grab the lone remaining mount and race to Naomi's defense, he heard a musket boom. The ball hissed by, barely missing his head, and thudded into the log wall behind him.

Charity gasped, then dived for cover.

Thorne darted aside to grab his ammunition bag and his rifle from the ground where he had laid them.

Charity's frightened pony nearly ran him down as it reared, wheeled and fled.

There was nothing he could do but follow Charity back inside and slam the cabin door.

"I'm sorry," Charity said, fighting to appear calm and failing miserably. "Naomi was coming with me. I know she was."

When Thorne made no comment, she assumed he was angry. Well, he had no right to be. She had done all she could. It wasn't her fault that she had failed. She was only one woman with two hands. She couldn't possibly have held on to the horse and Naomi at the same time.

Disgusted with herself, she sighed. No, she couldn't have. And in that case she should have chosen to drag Naomi into the cabin and let the horse be stolen. She realized all that now, when it was too late to do things differently.

"What now?" she asked.

He pointed. "Grab that old long gun standing in the corner and check that there's nothing blocking the barrel. I'll show you how to load it. The powder and ball are over here by me. The caliber should be close enough. You can add extra wadding if the ball seems too loose."

"Papa taught me how to load a gun," she said. "But how do you know this one is safe? It might blow up when you fire it if it's been sitting here rusting for very long."

"We'll have to take that chance." Thorne poked the barrel of his muzzle-loader out through a chink in the logs and sighted along it, waiting for a target.

"Maybe they were just after the horses," she ventured.

"Well, they have them now. And all our supplies."

Although he hadn't added, "How could you let them get away?" it was implied.

"I did the best I could," Charity insisted. "I know I should have let the mare go and held on to Naomi. She was right there, supposedly helping me. I never dreamed she'd run off like the Indian ponies."

"Did you see any special markings or clothing on the men? Anything that would help identify them?"

"No. Nothing. The horses got all het up and the next thing I knew, they were heading for the hills. Literally."

As she spoke she was checking the abandoned long gun by measuring the barrel with the ramrod to make sure there was no powder or ball already taking up space in it.

"This one isn't loaded," she said. "The rod goes in all the way to the percussion hole. Do you want me to load it for you?"

Thorne nodded. "Yes. Keep the first measure of powder on the light side till we see how it shoots."

She watched him sight his own rifle, hold his breath, then squeeze the trigger.

The gun went off with a boom that rattled the rafters and brought a shower of dust down on them to mingle with the cloud of pungent smoke from the burned gunpowder.

Jacob began to wail.

Charity was too busy to tend to him but she did call, "It's all right, sweetheart. Stay where you are. Uncle Thorne is taking care of us."

He passed her the first rifle to reload and took up the second one. "Wish me luck," he said, raising the stock to his shoulder and preparing to shoot again.

Charity chose to pray instead. *Father, help him. Help us. And please keep Naomi safe, wherever she's gone.*

There were more unspoken words, more silent pleas, and she didn't stop praying hard until Thorne had pulled the trigger of the second gun and its breech had held.

If it hadn't, she knew all too well that he could have had the whole side of his head blown off. That kind of accident had happened to careless men more often than she liked to recall, whether the metal was faulty to start with or they had thoughtlessly filled the breech with too much black powder.

Thorne fired, again and again, and Charity kept him supplied with loaded weapons. As she tore more pieces of fabric from her petticoat to make patches for the musket balls, she wondered what they'd run out of first. It didn't really matter. Once any of the other components, powder, ball or primers were gone, they would be defenseless.

The firing ceased as abruptly as it had begun. Charity froze, staring at Thorne and trying to read his unspoken assessment of their situation. He looked a lot less worried now than he had before. That was definitely a good sign.

"Are they gone?" she asked, reeling from fatigue and the effects of the fever she continued to deny.

"It looks like it." He straightened and propped the guns against the wall. "Keep everything loaded. I'll go have a quick look around."

"Take a rifle. You have to have something for protection."

"You keep them," he said, his gaze locking with hers as if he might never see her again. "If any Indians come through this door, don't let them take you alive."

"Whoa," she blurted, stunned. "I'd rather be a live hostage than a dead memory. Besides, I know you'd rescue me, no matter how long it took."

"I would, you know."

Her voice gentled as she reached up to cup his cheek with her palm and said, "Yes, Thorne. I know you would."

Though he didn't reply with words, the look in his eyes spoke volumes.

It wasn't until Charity was alone that she allowed herself to plop onto a rickety chair. Every bone in her body ached and she feared she was becoming very ill. That wouldn't do. Not at all. She must hold herself together and feign good health, at least until they reached Naomi's parents. After that she could let down her guard and allow her weakness to show.

Timidly, his cheeks streaked with tears, Jacob approached her. His voice was barely audible as he said, "Mama?"

Charity opened her arms and lifted him onto her lap. What could she say? How could she explain to the child that his mother was gone again and that it was her fault?

As her own tears began to fall, Charity held him close and laid her cheek on the top of his head. She was so weary, so spent she could barely think, let alone speak coherently.

Finally, she managed to say, "I'm sorry, sweetheart. I'm so sorry."

The little boy's response was both touching and heartbreaking. He wiggled and twisted till he could wrap his arms around her neck, kissed her damp cheek and said, "It's okay, Mama. Please don't cry."

Thorne returned after spending only a few minutes outside. "It's me. Don't shoot," he called before easing open the door.

Charity didn't rise to welcome him back. She wanted to run straight into his arms, regardless of the impropriety of such an action, but she simply lacked the strength to do so.

Jacob, however, had plenty of energy to spare. He shouted, "Uncle Thorne!" and raced toward him.

Catching the child in midstride, Thorne lifted him and swung him in an arc, sharing his joy as he glanced over at Charity. "I'm glad one of you is happy to see me."

"I'm happy, too," she said. "Honest I am." Getting to her feet, she swayed as a wave of dizziness and nausea washed over her.

Thorne hurried to her side and took her arm to steady her while he lowered Jacob to the floor. He peered at her. "You've been crying."

"I guess I'm not as strong as I thought I was."

"You're amazing. Most women I know would have fainted dead away at the first sign of Indian attack."

She blinked, trying to clear her head, and failed. The

room was spinning. Colored lights like the bits of sparkling glass in a kaleidoscope danced at the periphery of her vision. Blackness encroached.

She heard the rumble of Thorne's voice. It sounded so dim and far away she couldn't make out what he was saying.

One moment of peace. That was all she needed. She'd just close her eyes for a second and she'd be fine. She had to be. Failing to hold up her end of the bargain she'd made to care for the dear little boy and his mother was totally unacceptable.

Moisture flooded her already misty vision and tears once again slid down her cheeks as she recalled Jacob's words. He had called her *Mama*.

The importance of that choice was not lost on her heart or mind and that was all she could think of as she slipped further and further into the darkness that was waiting to give her rest.

Thorne caught her as she swooned and carried her to where he had placed his coat for the boy. Laying her gently atop the garment, he knelt at her side and began to pat her hands and rub her wrists.

At his side, Jacob was sniffling. "Is she sick?"

Thorne was about to assure him that Charity was merely overtired when it occurred to him that the boy might be right. He hadn't felt her forehead since the night before and it was possible she might have chosen to hide her infirmity rather than cause more worry.

His hand was shaking as he gently laid it on her forehead. She was burning up! His anger flared. The little fool hadn't given any indication that she was ailing or he would never have asked so much of her. Did she expect him to notice her feverishness on his own? Or was she purposely hiding those telltale symptoms to keep from causing a delay in their journey?

Any and all of those possibilities fit Charity's stubborn personality, he concluded. The question now was what should he do? If he tried to carry her the rest of the way to Olympia, or at least as far as the next farmstead, they would most likely be attacked en route. If that happened while they were out in the open, there was no way he could adequately defend both her and the boy, let alone get her to a place where she could be nursed back to health.

He looked around the cabin, assessing his options. They were meager to say the least. If they stayed there, he would have to find fresh water and food, which meant leaving Jacob and Charity unguarded for however long that quest took.

If he chose to stay inside and continue to protect them, they might all fail to survive without adequate provisions, especially water. It was a terrible choice to have to make.

Finally, in desperation, he took his questions to God. As he knelt beside the unconscious woman and bereft little boy, he closed his eyes and began to mutter a prayer. His plea was mostly centered on Charity, on the fact that he truly cared for her, although he did include the rest of his close family, including Naomi and Aaron.

Unashamed, he released the strong self-control on which he prided himself and bared his soul to his Heavenly Father.

As a man, he knew was out of options and saw no way to save his beloved.

As a Christian, he knew upon Whom he must rely if any of them were to survive.

Chapter Sixteen

The storm that had been heralded by the thunder began in earnest before another hour had passed. Heavy rain pounded against the roof of the cabin and trickled in through a myriad of chinks between the logs.

Desperate for water of any kind, Thorne placed the empty cooking pots where they would collect rain while he tried to keep their guns and clothing dry.

He'd built a fire in the stove using some of the furniture for fuel and was applying damp compresses to Charity's fevered brow. She lay wrapped in his overcoat, as well as her own, while he tried to sweat the fever out of her. So far, his method seemed to be working because she had passed through a slight delirium and was beginning to rest easier.

Thorne knew he should stop worrying but he could barely manage to breathe, let alone relax. The only time he had left her side was to stoke the fire or collect more cool rainwater with which to bathe her face and hands.

Jacob, bless his heart, had tried to help by moving some of the smaller pans beneath newly discovered leaks and Thorne had encouraged his efforts. As long as the boy was kept busy he was less likely to notice undue hunger or thirst.

It wasn't until Thorne noticed him taking secretive sips of the collected water that he realized he'd had an ulterior motive. That made him smile in spite of everything. Jacob was a chip off the old block, all right, a conniver with a penchant for doing as he pleased, even at such a young age.

Thorne no longer doubted that he was the child's true father. There were simply too many indications of it. Not only did Jacob look enough like him at that age to have been his twin, he was displaying many of the same mannerisms and attitudes. Even his lopsided smile was pure Blackwell, leaving Thorne torn between pride and a sense of wretched culpability.

"If only Aaron were here," he said softly. "I have so much debt to repay."

He glanced at the leaky roof and thought of other debts, mainly the thanks he owed to God for providing needed water. It sounded as if the rain was slacking off, but they had plenty saved to get them through the night and hopefully bring Charity's fever down. Beyond that, he dared not plan. Without horses and the guarantee of a safe passage, he'd be a fool to try to complete their journey, no matter how close they were to Olympia or Nisqually Flats.

There was also the matter of what may have happened to Naomi. If the Indians had stolen her, he had to attempt a rescue or at least try to buy her back from them before she was bartered to some other tribe. The Indians' practice of slavery among their brethren had surprised him the first time he'd heard about it but it was such a big part of their warrior culture he knew he'd have to play by their rules. Assuming they did have Naomi, that is. If she had simply wandered off and had had to weather the storm alone and lost, that might be even worse.

Jacob had laid himself down beside Charity when he tired and had quickly dropped off to sleep. Thorne had kept the fire going as he stood watch. Hour by hour, his fatigue grew. His eyelids felt leaden, his alertness nearly nil. He fought sleep rather then allow himself much-needed rest. He must not doze, he insisted. If he wasn't vigilant, anyone could sneak up on them.

Finally, he decided to hang some small tin cups above the closed door so they would clatter and rouse him if it was opened. Then he sat down on the dirt floor with his back to the wall and the rifles at hand.

In minutes after he'd rigged the alarm and settled his weary body comfortably, he nodded off.

Charity awoke to sunlight streaming through the cracks in the walls and ceiling. She was still a bit achy but her headache was gone and she could tell the fever had also passed.

"Praise God," she whispered as she left the still-sleeping child and got slowly, tenuously to her feet to check her balance. Thankfully, she seemed to be a bit weak but otherwise as well as could be expected. She didn't remember everything that had occurred the previous day but she did recall enough bits and pieces of it to realize that Thorne had nursed her through the crisis.

And sweet little Jacob had helped, she added. How hard and how sad it was going to be to bid that child farewell.

Looking around the room she saw Thorne dozing in

a seated position on the hard-packed floor. His coat was still on the ground where he had laid it for her and the boy and she knew he must be chilly, yet he was obviously sound asleep in spite of any discomfort.

Her mouth was dry, her throat parched. She found a pail of clean water with a dipper near the stove and slaked her thirst. Never had tepid water tasted so wonderful. The only thing better would be a bath. That was out of the question under these circumstances, of course, but she could clearly imagine its refreshing qualities.

She gently touched her wounded forehead. The place where the bullet had broken the skin was still tender but the surrounding skin felt cool, probably thanks in part to the pine bark Leschi had shown her how to steep and apply, as well as drink. That medicine was gone now, as was everything she owned, including her comb and brush, which meant that there wasn't a thing she could do to make herself more presentable.

If she hadn't been so glad to be alive, she might have fussed more. As it was, she knew there were far more important concerns to address, Naomi among them.

Thorne looked so peaceful, so dear, she yearned to let him sleep. Perhaps, if she eased open the door, she could make a silent trip to the facility out back and return without disturbing him. Since there didn't seem to be any other choice, she felt justified in doing so.

Charity didn't notice the tin cups balanced above the door until they clattered together.

Thorne was instantly awake. He jumped up, bracing for attack. When he saw who was standing at the door, he heaved a noisy sigh. "Oh, thank the Lord. How are you this morning?"

"Much better." She knew her smile was sheepish but she didn't care. She was so glad to hear his voice and look into his eyes she wouldn't have cared if he'd been yelling at her. "I was pretty sick, wasn't I?"

He nodded, his expression grave. "Yes."

"Thank you for taking such good care of me."

"I'm just glad my efforts were successful." Raking his hair back with his fingers he glanced at the floor where the boy slept. "Jacob's okay, too?"

"He seems fine. I'm sure my feverishness was due to the injury, not illness. I've never been shot before."

"And hopefully never will be again," Thorne said. "We should take whatever we think we'll need for the rest of our journey and get started as soon as possible, if you think you're up to it."

"I seem to be all right. I'm a little weak but not terribly dizzy the way I was." Reaching into the pocket of her coat, she withdrew a handful of crumbs. "I was going to offer you and Jacob some hardtack but I seem to have crushed it."

"You're the one who should eat it. You need to build up your strength."

Charity began to grin at him. "Are you being solicitous or is that your way of politely saying you don't want to share my crumbs?"

Laughing, he mirrored her broad smile. "I'm glad to see your sense of humor hasn't suffered. Don't throw that mess away till we get other food somewhere. We may end up eating it as a last resort."

Although she made a face she stuck her hand back into her pocket just the same. "All right. If you insist. I suppose it might not be too hard to take if we made it into a gruel. Where did you get all this fresh water?"

"The Lord sent it," Thorne said. "Right through the roof."

"I must have missed that."

"Undoubtedly. You were out of your head for hours."

Seeing affection and lingering concern in his eyes she wondered if she had babbled anything revealing during her delirium. She certainly hoped not. It was embarrassing enough to know that he—and Jacob, of course—had cared for her while she lay senseless.

If she had not trusted Thorne implicitly, she might have worried that he had taken advantage of her helplessness the way Ramsey Tucker once had. But that was not even a mild concern. She *knew* Thorne would never hurt her, never abuse her in any way.

That startling realization was so firm, so clear, her jaw dropped. She stared at him. The fear of being touched, at least by the man who was looking back at her so lovingly, was totally gone. What a wonderment!

"Are you sure you're all right?" he asked, starting to scowl.

"Oh, mercy yes." Charity beamed. "I'm fine. Never better."

"Good." His eyes narrowed further. "I think."

"In time I will share my private thoughts with you but for now I agree that we'd best get a move on." She looked away and blushed slightly. "If you will kindly watch for hostile Indians, I would like to use the facility."

"Of course." Thorne picked up one of the rifles, opened the door a crack to check the yard, then threw it open as he said, "All clear. Follow me and stay close. I don't want you going into that outhouse until I make sure it's good and empty."

Charity knew better than to argue. She would have preferred to take care of necessities without causing such a fuss but she knew Thorne was right to be cautious, especially in light of the Indian attack the day before.

Without hesitation she followed him into the sunlit glade. Wildflowers, nourished by the rain, were blooming in clusters of blue and yellow at her feet while birds soared in the cloudless sky or busily built nests in the nearby trees. It seemed impossible that there could be danger lurking in such a beautiful place but she knew it was not only possible, it was probable.

She had no sooner left the cramped facility and rejoined Thorne in the yard than she saw an Indian step boldly into the clearing. Her breath caught. Her heart raced.

The instant the man raised his hand in greeting she recognized Leschi. Behind him, one of his men was leading the runaway horses. Looking slightly soggy and every bit as confused as ever, Naomi was once again seated atop the black-and-white mare.

Charity was confused, too. She'd trusted the Nisquallies, as had Thorne. Was it possible that they had been the ones who had fired on the cabin?

No, she countered. If they had been the attackers, Leschi and his men would be long gone, not smiling and returning their horses and property.

Tears of gratitude filled her eyes and prayers of thankfulness filled her heart.

She stood back as Thorne cautiously approached the Indian. She could hear the men talking but couldn't make out every word. When Thorne lowered his rifle and offered to shake Leschi's hand, her fears were allayed.

God had more than answered her prayers for their deliverance, she mused, elated. He had not only given them water when they were in dire need, He had provided native guides again to lead them the rest of the way through the wilderness. Their troubles were over.

Olympia wasn't a surprise to Thorne because he had sailed close to that portion of the territories often while navigating Puget Sound. Charity, on the other hand, was clearly impressed. He had to smile at her enthusiasm.

"Look! Real hotels, just like in San Francisco," she said, beaming. "And see that sign? It even has a newspaper, the *Columbian.* We must try to get one and see what's been happening while we were traveling."

Thorne laughed. "I doubt the news will be as fresh as we were privy to in San Francisco. It would have either come by the same route we did or been sent overland, probably from New York. Either way, it's a long trip, even with the new railroad lines that run partway."

"I suppose you're right. How many people do you think live here?"

"One or two hundred, I imagine. Judging by the piles of spars, shingles and squared timbers stacked down by the docks, the lumber mills are going strong. There are undoubtedly a lot of folks living outside the city, too."

"Can we stay the night at one of the hotels?" Charity asked. "Our little man is badly in need of a bath. And so am I, I fear."

"You could have gone for a dip in any of the creeks we passed along the trail," Thorne teased.

"Brrr. You may be that hardy but the rest of us are

not, I assure you. Besides, the sooner we reach Naomi's parents the happier I will be."

"Amen to that," Thorne said seriously. "Leschi is going across to the west side of the bay to stay with relatives tonight. He said he'd call for us at the Sylvester Hotel at dawn. That's the big log building at the corner of Main and Second." He pointed. "Right over there."

Leading the way, Thorne rode ahead, trusting Charity to herd Naomi in the right direction. He knew she'd been terribly distressed to have lost track of his sister-in-law, because ever since they'd gotten Naomi back, Charity had hardly taken her eyes off her.

"I'll see about rooms and stabling for the horses," Thorne said. He took special pains to smile as he added, "Can you handle Jacob and Naomi?"

"Jacob, yes," Charity said. "As for Naomi, I will give it my best."

"As you always have, even when you were so ill you could hardly stand. I want you to know I don't blame you for her foibles. She is what she is. All any of us can do is our best."

Tarrying, Thorne decided to help Charity down after he had dismounted. He held up his arms, took Jacob from her and stood him on a low stump that protruded from the edge of the street in front of the hotel. Then he returned for Charity.

"I can manage," she protested.

"I know you can. However, there is no way you can preserve your modesty if you err in the middle of this bustling settlement so you may as well give in and accept my assistance."

It was all he could do to keep from laughing at her

expression of consternation. She knew he was right but she was still acting stubborn.

"Of course, if you want to try getting down by yourself, I can always stand back and watch," he added.

"I would rather you be close enough to cover my inelegance if I do show a bit of what's left of my poor petticoats," she replied, blushing. "I trust you will be enough of a gentleman to avoid staring."

"I shall be the soul of discretion," he vowed, chuckling as she leaned toward him and placed her hands on his shoulders.

She had already shed her heavy coat so he was able to grasp her thin waist. He lifted her easily, stepping back and sweeping her to the ground in one graceful swoop.

An instant later, as he lowered her feet to the dirt, he realized he'd made a terrible mistake. He never should have gotten that close to her again. She felt perfect in his arms, as light as a sunbeam and as beautiful as a butterfly. In contrast, he saw himself as clumsy and ill at ease. When he was this close to Charity Beal, he was no longer a shipping magnate or even an able seaman. He was an awkward boy longing for his first kiss from the woman of his dreams.

Ignoring the fondness he imagined in her lovely blue eyes, he set her away and quickly turned his attentions to helping Naomi.

From now on he would have to be even more diligent in regard to his actions, let alone his wayward thoughts. Charity was a lady of the highest order and deserved not only courtesy but honorable treatment. The more he grew to care for her, the more prudent he would have to be or he would surely alienate her.

Judging by the loathing she had demonstrated whenever she'd mentioned her late husband, he would have to be oh, so cautious. If he once stepped over the line and frightened her by making undue advances, no matter how gentle his approach, she might never be able to forgive him. Never be open to becoming a wife again.

When the right time came, when he was assured she would accept him, he would speak up and ask for her hand. Until then, he would keep his distance, for her sake and for the sake of their future happiness, even if the strain of biding his time was the hardest task he had ever undertaken—and he had little doubt that it would be.

Chapter Seventeen

True to his word, Leschi had appeared in the street outside the Sylvester Hotel at daybreak. Charity had already risen and seen to Jacob's immediate needs, as well as helping Naomi dress, so they were all ready to leave when Thorne called for them.

More time in the saddle did not particularly appeal to her but the weather was clear again and it felt good to soak up the sun's warmth as they rode Northeast across the rolling prairie.

By the time their mounted party reached the bluffs overlooking the place Leschi called Nisqually Flats, Charity understood why Naomi's parents and their neighbors had settled there.

The valley was a veritable Eden. Long, lush grasses waved like wheat in the cool breezes from the nearby ocean, and where there were cultivated patches of land she could see plots of healthy, farmed crops.

Charity had been balancing Jacob in front of her on the wide tree of the saddle and pointing out squirrels, rabbits and other wildlife along the trail, much to his delight.

When she reined in next to Thorne to gaze at the valley below, she was in awe. "It's beautiful. Look at all that grass. If Papa's old mule, Ben, were here, he'd think he'd died and gone to heaven."

"This place is like that to the Nisquallies," Thorne observed as their Indian guides left them with a parting wave and proceeded down a separate trail toward their own homes, as planned.

Thorne waited till Leschi and his tribesmen were a little farther away, then explained, "All they need or want comes right from the land. They tell me they harvest clams and oysters from the salt marshes, salmon from the rivers, wild berries and other fruits in summer, besides peas, potatoes and wheat from the tilled land."

"They're farmers? I had no idea. When I saw the crops, I just assumed they belonged to the settlers."

"Some of them do. The Nisquallies have worked for the British and Americans for years now and they've learned how to raise their own crops, as well as gathering the natural bounty from the sound and the surrounding forest."

"That's amazing."

She continued to sit there and drink in the view while Thorne scanned the trail behind them. Finally, he said, "I think we should be going."

"Why?" She tensed and looked behind her. "Did you see someone following us?"

"No. It's just a worrisome feeling I can't seem to shake. If there were any hostile Indians in this vicinity, I'm sure Leschi would have sensed it."

"Would he have said anything?" she asked, almost ashamed to be entertaining such suspicions.

"I think so," Thorne said. "But I understand what

you're asking. I suppose it's not wise to trust anyone too much. If I were in the Nisquallies' moccasins I don't know how hospitable I'd be to hundreds of newcomers."

"Surely, there's enough bounty in this land for all."

"At the present time, yes," Thorne said, "but I was speaking with some travelers at Sylvester's last night, after you and the others had gone to bed. They tell me there's talk of the United States' government drawing up a treaty as early as this coming winter."

"What kind of treaty?"

"It's apparently going to demand that the Indians west of the Cascades give up their homes and leave. That includes the Nisqually, Puyallup and Steilacoom tribes from right around here. Even if the chiefs refuse to agree to the terms of the treaty, it's a bad sign of trouble to come."

"Isn't there something we can do?"

"Yes. We can get Naomi and Jacob delivered to the missionaries, as planned, and catch the first available ship bound for San Francisco."

With that, he dug in his heels and urged his mount down the trail toward the American settlement.

Following, yet keeping to the woods to avoid detection, Cyrus Satterfield reined in his horse, yawned and stretched.

The lone Indian who had remained with him snorted in disgust. "They get away. They go to fort. You see?"

"All I saw was that there were too many Nisquallies with them for us to chance another attempt. I'm not worried. I'll get them eventually."

"How you know which woman?"

"Simple. The one with the child has to be his mother.

If I'm not sure when the time comes to take action, I'll kill them both and be done with it. Probably will, anyway."

"When? How? You go to fort?"

"I may, once I've scouted it out." He laughed at his companion's disconcerted expression. "I take it you're not coming with me that far?"

"No. Leschi go home, I go home."

"You never did tell me how you two are related."

"His mother Yakima. My father Yakima. Her brother."

"He knows you? Why didn't you *say* so? No wonder you didn't want to get close enough for him to see your face when we were chasing the woman and those fractious horses through the woods."

"Leschi a fool. He tillicum to King George men and Boston men. Make much peace. Patkanim say make war."

"And the rest of your tribe agrees, no doubt." He patted the leather pouch containing the roots the Indian had found and pounded into a pulp for him. "All right. I have the arrow poison and I've paid you every bit you're going to get from me. I told you long ago I could handle this myself. Go on home. I don't need you."

"You see Leschi, you no tell him," the wiry Indian warned, "or poison arrow find your heart, too."

Cyrus was still chuckling derisively as he watched the other man wheel his horse and disappear into the dense forest.

In Charity's opinion, the mission complex looked more like a farm than it did a church. A surprised Mrs. White, who bore a striking, though graying, resemblance to Naomi, greeted her daughter with tears of joy. After brief introductions all around, she graciously ushered the entire party into her modest log home.

When Naomi didn't answer her mother's simple queries, Mrs. White turned her attention to Charity and the child. "I can't believe our Jacob has grown so big already. Naomi often wrote me about him."

"He is a big boy," Charity said. "Heavy, too." Reluctant to let him go, she nevertheless presented him to his grandmother. "This is your granny White, Jacob. Remember? I told you all about her."

The child hid his face next to Charity's neck and continued to cling to her.

His understanding grandmother backed off. "Give him time. You've doubtless had a difficult trip." She nodded soberly toward her daughter. "What's wrong with my Naomi? Do you know?"

"I think so," Charity said, speaking quietly aside. "She was fine until her husband disappeared."

"Aaron? Where? When?"

While Charity remained in the parlor with Naomi and her mother to provide more details of their trials and tribulations, Thorne took Jacob outside into the yard.

"I want Mama," the boy whined.

"We'll go back in a few minutes. Aren't you anxious to meet your grandfather?"

"No."

Thorne huffed. "Well, nobody can accuse you of not being truthful, can they?" He saw a group of people hoeing in a nearby potato patch and ambled in that direction.

"Afternoon," the tallest man called. He removed his straw hat to mop his brow and Thorne could see that behind his thick, gray beard was the lighter but leathered skin of an aging settler.

"Hello. Mr. White?" Thorne asked.

"William White. That's me. What can I do for you?"

"I'd like you to meet your grandson," Thorne said with a grin. "This is Jacob Ashton."

"Well, well. God bless you for bringing him this far to see us." William offered his hand. "You must be Aaron."

"No. I'm his brother, Thorne. Half brother, to be precise. I'm afraid Aaron has been missing since before we left San Francisco."

"Is our Naomi all right?" the older man immediately asked.

"She's here, too, if that's what you mean." Thorne was sizing up the other farm workers as he spoke. Most were Indian women but a few were older Nisqually men. None of them were looking at him with nearly as much friendliness as Leschi had demonstrated.

Thorne understood that Rev. White was understandably confused and concerned. "Naomi's in the house with your wife. I know you want to see her but can we go somewhere private to have a talk first?"

"Of course, but…"

"It will all make sense once I've told you the whole story. At least I hope it will," Thorne said. "We made it this far only by the grace of God."

The reverend nodded and began to smile as he led Thorne toward the rudimentary barn. "That's the only reason any of us are here, son. I'm glad to hear you giving proper credit to our Lord."

Thorne reentered the house accompanied by Naomi's father. Jacob ran straight to Charity and hopped up into her lap while Mrs. White, who insisted on being called by her given name of Nancy, made the rest of the introductions.

"Pleased to meet you, Rev. White," Charity said, smiling at him. "Nancy tells me you have a preaching planned for tomorrow. You must not postpone it on our account."

"Never have and never will," he replied. "It's not exactly our usual camp meeting, though. One of my flock is marrying a Nisqually woman over by Fort Steilacoom and I've been asked to conduct a brief Christian ceremony for them in addition to the one the Indians plan."

Charity was taken aback. "A wedding?"

"Yes. I've seen one other like it since we've been ministering here and it's truly fascinating. I know you'll enjoy seeing all the Indian folderol."

"Oh, we couldn't intrude," she said, hoping the excuse was enough to deter the preacher. The last wedding she had attended, with the exception of her sister's, was the sham of her own marriage. The notion of celebrating the nuptials of strangers did not sit well with her. It had been hard enough to muster the fortitude to attend Faith and Connell's ceremony back in California.

"Nonsense," the missionary said. "The more the merrier is the way these natives feel. I suspect they'll even invite some of the British from across the sound. I've been trying to encourage that whenever the occasion arose. We all need to learn to get along."

Charity sensed that Thorne was looking at her as if he were waiting for her to make the final decision. Oh, how she wished everyone would simply allow her to abstain from joining in any such festivities.

"We—we were going to leave very soon. Mr. Blackwell has planned for it," she said, hedging as best she could. The silent plea she sent his way via her gaze was all she could politely accomplish. Unfortunately, Thorne did not seem to comprehend.

"There's no reason why we can't spare an extra day or two," he said. "Now that I see how much trouble Jacob is having settling in, I suspect it would be best to delay for a short while anyway." He smiled at the Whites. "And there may be questions you have that you've not thought to ask us yet. Miss Beal and I would be delighted to join you for the Indian wedding."

William White rubbed his hands together with delight. "Wonderful, wonderful. Folks will be coming from miles around. And afterward there will be a big, fancy meal. Nancy's been baking for days so she'll have something to offer the Nisquallies for their feast."

Sighing, Charity gave up searching for excuses. It was clear that they were all going to attend the wedding celebration whether she liked it or not. And she could understand why the Whites would want someone familiar to accompany Naomi and help them watch out for her, especially since she was going to be in a large crowd of strangers.

Plus, there was the problem of dear, bewildered little Jacob. Charity reiterated her vow to put his needs first. She would force herself to do whatever it took to help him adjust to becoming a permanent part of his grandparents' lives.

She blinked back unshed tears. Somehow, she must help the child get over his undue attachment to her and Thorne, so he would be able to accept his new living arrangements happily.

The task sounded daunting but she knew she was up to anything. After all, she had been shot, withstood an Indian attack and lived through a fever that could easily have taken her life.

Given that, how hard could it be to spend a hour or two encouraging the child to be more friendly while they watched some nuptial festivities?

According to Rev. White, Fort Steilacoom had been founded on the site of a failed farm belonging to an English sheep rancher named Joseph Heath. William had explained that the fort's construction encompassed quite a few of Heath's original buildings, as well as added blockhouses for the protection of settlers. At strategic places along the solid perimeter fence there were also observation towers from which soldiers with rifles could easily defend their outpost if need be.

The Whites owned a spring wagon and several strong teams of workhorses which were much more like those Charity was used to seeing than the Indian ponies had been. She had assumed it would be more comfortable to ride to the fort in the wagon than on horseback until she'd been bounced over the rough, rutted road from Nisqually Flats for what had seemed like hours.

Poor Nancy had fretted about her cakes and pies most of the way, worried they would be ruined by the buffeting. William had merely laughed and chided her for a lack of trust in the Lord.

When Nancy had snapped back, "It's not *God* I have a quarrel with. He's not driving this wagon through every pothole on the prairie," it had brought laughter all around and had further lightened Charity's anxiety. After all, she reasoned, she did believe in God. And she

could see that she had been rescued by divine providence more than once, especially of late. Therefore,
there was no reason why she should not be able to accept
whatever Rev. White said or did during the ceremony.

*I just hope and pray it doesn't make me remember
my awful wedding too well,* she added to herself. There
were some people, some things, she might never be
able to forgive or forget no matter how hard she tried.
And, in the case of Ramsey Tucker, she had to admit
she wasn't trying.

What she definitely did not want to hear was Bible
teaching that might convince her that she was wrong to
continue hating a man who was long dead. She wanted
to loathe him. It was her right. He had abused her and
she wasn't ever going to get over it.

Their arrival at Fort Steilacoom was heralded with
such excitement Charity had little time to continue to
brood. After she had helped Naomi and Jacob from
the wagon, she put them both to work carrying Nancy's baked goods into one of the blockhouses that was
being used to store the food the settlers were contrib-
uting for the coming feast. Tables inside were loaded
with fish, clams, oysters and stews. Besides the usual
side dishes of boiled potatoes, onions and bread, there
were some strange-looking baked roots one of the soldiers had told her were camas, a wild staple food that
the Indians loved.

It was hard for Charity to keep from staring at the
other women who were present. Although they were
dressed in calico instead of wearing triangular blankets over their shoulders and traditional bark skirts,
their hair and skin were much darker than hers, lead-

ing her to conclude that these were the Indian wives of settlers and soldiers.

She didn't begrudge them their happiness, assuming they were content, she simply wondered how hard they had had to work to make the transition from their old way of life to this one. Such changes could not have been easy. In comparison, the challenges of her own life seemed almost simple.

Chatting with the women, Charity learned that some had undertaken more than a day's journey to get there. Others had rowed across the sound or had taken a steamship from as far away as Whidbey Island, to the north. Their fortitude was certainly commendable, as was their friendliness. When a few of them mentioned being born Nisqually, she was pleased to tell them she had met their chief.

"Leschi is very wise but not chief," a young woman explained. "His father, Sennatco, is one of our chiefs."

"Oh, I just assumed…"

The woman smiled. "I understand. Every man trust Leschi, even King George men and Bostons. He is friend to Dr. Tolmie, too."

"A medical doctor? Here?" Charity asked.

Some of the younger girls giggled. "Not here. At Hudson Bay Company. Dr. Tolmie runs it."

"Oh, I see. There's certainly a lot to learn. I'm sorry to say I won't be staying long enough to figure it all out. We're leaving very soon."

"You and husband?" She looked pointedly toward the place where Thorne was helping unhitch the horses.

Charity knew she was blushing because her cheeks felt as if they were aflame. "Mercy, no. We're not married."

"You go with him? Stay with him? Reverend White say that wrong. Should marry." She glanced around at the other Indian women in calico as they all nodded tacit agreement. "We no sin. We marry like Holy Bible teach."

"I'm not... Oh, never mind. You wouldn't understand," Charity said with a shake of her head.

"I will pray for you," the Indian said with a gentle smile. "You not sin. Yes?"

"Yes, I will not sin," Charity said, humoring her the way she would have a child.

Yet something in the woman's words, in her sincerity, kept nagging at the back of Charity's mind for the rest of the long afternoon and try as she might, she couldn't seem to shake the conviction.

Chapter Eighteen

Thorne took it upon himself to stick close and keep an eye on the women and Jacob while Rev. White made his way over to the temporary Indian encampment on the banks of the Nisqually River, a stone's throw from the fort.

The way Thorne understood it, Indian marriage was arranged by barter between the young woman's father and the intended groom. Acceptance of the proposal was partly dependent upon the offering of suitable, valuable gifts, such as horses and blankets.

Both factions had been dancing to Indian drums and singing, accompanied by a soldier's fiddle music, the previous night. Come morning, an official exchange of the last of the promised gifts was made between the groom's side and the bride's side before everyone gathered in parallel lines bordering an aisle of woven reed matting and awaited the appearance of the bride.

Thorne herded Charity and Jacob into place along the aisle while Nancy White looked after Naomi. Together, they stood quietly, respectfully, and listened to Rev. White speak an opening Christian prayer. Breathtaking, snowcapped peaks of the Cascades and a cloud-less sky formed the perfect backdrop.

Thorne had noticed how quiet Charity had become of late and he was worried that she might be ailing again. When he had asked her, however, she had brushed off his concern as if she had never been racked by fever and delirium. Nevertheless, he held Jacob for her and stayed close enough to catch her if she swooned as a result of the hot sun or a return of her illness.

Charity pushed her bonnet off and let it hang at her back by its strings as an Indian maiden appeared and started to walk slowly, laboriously down the aisle. She was being escorted by several elderly Nisqually women. "Can that be the bride?" Charity asked aside.

"I assume so," Thorne bent closer to whisper.

"What has she got piled all over her?"

He stifled a chuckle before he answered, "Those blankets and shawls and all that finery are like her dowry. They'll take if off her and give it to the groom's people. Watch."

The Indians began to sing as other, younger women stripped away the layers of belongings to reveal a slim, lovely bride dressed in a tunic and leggings made of supple, white, fringed doeskin and trimmed with beads and tiny seashells. Instead of a veil, a closely woven hat of the same material as the mats sat atop her head. Her thick black braids hung below, entwined with thin strips of fur.

"Oh, my," Charity whispered. "She's beautiful."

"Aren't you glad you're here?"

"Yes. I must admit I am." Scowling, she glanced back at him a second time. "You knew I didn't want to come and you still refused to go along with my excuse. Why?"

"Because being here is the right thing to do."

He could tell she was less than pleased with his honest answer but he knew it was important that Charity be encouraged to share in the joy of matrimony, at least vicariously. It was no secret that her heart was badly scarred by her own marital mistake. He'd hoped that viewing the unusual ceremony would help her see that not all such unions were doomed to failure the way hers had been.

Charity sighed as she watched the elaborate ritual progress. Rev. White had completed his portion and had elicited the requisite "I dos." Then the Nisqually elders, all men, took turns speaking of the tribe's history and what they expected of the newly married couple.

The feast which followed featured the bride and groom eating from the same plate and sharing a drinking cup, which Nancy had explained was the Indian way of demonstrating that they were officially married. Besides the food the settlers had brought, there was fire-roasted salmon and trout, skewered bits of venison and elk and thick soups of clams and oysters.

Although Charity had not realized that personal trading among the women was also the custom, Nancy had provided extra ribbons and yard goods for her to offer the Nisquallies in exchange for shell jewelry and hand-woven baskets.

By the end of the day Charity was the proud possessor of lovely trinkets and a small, finely woven basket in which to carry them. She showed her prizes to Nancy and saw the other woman's eyebrows arch.

"What's wrong?"

"Nothing," Nancy said, smiling. "I just think it's interesting, that's all. Where did you get the hat?"

Charity peered at her treasures. "Hat? What hat?"

Pointing, Nancy explained, "This isn't actually a basket. It's a married woman's brimless, reed hat like the one the bride had. Any woman who wears one is announcing to everyone that she's spoken for."

"Oh, dear." Charity blushed. "I know who gave it to me and now I know why. It seems that some of the Nisqually women think I'm rather scandalous for planning to travel back to San Francisco with Thorne. I assured them I was not going to sin but they are apparently convinced I'm a terrible person."

"You sacrificed to care for my daughter and grandson. I don't think you could do anything that would make me think less of you or of Mr. Blackwell. However, I have seen the way that poor man looks at you and I suspect your standoffishness is hurtful to him."

"Surely, you must be imagining things."

"May I speak freely, as a mother would?" Nancy asked, sobering and taking Charity's hand.

"Of course."

"My grandson loves you, as does his uncle, that much I know." She paused and cleared her throat, obviously struggling to continue. "I have seen a miniature of my daughter's husband. Aaron is fair, like Naomi, and it seems to me that Jacob..." Nancy's lower lip trembled.

Charity patted her hand to comfort her and waited for her to go on.

"My daughter is not the obedient child her father and I would have wished her to be," Nancy said. "She wrote to me shortly before she married Aaron Ashton and confessed a sin which I strongly suspect has haunted her ever since."

"I don't understand."

"Perhaps it would be better if you did not, but William and I have talked this over and have prayed about it. We have decided that I should tell you what I know and let you form your own conclusions. But before I explain, let me assure you that Naomi was once a very rebellious girl and was fully capable of seducing any man."

Charity stared, wondering, dreading, that Nancy might say what she, herself, had been thinking. More than once she had noticed the resemblance between Jacob and Thorne, yet she had always set those suspicions aside, unwilling to entertain anything so shockingly unacceptable.

If she could have found her voice, she would have used it to silence the older woman. Unable to form coherent thoughts, let alone sentences, she merely gripped Nancy's hand more tightly and listened.

"Almost four years ago, when Naomi was engaged to Aaron Ashton, she—she consorted with another man."

"Thorne?" Charity's words were a hoarse whisper.

Clearly fighting tears, Nancy nodded. "Yes. And afterward, when she realized she was with child, she confessed it all to me in a letter. I don't think she ever told Aaron, let alone his brother, but now that I have seen the child, I have no doubts that Mr. Blackwell must be Jacob's father."

Thunderstruck, Charity just stood there, mute, and gazed at the distant, rugged mountains without seeing them. All the details, all the consternation, all the sibling rivalry and all of Naomi's guilty reactions suddenly made sense.

No wonder Thorne had seemed so overly concerned about Jacob's well-being. He wasn't his uncle, he was his father! Therefore, what about his feelings for Naomi? That was what hurt Charity the most. How could he have fooled her so completely? He'd seemed emotionally distant from Naomi and had pretended he was only looking after her because of a duty to his brother, while in reality he had fathered her only child.

Charity could not pretend she didn't care for one second longer. She'd been a fool. A stupid, gullible fool. How many times had she told herself it was insane to fall in love? Yet she had done it. That was the worst part of all this. She had fallen in love with a man who was unworthy of even the friendship and admiration she had bestowed. To *love* him, really love him, was an abomination.

Thrusting the basketry hat at Nancy, Charity broke away and ran, half-blinded by tears. She headed away from the encampment and toward the forest, the only place where she knew she'd find the privacy necessary to cry her heart out. She felt as if her best friend had abandoned her and that she had died as a result. Her hope *had*.

In a way, Thorne had died to her, too, she reasoned through her grief. He was a fraud. He had lied to her and led her on when all he'd really wanted was a nurse-maid for his illegitimate son.

It didn't matter that Thorne had been planning to leave Naomi and Jacob behind in the territories and return to the sea. That made his perfidy even worse. Not only had he behaved in a beastly manner once, he was about to do it again by callously abandoning his child.

Cyrus Satterfield watched from the guard post inside the fort, smiled and blew smoke from his cigar. He'd wanted to draw at least one of the blond women away from her companions and it looked as if he was getting his wish, although he would have preferred that she'd taken the brat with her to save him the trouble of seeking it out later.

He sighted on the clump of cedars into which she had fled and lined it up with the Indian encampment so he could be certain of finding the right place once he had descended to ground level. She wouldn't get away from him this time. He not only had his rifle and pistol, he was also armed with the poison. It would be easy to steal an unattended arrow from one of the reveling Indians, poison its tip and use it to stab the woman to death. If he failed to get close enough for that, he'd simply shoot her, instead. The plan was foolproof.

And then he'd go back and take care of the other woman and the boy.

Thorne frowned as he scanned the assembled crowd. He was certain he'd seen Charity speaking with Nancy White a few minutes ago but at present he couldn't spot either of them.

Naomi had joined her father and seemed to be getting along all right, considering, so Thorne scooped up Jacob and headed their way.

William nodded and smiled a greeting. "Hello there. I wondered where everyone had gotten to."

"I was about to ask you the same thing," Thorne said. "I've lost track of Char...Miss Beal."

"Ah, I see." He patted the place next to him, opposite Naomi. "Why don't you two share our blanket and take a load off. I'm sure the women are fine."

"I don't know. It's not like Miss Beal to wander away alone." Thorne sat cross-legged on the blanket and held

Jacob in his lap to keep him from running to join some older Indian boys who were chasing a playful, agile puppy through the milling throng of celebrants.

William nodded sagely. "I suspect Miss Beal wanted to do some serious thinking and praying."

"Why is that?" He didn't like the grave way the older man was looking at him. The perusal made him decidedly uncomfortable. When the reverend finally spoke, however, he understood the man's mood only too well.

"My dear wife has been telling your Charity a little about my daughter's past sins." Holding Naomi's hand in a show of support he pressed his lips together and nodded slowly, deliberately, as if he knew exactly what Thorne was thinking. "Our Naomi is many things but she has remained her mother's daughter. That's why she chose to bare her soul and ask our forgiveness before she went through with her marriage to your brother."

The older man directed a gentle, loving, knowing smile at Jacob. "We can see now that she was finally being totally truthful with us."

"I don't know what to say."

"You don't have to say a thing, son. 'All have sinned and come short of the glory of God.'"

Thorne hugged the child tighter. "I was not a Christian at the time. I don't know what I would have done if I had been."

"You are also a healthy young man. If my wife has the details right, you were not the instigator of the incident, nor were you unmoved by what you had done. She says you begged Naomi to marry you."

"Yes. I did," Thorne answered. He had been watching Naomi's blank expression and noted with relief that she seemed oblivious to what was being said. "My brother and I had a terrible quarrel when he saw her weeping afterward. As far as I know, she never admitted anything to him but Aaron must have known. How could he help but see the evidence in his son's face?"

"As have we all," White said. "Which brings me back to the matter of your Charity Beal."

"What about her?"

"Nancy has taken her aside and told her everything, discreetly I'm sure. If we are to carry out the plan we've been considering it was necessary that Charity be made aware of the entire story, first."

"No!" Thorne passed the child to William and leaped to his feet, scanning the crowd. "You don't know Charity the way I do. She won't be able to accept hearing something like that from anyone but me. I have to explain."

"Perhaps, if your intentions were as serious as I believe they are, you should have already done so."

"I was going to," Thorne said. "I was waiting for the right time."

"Then I suggest you find her. I'll watch the boy." He pointed. "Here comes Nancy. She should know where Charity has gone."

Thorne was beside himself. If Charity had been told all the sordid details of his past, she was probably never going to sit still long enough to listen to his pleas for forgiveness. He had no excuse for his behavior, nor had he ever had. It was just that he felt such news would have hurt less if it had come from him. Now that the damage was done, there was no telling how badly Charity had been hurt. Or what she might do or say as a result.

Running blindly, Charity tore through the mucky, grassy lowlands and straight into the forest. Her shoes were caked with mud, her skirt torn by brambles and her hands and face scratched, yet she pressed on.

The only pain she felt was in her heart and mind. "Oh, Thorne," she sobbed. "Why did you lie? Why didn't you tell me the truth?"

Because you would have hated me for it, came the unspoken answer.

Charity started to argue with herself, then realized that her conclusion was correct. She would have reacted in exactly the same way she was now, cut to the quick and blinded by tears.

Why weep for someone who was unworthy? Because, in her deepest heart and in spite of everything he may have done in the past, she was afraid she loved him still.

Gasping, she leaned against the trunk of a sturdy pine while trying to catch her breath. Why was she such a poor judge of men? She had idolized her father and he had abandoned her twice; once to go west in search of gold and again when he had as much as told her she wasn't important in his new life with Annabelle.

No thoughts of prior disappointments would be complete without considering Ramsey Tucker, too. He had taken advantage of her youth and inexperience to gain her trust and had abused her both physically and mentally while he was alive.

"But Thorne isn't like that," she argued, weeping and drawing in jerky breaths between sobs. "He isn't." He had always treated her kindly and fairly and with reserve, as a gentleman should. Even when she was half out of her mind with fever he had not done one thing that was out of line or could be construed as taking advantage of her.

If he's so perfect, why did he lie with Naomi? her broken heart asked. And why had he not made a clean break of his past?

That question brought her full circle to her original conclusion. When she barely knew him, such a confession would have kept her from agreeing to make the trip and care for the needy child. Later, when she had grown fond of Thorne, she would have been even less likely to accept his explanation no matter how fervently he had presented it.

Drawing another and another shuddering breath, Charity wiped her eyes on her sleeve and fought to calm herself. Other than a broken heart, a torn frock and a few scratches from her flight into the forest, she was physically unhurt. She would survive this trauma just as she had survived others. She would return to the Whites and act as if their news about Naomi and Thorne had not truly bothered her.

Will I be able to control my emotions when I look at him? she wondered. She doubted it but that did not negate her need to try to hold herself together, for her own sake as much as for that of Naomi's parents.

Oh, how she wished Nancy had not been so blunt. All the woman's words were awhirl in her mind, not making sense the way she wished they would. Nancy had said something about a plan and the necessity of revealing all, but for the life of her, Charity couldn't put those words into their original context.

Sniffling, she straightened, preparing to return to the wedding feast and face her disappointment. Turning in circles, she assessed the trees and blossoming blackberry thickets. It was impossible to tell which way she had come or even in which direction the fort lay.

Peering through the dense vegetation, she hoped to glimpse the snowcapped Cascade range and thereby get her bearings but the surrounding leaves and branches blotted out both the sun and the distant mountains. Worse, her headlong flight through the brush had not left enough damage to the vegetation to indicate her prior path.

Out of earthly options, she closed her eyes and laced her fingers together to pray for guidance. "Dear Heavenly Father, I've certainly gotten myself into a fine pickle, haven't I?" Her sigh punctuated the informal plea. "Please? I know You must be tired of rescuing me but I really need some help? Which way should I go?"

When she opened her eyes and spotted a man coming toward her through the woods she was instantly relieved and deeply grateful.

"Thank you, God," she whispered, starting toward her rescuer with a wave of her arm.

In response, the man raised a rifle and pointed it directly at her.

She froze, incredulous. Surely he couldn't be planning to *shoot* her.

The click of the hammer being cocked echoed in the silence. He fitted the stock against his shoulder.

The muzzle flashed.

At that very instant, Charity ducked.

Chapter Nineteen

Thorne heard the resounding echo of the gunshot. He'd entered the forest where Nancy had told him to but had soon lost Charity's trail. He was a seaman, not a tracker, a lack of useful training which he now regretted.

He stiffened and waited for further sounds. None came to him. If the shooter was a local hunter, it seemed odd that he'd be out prowling the woods instead of attending the Nisqually celebration the way most folks were.

What if someone was after Charity, instead? What if they had shot her? Thorne's gut clenched and his head pounded. He had been praying for her safety and well-being ever since he had left the others and although he was as undeserving of grace as any man, he couldn't believe God would have ignored his plea on her behalf.

Pressing on toward the direction of the shot, he prayed even more fervently. "Father, please help her. Keep her safe. Even if she never forgives me, please let me try to explain and tell her how much I love her. Please?"

Once again he paused and listened. Nothing. Dis-

heartened, he lowered his gaze. There were no foot-
prints visible on the dead leaves littering the ground
but a spot of brightly colored cloth did catch his eye.

He waded amongst the thorny brambles until he was
close enough to see that the torn scrap of fabric was of
yellow calico and bore the same tiny, flowered pattern
as Charity's skirt. Moreover, her discarded bonnet lay
on the trail just beyond.

"That way." he said aloud. "She went that way.
Thank the Lord."

Drawing a deep breath, Thorne shouted, "Charity,"
with all his might.

Instead of the reply he had expected, he heard her
distant, panicky scream.

"Don't bother yelling," Cyrus said cynically. "It
won't do you any good. It's just you and me. And pretty
soon it will be just me."

"Did Louis Ashton send you?"

"What if he did?"

"I'm not the one you want. I'm not Mrs. Ashton,"
Charity insisted. "You must know that. Look at me.
Don't you recognize me from San Francisco?"

"Maybe. Maybe not. I don't really care. I've been
watching you and that brat for hundreds of miles and
if you're not his mama you sure act like you are. If I
have my way, he'll be next."

"Jacob?" she gasped. "You wouldn't hurt an innocent child, would you?"

The assassin laughed. "I'd do in my own grandmother if it paid enough. Now, suppose you just hold
still and let me get this over with."

The notion of standing there, as meek as a lamb, and

letting him kill her was ridiculous. She didn't know what she was going to do or how she was going to escape but she did know she was not going to succumb without fighting back.

She cast around for a weapon. Anything would do. But other than a few fallen, rotten limbs there was nothing within reach that she could use for defense.

Trying to flee was also futile. Not only was she hampered by her voluminous skirts, she could already feel the creeping return of fatigue from the aftermath of her fever. She had spent—had wasted—what little strength she'd had in reserve and was now paying for her folly.

Backing away slowly, she decided to at least try to put a substantial tree or two between her and the evil man. That was when she noticed that he had propped his empty rifle against a rock instead of reloading it after he'd shot and missed. He was presently fiddling with an arrow though he had no bow that she could see. Surely, he didn't think he could seriously harm her if he couldn't fire that arrow.

Charity saw him open a pouch at his waist and stick the tip of the arrow into it with a stirring motion. Suddenly, she knew what he was planning. She'd heard tales of poisoned arrows from Leschi as they had traveled together and had felt sorry for the hapless game those arrows had brought down. Now, she feared she was about to find out exactly how the animals had felt as they had breathed their last.

No! her heart screamed. *I cannot die like this. Thorne will be devastated.*

The pure truth of that thought cleared her mind and forced her to see what her pride had made her keep denying. She *did* still love Thorne, deeply and irrevocably. In spite of his past, in spite of his deception, and in spite of, or perhaps because of, Jacob, she loved that stubborn, wonderful man with all her heart and soul and every ounce of her being.

"Get away from me. I told you, I'm not Naomi Ashton," she shouted at her attacker. "I'm Charity Beal. All I've been doing is helping take care of her and her little boy."

"That's really too bad. You see my problem, don't you? You know too much. I have no choice but to start with you and then go after the real Naomi, assuming you're not lying about who you are."

"I know who *you* are," Charity said, stalling for time. "You were a lodger at the Montgomery House hotel when the Ashtons were there."

"Now that you mention it, you do look a lot like that girl who worked at the hotel. She was paler and not nearly as able as you seem to be but I suppose it is possible."

"Of course it's possible, you dunderhead. I've been traveling with Naomi. We're both blond and blue-eyed and you've gotten us mixed up."

"Doesn't change anything," Cyrus drawled, displaying the arrow. "You hold still now and this will be over before you know it."

Charity fisted her hands of her hips. "I'll do nothing of the kind."

"Have it your way." With that he grasped the arrow as if it were a spear and started to close the short distance between them.

The gulp of air that filled her lungs was quickly expelled in a piercing shriek.

She turned at the same instant, hiked her skirts and ran for all she was worth.

* * *

Thorne heard Charity's scream. It made his hair stand on end. He braced, listened and heard more ruckus just ahead.

He shouted her name as he tore through the brush. If anything bad happened to her, he didn't know how he could go on, let alone find happiness again. She was everything to him. And she didn't even know it.

He broke through to a small clearing in time to see flashes of bright yellow moving in and out through the trees. *Thank God.* That was Charity's dress. He had almost overtaken her.

A man's coarse shout and muttered curses echoed back to him and chilled his soul. As he had feared, Charity wasn't alone. Someone was pursuing her.

Thorne doubled his efforts, moving so swiftly he felt as if his boots barely touched the ground. He traveled on pure instinct, without thought, without plan, without the least concern for himself.

Low-hanging branches slapped and scraped his face. He felt nothing, cared about nothing except reaching the woman he loved.

He shouted, "Charity," at the top of his lungs.

On the returning breeze he heard the sweetest sound of all. She called back, "Thorne."

If his name had not been so heavily tinged with panic, he would have rejoiced.

Spent and gasping, Charity nevertheless managed to answer Thorne's summons. She knew then that if she did not yield to the painful stitch in her side, she would soon collapse into a helpless mound of vulnerability. She could not go on like this. She had to rest, if only for a moment. And now that she knew Thorne was close by, she took the chance that he'd arrive in time.

Whirling and holding up her hands to fend off her attacker, she hoped and prayed he wouldn't prick her skin with the poisoned point of the arrow.

Now that she'd looked back, however, she could tell that the heavyset man was as winded as she was. Maybe more so. His round face was ruddy and flushed and his breathing was ragged. Staggering, he halted, still brandishing the lethal arrow.

"It's not too late to walk away," Charity managed to say. Her sides were heaving as she bent forward at the waist. The taste of bile filled her throat and she feared she was about to lose all the food she had recently eaten.

"I'm not going nowhere, lady. I came all this way to do a job and I intend to finish it."

"How much did Louis Ashton pay you? We'll double it."

"We? We who? I don't see nobody else."

Charity glimpsed a flash of movement in the woods directly behind him and her heart leaped. She straightened and smiled as she said, "You will. Praise the Lord, you soon will."

Thorne hit the other man a solid body blow and knocked him facedown on the ground before he had a chance to turn around and fight back.

"Watch out for the arrow," Charity shouted. "It's poisoned."

Forewarned, Thorne grasped the feathered end and whipped the shaft from Satterfield's fist. The sharp blade passed across the assassin's palm, slicing into the meaty flesh.

With a yelp of pain and shock the man grabbed his wrist and rolled onto his back as Thorne jumped away. The portly man ended up lying against the gnarled roots of a tree where he began moaning and thrashing.

Thorne hesitated only a few seconds, waiting to be certain Cyrus wouldn't recover and renew his attack, then threw the arrow aside and went quickly to Charity.

Neither of them spoke. She stepped willingly into Thorne's strong embrace, slipped her arms around his waist and clung to him as if nothing on heaven or earth would ever separate them again.

He held her close, his cheek pressed against her silky hair, then guided her away from their now-helpless nemesis.

"Are you all right?" Thorne asked.

Charity nodded and looked up at him, unashamed of the fresh tears in her eyes. "I am now. That man said he wanted to kill me. And Jacob. All of us."

Tightening his hold on her, Thorne swallowed hard. "What did he have on that arrow?"

"Some kind of poison. I think he must have gotten it from the Indians."

"Dear God," Thorne said prayerfully. "That could be you lying back there."

"Or you. But it isn't." She was teetering between the shock of her narrow escape and the joy of being reunited with Thorne. Her knees were wobbly and her vision misty. "Once again, I have you to thank for coming to my rescue."

"No. We both have God to thank," he said, his voice

choked with emotion. "I never stopped praying for you. All the time I was searching, I never stopped praying."

He placed one finger lightly beneath her chin and tilted her face up. "I know what Nancy told you. I was afraid I might never get the chance to say how sorry I was for keeping secrets when I should have spoken up."

"Is that all?" She was starting to smile.

"All? Isn't that enough?"

"No," she said tenderly as a solitary tear slid silently down her cheek. "You haven't told me you love me." Seeing his astonishment, she added, "I love *you,* you know."

"You do? Truly?"

"Truly. I didn't realize it until I'd nearly been sent to meet my Maker, but I finally figured it out. It doesn't matter to me what you did or didn't do in the past. If you've asked for the good Lord's forgiveness, that will be sufficient."

"I have. Many times over," Thorne said.

"Then I cannot deny you mine."

"Will you marry me?"

Charity was so overcome with happiness she was nearly unable to answer. The stricken look on Thorne's dear face as a result of her silence was what made her speak quickly and with assurance. "Yes. Oh, yes."

"When? Where?"

"Soon. Perhaps Rev. White will agree to perform the ceremony before we leave for California. I will be delighted to be able to inform my new Indian friends that I will not be tempted to sin."

She could tell by the strange way Thorne was looking at her that he was thoroughly confused.

Reaching up to pat his cheek, she grinned. "I have been instructed in the teachings of holy scripture by some caring Nisqually women. They also said they were praying for me because you and I were going to be traveling together and they were afraid I would be unable to resist your considerable charms."

To her delight, Thorne's face reddened and he began to give her his trademark, lopsided grin. "My charms?"

"Yes. In case you haven't noticed, I find you very appealing, Mr. Blackwell."

"Do you?" He arched an eyebrow. "In that case, perhaps we had best marry quickly, while you are still smitten."

"I suspect I will always be in love with you, sir."

Sobering, Thorne placed a tender kiss on her forehead before he said, "I know you were hurt before. I promise I will never harm you or frighten you. I would rather die than see you sad the way you used to be."

"It is a wonderment, but I don't fear you in the slightest," Charity said as she gazed into the depths of his dark eyes and saw all the love reflected there. "When we first met, I was not able to tolerate any man's touch without cringing, not even the innocent pat of my father's hand on mine."

Wrapping her arms around him once again and stepping into his embrace, she couldn't help smiling. "And now look at me."

"I am looking. And I think it would be best if we hurried back to the wedding feast," Thorne said, continuing to gaze at her with all the love he was feeling. "I made one big mistake in my life and I'm not about to make another."

"Did you love Naomi?" Charity felt his muscles tense beneath her touch.

"No. Never. I was acting the fool and I knew it, but I didn't have God's help resisting temptation the way you and I do now."

"I am resisting, truly I am. But it is not easy," she admitted with a blush. "If you will point me in the right direction, I will gladly rejoin the party. I can't wait to see the look on Nancy's and William's faces when we tell them we want to get married."

"Do you think they will be as surprised by it as you and I are?"

"I don't know about you," she said, taking his hand and letting him lead her away from the scene of mayhem. "But as Annabelle would say, I'm plum flabbergasted."

"Is that a good thing?"

Charity laughed again, positive she would never be happier no matter how long she lived. "It's a wonderment," she said. "A pure wonderment."

Their return to the wedding-feast grounds might have gone unnoticed if William had not insisted that some of the men from the fort form a search party. It was assembling and preparing to leave when Thorne and Charity stepped out of the woods together.

Thorne briefly explained what had occurred, then left Charity with the Whites and led a small group of soldiers back to take care of the body of Cyrus Satterfield.

The beaming smile Thorne saw on Charity's face when he returned made his heart lurch and his pulse pound. Judging by the expressions of satisfaction from the missionaries, they had been made aware of Charity's and his decision to marry before they left the territories.

William grabbed Thorne's hand before he could say more than hello, and pumped it briskly. "Congratulations, young man. Miss Beal told us everything."

"Will you perform the ceremony?"

"Of course. Would you like to make your nuptials a part of this celebration?"

Thorne looked to Charity and saw her shake her head. "I think it would be best if we did it back at your place where there's less distraction, if you don't mind," he said. "I want Charity to be comfortable." He looked over at the child who had again insisted that the future bride carry him. "And I want Jacob to be a part of the wedding. I think we both do."

"Yes," she said.

As she tenderly kissed the child's cheek Thorne could tell how badly she wished they didn't have to part from him. That was the only sorrow in the foreseeable future. Someday, perhaps, they would have a son of their own but that didn't mean it was going to be easy to leave Jacob behind, even if it was for his own good.

William cleared his throat and looked to his wife. Nancy nodded assent to his unspoken question and he began to speak.

"There is much unrest in these parts," White said. "I know everything looks peaceful right now, while everybody is celebrating, but there's an undercurrent of impending war with the Indians that can't be denied. Nancy and I will stay because it is our calling, and we will gladly assume the responsibility of our daughter's care, but we have decided that we cannot, in good conscience, let the child remain here with us. It's too dangerous. We are not able to guarantee his safety."

"What?" Frowning, Thorne stepped closer to Charity and put his arm around her shoulders to include both her and Jacob in a protective embrace.

"We know Jacob is dear to you both and since you are technically his father and Naomi is unable to even care for herself, let alone mind a lively little boy like him, we want you to take him. Make him your son, as he should be."

Charity was fighting tears. "But, he's not my son."

"He has already made the change, in his heart," Nancy said tenderly. "We've all seen it. He often calls you his mama, you know."

"Yes, but, he's just lonely and confused."

"And he needs a mother. He needs you. Of course, if you don't want him…"

"No! We do." She looked to Thorne. "Don't we?"

He could barely speak. "Yes. We do." More quietly he asked her, "Are you sure you don't mind?"

"I love him as my own. How could I mind? The only concern I have is what will happen to our plans if your brother returns and tries to reclaim him?"

"Don't worry. Before Aaron disappeared we had discussed the possibility of my taking custody of Jacob if anything happened to him and Naomi. I'm sure, if we can prove to Louis that the child poses no threat of inheritance, he will gladly forget he was ever born."

"And will Aaron?"

Thorne nodded sadly. "Yes. If I have to confess the truth to him to finish this once and for all, then I will.

I would rather have to live with my brother's lifelong hatred than jeopardize one hair on my son's head."

Looking down at Charity and the child in her arms, he knew he would gladly do whatever it took to guard and protect them for the rest of his life. And by the grace of God, he would succeed.

Epilogue

1858

Charity was glad Thorne had chosen to make San Francisco their permanent home, especially because doing so had brought her closer to her dear father and stepmother.

Though Thorne did occasionally sail on one of his vessels because he missed the sea, he had also built her a mansion overlooking the bay. When he was away she would often visit the "widow's walk" atop the roof and watch the harbor while she prayed for his safe return.

Jacob had matured to look even more like his father in the four years since they had unofficially adopted him. He was darkly handsome and every bit a Blackwell. So was his two-year-old baby sister, Mercy, who had been his shadow ever since she had first learned to toddle after him.

Charity sat knitting and smiled at her children as they played on the decorative Persian carpet at her feet. As usual, Jacob was acting the part of his sister's guardian, a role into which he had fallen as naturally as his father had when he had repeatedly saved Charity's life.

She was smiling and dreaming of Thorne when he appeared in the arched doorway of the parlor. Judging by the expression on his face he was privy to some news.

He waved a telegram and smiled. "Nancy White has accepted our invitation. She's coming to visit."

Charity laid aside her knitting and hurried across the room to see for herself. As she read the entire message she sighed. "That's wonderful. I was hoping she'd come. After all she's been through I'd wondered if she'd be up to it."

"I know. It had to be hard for her to give up her missionary work in the territories, but with William and Naomi both victims of the Puget Sound Indian war I can understand why she'd be ready for a change."

Charity slipped an arm around her husband's slim waist and stepped into the shelter of his embrace. "I was sad to read the news reports of Leschi's death, too. I had hoped his peacemaking would exempt him from the fighting."

"It should have," Thorne said soberly. "But in the end, I suppose he felt he had to side with his own people. I'm glad the hostilities are over. It's just too bad the war cost so many lives—on both sides."

His gaze went to his son. "Thank God, William was wise enough to send Jacob with us before the trouble started in earnest."

"I do thank God. Every day," Charity said. "And for you, too, husband. Do you think Nancy will agree to remain with us for a while? I'd love to have her here and I know she'll want to get to know her grandson better."

"We certainly have plenty of room," Thorne said.

"We do, don't we? And while we're on the subject, I think your mother might finally be ready to accept our invitation, too. You should ask her again."

Thorne hesitated, obviously mulling over the suggestion. "Really? After Louis died I thought she'd be eager to leave New York, but you know how she kept putting me off. What makes you believe she'd be willing to travel, now?"

"Because, as I told you when I received her last letter, I think she's finally accepted the fact she'll never see Aaron again. I know she was clinging to a faint hope he had somehow survived even though Louis was never able to locate any sign of him."

"And now she's let go? I hope you're right. I'll send her a telegram today. You're sure you don't mind having her and Nancy here at the same time?"

"Of course not. After all, they're both Jacob's grandmothers." She started to grin at him. "I am, however, beginning to feel as if I'm back in the hotel business."

Laughing, Thorne gave her a quick kiss before he said, "I promise you will not have to cook or make beds in this so-called hotel, my dear. We have servants for that, remember?"

"Yes, and you are spoiling me something awful," Charity replied. "I sometimes feel a bit useless. Since we're discussing changes, I suppose I should mention my plans to volunteer for several hours a week in the Orphan Asylum in the city." She watched his eyebrows arch in surprise but was pleased that he didn't argue.

"I worry about all those poor, lonely children," she went on as she gazed lovingly at her own. "There must be something I can do, besides donating money, to make their lives easier. I want to try."

Thorne pulled her closer and kissed her soundly before he said, "I would not expect anything less of you. And if you can manage to get Nancy White and my mother involved, too, I'm positive those motherless children will be blessed beyond imagination."

"What a wonderful idea! How did you get so smart?"

"The smartest thing I ever did was marry you," he said, smiling.

Charity returned his grin as she patted his cheek fondly and replied, "You have *never* been more right."

* * * * *

Janet Dean grew up in a family with a strong creative streak. Her father and grandfather recounted fascinating stories, instilling in Janet an appreciation of history and the desire to write. Today she enjoys traveling into our nation's past as she spins stories for Love Inspired Historical. Janet and her husband are proud parents and grandparents who love to spend time with their family.

Books by Janet Dean

Love Inspired Historical

Courting Miss Adelaide
Courting the Doctor's Daughter
The Substitute Bride
Wanted: A Family
An Inconvenient Match
The Bride Wore Spurs
The Bounty Hunter's Redemption

Visit the Author Profile page
at Harlequin.com for more titles.

COURTING
MISS ADELAIDE

Janet Dean

Bear with each other and forgive whatever grievances
you may have against one another.
Forgive as the Lord forgave you.
—*Colossians* 3:13

To my critique partner, Shirley Jump—her slashing red pen, savvy advice and endless support helped me become the writer I am today. To David Highway, president of the Hamilton County Historical Society—a big thanks for his assistance with my research. To my late parents, who never stopped believing I'd attain my dream. To my husband—a good man, a wonderful father and the love of my life.

Prologue

From the March 1, 1897, edition of The Noblesville Ledger:

WANTED: HOMES FOR CHILDREN

NOBLESVILLE—A company of homeless children from the East will arrive in Noblesville, Indiana, on Saturday, April 13. These boys and girls of various ages have been thrown friendless upon the world. The citizens of Noblesville are asked to assist the agents of the Children's Aid Society in finding good homes for the children.

Persons requesting these children must first agree to treat the children as members of their family, promising to feed, clothe, send them to school and church and Sunday School until they reach the age of seventeen.

Applications must be made to and approved by the local committee. Interviews will be held on Saturday, March 30, in Judge Willowby's chambers at the Noblesville County courthouse. The following well-respected citizens have agreed to sit on the local committee: C. Graves, J. Sparks, T. Paul and M. Wylie.

Distribution will be made at the Ward schoolhouse on April 13 at 10:30 a.m.

Chapter One

Noblesville, Indiana, spring of 1897

Adelaide Crum stepped to the open door and peered into the judge's chambers. Her heart hammered beneath her corset. Now that the moment she'd waited for had arrived, her courage faltered. She considered turning tail and scurrying home. But then she remembered the quiet, the emptiness of those rooms. She closed her eyes and sent up a simple prayer. *I don't ask often, Lord, but I'm asking today. Please, let them say yes.*

Squaring her shoulders, she crossed the room, then sat on one of the two chairs and faced the four men who held her future in their hands. To fill the vacant chair with something, she laid her purse on the seat, a seat that mocked her singleness.

Mr. Wylie, a large man who owned a farm north of town, folded his sausagelike fingers on the table. "I've dropped my wife off in front of your shop more times than I can count, Miss Crum." He chuckled. "Usually costs me, too."

She smiled a thank-you for his business.

Beside the farmer sat Mr. Sparks, the town banker. The little tufts of hair fringing his bald head reminded Adelaide of a horned owl. "Perhaps you'd better tell us why you've come, Miss Crum. Do you have recommendations for this committee?"

"I've come for myself." Adelaide laid a calming hand on her midriff to offset the growing urge to deposit her breakfast on the table in front of her. "To ask for a child."

Mr. Paul's nostrils flared, giving him an air of disdain, not a cordial expression for an elder at her church and the town's Superintendent of Schools. "For *yourself?* You're a single woman, are you not?"

"Yes, but—"

"I hope you can appreciate how unfair it would be to place a child in your home, where, if something happened to you, the youngster would be homeless."

"I'm in excellent health, Mr. Paul." She'd take this opening to plead her case. "I have sufficient funds to meet a child's needs. *And* a skill to teach, enabling a girl to make her own way. When I pass on, I'd leave her my worldly assets."

She took a deep breath, pulling into her lungs the overpowering scent of Mr. Paul's spicy cologne. "I'll see she's educated and brought up in the church. I've lived in Noblesville all my life. You remember seeing me in Sunday school, Mr. Paul. Mr. Sparks, I bank with you. Numerous people in town can vouch for my character." She'd rehearsed the words countless times and they tumbled out in a rush.

One man remained silent. Charles Graves. Her gaze darted to the new editor of *The Noblesville Ledger,* who sat at the far right of the table. Rumor had it he was single. Mr. Graves's generous mouth softened the square line of his jaw. Deep grooves marred his forehead, an indication, perhaps, that a newsman's life wasn't easy. And yet the cleft in the middle of his chin gave him a vulnerable air. Undeniably handsome, broad-shouldered and tall, he overshadowed the other men in the room.

He stared as if scanning the core of her, possibly looking for a flaw that would declare her unfit to rear a child. Their gazes locked and the intensity of his inspection sent a shiver down Adelaide's spine.

Mr. Paul rose and came around the table. "Miss Crum, I believe your character to be without blemish. I'm sure you can do all you say. However, the fact remains you're a maiden lady with no experience dealing with children."

"We have childless couples begging for a baby," Mr. Wylie added. "Couples, with acres of ground and not enough hands to till it, seeking boys. We have tried-and-true parents who've shown their abilities by rearing their own children."

Heat climbed Adelaide's neck. *Fiddlesticks! If I'd had the good fortune to be a tried-and-true parent, I wouldn't be here.*

How frustrating to have men make all the decisions, as they always had in Noblesville. She might be single, but that didn't mean she couldn't bring up a child. She had the capacity, the intelligence, to sit a committee like this one, to help make important decisions. Why couldn't men see women had a unique perspective with value, married or not?

"Gentlemen, I've proven my abilities by running a successful business while I tended to my sick mother. I can rear a child and do it well."

Her gaze collided with the editor's. Did she see compassion in his warm brown eyes?

Mr. Wylie pointed to the paper in front of him. "We'll only be getting twenty-eight children, mostly boys. We're unable to meet the demand. I hope you understand."

She understood all right. They didn't think she could handle the job. *Lord, give me the words to convince them.*

"Gentlemen, please hear me out. The fact I'm unmarried will give me *more* time to devote to a child. I realize boys are needed in the fields. My desire to rear a girl won't interfere with that." She bit her lower lip. "I'd be a good mother, if you'd give me a chance."

Arms folded across his chest, Mr. Paul leaned toward her. "The Children's Aid Society does not seek single parents, except in the rarest of cases. If we weren't overrun with applicants, perhaps we might consider your marital status more leniently."

She searched their faces for help. Mr. Paul's features appeared carved in granite. Mr. Sparks fidgeted in his chair. Mr. Wylie gave her a kind look, but showed no sign of intervening.

Mr. Graves wore a slight frown. He cleared his throat. "Miss Crum made some valid points about her suitability. Any chance, gentlemen, of stretching the rules?"

Adelaide held her breath. *Oh, please, God, change their minds.*

Mr. Paul tapped the edges of the paperwork in his hand. "Charles, we aren't here to make history. Just to make certain these children have good homes. Besides, placing a child in a fatherless home is unscriptural."

Mr. Graves arched a brow. "Would that be Third Timothy Four?"

Adelaide knew her Bible. There was no Third Timothy. Surprised at the jab and pleased he knew the Scriptures, she smiled at the editor. He winked. Warmth spread through Adelaide like honey on a hot biscuit. Could this handsome, successful man be on her side?

Mr. Paul harrumphed. "Perhaps you find that funny, Mr. Graves, but I do not. The Bible makes it clear the man is the head of the family. It isn't right to put a child into a home with no paternal guidance."

Adelaide tightened her hands into fists. Mr. Paul's fifteen-year-old son Jacob perpetually terrorized the town. A few months ago, she'd had to report him to the sheriff after she'd caught him setting fire to Mr. Hudson's shed. The boy had run off and thankfully, she'd been able to douse the flames. Yet, Mr. Paul had the gall to preach paternal guidance. "I had no father growing up. I'm no worse for it."

Mr. Paul leaned forward and patted her shoulder. "I didn't mean to insult you. There are circumstances over which we have no control, but that's not the case here."

Adelaide glanced at Mr. Graves. His gaze had narrowed but he said nothing. What had she expected? He didn't know her. None of them really did. They saw a spinster—nothing more.

"I'm sorry we can't help you." Mr. Wylie stood and walked toward the door.

She wanted to scream, but that would only prove her to be a hysterical female unfit to rear a child. She hated being powerless. Hated being at their mercy. Hated being unable to change a thing.

Adelaide grabbed her purse and rose. At the door, she looked back one last time, searching for some sign of softening on their faces, but no miracle came. Tears stung her eyes, but no matter what, she would not let them see her cry.

Mr. Wylie opened the door. "I'm sorry," he murmured again.

Unable to speak, she nodded an acknowledgment. Head high, she strode through the door into the waiting area, past her staring neighbors, and into the courthouse corridor, holding herself together with the strength of a well-honed will.

Every step pounded in her head, reiterating again and again and again. *I failed. I failed. I failed.*

In the hallway, she sidestepped a couple blocking her path.

"Please, Ed, we can't replace our boy. I'd like a girl—"

"A boy is what we agreed on," the man snapped. "I'm trying to put this family back together, and all you do is whine."

The woman's gaze darted to Adelaide, and then dropped to the floor. Frances. Before Adelaide could greet her, Frances followed her husband to the door. Ed turned to open it, giving Adelaide a glimpse of his face. Anger blazed in his eyes. Then, like a shade dropping over a window, he controlled his expression, leaving his countenance smooth and pleasant.

"Miss Crum," he said, giving her a friendly nod.

Adelaide couldn't believe this irate man could be the same person who'd picked her up after a childhood tumble and declared she'd be fine. All these years later, she still remembered his kindness, the gentle way he'd cleaned her scrapes with the red bandanna he'd dampened at a nearby pump.

Losing their son must have changed him. Whatever the cause, if Ed carried that much anger, the Drummonds shouldn't be considered for a child. But they probably would be, since marriage seemed to be the committee's only condition.

The pain of the rejection tore through her. Adelaide bolted for the entrance. She shoved open the heavy door, gulping in air. As she started down the steps, low-slung clouds released their moisture, spattering her face as if nature shed the tears she would not weep. Lightning zigzagged overhead and thunder rumbled, then the sky burst under the weight of its watery load.

In the deluge, her sodden garments grew heavy, but didn't slow her progress. With both hands, she hiked her skirts and hustled across the street. As she trudged to the back of her shop, closed for this momentous day, the mud grabbed at her shoes. Her shoulders heaving with exertion, she pried the dirty shoes from her feet and dropped them outside the door, indifferent she'd ruined their fine leather. Then climbed the stairs to her quarters above the shop.

She removed her soggy skirt, and then wilted onto the bed, dropping her hat on the floor. A curtain of rain veiled the window, darkening the room. Her mother's words echoed in her head. *It's a man's world, Adelaide. If you think otherwise, you're in for a rude awakening.*

Today, four men had found her unworthy to rear a child. She'd built a successful business, had taken care of herself and her invalid mother, and all without a man's help. But what she wanted most, a child and family, she couldn't have without a man, without a committee of men.

"Why, Lord? Why was the answer no?" No reply came.

There would be no little girl to sew for, no little girl to love. No little girl, period.

A sob ripped through her, then a piercing wail. She burrowed her face in the pillow to muffle the sound, but then remembered she had no one to hear. No one to see. No one to care.

The dam she'd built to hold back her emotions crumbled, releasing a flood of tears. As she wept, spasms shook her body until, long minutes later, exhaustion quieted her. Every part of her echoed with hollowness, emptiness. For the first time in her thirty-one years, she felt old. Old, with the hope squeezed out of her.

But then she remembered Mr. Graves's wink.

Somehow the gesture had united them against the others. He appeared to have confidence in her ability to mother a child. Like butter on a burn, the thought soothed her wounded heart.

But even if no one else did, Adelaide had faith in herself. And even a stronger faith in God. God would sustain her.

What if the committee's decision wasn't God's final word?

At the thought, Adelaide sat up on the bed. Her chest swelled with hope and her mind wrapped around a fresh determination. The committee's rules weren't etched in stone like the Ten Commandments. She'd never believed all the conventions in her world concurred with God's plan. Until she knew in the core of her being God didn't want her to mother a child, she would not give up hope. She would believe a child waited for her, waited for the comfort of Adelaide's arms.

Charles couldn't get the memory of Miss Crum out of his mind. He wished he hadn't agreed to sit on this committee. He wanted no part in impersonating God.

No part in causing the kind of pain he'd read on Miss Crum's face.

If Charles understood anything, he understood pain.

He forced his attention back to the discussion, chagrined to discover everyone looking at him, waiting for him to speak. "I'm sorry. Would you repeat that?"

"We were saying the Drummonds have the ability to train a boy in farmwork. They lost their only child to a stove fire a few years back. A terrible tragedy."

Charles examined the burly man and his timid wife. From the little he'd listened to, Mr. Drummond had done all the talking. The man seemed affable enough, but during the interview, his wife had avoided eye contact. Perhaps she was merely shy. "Mrs. Drummond, you haven't said. Do you want a boy, too?"

She looked to her husband, hesitating a moment. "I'd be open to a girl." Her voice quavered, but for the first time she met Charles's eyes. He saw a flicker of hope, and something else, something that gnawed at his memory. Before he could identify it, she lowered her gaze.

Mr. Wylie checked a list. "We've been told to expect a brother and sister. Would you be willing to take both of them?"

Mrs. Drummond's gaze darted to her husband.

"How old are they?" Mr. Drummond asked.

"The boy is ten, the girl is, let's see…" Wylie scanned a paper in front of him. "Seven."

Mr. Drummond rubbed his chin. "Two pair of hands *would* be a help," he said, considering. Then he smiled. "The missus would like a girl. We'll take them both."

"Excellent. We don't want to split up siblings unless we have no choice."

Mr. Drummond nodded. "Family means everything. Husband, wife…" He hesitated, his tone emotional. "Children. Nothing should divide a family."

Mr. Wylie pushed the papers away and looked at Charles. "Any objections, Mr. Graves?"

The couple had the proper references, had said all the right words, but what did that prove? The entire exercise was ludicrous. But perhaps no more so than nature's method of selecting parents guaranteed they'd be adequate for the job.

Yet some kind of sixth sense twisted a lump in his throat, made him hesitate, but just as quickly, he dismissed it. The others knew them, had greeted them warmly.

For the hundredth time he questioned why God, all powerful and all knowing, allowed unsuitable people to have children. He could only be certain about one thing. A child would be better off living in Noblesville than roaming the streets of New York City or living in one of its crowded orphanages. "I have none."

"Good!" Mr. Wylie sent Mr. Drummond a smile. "I've been meaning to thank you, Ed, for helping fix the church roof."

Ed nodded. "Glad to do it. We can't expect the parson to hold an umbrella over his head while he's preaching."

While Wylie ushered the Drummonds from the room, Charles rose from his chair and crossed to the window. Even in the sudden downpour, the streets crawled with horse-drawn wagons and buggies. A typical Saturday, the day area farmers came to town to transact business or sell produce.

Like most county seats, the courthouse dominated the square, giving a certain dignity to the mishmash of architecture surrounding it. Noblesville was a nice little town. The decision to move here had been a good one. He'd been able to help his brother's family and to bring *The Noblesville Ledger* back to life. That had been his father's plan, but long before that revelation, owning a paper had been Charles's dream, a dream he'd soon achieve.

His hand sought the telegram inside his pocket, notification his father had died peacefully in his sleep. Charles crushed the flimsy paper into a tight ball. Maybe now, he could put his past to rest.

He looked down the block to *The Ledger,* then across the street to Miss Crum's millinery shop. She wanted a child to love, not a worker for her store.

Charles turned from the window. "I'm uncomfortable placing these youngsters to be laborers on farms."

"Work never hurt anyone." Wylie hunched forward, biceps bulging in his ill-fitting coat until Charles expected to hear ripping fabric. "Hard work builds strong bodies, sound minds."

"Some of these 'Street Arabs' have been pickpockets and beggars," Paul spoke up. "We're saving them from a life of crime. If they work hard, they'll make something of themselves."

Charles's thoughts turned to Miss Crum, an easy task. She stuck in a man's mind like taffy on the roof of a tot's mouth. Her eyes had captured him the first moment he saw her. A dazzling blue, they were deep-set under straight, slim brows, gentle, intelligent eyes. Her hair, the color of pale honey, had been smoothed back into a low chignon. Clearly a proper, straitlaced woman, the kind of woman who attended church on Sunday wouldn't abide a man like him.

She'd shown a passel of courage facing the committee, even more strength of will when she'd left with her dignity pulled around her like a cloak. Of all the women he'd met that day, Miss Crum was the only one he felt certain would give a child the kind of home he'd read about in books.

He might have fought more for her, but thoughts of his widowed sister-in-law's struggles had stopped him. Besides, to object further would have been a waste of time. He'd soon discovered folks in Noblesville resisted anyone who challenged their customary way of life.

By noon all the children had been spoken for. The actual selection of the orphans would take place in two weeks on the day of distribution. The four men shook hands, relieved they'd finished their job, at least for now. After the distribution, the committee had agreed to keep an eye on the children and their guardians as best they could.

A fearsome responsibility.

Outside the courthouse the men dispersed. Charles pulled his collar up around his neck and dashed to the paper in the pounding rain, splattering puddles with every footfall. Ducking into the doorway of *The Ledger,* he removed his hat, dumping water on his shoes, his spirits as damp as his feet.

His gaze shifted across the street to the CLOSED sign in the window of Miss Crum's millinery shop. In the months he'd been here, he'd never seen the shop closed on a Saturday.

As he opened the door to the paper, he couldn't help wondering what Adelaide Crum was doing right at this moment, after four men had dashed her hopes as surely as the sudden storm had wiped out the sun.

Chapter Two

Adelaide woke with a start, bolting upright in bed. Something important was to take place today. Then the memory hit and she sank against the pillows. The children would arrive today.

For her, another ordinary day; for twenty-eight couples, this day had blessed them with a child.

The past two weeks, she had relived the meeting with the committee numerous times, trying to see how she could have convinced them. Wasted thoughts. Wasted hopes. Wasted tears.

She'd been certain God approved of her desire to rear a child, yet the committee had turned her down. Could she have been wrong? Didn't God want her to mother an orphan? If not, why?

I'd be a good mother. I'd never be like Mama— crabby, critical, always taking the pleasure out of everything.

After a decade of caring for her mother and running the shop, at first her mother's death had been a relief. The admission put a knot in Adelaide's stomach, and she said a quick prayer of repentance.

Shaking off her dark thoughts, Adelaide held up her left thumb. "I'm thankful, God, for a thriving business." Lifting her index finger, she continued, "I'm thankful for these comfortable rooms that give me shelter." Then, "Thank you, Lord, for good friends." Touching each finger in turn, she found, as always, many things for which to give thanks.

But today, it wasn't enough.

She climbed out of bed and shoved up the window. The clatter of wheels, a barking dog and a vendor's shout brought life into the room. She walked to the dresser mirror and picked up her brush. In her reflection, she found no ravages of age, no sign of crow's-feet. Her nose was clearly too long, but, all in all, a nice enough face.

Nice enough for a handsome man like Mr. Graves to admire?

Adelaide blinked. Where had that thought come from?

She laid down the brush and leaned toward the mirror, then crossed her eyes. *If you don't stop that, Adelaide, your eyes will get stuck there.* Recalling her mother's warning, a smile tugged at the corners of her mouth.

Feeling better, she dressed, then hurried to the kitchen and made coffee. As she sipped the hot brew, her gaze traveled the room, pleased with the soft blue walls above the white wainscoting. Blue-and-white checked curtains, crisp with starch, hung at the window over the sink. This would be a cozy place for a child to have breakfast. The oak pedestal table circled with four pressed-back chairs, plenty of seating for a family.

Neither a crumb littered the floor nor did a speck of dust mar the table. She sighed. All too aware, she lived in the perfect, uncluttered home of a childless woman.

Enough of self-pity. Time to open her shop. Downstairs, she flipped the sign in the window and sat down to mend a torn seam when the bell jingled.

Sally Bender, dressed in drab green with her gray hair stuffed beneath a faded blue bonnet, tromped into the shop. "Land sakes, Adelaide! Are you buried alive under all these hats?" Before Adelaide could answer, Sally went on, "It's high time you got out your frame so we can finish that quilt."

Adelaide's mother's declining health had ended the quilting bees. "Good morning to you, too, Sally," Adelaide said with a teasing grin.

"Oh, good morning." Sally smiled sheepishly, but then parked fisted hands on her hips. "You know I'm right. It's not good to mope like this."

"I'm sewing, not moping."

"You can't fool me, Adelaide Crum. You're hiding out here. The 'Snip and Sew' quilters haven't met in months. Why, the church auction will come and go before we finish that quilt." A spark flared in Sally's eyes. "Is it man trouble?"

"No, just work."

"Then start having some. Ask Horace Smith to the church picnic. Give me something to think about besides this unseasonable heat."

Old enough to be her father, the town's mortician looked barely more alive than his clientele. "If you're relying on me for excitement, you'll expire from a bad case of monotony." She chuckled. "No doubt Horace would thank me for the business."

Sally poked her arm. "Now you sound more like yourself."

Putting aside her sewing, Adelaide rose. "I'll set up

the frame. We can start a week from Monday at ten o'clock."

"Good. On the way home, I'll stop and tell the others." She drew Adelaide into a hug. "I've missed you."

"I've missed you, too."

Sally spun out like a whirlwind. Adelaide whispered thanks for a caring friend.

Adelaide kept busy, but the morning dragged. Unable to concentrate, she had to rip out rows of stitches in Mrs. Willowby's bolero jacket and jabbed herself twice with the needle. She laid the garment aside, then stuck the pricked finger in her mouth as she ambled over to the window.

The street was exceptionally busy, even for a Saturday. No doubt twenty-eight of these conveyances held those fortunate couples who'd been given a child.

What if an unexpected child had ridden the train? Maybe I'm supposed to be at the distribution, taking an opportunity God provided.

Adelaide whipped off her apron and raced upstairs for her hat and gloves.

Charles walked the few blocks to *The Ledger,* his stride brisk. Under his hat perspiration already beaded his forehead. He neared Whitehall's Café and the aroma of strong coffee wafted through an open window, tempting him. Up ahead, a group of people huddled, heads bent, talking, unusual for an early Saturday morning. Coffee could wait.

As Charles neared the paper, his reporter came running from the opposite direction, his lanky legs skidding to a halt in front of him. "Mr. Graves, Sarah Hartman hung herself from a rafter in her barn!"

"What can you tell me about her?"

"Nothing except she's an old lady who lived on a farm outside of town. Must've gone daft. Her daughter found her this morning."

"Too bad," Charles said without a trace of feeling. Long ago, journalism had taught him to distance himself from tragedy, to look at events as part of the job, not troubles affecting people's lives. Otherwise, every death would have him bawling like a baby. Though, upon occasion, the sum of all those tragedies circled over his head like buzzards converging on the kill, disturbing his sleep.

"Did the *sheriff* say it looked like suicide, or the town gossips?"

James thrust out his chin, annoyance etching his brow. "The sheriff did. He found a crate kicked over beneath the body."

Charles nodded his approval. "Good work. Get the sheriff's statement. Interview the daughter. While you're at it, ask about funeral arrangements for the obit."

"Mrs. Hartman had one child." James checked his tablet, clearly proud of his reporting skills. "Frances Drummond."

Drummond? Charles had no idea why, but hearing that name left him feeling uneasy.

A crowd gathered as Adelaide slipped into the schoolhouse. Across the front of the room, the orphans sat in two rows of chairs, their young faces etched with uncertainty and a glimmer of hope. Adelaide counted nineteen boys and nine girls. Twenty-eight, the exact number the committee had expected. Her heart plummeted. Still, she couldn't drag herself away.

She studied each child in turn. Some appeared to be in their early teens, others quite young; their small feet dangled above the floor. Though rumpled from travel, all wore proper clothing, with hair combed and faces scrubbed.

They were beautiful, every single one of them.

Across the room she caught the eye of Mr. Graves. His quick smile made her feel less alone in this room of instant families.

Adelaide's gaze returned to a young girl of six or seven. Fair and blond, she leveled aquamarine eyes on the crowd. A brave little thing or maybe merely good at hiding her fear.

"Miss Abigail, what on Earth are *you* doing here?"

With huge proportions and a voice to match, Viola Willowby loomed over her. That a steady customer persisted in calling her Abigail, even though Adelaide's Hats and Sundries hung in bold letters over her shop, set Adelaide's teeth on edge.

She lifted her gaze, forcing up the corners of her mouth into something she hoped resembled a smile. Atop Mrs. Willowby's head perched one of Adelaide's finest creations—a floppy straw hat bedecked with pink cabbage roses.

"Hello, Mrs. Willowby."

"I saw you leave the orphan interviews. Why were you there?"

"For the same reason as you."

Mrs. Willowby gasped. "You can't be serious! It… it wouldn't be proper." Mrs. Willowby pulled a lace-edged hanky from its hiding place in the depths of her ample bosom and touched the linen to her nose, as if she feared catching some dire malady that would render her as irrational as she obviously thought Adelaide to be.

Adelaide looked her square in the eye. "And why not?"

"You're a spin—" Mrs. Willowby's face flushed, unable to get the heinous word past her lips. "A maiden lady."

Adelaide wanted to rip the stunning hat off her customer's head and swat her across the face with it. But then she sighed, ashamed of herself. A Christian shouldn't think that way. Besides, Mrs. Willowby represented the thinking of the committee, probably of their church, even the entire town. "You needn't worry. They denied my request."

"Well, I should think so!"

Judge Willowby, an equally large man, tapped his wife on the shoulder. "I'm sure Miss Crum is quite capable of rearing a youngster, Mrs. Willowby." While his wife sputtered like an overflowing teakettle, he motioned to two chairs. "It's time to start." He turned to Adelaide. "Nice to see you, Miss Crum."

Adelaide smiled at the judge. Clearly he found some good in his uncharitable wife.

Adelaide could understand why the Willowbys had been given a child. Years before, they'd lost their two children to diphtheria. Well-heeled, after finding natural gas on their property, they wielded a lot of influence in town.

While she… Well, truth be told, she *was* a spinster. How she disliked the word, but at thirty-one years of age, soon to be thirty-two, Adelaide had to accept it applied to her.

She moved to the back of the room and took a seat,

recalling some years back her chance at marriage. She hadn't loved Jack, the man who'd asked. Had her refusal been a mistake? Young at the time, she'd foolishly expected to fall in love. It hadn't happened.

Keeping busy hadn't been a problem. She faithfully attended the First Christian Church, went to prayer meetings on Wednesday nights, where she communed with the Lord, but with not one eligible bachelor. Within the pages of books, she found adventure, but put little stock in the fictitious men who whisked women away to live happily ever after. No, Adelaide lived in the real world, had her feet planted firmly on the ground. Men couldn't be counted on. Her chest constricted. Her mother's life had proved that.

Her gaze returned to Mr. Graves. Light streamed through the window behind him and the rays caught in his thick hair, giving him a halo of sorts. Though with that strong jaw and stern expression, he hardly looked like an angel. But he did, she had to admit, look fine.

Mr. Wylie walked to the front and asked for quiet, then introduced Mr. Fry, an agent of the Children's Aid Society.

A thin fellow with slicked-back hair and a hooked nose walked to the podium, eyeing the crowd over his reading glasses. "Ladies and gentlemen, the Children's Aid Society is grateful for your interest. Many of these children were homeless, sleeping in doorways and privies, selling matches or flowers, working as shoeshine or paperboys. Some begged for food. When they came to us, many wore filthy rags infested with vermin."

The children sat unmoving, staring ahead with somber gazes, showing no reaction to Mr. Fry's words. "You may wonder why New York City has such a vast number of orphans." His hand swept over the children. "Some of these children aren't, in fact, orphans. When John's family—" a thin boy scrambled to his feet "—immigrated to this country, he and his family became forever separated." John sat down.

"Death or desertion of one parent left eight of our twenty-eight children with no one to care for them. Unwed mothers left a few on our doorstep."

Someone murmured, "Poor things."

Tears stung Adelaide's eyes. More than anything, she wanted to take every last one of these children home and try to make up for the deprivation of their young lives with warm hugs and fresh-baked cookies.

"In some cases, family members brought them to us, trusting we could provide them a better life, which, with your help, we're attempting to do."

Adelaide couldn't imagine giving up a child. Nothing could make her do such a thing.

"Mr. Brace, our founder," Mr. Fry continued, "realized we couldn't handle the problem alone. He devised this plan to place the ten thousand orphans we presently have into rural areas and small towns, where they'll receive an education and enjoy the benefits of a healthy environment and family life."

The numbers boggled Adelaide. Surely with that many homeless children, there'd be *one* child for her.

Perhaps if she went to New York—

"Your local committee," he said then consulted his notes, "comprised of Mr. Wylie, Mr. Paul, Mr. Sparks and Mr. Graves, has approved the eligibility of your homes."

Involuntarily, Adelaide's gaze again sought Mr. Graves. Even from this distance, the sight of his determined, serious face shot little pricks of awareness through her limbs.

She forced her attention back to Mr. Fry.

"I've been told more requests were made than we could provide on this trip. Perhaps in the future as more children come to us, we can remedy that situation."

Adelaide caught her breath. If they came again, then, next time she might convince the committee.

Who was she fooling? No one in Noblesville, or New York, would give a single woman a child. If only she could give her world a twist and watch it transform like the bits of colored glass in the kaleidoscope she'd seen at the mercantile. Maybe then, she'd change a few stubborn minds.

"Along with periodic visits by one of our agents, these gentlemen have agreed to oversee the children's welfare. At any time, the agreement to care for a child can be broken, either by the family or by the child."

Perhaps a little girl would be unhappy in her new home and the committee would reconsider their decision.

He cleared his throat. "Now, let's meet the children."

Mr. Fry introduced the bigger boys in the back row. Half listening, Adelaide's eyes remained riveted on the little blond-haired girl. At last, Mr. Fry gave her name. She stood along with an older boy beside her.

"Emma and William Grounds are brother and sister. Emma is seven, her brother, William, ten. Their father deserted his family years ago and their mother recently died. Both youngsters are in good health." Emma and William clutched each other's hands, their eyes conveyed a warning—they were a matched pair, not to be separated.

Mr. Fry continued down the row and the Grounds children sat down. Laying her head on her brother's shoulder, Emma stuck two small fingers in her mouth. Two precious German children, whose father had left them, as hers had done. Adelaide yearned to pull them into her arms until that longing bordered on pain.

Oh, Lord, please bring these children into my life.

Mr. Fry instructed the selected couples to seek out the children and the meeting ended. Almost against her will, Adelaide moved toward the Grounds siblings. She froze when she spotted Frances and Ed Drummond, wearing black out of respect for Mrs. Hartman's untimely death, talking to William and Emma.

As Adelaide watched, Emma tentatively took Frances's hand. William sat silent, his arms hanging limp. A woman who'd accompanied the orphans on the train joined the couple and spoke to William. Apparently overcoming his hesitation, he took his sister's other hand.

Disappointment slammed into Adelaide's stomach. She swayed and sank onto a nearby chair. *Her* children were going to live with that angry man and his spiritless wife. Helpless to act, she watched the four of them cross to the registration table. The Drummonds signed a paper and left the room before a miracle could bring those children into her arms. Didn't God care about them? About her?

Across the way, Judge and Mrs. Willowby left with a dark-eyed, curly-haired boy in tow. The same process repeated all around the room. Soon all the orphans were spoken for and on their way to new homes.

A heavy stone of misery sparked a sudden, uncustomary anger. Adelaide approached the table where the men who'd denied her application sifted through paperwork. "How could you allow the Drummonds to have the Grounds children?"

Mr. Paul, his face turning a deep shade of crimson, leapt to his feet. "Now see here, Miss Crum, it's not your place to criticize the decisions of this committee!"

Mr. Wylie took Mr. Paul's arm. "No need to raise your voice, Thaddeus." He turned to Adelaide. "The Drummonds are fine people. Ed sits on the county council, helps his neighbors. You probably heard Mrs. Drummond recently lost her mother." He grimaced. "A few years back, their only child died in a horrible accident. They deserve this new beginning."

Face pinched, Mr. Sparks came around the table. "You're mistaken about the Drummonds. They pay their bills and attend church."

Adelaide wanted to challenge their view, but that meant butting her head into that stone wall of men. Without a doubt, Frances was a good person, but she'd changed into a colorless, weary creature, perhaps downtrodden by her husband.

"Do you have proof they're unsuitable?" Mr. Graves asked.

Adelaide moved forward. "The day of the interviews, Mr. Drummond looked very angry—"

"If that's a crime, we'd all be in trouble." Mr. Wylie chuckled. "I know you've never been married, Miss Crum, but it's not uncommon for husbands and wives to argue."

She tamped down her annoyance. They hadn't seen Ed Drummond's expression. But they'd already gone back to their paperwork, dismissing her with silence.

All except Mr. Graves, who studied her with dark, somber eyes. But he remained mute.

She turned to leave, then stepped into the bright sunlight, watching wagons and buggies roll away from the schoolhouse. Her gaze lingered on the smiling couples with youngsters.

For a moment, she regretted refusing Jack's offer of marriage.

But then she remembered how he'd gobble dinner, barely speaking a word, and later, hands folded over a premature paunch, would fall asleep in the parlor until he roused enough to go home. No sharing of dreams, no laughter, no connection. His only thank-you for the meal was an odorous belch.

Without a doubt, her main appeal to Jack had been the income from her shop. Adelaide lifted her chin. If marriage offered no more than that, she could manage nicely without a man. But a child... A child was different.

Charles watched Miss Crum leave. What had she seen or heard that upset her enough to challenge the committee? With his own misgivings needling him, he followed her. "Miss Crum!"

She pivoted. His heart stuttered in his chest, a warning that when it came to Miss Crum, he was fast losing his objectivity. "I need to ask. What made you say the Drummonds wouldn't make good parents?"

She met his gaze with an icy stare. "I've seen Ed's temper. Frances appears heartbroken, unable to care for two children."

"That's understandable. She lost her mother—"

A light touch on his arm cut off his words.

"Have you ever had a bad feeling about anyone, Mr. Graves?"

"Sure."

"Then you can understand my concern. I have a bad feeling about that man."

As a newsman, he might use intuition to guide him, but he needed tangible evidence, not the insight of one disgruntled woman. "With nothing to base it on—"

"I know the committee's position. They made it clear the day I applied." She gave him a curt nod. "Good day."

Watching her leave, he regretted the committee's decision. No point in getting sappy about it. He wasn't in the business of securing everyone's happiness, even the happiness of a woman with eyes the color of a clear summer sky.

Crossing the street, he slipped between a buckboard hauling sacks of feed and a dray wagon. The image of Adelaide Crum nagged at him with a steadfastness that left him shaken.

Yet, the lady saw things as black and white, right or wrong, while he found areas of gray. Not that it mattered. He had no intention of getting involved with her, with anyone.

He had all he could do running the paper and helping his brother's family. He didn't want another complication in his life, in particular a complication of the female sort.

Yet something about Adelaide Crum made him question his decision.

Chapter Three

Tuesday morning Adelaide sewed pink ribbons on to a child's bonnet, each tiny stitch made with infinite care. On the table beside her, her Bible lay closed. Unread.

As she worked, she pictured Emma Grounds, the little German girl, wearing this hat as they picked day-lilies out back. She imagined bending down to gather the girl to her, nuzzling her neck, inhaling the scent of warmed skin, the scent of a child.

Sighing, she pinched the bridge of her nose, fighting tears, then knotted the final thread, snipped off the ends and laid the finished hat on her lap. In reality, a customer would buy this bonnet for her daughter or granddaughter and it would be gone, out of Adelaide's grasp as surely as Emma.

She removed her spectacles and laid the hat on the counter. The bell jingled over the door. The sight of Laura Larson brought a smile to Adelaide's face. Laura's youthful spirit might be encased in a plump, matronly body, but her laughter lit up a room like firecrackers on the Fourth of July. Without her help, Adelaide couldn't have managed the shop during her mother's illness. "Hello!"

Laura strolled toward her, her gaze sweeping the shop. Slicked back into a bun, some of her salt-and-pepper curls escaped to frame her round unwrinkled face. "My, my, haven't you been busy."

Leaning on the counter, Adelaide viewed her surroundings through Laura's eyes. Hats lined every shelf and perched on every stand. Already full when she'd become work-possessed, display cabinets burst at the seams. "I guess I'm overstocked."

Laura giggled, sounding more like a young girl than a grandmother in her fifties. "I'd say so. Do you have some hat-making elves tucked away in the back?"

Adelaide smiled. "No, I made them all."

"Why so many?"

What could Adelaide say? She'd been drowning her sorrow in hats? That for the past two weeks she'd been sewing, rather than praying about her problems? "Would you like some tea?"

"Tea sounds wonderful, if you have the time."

Adelaide headed to the kettle on the tiny potbellied stove in the back. "One thing I have plenty of is time."

"What you have plenty of, dear, is hats," Laura said, following her.

Pouring steaming water into a prepared teapot, Adelaide chuckled. For a moment, the sound stopped her hand. How long had it been since she'd laughed?

Adelaide gathered two cups with saucers and added a teaspoon of sugar in each, the way she and Laura liked their tea. She carried the tray into the showroom.

Laura joined her at the table, a cozy spot where her

customers leafed through copies of *Godey's Lady's Book* while enjoying a restorative cup of tea.

"Why not mark them down and run an ad in the paper?" Laura said. "You'll need the space when it's time to display wools and velvets."

Running an ad meant seeing Mr. Graves. She would like to strategically poke a hatpin into every member of the committee, even *The Ledger*'s editor. Of course, she'd do no such a thing.

Filling Laura's cup, Adelaide sighed. "I'll run an ad."

Laura took a sip, and then rested her cup in the saucer. "You missed Wednesday night's prayer meeting. Again." Laura touched her hand. "Tell me what's wrong."

Adelaide lifted her head, meeting Laura's gentle and accepting, ready-to-listen eyes. Her gaze skittered away and settled on the bonnet lying on the counter, then over to her unread Bible.

She considered telling Laura about her struggles, but it might sound as if she blamed God. And she didn't. It was her fault she resisted His will for her life. Or was it the committee who refused His will? Her mind had been so full of hurt and discouragement she no longer heard with certainty the quiet, inner voice that had guided and sustained her.

Laura gave her hand a squeeze, but said nothing, simply waited. Tenacious as a bulldog tugging at a trouser leg, Laura wouldn't let go until she got the story.

"A couple weeks ago, I asked to care for one of the orphans coming to town on the train, and the committee turned me down."

"Oh, no."

"Afterward—" She bit her lower lip until she could continue. "To keep busy, I made hats."

Laura turned over Adelaide's hand. "Which explains your rough palms and bloodshot eyes."

"It's been…a difficult time."

"Yes, I see—"

"Do you? Do you see this was my last chance—" Adelaide blinked hard and pulled away her hand.

"I'm sorry, dear," Laura said, her heartfelt tone bringing a lump to Adelaide's throat.

"No, I'm the one who's sorry for burdening you with this."

"Don't be silly! I'm your friend." Laura slapped the table. "That committee is made up of nitwits."

"Some nitwits. Only the superintendent of schools, the president of the bank, the editor of our newspaper—"

"Mr. Graves?" Laura scooted to the edge of her seat.

"None other."

"Now *there* is a handsome man," Laura said, with a grin. "Looks like his father."

Adelaide gasped. "You knew Mr. Graves's father?"

Laura nodded, her eyes shining like a brand-new penny. "He grew up in Noblesville. Back then, I had a huge crush on Adam Graves. But he only had eyes for your mother."

"My *mother?*"

"Yes, dear, it might astonish you to hear this, but as a young woman, Constance Gunder reigned as belle of the county."

Her mother had been an attractive woman, but the pained expression she'd worn as long as Adelaide could remember suggested Constance had never known a happy day in her life.

"For a long while, Adam and your mother were inseparable," Laura continued. "Everyone assumed they'd marry."

Adelaide hadn't been told any of this. Why had her mother gone from belle to bitter? "What happened?"

"Constance fell in love with your father. Not a staying kind of man, but he swept your mother off her feet." Laura sighed. "Adam moved away right after that. Landed in Cincinnati, I believe. Your folks got married. As far as I know, Adam never came back, not even to visit his parents before they died."

"That seems callous."

"A broken heart can change a man—and a woman. I've always wondered if that's what damaged your mother."

Adelaide shook her head. "My mother never opened her heart enough to get it broken." She ran her finger around the cup's rim. "Did you know my father?"

"Not really. A fun-loving, charming traveling salesman with dimples—that pretty much describes Calvin Crum."

"Do you know why he left?"

Laura shook her head. "Constance never confided in me." Laura pursed her lips, as if cutting off something she wanted to say, then brightened. "Well, all that's water under the bridge." She waggled her brows. "I understand Adam Graves's son is available."

"For what?"

"For your ad, what else? And you better get over there, before all these hats start gathering dust." Laura returned to her tea, her face the picture of innocence, knowing full well she'd used the exact words that would convince Adelaide to place the ad and put her into the presence of Mr. Graves.

Whether Adelaide wanted to deal with the editor or not, she needed cash to buy supplies. She couldn't afford to dip into her meager savings.

Besides, she had another pressing reason to see him. "I *do* owe Mr. Graves and the entire committee an apology."

"Why?"

"I lost my temper at the distribution of the orphans." Adelaide glanced at her hands.

"I'd have wanted to give them a piece of my mind, too."

"Yes, but you wouldn't have. I've asked God's forgiveness." She swallowed. "But I've put off the next step."

Laura nodded. "You'll be doing the right thing. You can place the ad as an act of repentance *and* good business." Laura smiled, then rose to give Adelaide a quick hug. "I'll be back to quilt on Monday. I'm only blocks away if you need me," Laura said, then left.

Adelaide restored order to the shop and then climbed the stairs, her stomach lurching at the prospect of facing Mr. Graves and the entire committee. If she had more say in what happened, maybe she wouldn't be in this mess. In her world, an unmarried woman couldn't discern anger in a man, couldn't challenge the decisions of men. Couldn't be deemed fit to rear a motherless child, though countless widows raised their own children.

If only I had a way to get through to these men, to let my voice be heard.

Then maybe—

"Oh, why am I even bothering to dream about what can't be undone?" she said to the empty room.

Adelaide whipped off the apron, smoothed her navy skirt and then donned hat and gloves. Mr. Graves would not see how dejected she'd been since the committee's decision.

In fact, she wouldn't let Mr. Graves see her heart at all.

Downstairs, she flipped the sign in the window to CLOSED, left the shop and stood at the edge of the boardwalk, waiting while horses of every description clopped past. The sight of the huge animals always left Adelaide weak in the knees. Would she ever get over her fear of horses?

Seeing an opening, she hustled across the street, holding the hem of her skirt out of the dust. Arriving safely on the other side without being crushed by the temperamental beasts, she heaved a sigh of relief. In front of *The Ledger,* she took a moment to slow her breathing. Grasping the handle of the door, she turned the knob when the door burst open.

A young man slammed into her. The red-faced youth steadied her with his hand. "Excuse me, miss! Are you all right?"

Adelaide fluffed her leg-of-mutton sleeves. "I'm fine."

"I'm sorry, I didn't see you. I'm rushing to get to the courthouse. A horse thief is being arraigned today, and I'm sitting in on the trial." Holding a pad and pencil aloft, he puffed out his chest like a bantam rooster. "I'm a reporter."

"Not apt to be one for long if you knock down a loyal

reader, James," warned a deep masculine voice, a familiar voice that sent a wave of heat to Adelaide's cheeks.

The young man's complexion also deepened to the color of beets. The editor smiled, softening the harshness of his words, and gave Adelaide a wink. The second time he'd winked at her. Despite everything, she couldn't help but smile back.

"Don't worry. I'll take care of Miss Crum."

Adelaide's gaze darted to the editor. Heavenly days, no one took care of her. Even hearing the words unsettled and somehow thrilled her, too.

"I'll expect a full report on the proceedings, James."

The young man nodded, then took off at a run across the street, his long legs dodging buggies and wagons on his way to the courthouse.

Adelaide turned back to the editor. "I don't believe his feet touched the ground."

Brown eyes sparkling with good humor, Mr. Graves chuckled. Without a coat, attired in a pin-striped vest and white shirt, he'd rolled his sleeves to the elbow giving her a clear view of muscled forearms. His broad shoulders filled the doorway.

The kind of shoulders one could lean on, tell every trouble to, a luxury Adelaide had never had.

Laura had said Charles looked like his father. Adelaide resembled her mother. Odd, history repeating itself that way.

He gestured for her to enter ahead of him. "Come in."

The instant Adelaide stepped inside, the odor of ink filled her nostrils. With the presses running, the noise level forced her to raise her voice several notches, disconcerting her. But not nearly as much as the man beside her, who looked more male than any man she'd ever met.

"Your reporter seems like a conscientious young man."

"Yes, but a bit out of control."

Exactly how Adelaide felt at the moment.

He led her to a desk the likes of which she'd never seen. Newspapers, books and a jumble of paper littered the surface and spilled over onto the floor. Her gaze surveyed three coffee cups, two tumblers, one filled with water, the other with pencils, an ink well, scissors, a glue bottle, a crumpled rag stained with ink, rubber bands, an apple and, gracious, the remainder of a half-eaten sandwich.

"Oh, my."

Mr. Graves stiffened. "Something wrong?"

"Nothing really." Adelaide clasped her hands together to keep them from organizing the desk and then giving it the dusting—well, more like the good scrubbing—it needed. That Mr. Graves could work amidst such a mess amazed and baffled her.

He motioned to a chair. "Please, have a seat."

She glanced at the chair he'd indicated, only to find it piled with newspapers. With a boyish grin, Mr. Graves removed them, obviously unconcerned with disarray. She started to sit when she spotted the crumbs.

He followed her gaze. "Let me take care of that." He took out a handkerchief and swiped it over the seat, sending crumbs tumbling to the floor.

She cringed. Heavenly days, fodder for bugs, or worse, rodents. But then he bent near and she caught the smell of leather and soap mingled with ink and filled her lungs, reveling in the scent of him. Suddenly woozy, she dropped into the now tidy seat before she did something foolish, like telling him how good he smelled.

The fumes must have made me light-headed.

The editor cleared a space, then perched on the corner of his desk. His dark gray pants and vest hugged a flat midriff with nary a sign of a potbelly. Her gaze lingered on his hands. Ink-stained, the tips of his long fingers fascinated her. Large, capable, strong—a man's hands, not at all like her own.

With great effort, she pulled her gaze away to look into his eyes and caught him studying her, a puzzled look on his face. Heat climbed her neck. What was the matter with her? She was behaving like a schoolgirl, as if she'd never seen a man.

"Miss Crum? You're here because…?"

Her hand fluttered upward, easing her collar from the heat of her neck. "I want to place an advertisement in your paper."

He folded his arms across his chest. "I'd welcome your business, but I believe you already advertise with us."

He'd paid attention, knew she ran a monthly ad, but then that was his job. "Yes, but I need a special advertisement to promote the sale of my latest creations." She worried her lower lip. "I'm overstocked."

"I see. Perhaps a larger, eye-catching ad would bring in those ladies who didn't get a new bonnet for Easter?"

Adelaide smiled. "Exactly."

"Let's check our type selection for a suitable hat."

Adelaide took in a deep breath. "Before we do, there's another reason I've come, a more important reason."

"More important than business?" He gave her a teasing grin.

"Much." She swallowed over the lump in her throat. "I, ah, owe you an apology."

He raised a brow. "For what?"

"For my outburst the day of the distribution. I don't know what got into me." She sighed. "I behaved badly and I'm sorry."

"You surprise me, Miss Crum."

Adelaide glanced at her hands, then met his gaze. "When I've done wrong, the Bible teaches me to apologize."

His eyes searched her face. "Apparently you do more than carry that book on Sunday mornings."

What a strange comment. One he wouldn't have made if he knew how she'd struggled of late with reading the Bible. "The Bible also says you're to forgive me."

"Yes, if need be, seventy times seven." A smile took over his solemn face. "Forgiving you is an easy task, Miss Crum."

Like rainfall after a drought, his words seeped into her thirsty heart. "Thank you." She shot him a grin. "Though, I trust my behavior won't require quite that much clemency."

He leaned toward her. "That's too bad."

Adelaide's mouth went dry. What did he mean? She lurched from the chair. "I'd like to look at your hat selection."

He smiled, and then with a hand on her elbow, led her to an enormous array of type fitted into shallow drawers. The presses pulsated through the wooden floor into the soles of her shoes and up into her limbs. That had to be why she felt shaky on her feet. Not because of Mr. Graves's touch.

The presses came to an abrupt halt.

The editor stopped his search and faced her. "Perhaps I'm out of line, but I feel compelled to say I disagreed with the committee's decision." He took a step closer until she could see the length of his lashes, became aware of the rise and fall of his chest as he breathed. "I saw the logic in the astute arguments you made regarding your suitability."

Compliments on her cooking she'd had, but no man had ever praised her intellect. Still… "Then, why didn't you speak up?"

"I thought about the burdens my sister-in-law carries rearing her boys alone. Too late I realized that even with her hardships, Mary is an excellent mother." He stepped closer yet, until she could feel heat from his body, could see gold flecks in his dark eyes. "I'm sure you'd be a good mother."

Sudden tears filled her eyes and she looked away.

He touched her arm. "I think I know how much the committee's decision has hurt you."

Adelaide noticed his assistant watching the exchange with interest. Teddy Marshall would be telling his wife about this visit at noon and the whole town would know by nightfall. She smoothed her skirt, then her brow. "Whether it hurt me isn't the point. It wasn't fair."

His gaze locked with hers. "Life is often unfair, Miss Crum," he said, and then returned to his search of the boxes.

From his tone, Adelaide suspected he wasn't simply talking about her situation. Did he have a message in there? Some lesson to learn? If so, she wasn't ready for it. Not with her heart burning with want for something she couldn't have.

He held out two blocks for her to examine. "Here you are."

Adelaide pulled her spectacles from her bag to peruse the blocks, glad for the distraction from all the confusing feelings rushing through her. With Mr. Graves standing near, she found it difficult to concentrate. Taking an eternity to make a simple decision wasn't like her. She forced her focus on business, not on the man at her side.

At last, she selected the larger block engraved with a most fetching hat, complete with feathers. "I'd like to use this."

Remembering her mother's words, she removed her wire-rimmed eyeglasses and stuffed them into her purse.

"Your eyes are pretty either way," he said softly.

Is he teasing me? "I've been told spectacles give me the appearance of an old maid schoolmarm."

"They give you an air of intelligence." He met her gaze. "I find intelligent women attractive."

She fingered the ribbed edge of her collar, her mind whirling around the compliment.

A door slammed. Fannie Whitehall crossed the room, her curly red hair poking out from under a big-brimmed straw hat.

Fannie said hello, and then brushed past Adelaide with as much interest as she'd give a fencepost. She held out two jars topped with a thin layer of paraffin and thrust them into Mr. Graves's hands. "I brought some of my preserves like I promised."

Charles looked at the jars like he'd never seen jam before. "Thank you, Miss Whitehall."

"That jam's mighty fine on biscuits."

He gave a lopsided grin. "I'm sure it is, but I'm not much of a cook."

"I'd make you a batch, but you'd have to bake them." Fannie let out a giggle. "I always burn the bottoms."

"Biscuits are my specialty." The words tumbled out of Adelaide's mouth. Had she actually said that? Out loud? Apparently she had, judging by the startled expression on both Mr. Graves and Fannie's faces. "Ah, as a thank-you for the time you spent on my ad."

"That's kind of you, Miss Crum," Mr. Graves said.

Her gaze collided with his and held for several moments, then darted away, then returned. He gazed at her with an intensity that suggested something important was happening, something significant. No man had ever looked at Adelaide like that before. Her hands trembled and she clasped them together, trying to gain control over her traitorous body, especially with Fannie's sharp-eyed scrutiny.

"I… I'd best be…going," Adelaide stammered. "I need to get back to the shop."

"Let me walk you out." The editor gently guided her by her elbow to the door and then opened it. "I'll write up the ad and have it ready first thing tomorrow morning."

The huskiness in his voice set her insides humming and brought an odd tightness to her throat. "I'll stop by the paper to look at it before I open the shop."

They said goodbye. Once outside, the sun shone brighter and the sky appeared shades bluer than when she'd walked over to *The Ledger*. Finding a break in the traffic, she scurried across the street and entered her shop, then glanced back.

Mr. Graves remained in the open doorway where

she'd left him. He'd complimented her eyes, even said her spectacles gave her an air of intelligence. No one had ever said anything nicer to her in all her days. Joy zinged through her chest, pushing against her lungs until she could barely breathe.

Then Fannie joined Mr. Graves in the doorway, deflating Adelaide's mood faster than a burst balloon.

Charles watched Miss Crum cross the street and enter her shop. As the door closed behind her, he detected a little twinge of disappointment. Silly. The lady was a client, nothing more.

Beside him, Fannie cocked her head. "Promise you won't forget to take the jam home. I put it on your desk."

"How could I forget?"

She giggled, and then jiggling her fingers at him, she flounced down the walk.

Charles let out a gust of air. He needed to help Teddy get the presses running, but he stayed at the door, thinking not about Fannie, but of Miss Crum.

With his office directly across the street from her shop, he'd noticed since the interviews how little she went out. When he worked late, he'd observe her lamp lit well into the night. After seeing her today, he guessed Miss Crum was a workhorse or an insomniac. Under her pretty blue eyes, dark smudges marred her creamy skin. If he was any judge of people, and in this business he made it a point to be, Miss Crum still suffered from the committee's rejection.

"Miss Crum's a looker, though kind of standoffish."

Charles hadn't heard Teddy come up behind him. For a burly man he had a light step. Charles purposely turned a cool eye on his assistant, hoping to stop what was coming.

"Yes, sirree, she's one fine-looking woman. Thinking about courting her?"

Charles scowled. "Where did you get that idea?"

Teddy smiled, putting his whole face into it, annoying Charles. "Oh, I've seen you watching her comings and goings. It's time you quit thinking about asking her and do it."

"My priority is to get this newspaper in shape."

"Which you've done. Since you've taken over, the paper comes out on time and has another section. Why, it looks downright citified." Teddy swept his arm over the room. "You've made this your life. A lonely way of living, that's sure."

The truth slammed into Charles. He *was* lonely. Since he arrived in town, Fannie had come by the paper with one excuse after another. But her giggling and incessant chatter put a knot in his stomach. From what she'd said, she didn't even read the newspaper.

No, he liked the appearance and manner of Miss Crum. "I've considered asking her to dinner," he said before he thought.

"Miss Whitehall or Miss Crum?"

"Miss Crum."

Teddy raised his brows. "So, what's stopping you?"

"A woman who applied for an orphan would have only one thing on her mind—getting married and having babies of her own. I've no intention of tying that knot."

Teddy scratched the back of his neck, peering at him with mild hazel eyes. "You running away from matrimony, boss?"

Shoving his hands into his pockets, Charles studied the floor, and then raised his gaze. "In my experience, Teddy, if you smile twice at a woman, she starts planning your wedding." His hand left his pocket and pushed through his hair. "What makes women think they know a man better than he knows himself?"

Teddy hooted. "They do, that's a fact." His eyes disappeared in a lopsided grin, a grin fading faster than morning glories at noon. "What's wrong with marrying? My Grace is a good woman, takes care of me just fine. Gave me four sons," Teddy said, his tone laced with pride.

Countless Sunday mornings, Charles had seen Miss Crum set off for church, dressed to the hilt from the shiny tips of her shoes to the top of her elaborate hat, clutching the Good Book. Yes, a fine Christian woman. As different from him as any woman he'd ever known. Exactly why this sense of a connection between them wasn't logical.

If Charles really cared about Miss Crum, he'd stay away.

But he had no intention of sharing that with Teddy. "We'd best get to work or we won't get this edition out."

Teddy gave him a long, hard look before heading inside. Once they had the presses running, Charles strode to his desk. Miss Crum's dismay at the disorder he worked in made him as uncomfortable as having his knuckles rapped by his first-grade teacher. He began organizing the clutter and then stopped.

He wasn't going to let any woman walk in here and, with one disapproving glance, change the way he ran his office. If he did, next thing he knew, she'd be running his life.

Tousling the paperwork, he restored the desk to its original state and for good measure, dumped the cup of pencils. Slumping into his chair, he eyed the mess with grim satisfaction, promising to steer clear of Miss Crum.

Yet loneliness washed over him, leaving him hollow. Empty. Unlike Fannie, unlike any woman he'd known, Miss Crum captivated him. Though he fought it, he craved substance. Biscuits instead of jam. But that meant letting someone get close. Even a woman like Miss Crum, whose guileless blue eyes tugged at the rusty hinges of his heart, needed to be held at arm's length.

For her sake, more than his.

Chapter Four

That morning, Adelaide awakened with a sense of anticipation. How much did her excitement have to do with seeing Mr. Graves that day? Everything. That realization scared her more than horses, more than tornadoes—her worst fears…until now.

No, spending her life alone terrified her more than anything.

With God only a whisper away, shame lapped at her conscience. A Christian could never be alone. Still, hadn't God intended His children to walk two by two?

Forcing her mind away from the editor, she picked up her Bible and opened it to the pink crocheted bookmark, a bookmark she hadn't moved in weeks. She had a lot of catching up to do. "Forgive me, Lord," she whispered, then began to read.

The clock struck nine. Adelaide jumped, then closed her Bible, amazed she'd read for an hour. Within these pages, pages she'd neglected, she found peace and comfort and strength. No matter what happened, she would never again make the mistake of neglecting Scripture.

She donned gloves and her latest hat, harboring butterflies in her stomach instead of the peace her Bible reading had given her, all because of Mr. Graves.

Minutes later Adelaide walked through the door of *The Ledger.* Mr. Graves and Teddy leaned over the boxes of type, selecting and then sliding them into place on narrow racks. When the door shut behind her, Mr. Graves's gaze met hers.

Teddy threw up a hand. Adelaide waved back, excited to be in this fascinating world of words. Until Mr. Graves's friendly smile put a flutter into the rhythm of her heart.

They met at his desk, a desk with less clutter and no stale food or empty coffee mugs. Adelaide bit back a smile.

The editor stuck his hands into his pockets and tipped forward on the toes of his shoes. "You look festive today."

"Thank you."

Amusement warmed his chocolate eyes as he viewed her hat with its nested bird. "Looks like some baby birds are about to hatch in that bonnet of yours."

Laughter bubbled up inside Adelaide. She pressed her lips together, trying to keep her mirth inside, but a most unbecoming giggle forced its way out. Heavenly days, she sounded like Fannie. "I like birds."

"Hopefully that fruit is *fake* or the birds you so admire might put your hat on the menu."

"I'll have you know my hat is in vogue," she said, the hint of a tease in her voice. "What you need is someone to teach you and your readers style."

He smirked. "I can't see farmers reading it."

"Well, no. But farmers' wives spend money in town—"

"On birds for their heads," he said.

She raised her chin. "Are you poking fun at me, Mr. Graves?"

His gaze sobered, something deep and mysterious replaced the mirth and sent a quiver through Adelaide. "Not at all, Miss Crum. Not at all."

She glanced away from that look and the unspoken words it contained. "Good because I'd like to write a fashion column for the paper." She covered her mouth with her hand, but the half-baked idea she'd been considering had already escaped. Being around this man scrambled her orderly mind.

Considering her proposal, Mr. Graves tapped a finger on his chin, very near the cleft. "I couldn't pay much—"

"One free ad per column will do."

"You're a shrewd businesswoman. A fashion column isn't a bad idea. Could you give me a sample? Say, by Monday?"

She beamed, barely able to keep from hugging him for this opportunity. A column would give her shop publicity. Perhaps increase sales, something she needed badly. An article would also give her a voice—granted one about style, but still a published voice. "It'll be exciting to see my name in print."

"You and I seem to be kindred spirits."

He cleared his throat, pivoted to his desk and grabbed a piece of paper. "I have your ad right here. Have a seat."

Adelaide glanced at the chair across from his desk, pleased to see it cleared of books and crumbs. She shot him a grin. "It appears you've made a few changes."

"Nothing of consequence." His mouth twisted as if he tried not to smile. "It merely made sense to have one chair fit for subscribers."

She cocked her head at him. "That's very astute of you."

"Under that proper demeanor, you have a feisty side, Miss Crum, a side that keeps a man on his toes."

Adelaide lifted her chin and reached for the ad. "Stay on your toes if you like, but I prefer to be seated."

His laugh told Adelaide the editor had gotten her attempt at humor. How long had it been since she'd made a joke? Felt this alive?

She tamped down her unbusinesslike feelings. After putting on her spectacles, she read the ad, and with an approving nod, returned it to him. "This is perfect."

Mr. Graves sat on the edge of his desk. He leaned toward her, a wide grin spreading across his face.

Something about this man made her feel content, like she did in church, but had never experienced in her home growing up. She hardly knew him, so the thought made no sense. And Adelaide prided herself on being a sensible woman.

"I'll run this in the next edition," Mr. Graves said.

"And I'll deliver my column personally. On Monday. If you print it, the column should take care of the bill."

He nodded. "Are you always this efficient?"

"I take my work seriously."

"Ah, a woman after my own heart."

He'd called them kindred spirits, declared her to be a woman after his own heart. The words ricocheted through her and left a hitch in her breathing and a huge knot in her stomach. Dare she hope for something too important to consider?

On Monday Adelaide once again sat across from the editor, this time with her fashion column clutched in her palm. When she handed it over to Mr. Graves, her heart tripped in her chest. Why had this column become so important?

"Neat, bold strokes, a woman not afraid to share her mind." He grinned, settling behind his desk to read.

Across from him, Adelaide fidgeted like a student waiting outside the principal's office while Mr. Graves bent his head to read. After he finished, he smiled. "Your assessment of women's fashions is written with the wit and flair I'd only expect from a professional journalist. I'll run it in the next edition."

"I loved writing it."

"If you want another article, let me know."

"I'd hoped you'd want a monthly column."

Mr. Graves ran his fingers through his hair. "Well, perhaps. Let's see how this article is received first."

"Fair enough."

"I'm guessing we'll get positive feedback from the ladies. Who knows? Maybe the men, too." He tapped the paper. "You have a gift for words."

Slowly a smile took over his face. "Would you be my dinner guest Saturday evening?"

Adelaide blinked. Had he asked her to dinner? She gulped. "Dinner? Saturday?"

"If that isn't a good night…"

He must think I'm an idiot. "Saturday will be fine."

A strange tightness seized her throat. How long since she'd shared a meal with a man? Years. And never with a man this attractive, this intelligent. A man, who had only to smile in her direction to set her heart hammering.

Evidently from his calm, easy demeanor, Mr. Graves

often asked a woman to share a meal. Something she'd best remember, lest she make too much of the invitation.

"I'll call for you at seven," he said.

"Seven," she repeated.

"I thought we might go to the Becker House."

She nodded, recovering her wits and her manners. "The Becker House would be lovely."

"When I arrived in town, I stayed there, so I speak from experience. The food *is* great."

The door rattled shut. A rotund gentleman dropped the briefcase he carried, then shoved his hat back on his head and mopped his forehead with a handkerchief. "Whoo-ee, it sure is hot for April. Never thought I'd complain about the heat after the winter we had, but this day is an oven, and I'm the hog roasting inside."

Charles crossed to the stranger. "May I help you, sir?"

"You can indeed. I'm looking for Mr. Charles Graves."

"You've found him."

"Excellent! Saves me a trip back into the sun." He stuck out a palm. "I'm Spencer Evans, your father's attorney. My condolences for your loss."

Adam Graves had died? Adelaide's gaze darted to the editor. Mr. Graves gave a curt nod. She hadn't seen anything about it in the paper. Nor did his son act grieved, but from her limited experience, she realized men didn't carry their feelings on their sleeves.

"I'm sorry about your father, Mr. Graves." Rising, Adelaide tucked her spectacles into her bag. "I'd best be going."

"I'll see you Saturday evening, Miss Crum."

"Did you say Miss *Crum?*" Mr. Evans turned toward her. "Could you be *Adelaide* Crum?" When she nodded, the lawyer slapped his hands together. "It's a piece of luck finding you here. A sure piece of luck."

"I'm afraid I don't understand—"

"Of course you don't. I apologize for being obtuse. This unseasonable heat must be muddling my brain, what there is of it." He chuckled. "As I said, I'm Adam Graves's attorney. If I locate all the heirs before I melt, I'd like to read his will at one o'clock this afternoon. If you both are available, that is."

Adelaide looked at Mr. Graves, then back to Mr. Evans. "There must be some mistake. I didn't know Adam Graves."

The editor frowned. "Are you certain of your facts, Mr. Evans?"

"I make it a point to be certain of my facts." Mr. Evans gave a nod toward the stack of newsprint. "I'm sure in your business, you do the same. Adelaide Crum is one of Adam Graves's heirs, as is one Mary Graves. Do you know where I can find her?"

Mr. Graves nodded. "Mary lives on South Sixth Street between Maple and Conner. If you'd like, I can take you to her place right now."

Filled with unspoken questions, the editor's gaze locked with Adelaide's. Baffled by the turn of events, she looked away.

"I'd appreciate it." The lawyer turned to her. "We'll meet in the private dining room of the Becker House this afternoon at one o'clock, Miss Crum. That way I can take the morning train back to Cincinnati tomorrow." He shoved his hat back in place.

Adelaide looked at the clock on the wall. "In less than an hour, Mary will be coming to my shop to quilt."

"Wonderful. That'll give me time to speak to her before she leaves. Whoo-ee, it is indeed my lucky day!" Mr. Evans turned toward Adelaide. "And yours, too, Miss Crum." He gave her a jaunty wave. "See you this afternoon."

Then he and Mr. Graves were gone, leaving Adelaide with an uncomfortable feeling that this was not her lucky day. Not her lucky day at all.

Adelaide laid out scissors and thread, and then prepared a sandwich for lunch. While thinking about the odd meeting with the lawyer, she layered ham and cheese on two slices of bread. With so much on her mind, she had no interest in food or quilting. But company might take her mind off the one o'clock appointment.

At exactly ten o'clock, the "Snip and Sew" quilting group, carrying lunch pails and sewing baskets, pushed through the shop door, the four women clumped together as if they'd been stitched at the hips. They chattered and laughed, except for Mary, who gave Adelaide an encouraging smile.

Tension eased from between Adelaide's shoulder blades. At least, Mary didn't appear disturbed that she'd be at the reading of Adam Graves's will.

Bringing up the rear came a fifth woman, the one person Adelaide had least expected to be interested in quilting.

Fannie Whitehall.

Sally pulled Fannie forward. "Fannie's joining our group. She's not a quilter, but she can stitch a fine hem."

"How nice of you to help, Fannie," Laura said.

The others greeted Fannie, friendly as birds on a branch.

The news thudded to the bottom of Adelaide's stomach. From seeing Fannie at *The Ledger,* Adelaide knew the girl hankered to play husband archery, and Mr. Graves was the target. Still, money raised from the sale of the quilt would buy supplies for the Sunday school. Only a selfish woman would resent another pair of helping hands. She swallowed her reservations and offered a smile. "Welcome, Fannie."

"Well, shall we get started?" Laura said.

Adelaide led the ladies to where she'd assembled her frame and had attached the Dresden Plate quilt. The pastel petals and yellow centers looked pretty enough to attract bees.

Adelaide grabbed a chair for Fannie, then she and Mary put away the ladies' lunches.

"Charles brought Mr. Evans by," Mary said in a low voice. "He told me you're one of the heirs."

"I can't imagine why."

"We'll find out soon enough."

Adelaide's stomach knotted. Whatever happened at the reading of the will, there'd be consequences.

By the time Mary and Adelaide took their places around the frame and threaded their needles, the chatter had ebbed and all heads bent over their work.

Fannie sewed beside Adelaide, taking each stitch with care, surprising Adelaide, who'd expected the girl's workmanship to be shoddy. At the thought, Adelaide's needle pierced the layers of fabric, pricking both her finger and her conscience.

Pausing in the middle of a stitch, Fannie looked at Mary with big, innocent eyes. "I'm hoping you can help me, Mary."

Mary tied a knot in her thread. "You're doing a fine job."

"I don't mean help with quilting." Fannie sighed. "I mean help with men. Well, not all men, only one. Charles Graves."

Adelaide missed the eye of the needle with her thread.

Mary shrugged. "I can't be much help. My brother-in-law is a mystery, even to me."

"Adelaide, you were talking to Mr. Graves." Fannie whisked her gaze over Adelaide either sizing her up as the competition—or fitting her for a very tight seam. "You—" Fannie hesitated "—don't have designs on him, do you?"

Adelaide's pulse skipped a beat. "Designs?"

Every hand hovered over the quilt, all eyes riveted on her and Fannie. Adelaide shook her head.

"I didn't think you did. I told Mama, 'Adelaide Crum is too levelheaded for a man like Mr. Graves.' I can't imagine you two courting." Fannie's eyes narrowed. "So you were at the paper on business. Nothing else?"

Heat filled Adelaide's veins. "Yes, business for the shop."

Fannie beamed. "Oh, I'm glad. I'm mad about Mr. Graves. Mama says he'd be quite the catch."

With her teeth, Sally broke off a length of thread. "Are you doing a little fishing, Fannie? Over at *The Ledger?*"

The women chuckled.

Fannie sighed. "I'm not sure you noticed, Adelaide, but Mr. Graves didn't seem all that eager to try my b-biscuits." Her voice quavered. "I don't understand what I'm doing wrong."

As much as Adelaide didn't want to, a thread of sympathy tugged between her heart and Fannie's. The girl meant well, even if she didn't see the consequences of her words or actions.

"Maybe your reputation as a cook is scaring him off," Laura said, one brow arched.

"Well, it's hard to get the temperature right in that huge cookstove of Mama's. But how would Mr. Graves know that?"

"You told him," Adelaide reminded her.

"I did?" Fannie thought a second. "Oh, I did!" Her green eyes filled with tears. "I've ruined my chances with him, exactly like I ruin my biscuits."

Adelaide laid down her needle. "That's no reason to cry."

"I'm sorry." Fannie dashed away the tears slipping down her cheeks. "It's just that I'm getting…well, desperate."

Martha harrumphed. "Desperate? How?"

"In three months, I'll be twenty. I've always planned to be engaged by my twentieth birthday. I'm getting old!" she wailed.

Fast losing sympathy for the girl, and with her own birthday looming, Adelaide bit back a retort.

Laura shook her head. "Fannie, dear, I'm sure you don't intend to, but you have a way of making me feel ancient."

Fannie gasped. "Oh, chicken feathers, Laura. I'm sorry."

"Why are you in such a rush anyway?" Martha asked, smoothing her dress over her bulging belly. "If you ask me, men are like flies. You trap yourself one, only to learn he can be a pest."

"Appears to me, yours has been pestering you

plenty," Sally said and the room once again filled with laughter.

Fannie took up her needle again. "I'll lose my looks soon."

Sally waved a dismissive hand. "Phooey! You're pretty. I look like a possum and I still managed to get a husband."

Adelaide gasped. "You do not look like a possum!"

"I do," Sally said, stitching along a rose-sprigged petal. "Small beady eyes, long nose, gray hair. Why, with my sons toting guns everywhere, I rarely venture out after dark."

Chuckles bounced off the high ceiling. "You're making fun, but I'm serious," Fannie moaned. "What am I doing wrong?"

Laura rose and stepped around the frame, then tilted Fannie's face to hers. "You're too eager. Let the man take the lead."

"I'm only being friendly," she said dismissing the comment. "What I need is a new hat, maybe a new way to style my hair. You always look fashionable, Adelaide. Will you help me?"

Adelaide thought of telling Fannie to leave the editor alone, but that wasn't her place. Nor did she care who he courted, though she had questions about the man. Even more about Adam Graves's will.

Sally gave Fannie a wink. "Play possum more, Fannie."

"Play possum?"

Sally nodded. "When you chase the men like a hound dog after a fox, why, you take all the fun out of it. Pretend you don't care. Pretend you wouldn't feed them a biscuit if they were the last to arrive for the fishes and loaves."

Fannie turned to Adelaide. "You're the best possum I know. Would you help me become more...?"

"Demure," Laura provided.

"Demure?" Fannie smiled wide. "I like the sound of that."

Had Fannie compared her to a wild animal that hung from a tree by its tail? Adelaide worked up a smile before she injured Fannie with her needle. As much as Fannie grated on her nerves, if she refused, the ladies might decide she had an interest in Mr. Graves. "It would be my pleasure."

"With your help, Adelaide, Charles Graves will fall in love with me, and I'll soon be a married lady."

As Adelaide listened to Fannie chatter on about his virtues, she realized her help meant trying to get Fannie a husband and children. She had to wonder—

What kind of bargain had she struck? And what would it cost her in the end?

Charles paced the private dining room at the Becker House. His sister-in-law, wearing her best finery, sat watching him, her expression wistful. Could she be thinking Sam should be sitting beside her, instead of lying in Crownland Cemetery?

He'd wanted to rip into Mr. Evans's briefcase to look at the terms of his father's will. When it came to legalities, the gregarious attorney kept a tight rein on his mouth and skillfully sidestepped every question Charles had slung at him, giving no hint why Adam had mentioned the milliner in his will.

At exactly one o'clock Mr. Evans ushered Miss

Crum, looking as perplexed as he felt, into the room. She glanced at him, her eyes filling with sympathy, probably for his loss. She couldn't know grief was the last emotion his father's death elicited.

She still wore the bird nest hat. On her, the silly hat looked good. Every hair in place, her clothing spotless, Miss Crum appeared serene. Only a heightened color in her cheeks suggested either the heat or an inner turmoil bothered her.

Well, she wasn't the only one stirred up by the chain of events. His father was no philanthropist. He'd never cared about the financial problems a woman might have either running a business or raising two children alone. He'd never cared about anyone.

Mr. Evans stepped forward. "Miss Crum, I believe you said that you and Mary Graves quilt together."

Miss Crum smiled. "Yes, and we attend the same church. Mary's father is my doctor."

"This is indeed a small town." Mr. Evans grinned, motioning to the table. "Well, since we're all here, let's take seats and get down to business before we roast and find ourselves on the hotel bill of fare." He chuckled, but no one else laughed.

Miss Crum took a chair across from Mary. Charles strode to the other side of the table and sat beside his brother's widow.

After sitting at the head of the table, Mr. Evans unlocked his briefcase and took out a sheaf of papers. "I have here Adam Graves's last will and testament."

Charles shifted in his seat.

"'I, Adam Graves, being of sound mind, do hereby bequeath to my son, Charles Andrew Graves, and to

Mary Lynn Graves, my son Samuel Eugene Graves's widow, my house in Cincinnati and its contents.'"

Apparently his father had kept his boyhood home. Nothing could ever make him step inside that place.

Mr. Evans glanced at him and Mary. "If neither of you want to move in…"

Both Mary and Charles shook their heads.

"Then I suggest the house and belongings be sold at auction. My assistant can ship personal items you might want."

"Sell them all," Charles said, his tone filled with bitterness.

"If Mary agrees, I can do that, except for this." He took a silky pouch from his briefcase and removed a gold pocket watch, the fob hanging from a thin chain. "When Adam made out his will, he asked me to give this watch to you personally."

Taking the watch, Charles felt the weight of it in his palm and took in the intricate engraving on the lid. His gaze dropped to the fob. He pictured Grandpa Graves, a large man with a hearty laugh, dangling the fob from callused hands, coaxing Charles and Sam onto his lap. His grandparents' rare visits were peaceful times. He tucked the watch in his pocket.

"'I bequeath Charles Graves the sum of two thousand dollars,'" Mr. Evan continued, "'and fifty percent ownership of *The Noblesville Ledger.*'"

Charles's jaw tightened. Leaving half ownership of the paper to him and half to Mary wasn't good business, but at least Charles knew his sister-in-law wouldn't interfere at the paper.

Mr. Evans handed over the bank draft. "In a moment, I'll go over the ownership papers." Evans turned to the will. "I hereby bequeath to Mary Graves the sum of five thousand dollars."

Charles squeezed Mary's hand, pleased his father had realized she needed money more than he. The money would come in handy in the years ahead, raising Sam's boys. And would give Mary the security she lacked since his brother had died. Weeping silent tears, she took the bank draft with trembling fingers.

Mr. Evans focused on the page in front of him. Charles's pulse kicked up a notch.

"'I hereby bequeath to Adelaide Crum, daughter of Constance Gunder Crum, fifty-percent ownership of *The Noblesville Ledger*.'"

Constance Gunder? Air whooshed out of Charles's mouth and his gaze settled on the woman across from him.

"Me? Why? I don't understand any of this," Miss Crum said. "Why mention my mother?"

Constance Gunder, the name Charles's mother had hurled in his father's face after Adam had accused his wife of flirting in church. Charles had never forgotten the name—or his father's reaction. Adam had backhanded his mother, knocking her to the floor, and then stood over her, shouting she wasn't worthy to wipe Constance Gunder's shoes and if she ever spoke that name again, he'd kill her. Charles had known then that somehow this woman had been at the root of Adam's anger, anger he expelled through his fists.

Constance Gunder, the woman Charles learned to despise—could she really be Miss Crum's *mother?*

How could his father do this? Was this one last ha-ha from the grave?

"Furthermore—" Mr. Evans began.

Charles jumped to his feet. Mary laid a hand on his wrist, but he jerked away from her touch. "What's going on here?" His voice sounded gruff and he cleared his throat. If only he could clear this nightmare his father had concocted as easily.

"It's quite simple," Mr. Evans said, nonplussed by Charles's reaction. "You and Miss Crum are half owners of *The Noblesville Ledger*."

"That's ridiculous!"

Mr. Evans's gaze returned to the will. "There's more."

"More?" Unable to sit, Charles strode to the fireplace, putting him across from Miss Crum, the woman who'd made a crack in his frozen heart. *What a joke on him.*

Miss Crum's eyes were wide, probably seeing dollar signs. Yet, even as he thought it, he knew the accusation wasn't true. Still, the idea clung to his mind like a burr under a saddle.

Mr. Evans bent over the paperwork. "'The equal shares of *The Noblesville Ledger* are not to be sold by either Charles Graves or Adelaide Crum for a period of two months. If either heir goes against my wishes, and sells his or her half of *The Noblesville Ledger* before the end of a two-month waiting period, the equipment and building are to be sold, all proceeds going to charity.'"

Charles stalked back to the table. Mary met his gaze with a worried frown. "He promised the paper to me! Why did he leave a perfect stranger half of *my* paper? Then force us to keep this ludicrous arrangement for months?"

Mr. Evans tipped his head between Charles and Miss Crum. "Perhaps she isn't a stranger, at least not to your father."

Color climbed Miss Crum's neck. "I'm not sure what you're suggesting—"

"My father returned to Noblesville only once—four years ago, when he bought *The Ledger*." Charles turned to Miss Crum. "Did you two arrange this then?"

Miss Crum gasped. "I've never even met your father."

"Adam didn't share his motives with me, but rest assured, knowing your father, he had his reasons. Where there's a will, there's always a reason." Mr. Evans chuckled to himself.

Charles scowled. "Have you considered joining a minstrel show, Mr. Evans?"

The attorney sobered. "I apologize." He handed Mary and Miss Crum a copy of the will, then laid the third copy where Charles had been sitting. "This lawyering can get dry as dust. I can see this is no laughing matter."

"Surely we can make this partnership work for two months," Miss Crum said, as if her ownership was of no consequence. "I won't be underfoot at *The Ledger*. I have my own business to run."

"Charles, sit down," Mary said, tears brimming in her eyes.

But he couldn't sit. Just when Charles had found some measure of control over his life, his father yanked it out of his hands. Even from the grave, Adam managed to control—no, punish—him.

His gaze sought the milliner's. "If you're expecting this business relationship to be pleasurable, Miss Crum, you're mistaken. As soon as I can, I'll buy you out. In the meantime, I promise, this will be the longest two months of your life."

Chapter Five

Minutes later Adelaide stormed out of the hotel and strode up the street. How dare Charles Graves act as if she'd robbed him? She'd considered him a friend, but he'd treated her like an enemy. True, he'd been denied half ownership of the paper, a sizable financial loss, but that hadn't been her doing.

Adelaide dodged a woman holding a towheaded boy by one hand. The sight of the child put a catch in her throat. But she wouldn't think about that now, not when her mind couldn't grasp Charles's hatred of her mother, a woman he'd never met.

She'd get to the bottom of this. No more guessing about her mother and father, about her past. But where should she begin?

Before taking sick, once or twice a year her mother had cleaned the attic. Now that Adelaide thought about it, she always gave an excuse why she didn't need help. The last time Adelaide had been up there, she'd stored equipment used to care for an invalid. She'd seen a few pieces of furniture, a couple trunks. Could the trunks hold the answer?

About to turn the corner onto Ninth, she heard a shout.

"Adelaide, wait!" With one hand clamped on her bright green hat and holding her billowing skirts with the other, Mary rushed toward her. Adelaide slowed her steps.

"You're—a fast—walker," Mary said, her words uttered in hitches as she came alongside.

"Only when I'm angry."

Mary sighed. "I'm sorry about Charles's reaction to the will. He'll get used to sharing the paper."

"I doubt that."

"He calls the paper his dream, but really it's his refuge."

Two men strolled past, discussing the rising price of seed. Once out of earshot, Adelaide leaned closer to Mary. "Do you understand why Adam Graves left me half the paper?"

"I have no idea. I never knew Sam's father, only met him once—at Sam's funeral. He came up to the casket, spoke to me and the boys, and then tried to have a word with Charles. That didn't go well, and Adam left immediately, didn't even attend Sam's graveside service. He never contacted me after that, not even to check on his grandsons."

Mary fell in beside Adelaide and they began walking again, but at a slower pace. When they reached the Masonic Lodge with its impressive gables, Mary cleared her throat. "If you never met Adam, then the connection had to have been between your mother and Adam."

"My mother never mentioned him, but a friend said they were childhood sweethearts. I don't understand any of it, but I'm going to search the attic to see what I can find."

Mary laid a hand on Adelaide's arm. "Do you want company?"

At the gesture, Adelaide blinked back sudden tears. "That's a kind offer, but…why would you want to?"

"I wouldn't want to poke around in the past alone. Plus, I knew Sam, and I know Charles. Perhaps I can give you insight."

"I'd appreciate it," Adelaide admitted, then led the way to her shop.

Inside, they found Laura helping a shopper try on a hat. "Back already?"

Adelaide took Laura aside. "Thanks for tending the store. Would you mind staying while Mary and I have a visit?"

Laura greeted Mary, and then smiled. "I'd love to stay. I've missed the shop."

Adelaide ushered Mary up to her quarters, then lit the lantern and opened the door to the attic. Adelaide climbed the stairs with Mary close behind. In the dim light, Adelaide didn't see the cobweb until it plastered against her face, a sticky reminder of the attic's neglect.

At the top of the stairs, the scent of lavender permeated everything her mother had touched, now mingled with the musty smell of age. Regret she and her mother hadn't been close laid heavy on her chest. Maybe here she'd find the clue to her mother's aloofness.

Mary looked around the stand-up attic. "This is huge," she said, then sneezed.

"I'm sorry, it needs cleaning."

Mary laughed. "With two boys, I'm used to a little dust."

Along one wall stood makeshift shelves filled with long forgotten fruit jars, crocks, a glass butter churn with a wooden paddle, a jar of buttons. Across the way sat a dressmaker dummy and an elaborate wicker carriage.

Under the window, Adelaide spied the large camelback trunk.

Dropping to her knees, Adelaide blew a layer of dust off the lid, and then raised it carefully. She removed an old rust-stained quilt then pushed aside a stack of linens. Underneath she found a celluloid-covered box. She tugged it out, and then lifted the tiny brass catch to reveal a stack of handkerchiefs. "Granny must have tatted these."

Mary fingered the lace. "They're lovely."

A visit from her grandmother had been an oasis in the desert of her life. She put the box aside to take downstairs.

Still, no hint here to what went before. Adelaide led Mary past a dresser. Tucked behind a hall tree, she found the small trunk. She rolled it out, its metal wheels squeaking, and then opened the latch. Inside she found another quilt, a half-finished pillow slip, a Bible—Granny's.

Had she been foolish to think she'd find anything that would reveal her mother's past in this dirty, stuffy place?

About to give up, her hand brushed against paper, paper that crackled with age. "Oh, it's my parents' marriage license."

The license promised "until death do us part," yet her parents' marriage had ended nearly as quickly as it began. Her gaze swept over the wedding date. She

gasped. January 17, 1866, not the October date she'd
been told.

"Is something wrong?"

Adelaide's fingers flew to her mouth. "They married
six months before my birth. I didn't know."

A spark of insight ignited in Adelaide's heart. Her
mother's warnings about men now made sense.

*Oh, Mama, did my conception end your hopes and
dreams?*

The afternoon sun glinted in through the window,
sparking off an old mirror in the corner. Adelaide rose
and walked to the window facing the street, thinking
about her mother's loss of independence and the load
of responsibility she'd carried alone.

A woman and small child, their eyes downcast, came
into view. Adelaide's pulse tripped. Emma, the orphan
girl, held Frances Drummond's hand. Dressed in black
from head to foot, a veil covered Frances's face. They
stopped in front of *The Ledger,* then disappeared inside.
Perhaps Frances had a delivery problem with the paper.
Yet, something about the two troubled her.

Adelaide turned back to Mary. "Your boys will be
home from school soon. Maybe we should continue
the search later."

Mary looked at the watch pinned to her bodice.
"Oh, I should be going, but we haven't found what you
wanted."

"I'll look another time." She smiled at Mary. "But
thanks, I'm grateful for your company."

Closing the lid of the trunk, and gathering the box of
hankies and the lantern, they returned below.

Later, Adelaide waved goodbye to Mary and Laura,

then stood at the window, waiting for Frances and Emma to leave *The Ledger*.

Charles threw down his pen and shoved aside the copy he'd tried to edit for the past hour. Even with his insides twisted into a pretzel over losing control of the paper, he couldn't put Miss Crum out of his mind. He'd not soon forget her anger-filled eyes tinged with hurt.

The door opened and he lifted his gaze from the paperwork, half expecting, even half hoping to find Miss Crum standing there. It wasn't. A twinge of disappointment settled in his gut.

His visitor wore a black gauze veil attached to her hat, hiding her face, making it difficult to identify her—until Charles spotted a little girl he *did* recognize peeking around the woman's skirts—one of the orphans. Charles rose and went around his desk.

Carrying a satchel, the woman approached with cautious steps. "Mr. Graves, I'm bringing Emma to you."

He leaned closer. "Mrs. Drummond?"

"Yes." Her hand fluttered to the veil. "I'm feeling poorly…since Mama died. Not up to caring for Emma right now."

"I see." But he didn't see at all. "What about William?"

"Ed needs William on the farm. But Emma…" She hesitated. "Emma needs someone to see she eats right and keeps up with her schoolwork, needs someone to braid her hair." With a gentle touch, she ran work-worn fingers over Emma's silken plaits. "I hope you might know a good place for her until I'm on my feet."

Charles saw Mrs. Drummond's obvious reluctance

to let Emma go and her responsibility for Emma shifted to his shoulders.

"I'd be glad to help." This poor woman carried a heavy load. "I'm sorry about your mother's...death."

"I can't believe she'd..." Her shaky voice trailed off.

Neither spoke the horrifying truth lingering beneath the conversation—suicide. He could imagine Mrs. Drummond's regrets; guilt for not having seen it coming, for not having done more to prevent such a loss. "Can I do anything else?"

"No." She bent close to Emma, emitting a soft moan, and then kissed the little girl's forehead.

Charles took a step closer. "You seem to be in pain."

"I wrenched my back, but I'll be fine." Mrs. Drummond handed Emma the satchel. "Remember what I told you." The little girl bobbed a promise, her face melancholy. Mrs. Drummond's fingers skimmed over Emma's cheeks. "I'll be going, then." With a hurried step, she walked out the door, leaving Emma behind.

Emma stared after her until the door closed, then turned to him with sad eyes. Where was his assistant? "Teddy!"

"Yeah, boss?"

"Run to the bank and then on to the superintendent's office and ask Mr. Sparks and Mr. Paul to come as soon as they can."

"Sure." Unspoken questions packed Teddy's gaze, but he headed out the door.

Charles cleared his throat. "Emma, I'm Mr. Graves."

She looked back at him, her blue eyes swimming with tears, twisting his innards into a knot. He patted her shoulder awkwardly. "Don't worry. Everything is going to be fine."

He had no idea how to keep his promise.

Tears spilled over her pale lower lashes, becoming visible now that they were wet and spiky. If he didn't do something, she'd start bawling. The prospect sent him behind his desk. He jerked open the top drawer and rummaged through it until he found what he sought— a bag of peppermints. "When I was a youngster," he began, "on my way home from school, I'd pass Mrs. Wagner's house. She'd be rocking on her porch, wearing a gray tattered sweater, no matter how hot the day…"

Emma stopped crying, but looked far from cheerful.

"She'd call me up on the porch, ask if I was studying and behaving. Then, she'd reach into the pocket of her sweater and pull out a peppermint." Charles took a candy from the bag. Emma's eyes widened. "She'd say, 'You're a smart boy, Charles. Work hard and one day you'll make something of yourself.' And, she'd drop the candy into my palm—like this."

He opened Emma's small hand and let a peppermint fall into her palm. When the corners of her mouth turned up in a smile, a peculiar feeling shot through him. As it had for him all those years ago, the candy once again worked wonders.

His entire adult life, he'd kept a stash of peppermints around to remind him of Mrs. Wagner, the one person who had believed in him, who'd given him a desire to improve his lot. The candy still tasted as sweet as her words. But even while Emma sucked on the treat, worry etched her face. Paul and Sparks better get here fast. He only had so many peppermints.

Twenty minutes later, Thaddeus Paul and John Sparks entered the office.

Sparks's gaze settled on Emma. "What's the emergency?"

Charles bent down to Emma's eye level. "I need to talk to these gentlemen. Will you be all right until I'm back?"

She nodded, though her gaze lingered on the bag of candy. Charles fished out another peppermint and then motioned for the men to accompany him into the back room.

As soon as they followed him in, Charles closed the door. "Grief stricken over her mother's suicide, Mrs. Drummond is unable to care for Emma Grounds. Her husband is looking after the boy. We need someone to take Emma in temporarily."

Thaddeus frowned. "Any idea who?"

Sparks shoved his bowler back on his forehead. "We turned away a few couples from the area, but it'll take a day or so to get her settled." His brow furrowed. "She needs a place now."

Charles had an idea, one that nagged at him. As a member of the committee, finding someone to take care of the child had to be his first consideration, even if that someone owned half the paper. Still, no one would be more conscientious than Adelaide Crum. He had an even stronger conviction she'd be a good mother—even if her own mother had ruined his family.

Is it my fault I'm Adam Graves's son?

The truth zinged through him. No, no more than Adelaide could be held accountable for the hell Charles called home. He took a deep, cleansing breath. "How about asking Miss Crum?"

"Hmm." Sparks pursed his lips in thought. "Well,

her recent apology exemplifies her character. What do you think, Thaddeus?"

Paul frowned. "Can't we find a *married* woman?"

"None of us has time to deal with this," Sparks said, his tone exasperated. "Miss Crum is right across the street. The arrangement isn't permanent, so I have no problem with it."

Paul shoved his glasses higher on his nose. "That would be the easiest solution."

"Then it's settled, if she's willing," Sparks said, his gaze sweeping Charles's face, then Paul's. They all nodded.

"Who's going to ask her?" Sparks plopped his hat back in place. "I shouldn't be away from the bank."

Already heading for the door, Paul turned back. "I need to get back to the office, too. Can you see to it, Charles?"

He'd done the least legwork for the committee so it was only fair he ask Miss Crum. His wayward pulse leapt at the prospect of seeing her, giving her this news. Nodding his acceptance, he walked the men into the main room and out the door, both obviously relieved to dump the matter in his lap.

Charles grabbed his coat and shrugged it on. Without a doubt, Miss Crum would take care of Emma. But the more he thought about it, the more he suspected that once she had a taste of mothering, she'd be starved for more when the child left.

What had he been thinking when he suggested her?

He'd been thinking how she'd look when she heard the news, the sparkle his words would put into her clear blue eyes. He'd taken part in hurting her, both with the committee and now over the ownership of the paper, and he wanted to make amends.

Grateful for Teddy's experience with children, Charles said, "Keep an eye on Emma, will you?"

With a grin, Teddy hunkered down beside the little girl. "Sure thing, if she'll share a peppermint with me."

Charles strode to the door, knowing he danced dangerously close to a web of entanglements. Every instinct warned him off, told him to stay clear of Miss Crum, while every muscle and tendon in his body moved him out of the office and across the street.

Adelaide knotted the end of the thread and then snipped it. Earlier, she'd watched Frances leave *The Ledger* without Emma. She'd wanted to call out to Frances, to ask what was going on, but her classmate's slumped posture had kept Adelaide silent. Clearly, something had happened, but what? And what part did Mr. Graves play?

His last words rattled through her mind, ...*expecting this business relationship to be pleasurable, you're mistaken...buy you out...longest two months of your life.*

He'd failed to see she couldn't fix the past, especially a past she hadn't shared. She couldn't even fix her own problems.

He detested the idea of her involvement at the paper, but she didn't have time to run her shop and work at the paper, too. Still, as part owner of *The Ledger,* she *could* have a voice. Express some important ideas. Maybe make a difference for the women in town. That much she could—and would—do. Whether Charles Graves liked it or not.

The bell jingled bringing Adelaide to her feet. Mr.

Graves, his expression solemn, walked to the counter where she waited, her pulse tap-dancing in her temples. If he had come here to berate her mother, she wouldn't listen.

He met her gaze. "I'm glad we're alone. We need to talk."

Adelaide hadn't realized she'd been holding her breath until it came out in a gust. "About you hating the sight of me?"

He had the decency to look discomfited. "I don't." He drew in a breath. "I'm sorry about my outburst. I realized a truth earlier. You can't help that you're Constance Gunder's daughter, any more than I can help being Charles Graves's son." He plowed a hand through his thick hair, leaving furrows deep enough to plant seed in. "I've been a bear. Will you forgive me?"

Adelaide saw something wounded and raw in his eyes, telling her Mr. Graves had suffered. "I forgive you." She smiled. "But you're right, you were a bear."

"Maybe you'll be happier with me when you hear the main reason I've come." He took a step closer, his brown eyes filling with light. "Mrs. Drummond isn't well and needs someone to look after Emma Grounds. The committee thought of you."

She pressed a hand to her heart, for surely if she didn't, it would leap from her chest. Never in her wildest dreams had she considered this possibility. "Emma, come *here*? To live with *me*?"

"Yes." The corners of his eyes crinkled with a grin.

Why? Why had the committee given her this chance? Then she knew. *Thank you, God.* "It's an answer to prayer."

He frowned. "It's the committee's doing, not God's."

She shook her head, a smile riding her lips. "Oh, Mr. Graves, you have a lot to learn about the power of prayer." But she wouldn't worry about that now, not when she had a child to love. Oh, maybe two. "What about William?"

"Mr. Drummond is looking after him." Charles lowered his head and looked her straight in the eye. "You understand this arrangement is *only* until Mrs. Drummond gets back on her feet?"

Adelaide came around the counter. "Of course."

His eyes narrowed. "Do you? Really?"

"Yes, yes!" For however long He willed it, Adelaide was going to treasure this gift from God. The possibilities raced through her mind—sharing meals with Emma, reading her bedtime stories and teaching her to sew. Adelaide's breath came in gulps and her lungs expanded until they felt ready to explode. "When will she arrive?"

"Is now convenient?" A grin curved across his face.

"Yes! Oh, thank you!" In a second of wild abandon, Adelaide threw her arms around him, giving him a fierce hug. His torso felt hard and wide, masculine. A realization struck—she'd never hugged a man before, nor acted so impetuously. Heat climbing her cheeks, she stepped back. "I shouldn't have done that, Mr. Graves."

He moved closer, until the warmth of his breath drifted along her chin. "No need to apologize. And please, after that hug, I think you should call me Charles."

"Charles." She tasted the sound of it on her tongue. "Will you...call me Adelaide?" A forward suggestion, but given the circumstances, it felt right.

His gaze swallowed her up, left her breathless.

"Instead, may I call you Addie?"

"Addie?" No one had ever given her a nickname or a pet name before. It made her feel special. Her hand drifted to her chignon, fussing with it like an old maid. She quickly lowered her hand to her side.

"If you don't like it—"

"Oh, but I do." To her, Adelaide sounded like a hair-up kind of woman, while Addie seemed like a hair-down kind of gal. The kind of woman she'd always wanted to be.

"Then Addie is what I'll call you."

She smiled, feeling feminine, alive and—oh, my—cherished.

To keep her hands from straying to him, she clasped them together. For now, she'd focus on Emma. She, Adelaide Crum, would be taking care of the little girl she'd sensed a kinship with from the first moment she'd seen her.

"Emma's waiting in my office. I'll bring her to you."

"I'd like to get her myself."

He looked around the showroom, empty of customers. "Can you leave the shop?"

In answer to his question, she walked to the door, lowered the shade and flipped the sign in the window to read CLOSED. Dusting her palms together, she grinned. "I'm the boss."

Charles chuckled. Adelaide joined in.

Filled with gratitude to God, she did something totally out of character, something she hadn't done since a little girl. Hiking her skirts to keep them from snaring her feet, she dashed out the door and ran across the street without her hat and gloves.

Chapter Six

Charles caught up with Addie when she stopped in the middle of the street. She glowed with happiness. No doubt about it, the lady was headed for a fall. Especially if she thought this child heaven-sent. When the Drummonds wanted Emma back, how would she cope? How would God answer her prayers then?

She turned to him, a question on her features. "Charles?"

His given name, almost a caress, slipped off her tongue and warmed him. If only he could forget what stood between them. A dozen issues separated him from Addie. Her mother had destroyed his family. She held beliefs he hadn't shared since his childhood prayers had gone unanswered. She had needs he couldn't meet.

And he was his father's son.

A warning shout made Charles jerk to the right in time to see a team of horses barreling down on them. His stomach in his throat, he scooped Addie up in his arms and dashed for the safety of the walk, barely escaping the hooves. The wagon rattled past, kicking up dust; the driver raised his fist at them, shouting obscenities.

But with Addie cradled in his arms, fitting in the niche as if she belonged, Charles barely noticed. He quickly set her on her feet. She tugged at her clothing, her face flushed.

She splayed shaky fingers across her bosom. "Whew, that was close!" She gave him a weak smile. "Thank you, Charles."

He grinned. "The pleasure was mine."

"Before you rescued me, I started to say—the committee didn't suggest me. You did." She laid a hand on his sleeve. "Am I right?"

Charles nodded.

Tears filled her eyes. "Thank you again."

"You're welcome." Those eyes would be his undoing. He pulled his gaze away and cleared his throat, motioning toward the door of the paper. "Before we go in, I want to warn you Emma is upset. Mrs. Drummond's misery may be affecting her."

"Could be. Suicide has to be far worse than any natural death. I went to school and to church with Frances, so I knew her mother well. Sarah Hartman was a good woman."

Charles glanced over at the trim figure beside him, with her straight posture and youthful glow. "Mrs. Drummond looks old, worn down. I can't believe you two are the same age."

"Farm life must have taken a toll on her, or maybe it's that grouchy husband of hers."

He raised a brow. "You're very outspoken."

"Well, it's true, though I doubt her husband is the entire cause. I can't imagine losing a child." She paused, sympathy taking over her gaze. "Eddie's death had to cost Frances more than hard work or a disagreeable spouse ever could."

"I'm sure you're right." He wouldn't gain favor by harping on it, but the mention of Mrs. Drummond's lost child hammered home the need to warn Addie about the brevity of Emma's stay. "I'm concerned about your taking in Emma."

"Are you saying I'm not competent to care for a seven-year-old child, even for a while?"

He heard the irritation in her voice, the underlying pain of what she perceived as doubt. "Of course not, but when Emma returns to the Drummonds, there's a good chance you'll be hurt."

Adelaide pulled her arm from his grasp. "I'm a grown woman, Mr. Graves. Your concern is touching, but unwarranted. Besides, this is part of God's plan. I'm sure of it." She moved toward the door. "If you're finished, I'd like to get Emma settled."

Charles noted her formal address, the sharpness in her tone. She had every right to be annoyed. He'd suggested her, had dashed over to tell her and then had ruined the moment. "Addie."

She turned back, her expression cool.

"Emma's fortunate indeed to have you to look after her."

Her features softened and a smile crept across her face, lighting up her eyes. "Thank you, Charles."

Her grin touched his heart, tempting him to forget all those reasons he shouldn't get involved, but sanity reigned and he walked her to the door of *The Ledger*.

Inside the office, they found Emma rocking in his desk chair. With eyes closed, head lolling against the slats, her wide grin revealed two missing teeth. While he and Addie watched, the chair slowed and Emma's eyes popped open. Her gaze darted from Addie to Charles and the smile faded.

Addie knelt beside her. "I'm Adelaide Crum. I remember the day you came to town." She motioned to the chair. "Is that fun?"

The little girl's head bobbed.

"Do you suppose I could have a turn?"

Emma hesitated and then scooted to the side, making room.

"I won't fit, but if you sat on my lap, we could both rock."

Charles's jaw fell open when Emma hopped down and climbed into Adelaide's lap. Soon, she and Emma giggled in the swaying chair, with its spring squealing, the awkwardness of their meeting forgotten. Watching them, something tightened in Charles's chest. How long since he'd heard joy like that?

Stored deep in his memory lived shrieks of terror, sobs and groans—the sounds of his childhood. Charles bit the inside of his cheek, fighting for control, mourning the loss of something he'd never had. Happiness. True happiness.

Pain came in many forms. Charles had thought he'd experienced them all. He'd put them behind him—or so he'd thought. Yet, deep inside he knew he hadn't let go of the past. How could he, when the past lived in him still?

He saw the hope—the faith—in Adelaide Crum and wondered how anyone could have such a thing.

Adelaide brought the chair to a halt. Leaning her chin atop Emma's head, she mouthed a thank-you, widening the crack in Charles's heart. Suddenly, he didn't want their time together to end. "Would you ladies like to walk to the livery to see my horse? We can drop Emma's satchel at the shop first."

Emma bounced off Adelaide's lap. "The livery!"

Addie rose and knelt before the little girl. "Let's get you settled in. We can visit the livery another time."

Emma sighed and gave a sad nod.

Addie studied Emma's rag-doll posture, then chucked her under the chin. "Getting settled can wait."

A look of surprise took over Emma's face, and then slid into a smile.

Charles grabbed a handful of sugar cubes from a bowl near the potbellied stove. "Let's take Ranger a treat."

Emma's hand darted out, palm cupped, and Charles dumped the sugar into it.

Emma beamed. "Ranger is a nice name."

Adelaide took Emma's free hand and Charles offered Adelaide his arm. When she slipped her hand into the bend, she looked up at him, her expression happy, grateful and full of optimism. The idea he could have a family ricocheted through him. He quickly dismissed the notion. He resolved to keep things impersonal, as he always had, but something sharp panged in his chest.

As Adelaide stepped inside the dim, cavernous stable, dust motes floated in the sunlight streaming through the open doorway. The pungent odor of manure and hay filled her nostrils. A horse nickered in a nearby stall, raising the fine hair on her nape. With Emma skipping at her side, Adelaide followed Charles to a stall midway down the aisle. He opened the door and led out a huge brown horse. Adelaide took a step back.

"Ladies, meet Ranger," he said, tying the horse to a post.

Emma gazed at Charles, a look of pure awe on her face. "Ranger's your very own horse?"

Charles grinned down at the little girl. "Yes, he is."

Watching them at a distance, tenderness for this child and this man filled her heart. Then the huge creature shook his head and stomped his hooves, rattling the floorboards—and Adelaide.

"I love horses." Emma patted Ranger's wide back.

"Hold out your hand," Charles said, demonstrating, "flat like a board, so he can see what you've got for him."

When Ranger's lips curled around the treats, Emma gasped, then giggled. "That tickles!"

Charles slipped out of his coat, hanging it on a nearby peg. "Would you like to help groom Ranger, Emma?"

In minutes, Emma teetered on a crate, clutching a brush bigger than both her hands. Charles showed her how to hold it, laying his large hand over Emma's much smaller one, helping her move the brush down the animal's coat.

When he stepped away, leaving Emma to do the job, Adelaide reminded herself not to trust this happy scene. Not to trust Charles. Oh, but the pull to do so wrapped its tentacles around her and squeezed.

Emma made long strokes, then shorter ones until the animal's coat gleamed. She looked at Adelaide over her shoulder. "Don't you want to brush Ranger, Miss Crum?"

Charles glanced at her. "Yes, Addie, don't you?"

A lump the size of a melon formed in her belly. She'd been ten when she'd tumbled from a horse, breaking her leg and nearly getting her head stomped by the hooves. She'd steered clear of horses ever since.

Adelaide looked into two pair of eyes—one pair dancing with excitement, the other issuing a challenge. With God's help, she'd show this man her strength, her ability to overcome her fear, to be an example of courage to this child.

Raising her chin, she approached the horse gingerly, edging her hand closer. The huge animal raised a hoof, slammed it down, stalling Adelaide's hand midair. Ranger's dark brown tail swished at the flies pestering its hindquarters. Sucking in a gulp of air, she again reached a palm. The horse snorted. She withdrew.

Charles took Adelaide's hand and led her closer. "There's nothing to fear."

Oh, but she knew differently. And it wasn't only the four-legged animal in front of her.

Emma handed Adelaide the brush, leaving her little choice. "Here, Miss Adelaide!"

Charles sent her a gentle look of encouragement. "No rush. A big animal like Ranger takes getting used to."

Adelaide lifted her chin. She'd show him Adelaide Crum had courage. She laid the brush against Ranger's side, slowly moving the tool downward, careful not to press hard. Beneath the bristles the flesh on the horse's belly quivered, but Ranger didn't move.

Emma laughed. "Look! He's ticklish!"

Charles patted Emma's shoulder. "So he is. Maybe it's Miss Crum's touch."

Adelaide ran the brush along Ranger's back and once

again down his sides, then stood back and cocked her head at Charles.

"This is fun!" Emma's eyes danced with delight. "Let's visit Ranger every day."

"I know Ranger would love seeing two such pretty ladies." He turned back to Adelaide, eyes gleaming with mischief. "Now that wasn't so bad, was it?"

"No, he's a beautiful animal."

Charles ran a hand along Ranger's dark brown mane. "He's alone too much. That's not good for a horse."

"That's not good for anyone," Adelaide said quietly.

Charles, looking eager to put distance between them, hurried to put the brush away, then led Ranger to his stall and secured the door.

Fine, she didn't want to get involved with a man. Not even this one. She knew firsthand the pain a man could cause. Her father had left her mother, hadn't cared enough to see his daughter again, not even once, as if she were unworthy, unlovable. With God's help she'd become strong, able to stand on her own two feet, all without a man.

So why had she accepted Charles's supper invitation? Loneliness. The answer tore through her, forcing her to take a steadying breath. No amount of hard work, praying or sharing with friends could fill the empty spot inside her.

Charles returned and the three of them stepped outside. Emma ran to the hay mound and then sent a questioning glance over her shoulder.

Adelaide nodded approval. "Go on. That looks like fun."

Emma flung an armful of hay into the air, squealing as it showered down on her upturned face. Grabbing more, she tossed it at Charles, the pieces scattering at his feet. Laughing, he scooped up an arsenal and chased after her. Emma raced behind Adelaide's skirts, at the exact moment Charles tossed the hay.

When the itching strands hit her face, Adelaide yelped, the fun, the sheer freedom of it leaping in her chest. "You're going to be sorry!" She ran toward the hay mound for ammunition.

"Oh, no you don't." Charles dove after her, tugging her down on the hay.

Suddenly he stopped, gazing down at her. With his face only inches away, close enough to touch, close enough to kiss, she froze, her breath caught in her throat.

Even she, a woman who knew nothing of men, recognized longing in his eyes, in the tiny specks of gold in their depths.

"Here I come, ready or not!" Emma tumbled down, pelting them with fistfuls of hay.

Charles and Adelaide sprang apart, the mood broken. For a split second, she'd forgotten Emma and exposed her to unseemly behavior. Thankfully, Emma didn't appear to have noticed.

Charles's gaze shifted to Emma. His hand shot out and tickled her.

The little girl shrieked and scrambled out of his reach, tossing more hay their way. "You can't get me!"

"I will. Just wait." Charles jumped to his feet, and then pulled Adelaide up after him. "Are you all right?"

"Yes." Adelaide's world tipped off balance. Since she'd met Charles, her tidy life had turned upside down, inside out. Her inhibitions had crumbled, as well, turning her into someone carefree and full of life—Addie, the hair-down woman.

Charles took off after Emma and scooped her up. "I'm too fast for you, Emma," he teased, swinging her in front of him.

When he turned to Adelaide with a grinning Emma nestled on his arms, both looking more like scarecrows than themselves, Adelaide ached to enfold them in her arms. Maybe then, she would find the sense of family she'd been looking for her entire life. But she had no trust to give.

Emma burst out laughing, pointing first at Adelaide, then at Charles. "You look funny!" she crowed.

Charles bounced her on his arms, sending pieces of straw fluttering to the ground. "No funnier than you, cupcake."

The little girl giggled. "I'm not cupcake. I'm Emma!"

Charles put Emma down, grabbed a pitchfork leaning against the side of the stable and repaired the mound. Adelaide brushed hay from Emma's hair, then from their shoulders and skirts.

"Can I climb on the fence?" Emma said.

Adelaide nodded and Emma raced off. Charles crossed to her side. "You missed some." With gentle fingers, he pulled strands from her hair. She couldn't meet his gaze.

Adelaide's chignon had pulled loose, and her clothing was in disarray, totally unlike her finicky nature. "Thank you."

Charles tucked a loose curl behind her ear, the movement of his hands sweet and tender. "You're a mess."

Adelaide's hands flew to her hair, but he clasped them in his, stopping her. "I like you that way."

Their gazes locked; her mouth went dry.

What if someone had seen their silliness in the hay? If so, the committee might hear of it and take Emma. Hands shaking, she tugged the hairpins from her hair and pulled it into a knot, securing a proper demeanor right along with it. "I apologize. Our behavior wasn't suitable."

With a curt nod, he took a step back. "We'd best be going."

Adelaide called to the little girl a few feet away. "Emma, Mr. Graves and I need to get back to work."

With Emma chattering between them, they sauntered down the walk. A robin, with a morsel in its beak, swooped into the leafy branches of the tree they passed, silencing frantic chirping coming from an unseen nest. The scent of fresh-mown grass carried on the breeze. The beauty of the day and Emma's contented expression restored Adelaide's serenity.

Until Mrs. Willowby, the feather on her hat bobbing in rhythm with her stride, headed toward them, holding the hand of the little orphan boy. "I'd like you to meet our Ben," Mrs. Willowby said, her tone laced with pride.

Ben ducked behind his mother's skirts, then peeked around.

Adelaide smiled. "Hello, Ben. Do you remember Emma?"

Mrs. Willowby's gaze roamed over them. "My, don't the three of you look like a family?"

Charles took a step over, separating himself from the two of them, from the image.

Adelaide kept walking, tugging Emma along with her. "Have a good day, Mrs. Willowby. You, too, Ben."

Once they were out of hearing distance, Adelaide slowed the pace. Emma was coming home with her. The thought sung through her. Nothing Mrs. Willowby could say could change that fact.

"Ben looked happy." Emma sighed. "I wish we were a family, like that lady said. Then William could come live with us."

Charles squatted down beside Emma. "You have a family, the Drummonds. Don't you like living with them?"

Emma shook her head.

Charles chucked Emma under the chin. "Why not?"

Adelaide held her breath and waited for Emma's answer, hope rising and falling in her chest like the bobber on a fishing line. But Emma shook off Charles's hand and ran off to examine a rock alongside the road.

Charles nodded toward Emma. "She's a great little girl. Everything delights and fascinates her. She gives me a new view on the world, a world I've tended to see through jaded eyes."

"Jaded? Why?"

A shadow passed over his face and he looked away. "Nothing specific, simply some of the things I've seen."

"Saturday's dinner invitation didn't include Emma," she said. "Perhaps we should cancel our plans." At the prospect, disappointment ached inside her and she hoped he would disagree.

His gaze went to her. "No," he said, the word echoing with finality. "I don't want to cancel."

He held out his arm. Adelaide hesitated, and then slipped her hand through the crook. He drew her close, his hand resting lightly on hers. Adelaide's stomach hadn't rolled like this since she'd won the county spelling bee in the eighth grade.

"It'll be fun to take Emma to a restaurant," Charles said.

"A restaurant?" Emma had rejoined them, a small, smooth rock cradled in one hand. "I've never eaten in a restaurant before."

Charles smiled. "Then it's time you did."

Adoration filled Emma's gaze. Did Charles have any idea how much he mattered to Emma?

They parted ways, Emma and Adelaide to the shop and Charles back to the paper. Despite her resolve, Adelaide missed him already. She sighed. If only she could get inside his head, understand his thoughts. Like a locked door, she had hints of what was on the other side, but until the door opened, she couldn't be sure.

She'd have to find the key. No, better to leave that door locked. Opening her heart to a man would only lead to heartbreak.

Chapter Seven

Inside Charles's office, the noisy newspaper was down-right quiet compared to his afternoon with the gregarious seven-year-old girl. Still, he knew Emma's absence hadn't brought this sense of emptiness. He wanted to be with Addie. Too much. He felt split down the middle, with one side, the rational side, telling him to run the opposite direction, while the other side hungered to see Miss Crum, to savor her goodness. But he didn't dare.

Not when a monster crouched inside him.

People said he looked like his father. When he shaved, his father's face looked back at him—the public face his father wore in town. Charles could still remember his father's gentle touch as he'd run his fingers through Charles's hair during church service. When Adam Graves wasn't drinking, he'd been an affectionate man and Charles had loved him with all his being.

But the years passed and his father drank more and more, quoting Scripture and beating his family. Many a Sunday following a thrashing with a razor strap the day before, Charles and Sam had sat cautiously in the pew. Until the time when Adam quit attending church and his family saw only his private face—that of a man filled with hate.

His father appeared in his mind's eye, as plain as if he stood before him. Lips curled in a snarl, eyes bulging with rage, mouth spewing curses, veins bulging in his neck mere seconds before he'd start hitting. The sounds of fists meeting flesh ricocheted through him with such vividness Charles discerned the familiar metallic taste of blood upon his tongue.

Unseen fingers closed around his windpipe, suffocating him until bile rose in Charles's throat. He leapt from his chair and dashed for the privacy of the alley.

Teddy blocked Charles's exit. "You all right, boss?"

"Don't you have enough to do around here besides poking your nose in my business?" Charles growled, sidestepping him.

In the alley, with sweat beading his forehead, Charles leaned against the brick and struggled to slow his breathing. *Inhale. Exhale. Inhale.*

But childhood memories continued to slam into him with the same brutal force his father had used to subdue his family.

Until the worst memory of all exploded in his brain with such power he could no longer resist—the memory of *that* night.

Even all these years later, Charles could not forgive himself.

He'd better get a grip on his life, on his mind. He had a business to run, Sam's family to help.

Yet, his hands balled at his sides. Adam Graves had been the reason his brother drank. If Sam hadn't been in that barroom brawl, he'd be alive today. Sam had inherited the family legacy of bitterness, distrust and booze.

Wiping his brow, Charles took in a gulp of air. He couldn't change the past but he could leave it there, far from the present, far from everything he'd worked hard to gain.

But images from that night popped up again and again, released by the reading of his father's will and the insane hope he could have a normal life.

Blocking thoughts of Addie, thoughts tempting him to indulge in the fantasy of a family, Charles pushed away from the brick and started inside. After dinner on Saturday, he'd make no more plans with Miss Crum. He wouldn't open her to the pain and anguish of his past, wouldn't taint her pretty world.

From the shop window, Adelaide glanced at *The Ledger*. That simple act set her heart humming. She brushed her fingertips across her lips, reliving the almost-kiss in the haystack. Charles Graves had feelings for her, but only a foolish woman would believe those feelings involved a future. He didn't want that any more than she did.

For now, God had given her Emma, bringing joy into her life. She'd be the best mother she could be. And make sure Charles noticed at supper. If Frances couldn't care for Emma, then surely Charles would support her with the committee.

She turned away from the window and watched Emma roam the showroom, examining the array of adorned hats, captivated by the fruit, plumes and flowers.

Adelaide joined her at the display. "Want to try on a hat?"

Emma beamed. "Could I?"

Adelaide lifted a bonnet from the stand, the one she'd visualized Emma wearing that day in the shop, the same day Laura had bullied her into placing an ad, bringing Charles into her life, and through him, Emma. *I owe Laura a new hat.* With damp eyes, she placed the bonnet on Emma's head. "I designed this especially for a young lady like you."

Checking her reflection in the mirror, Emma's eyes sparkled. "Oh, it's pretty!"

Amazing how the proper hat affected a female's outlook, no matter her age. "It's perfect for you." Adelaide tied the pink ribbons under Emma's chin. "You must have it."

"I don't have any money."

Adelaide cupped Emma's chin in her hand. "It's a present."

Emma's mouth drooped. "It's not my birthday."

"The best presents are given for no reason."

"I can keep it, even when I go back to the Drummonds?"

The reminder tinged the day with a touch of gray but Adelaide shook off the feeling. Emma wasn't going back for days, maybe weeks. God had a plan. "Yes, and I'll make a bonnet for Mrs. Drummond, too. Would you like to help?"

"Yes!"

Adelaide smiled and then checked the clock on the wall. "It's getting late. That will have to wait until another day."

Emma folded her thin arms. "I don't want to wait."

"You can help me fix dinner. Do you like fried chicken?"

The little girl nodded, her petulance gone. "Yum!"

The tension in Adelaide's shoulders eased, relieved Emma's stomach tempered her apparent strong will. She picked up the satchel and with Emma scampering up the stairs beside her, explained the shop hours.

"I can sell lots of hats," Emma predicted with confidence.

"Perhaps, but you'll have homework to do."

Emma wrinkled her nose. "I don't like homework."

Adelaide's stomach clenched. Would this be a daily battle? She'd always loved her lessons. "Is the work hard for you?"

Emma's gaze sought the floor. "Mama got sick and William and I didn't go to school. The girls in my grade can read better than me, but I don't care. Who needs to read anyway?"

Adelaide tilted Emma's chin. "If I couldn't read, I couldn't run the shop. You'll catch up. I'll help."

Taking her hand, Adelaide led Emma to what had been her mother's room. A resplendent rainbow-hued quilt covered the double bed. White ruffled curtains crisp with starch adorned the window. How had her mother been gloomy, awakening in such a cheerful room?

From the satchel, Emma retrieved a rag doll, mended and clean with a stitched jolly smile and button eyes. After tucking her doll against the pillows, Emma danced around the room, inspecting each nook and cranny. Seeing Emma chasing out the shadows of her mother's illness brought happy tears to Adelaide's eyes.

Adelaide tucked the little girl's things in an empty dresser drawer and then gave a tour of the rest of the rooms, including her own.

"Your room is smaller than mine," Emma said with the candor of a child. "But it's pretty."

"Thank you. My grandmother made the quilts. She knew how to use a needle. Guess I take after her." Adelaide sat on the bed, patting a spot beside her. Emma joined her, sitting up close. "This quilt pattern is called Ocean Wave. See how the blocks look like the sea?" Emma traced a finger around a triangle-shaped snippet of navy fabric.

Adelaide had started sewing doll clothes when she'd been about Emma's age. She'd teach Emma some basic stitches. Together they'd make a dress for her doll. Adelaide had so many plans.

Taking Emma by the hand, they walked into the parlor. Emma stepped between two chairs to look at the pictures arranged on the marble-topped pedestal table.

Emma pointed to a daguerreotype. "Is this your mother?"

"Yes, and those are my grandparents."

Emma looked around her. "Where's your papa's picture?"

"I… I don't have one."

"Did he run away, like my papa?"

"Yes, I guess you could say that."

Emma considered this for a moment, her face sober, as if trying to figure out something Adelaide had never understood.

Emma saw the upright piano and brightened.

"If you'd like, I could teach you some simple songs."

"You know how to do a lot, Miss Adelaide."

After years of criticism, the remark slid into the marrow of Adelaide's bones and she gave the little girl's hand a squeeze. "Why, thank you."

In the kitchen, Adelaide heated leftover fried chicken and potato cakes while Emma set the table. At dinner, Emma ate heartily, leaving some crumbs under her chair. They established a pattern for their future evenings, however many there might be. While Emma completed her homework at the kitchen table, Adelaide cleaned up the dishes, helping with schoolwork only if asked.

Emma asked for a pencil and paper, then hunched over it, working feverishly. Soon, she folded the paper and smiled up at Adelaide. "I made you something."

Adelaide's eyes stung. "You made something—for me?"

Emma unfolded the paper and smoothed it flat. "A picture!"

Adelaide stepped behind her to get a better view. Four figures drawn with a childish hand stood outside a house. A tree grew alongside. A smiling sun hung in the sky. "Who are they?"

"That's William," she said pointing to the figure dressed in pants. "That's me." She indicated the shortest figure in a skirt. "This is you, and this is Mrs. Drummond."

All the faces sported big smiles. Adelaide couldn't have been more pleased with an original Rembrandt. "That's a lovely picture. Thank you." She patted Emma's hand and the little girl beamed. "Where's Mr. Drummond?"

Emma's smile turned to a frown. "I don't like him."

"Why?"

"He yells and stuff."

Adelaide knelt in front of Emma. "What do you mean?"

"I wish he'd run away like my papa and your papa," she muttered, smoothing the drawing again and again with her hand.

Though Adelaide tried to find out more, Emma only shrugged, putting up an invisible wall to Adelaide's quest for answers.

"Can I play the piano?" Emma asked.

Adelaide led the little girl to the parlor. They sat side by side on the bench as Adelaide guided Emma's fingers to play "Mary Had a Little Lamb."

The clock struck half past nine. "Oh, my! Time for bed."

Emma pounded the keys. "Mama let me stay up really late."

"That's probably because you weren't going to school."

"I don't want to go to school." Emma's gaze sparked defiance. "You can't make me."

Adelaide sucked in a gulp of air, unsure how to handle Emma's challenge. But then the Bible's admonition for children to obey their parents stiffened her backbone. "I like having you here," Adelaide said, "but while you're in my house, you'll do as I ask." Then she gave Emma a bright smile. "Let's get you ready for bed."

Though Emma's chin hung to her chest, she followed Adelaide to the bedroom. Later, the conflict forgotten, Emma nestled under the covers, embracing her doll as Adelaide read from her childhood Bible storybook, then listened to her prayers.

"Good night, Miss Adelaide," Emma said, yawning.

Looking at Emma's sweet face, a coil of warmth slid through Adelaide and she kissed her cheek. "Sleep tight," she said, slipping out of the room.

Adelaide had never been part of a real family and now it was within her grasp. She would give Emma attention, hugs and kisses, things she'd never had growing up, for as long as God granted her this gift.

Her mind flitted to Charles. If only—

She didn't dare finish the thought. She'd always been careful what she hoped for, the only way to avoid heartache.

She would savor this moment, not looking forward or back, because she was the happiest she'd ever been in her life, right now, in the present. God had given her this precious girl, and she'd be forever grateful. Forever changed. In a matter of hours, Emma had become firmly entrenched in her heart.

In the middle of the night, something jolted Adelaide awake. She heard Emma crying. She leapt out of bed and raced down the hall to find the little girl thrashing about in bed. Adelaide sank to the mattress beside her and laid a gentle hand on Emma's forehead. No fever. Probably a bad dream.

Adelaide stroked her palm across Emma's temples, offering comfort, until the little girl's breathing slowed and her body relaxed. She remained several minutes longer to ensure Emma would not awaken, and then tiptoed back to her bed.

But sleep eluded her. Could Emma be missing her real mother or William? Or were there other nightmares an orphaned seven-year-old might have, agonizing dreams Adelaide couldn't even begin to imagine? A nagging sense of doubt planted itself in her midsection. What if she couldn't give Emma comfort and security?

Scrunching her pillow, Adelaide recalled years of craving the simplest touch and a kind word. She'd give

Emma what she'd missed growing up. After all, she had hugs in abundance and limitless love to share. She prayed that would be enough.

The next morning motherhood required every ounce of Adelaide's patience. Emma dawdled at breakfast and dressed with the slowness of a tortoise. Thankfully, they reached Second Ward School, a few blocks away, right as the bell rang. Adelaide explained the situation to the teacher and then hurried home, vowing tomorrow would go more smoothly.

Adelaide made Emma's bed, then walked to the kitchen and poured steaming water from the teakettle into a dishpan. As she scrubbed the dishes, she remembered where she'd seen this kind of disarray. She'd been eight, when her mother, sick with influenza, sent Adelaide to stay with Winifred Cook's family. Disorder reigned in the Cook household, but Winnie's parents tucked the children into bed with a prayer and a kiss. What a revelation to discover not all children lived in a neat but silent house.

For weeks after returning home, Adelaide's skin ached to be touched. She'd tried to keep the warm feeling by stroking her arms and hugging herself, but it hadn't been the same. Cleanliness was next to godliness, or so her mother said, but neatness wasn't important to children.

Maybe Adelaide needed a little disorder in her very tidy life, too. Hadn't Charles hinted at that yesterday?

The clock struck ten. Adelaide jumped. *Fiddlesticks, I'm late.* She finished wiping the dishes and then raced downstairs. As the clock struck a quarter after the hour, she grabbed the broom, flipped over the sign in the window and opened the door.

She'd no more than stepped onto the boardwalk when Charles appeared at her elbow in shirtsleeves and vest. "Is everything all right, Addie?"

At the sight of him, delicious warmth spread through her and the morning's tension vanished. "Why would you think it wasn't?"

"Why?" He lowered his face to hers, brown eyes dark under knitted brows. "In the three months I've been at the paper, I could set my watch by when you came outside toting that broom. Exactly five minutes before ten, every morning." He stuck his pocket watch in front of her. "It's now twenty minutes after ten, Addie. *Twenty minutes.* That tells me something's wrong."

Gracious, Charles knows exactly when I make my appearance on the walk every morning. He's been fretting about me.

As far as she knew, no man had ever worried about her. Speechless, her hand splayed across her bosom.

Charles dropped the watch into his pocket. "Is it Emma?"

"Is what Emma?"

"Adelaide Crum, you can be the most exasperating woman. Is something wrong with Emma?"

"She's fine and in school. We were running late." She gripped the handle of the broom, smiling up at him. "I had no idea you're such a worrier, Charles."

He harrumphed. "I'm not, but this *was* your first day with Emma. Naturally I'd wonder how you two were managing. Then you're late, ridiculously late—"

"Twenty minutes is not ridiculously late. Why, I've seen you darting into the newspaper at half past eight."

A sheepish look came over his face. "Here, let me do that," he said, taking the broom from her hands. "You probably have things to do to open the shop."

"Well, thank you." Adelaide walked inside, but didn't dust the counter, didn't wash the windowpane. Instead, she stood transfixed, watching Charles's muscles as he pushed that broom like a madman.

A desirable, intelligent man cared enough about her to worry, to take a burden from her shoulders.

Like a husband would.

The thought took her breath away, zinging a feeling of hope through her, hope for a husband, and hope for children. She shoved it down. She had no claim to Charles, no need of a man. She took care of herself. And if God willed, she could take care of a child, too.

But oh, for a moment, she wanted to believe in the fantasy.

Charles appeared in her doorway and held out the broom. As she took it, their fingertips brushed. He yanked his hand away as if he'd been burned. "I'd, ah, better get back to the paper."

"Thank you for…" But she couldn't go on. She dared not voice the thoughts filling her heart. *Thank you for noticing, for caring, for making me feel like a woman.*

He turned to leave, then swung back to face her. Adelaide wanted to lean against his broad chest, to feel those strong arms around her, but she looked away, lest he read the longing in her eyes.

"Well, good day, then," he said.

He crossed the street, moving out of her reach, leaving her standing there, heart pumping wildly.

What had gotten into her? She couldn't trust these fierce feelings. Even her parents must have had attraction…for a while. Her mother constantly drilled fear of abandonment into her, honing her skill at keeping her emotions locked inside.

Until she met Charles.

She hurried to the window and caught a glimpse of his retreating back. Optimism rose up within her. Could Charles be part of God's plan for her?

Chapter Eight

On Saturday night, precisely at six, Charles stood in Adelaide's shop, basking in her smile, a smile that told him the ownership of the paper hadn't built an insurmountable barrier between them. Emma smiled at him, too, looking confident and happy. Not at all the weepy little girl Mrs. Drummond had brought to him.

He knelt in front of her. "My, don't you look pretty."

"See my new hat?" The little girl twirled, sending the pink ribbons under her chin flying.

"Very attractive." He rose and turned to Addie. Her dazzling indigo eyes sparkled.

Bending down, Addie gave Emma a kiss on the cheek. "You look prettier than irises in springtime, sweetie."

Emma rose on tiptoe and kissed Addie's cheek. With a palm, Addie caressed the spot. Her damp eyes met Charles's and her wordless thanks clutched at his heart.

Planting a fist on her hip, Emma eyed him. "You think Miss Adelaide looks pretty?"

Color dotted Addie's cheeks. "That's not polite, Emma."

The little girl looked baffled. "Why not?"

Addie laid a gentle hand on Emma's cheek. "It's fishing for a compliment and puts Mr. Graves in an awkward position."

Pretty hardly described Addie's softly flushed cheeks, her full lips and the regal tilt to her chin. "Actually, I don't feel the least bit awkward, Emma. Miss Crum looks lovely."

Taking a cue from Addie, Emma took an arm, looking pleased at being treated like a lady. Addie locked the door and took Charles's free arm. As they left the shop, something inside him bubbled like mineral springs in Florida. Something so new, he barely recognized the sensation, but thought it might be akin to joy.

When curious passersby stared at the threesome, greeting them with a questioning air, the feeling ebbed, replaced with a twist of uneasiness. In small towns, people poked their noses in other people's business. He hoped rumors wouldn't take wing and plant the idea he'd be part of a family.

But then he glanced down at Addie, took in her smile and radiant eyes and suddenly it didn't matter what anyone thought. Tonight he'd give her the evening she deserved. He'd let nothing spoil it, not even his disquiet at getting too close.

Charles pushed open the door of the hotel and ushered the ladies inside. The mahogany registration desk gleamed, colorful carpets covered the plank floor and a gas-lit chandelier twinkled overhead. Emma stood openmouthed.

The rotund waiter barreled over. "Mr. Graves, may I seat you by the window?"

"Thank you, Arthur."

Arthur grabbed a stack of menus. "This way, please," he said, leading the way into the dining room.

Charles steered Addie past a few tables occupied by no one he knew. At the window, he pulled out a chair first for her, then for Emma, before taking a seat between them. Arthur handed out huge menus, so large, Emma's hid her from view.

Arthur returned with a water pitcher and filled their glasses. Charles leaned toward the little girl. "That menu is bigger than you are. Here, let me take it before—"

The heavy volume slipped from Emma's fingers, knocking over her glass of water. Charles rose to wipe up the spill with his napkin. Emma cringed, shrinking into her chair.

An instinct flared. Charles *knew* that reflex. "It's all right, accidents happen," he said, his voice soft, without a hint of reprimand.

Surveying the mess, tears filled Emma's eyes.

Addie patted her hand. "No damage done, sweetie."

Arthur mopped off Emma's menu and tucked it under his arm. "It's my fault, miss. The menu is too large for you to manage. I'll get more napkins." He walked toward the kitchen.

Who had punished this child for making a mistake? Had the Drummonds mistreated her, or her own family in New York, or possibly someone at the orphanage? He recognized the signs—the shrinking away, the fear. Or could he be overreacting because of his past? Seeing abuse where none existed?

Adelaide picked up her menu and helped Emma make a selection. Arthur returned and took their order and they all noticeably relaxed.

Adelaide put on a bright smile. "Emma, tell Mr. Graves about our day at the store."

"Miss Crum sold five hats!" Emma boasted. "And..."

But Charles didn't hear what the child said. He couldn't take his eyes from Addie, the glow of her creamy skin and her shimmering eyes reflecting the light from the chandelier overhead.

"Mr. Graves, did you hear?" Emma's impatient voice cut into his thoughts. "Miss Crum sold five hats."

Charles swallowed, struggling to get back into the conversation. "That's good news. I'm, ah, glad the ad helped."

Arthur appeared with a glass of milk for Emma. Soon, the waiter set plates of steaming food before them.

Adelaide bowed her head and whispered a prayer for them all, then took a bite of chicken. "Delicious."

Obviously determined nothing else would go wrong, Emma ate with exaggerated care, wiping her mouth with her napkin whenever Adelaide did. She took small bites and steered clear of her milk; evidently considering the large glass too risky.

But, not nearly as risky as Charles felt it was to spend an evening with Addie. He'd better watch out or he'd start to care about this woman.

Adelaide had trouble keeping her mind on eating and her eyes off her dinner companion, who looked distinguished in a dark suit and crisp white shirt. Even the movements of his hands fascinated her.

Reaching for the salt, their hands brushed each other. She clutched the fork so tightly the tines scraped across the plate.

"Sorry," she said, putting down the fork and laying her trembling hands in her lap. "I finished another fashion column, Charles."

"Good, bring it by."

Then silence as they stared into each other's eyes. She groped for a topic of conversation. "Where did you live before moving here?" she asked, her voice unsteady.

He cut a bite of steak. "In Cincinnati."

"Oh, of course." Feeling foolish to have forgotten, Adelaide took a sip of water to ease the unaccustomed dryness of her mouth. "So you moved here because of *The Ledger?*"

Charles laid down his utensils. "My father asked me to get the paper on solid footing. Owning my own paper has been a dream of mine so I jumped at the chance."

An awkward silence followed. Best to change the subject and seize the opportunity to show him how competent she would be as a mom. Adelaide said, "The shop is my dream. In fact, I plan on teaching Emma how to sew and make hats. Who knows, one day that might lead to some dreams of her own."

"Just watching you run the shop should be an education. Your success is a terrific example for her."

"Thank you," she said, pleased Charles had seen what she could offer Emma.

In companionable silence, they concentrated on their food, but she didn't have much of an appetite. "Compared to Cincinnati, Noblesville is small."

"True, but since my brother's family lives here, I already knew something about the town. And with the state capitol only a few miles away, I had no concern about missing the city." He toyed with his fork. "Not that I've had the time. There's always too much to do at the paper. I suppose it's the same for you."

She nodded. "The shop ties me down. I order supplies through the mail or purchase them from salesmen."

"I'm helping Miss Adelaide make a hat for Mrs. Drummond," Emma piped up, her smile wide.

"That's great, Emma." He turned to Adelaide. "You ought to get a clerk to help out. All work and no play…"

"When my mother was ill, at the last, I hired Laura as a part-time clerk, but after Mama passed, I had no reason to keep her on."

Charles's gaze locked with hers. "Perhaps you need to rethink that."

Was he suggesting they spend more time together?

"Miss Adelaide, don't you like your food?" Emma said, breaking the link between them. "Remember 'waste not, want not' like your mama always said?"

Noticing Charles's clean plate, Adelaide flushed. Charles pushed back from the table and laid an ankle across his knee, looking more at ease than she'd felt in her entire life. Horrified this man could turn her into a stammering mass of nerves when she intended to show him she could take care of herself and a child, she fought his charm.

"The food's delicious." Though, she could barely remember what she'd eaten. "I'm taking my time, enjoying every bite."

"No hurry." Charles patted his torso. "We need to digest our food so we have room for dessert."

"Do they have chocolate cake?" Emma asked.

"Yes. Pie, too. The hotel's cream pies melt in your mouth."

With the promise of dessert, Emma got to work on her meal.

Charles turned back to Adelaide. "Tell me something about you. You don't have any living family?"

"No, no one." Adelaide took a sip of water. "How about you?"

He straightened and dropped his foot to the floor. "You probably know Sam died two years ago," he said his tone subdued.

Adelaide nodded.

"My mother died when I was sixteen. So all I have is Mary and her two boys.

"I got a brother," Emma chimed in. "William and me slept on the floor. He told me stories." She sighed. "Papa left us and then Mama died…." Tears welled up in the little girl's eyes.

Adelaide's gaze collided with Charles's look of dismay. "Before you know it, you'll be back with William," Adelaide assured her, dreading the prospect.

"Why can't William live with us?"

Adelaide's heart went out to the loneliness in the girl's voice. "Rules, sweetie." She hated those rules herself, rules preventing her from having Emma permanently.

"How about ordering that cake?" Charles said, his words putting a smile on Emma's face.

Charles summoned the waiter and ordered dessert. Emma clanked her fork and spoon together a few times, then rose from her seat, almost tipping her chair.

"Sit down, honey," Adelaide said.

"I'm tired of sitting," Emma whined.

"I know, but you want that chocolate cake, don't you?"

Emma nodded and returned to her seat. Soon Emma swung her feet against the rungs of her chair, the sound echoing through the quiet, high-ceilinged room. Adelaide bit her lip, trying to hide her disquiet. She'd hoped to show Charles her mothering skills, not to look inept.

Across from her, Charles reached into his coat pocket and brought out a pad of paper and pencil. "As a boy, I had a dog I called Rusty. Part Irish Setter. He had long ears like this."

Emma's feet stilled as Charles began sketching the dog, his hand moving quickly across the paper. She slid from her chair to stand beside him, watching him draw one animal after another.

His delightful little drawings charmed Adelaide as much as they did Emma. "I didn't know you were artistic. Do you draw the political cartoons on the editorial page?"

Charles glanced up. "Yes, I do."

"I'm impressed."

He gave her a small pleased smile. "Thank you."

The man had many layers. Each time she saw him, Adelaide discovered something that added to her appraisal. He'd been able to calm Emma when she had not, yet she doubted he'd lowered his opinion of her as a mother.

Still, he remained a man. Even as she thought it, she knew this mistrust of men came from her mother. She needed to evaluate things on her own.

The waiter arrived, carrying a tray with Emma's dessert and two cups of coffee. Emma scrambled back into her chair, Charles's drawings forgotten. In minutes, Emma's unrest vanished as quickly as her dessert.

Eager to know the details that made up Charles's past, Adelaide said, "Tell me more about your dog."

"We had lots of dogs, not only Rusty, sometimes two or three at a time. They lived out back in a pen." Charles took a sip of his coffee. "Did you have a dog, Addie?"

"No, I wanted a cat, but Mama couldn't abide cat hair on her furniture. I found a toad once and kept it in a box in my room. Until Mama found it and said it'd give me warts."

"Me and William had a kitty," Emma said. "Mama called Felicia the best mouser in the building. Will you draw my cat?"

"Sure, what did she look like?"

A smile spread across Emma's chocolate-speckled face. "Like a gray-and-white striped tiger with white patches on her front feet and here." Emma pointed to her forehead and then her torso. "Mama said Felicia wore a bib so when she ate, she wouldn't get dirty.

Charles smiled. "She sounds like a beauty."

Emma twisted her napkin. "We gave Felicia to a neighbor, 'cause we couldn't take a cat to the orphanage. I miss her."

Adelaide's throat tightened for Emma's many losses.

"I can see why." Charles reached over and patted Emma's hand, then drew a curve that quickly turned into the body of a cat, sitting on a stool. On the face, he added two triangular ears and an upside down triangle for a nose.

Watching them, Adelaide marveled at how Charles related to children. Emma had taken a liking to him right away. Charles Graves was a kind man. Adelaide could think of no higher compliment.

With Emma in the middle, they walked home in the

dark, their way lit by gaslights along the street. The soft night air between her and Charles crackled, leaving Adelaide shaky but feeling alive.

"Here we are," Charles said, reaching the door of her shop.

She dug into her bag and retrieved the key. All thumbs, she dropped it, and then bent to retrieve it, just as Charles reached to snatch up the key. The two of them almost collided and both let out a little shaky laugh. In the dim light, they stood facing each other, close enough to touch, to reach out....

Adelaide's stomach dropped like it had when she'd swung out on a rope over Phillip's Creek. But she wasn't a child now. Dangling from anyone's rope posed a risk she would not take.

He reached past her, his arm brushing hers, turned the key and opened the door.

"The meal was delicious," she said, though she didn't remember eating a bite.

"I'm glad you enjoyed it."

"Well...thank you for a lovely evening."

"I should be thanking you," he said softly, "both of you," he added, his gaze taking in Emma, too.

She and Emma stepped inside the shop. Adelaide chanced one last glance back at Charles. Having a man in her life didn't mean she wouldn't be lonely—Jack had proven that. He'd claimed he wanted to marry her but never exhibited an interest in anything about her, except her cooking and the profits from her shop. Besides, she couldn't be involved with a man who had issues with his faith.

"Would you accompany us to church tomorrow?"

His gaze dropped to his feet. "Mary's expecting me for dinner."

"Mary and the boys will be at church. I'm sure they'd love to have you join them."

He tightened his jaw. "Church and I aren't a good mix."

Hope she hadn't realized she held tumbled from its lofty perch. "Well, if you change your mind—"

"I won't. Good night, Addie." He turned and walked away in the direction of his house.

Charles had used his sister-in-law as an excuse. Why did he avoid church? Perhaps, God had placed her in his life so she could help him find his way back. If so, how?

Chapter Nine

The morning of Decoration Day, most of the shop-keepers in town had locked their doors. Nobleville's citizens headed first to Riverside Cemetery and then on to Crownland Cemetery to listen to the speeches and honor the country's fallen heroes. A cool breeze fluttered the flags.

Charles waved at James across the way as he scribbled notes for the paper, and then slipped in beside Addie and Emma. Addie's welcoming smile dazzled him. On this beautiful, celebratory Monday, he wanted to throw caution to the wind, to pretend he'd have tomorrow with Addie and every day after that. He tucked her gloved hand into the crook of his arm and watched the Union soldiers honor their dead.

Emma tugged at his sleeve. "Who are they?"

"Those men fought in the Civil War," he said, bending down to speak into her ear. "See their uniforms? They…"

But, Emma's attention had latched on to a dog that joined the parade. Charles returned his gaze to Addie. In the misty depths of her eyes, he saw an understand-

ing of the sacrifices these men had made for their country, along with the countless thousands on both sides
who'd died during that hideous war.

The more he knew Addie, the more he perceived
the depth of their connection. As much as he knew
Addie deserved a better man, she'd taken residence in
his mind. And, could it be, even in his heart? No. He'd
only bring her trouble. In the end, he'd draw the joy
from her life.

After the last speech, men in faded overalls, women
wearing sun-bleached bonnets and children itching to
shuck high-top shoes flowed across the street or stopped
to chat with friends.

As they strolled toward Addie's shop, Charles pulled
a lollipop from his coat pocket and handed it to Emma.
She rewarded him with a huge smile.

Addie whispered in Emma's ear and the little girl
pulled the treat out of her mouth. "Thank you, Mr.
Graves," Emma said, then popped the sucker back in.

Charles smiled. "You're welcome. Are you enjoying
your day out of school?"

"Yes!" The little girl twirled in front of them. "I
don't have to do math or read or *anything*." Emma said
between licks. "And Miss Adelaide's shop is closed all
day."

"Aren't you the lucky ladies?"

Emma's eyes sparkled. "And guess what? Miss Adelaide is going to buy me a doll that gots a china head!"

Addie smiled. "Mr. Hudson offered to open the
store."

"With all the farmers in town, Mr. Nickels decided
to keep the feed store open, too. Not sure our veterans
would approve."

"Well, Emma's glad." Adelaide smiled down at her. "Every girl needs a special doll."

"And you want to make sure she has one."

Addie laid a gentle hand on Emma's shoulder. "Yes."

Charles dropped them at the door of the shop "I best get back to the paper," he said, sorry to see the morning end.

Addie cocked her head at him. He assumed a few well-placed hatpins kept the wide-brimmed straw hat from swaying on her head. "I'm sorry you have to be inside on such a pretty day," she said.

Wish I could spend it with you. Instead he said, "Me, too."

He walked to his office and while Teddy set type, he tackled his editorial, glad to focus on work instead of the lady across the street. As he finished, the door opened.

Charles greeted Roscoe Sullivan, the previous editor of *The Ledger.* Roscoe pulled at the suspenders that held up his pants. "Too bad you're cooped up on such an afternoon, Mr. Editor."

Charles grinned and stretched his muscles, glad for the company. "I managed to take in the parade this morning."

Roscoe removed his straw hat, the band stained with sweat, and dropped into the chair across from him. "I've been keeping tabs on the paper." He tapped a nearby issue. "I like how you've used the editorial page to instigate reform, like cleaning up our streets and getting support for building the new school."

"I appreciate that," Charles said. "Say, how's retirement?"

"Not sure I like it much, though I hear the fishing

is good up on White River." Roscoe flipped a wrist, throwing out an imaginary line. "The main reason I came by is to say thanks for seeing that my nephew got those orphans."

"I didn't do anything special. The decision was unanimous."

"Ed's all the family I've got. When little Eddie died, it about killed Carrie and me." Roscoe shook his head. "Then Frances's mother commits suicide. Life's given Frances one too many kicks in the stomach, but she'll get back on her feet."

"I think you're right." He wished Mrs. Drummond well, but when she recovered, she'd want Emma. The thought cooled his mood faster than a winter dip in the Ohio River.

Roscoe slapped his hat on his head. "Best get a move on."

The two men walked to the door. As if he'd conjured her up, Adelaide left her shop with Emma chattering alongside, probably on their way to buy Emma's doll. They saw him in the open doorway and waved. Charles waved back.

"Ed told me Emma's staying with Miss Crum for now," Roscoe said. "It appears she's doing a right good job."

"Yes, she is."

"Heard tell you were spending time with the lady. Keeping an eye on Emma, huh?" Roscoe thumped him playfully in the arm. "Unless there's another reason for your attention?"

Charles opened his mouth to protest, but thought better of it. There wasn't much he could say to stop the talk; protesting only increased the gossip.

"She's a fine woman," Roscoe continued. "Always wondered why some swain hadn't snapped her up. Maybe you're the one."

Charles put up his hands. "Not me. I'm too set in my ways."

"A woman has a way of changing that." Roscoe chuckled. "Marriage can bring a lot into your life— good cooking, companionship. Not a day goes by I don't miss my Carrie." Roscoe's eyes misted and he made a production out of adjusting his hat, then shoved away from the door. "I'm off."

Charles cleared the sudden lump in his throat and returned to his desk and the pile of work awaiting him. By the look of things, he'd be here for hours. And at the end of the day, all that would greet him would be some poor excuse for a supper.

For a moment, he tried to imagine what it would be like to have a wife to come home to, welcoming him with a smile, and a home-cooked meal on the table— a table surrounded by the freshly scrubbed faces of their children.

His life had left him cynical about marriage. Apparently, a few—Teddy and Roscoe, if he could believe what they said—had enjoyed domesticity. But without a framework for such a life, Charles could barely imagine it.

At the memory of his boyhood home, tension crept into his shoulders and up his neck muscles. No, having a wife and children gathered around a table didn't ensure a happy home.

Until he had an idea what did, he had no business picturing a future with Addie. She deserved a better man, a man who could give her happily ever after.

* * *

Adelaide detected a tug on her hand, but deep in thought about Charles, she ignored it.

"Look! It's William." Emma dropped Adelaide's hand and ran toward her brother. "William!"

Toting a sack of feed big enough to topple him, the boy's face broke into a lopsided grin.

Emma huddled close to her brother. "Is Mrs. Drummond better?" she asked, her voice almost a whisper.

William juggled the sack of feed and shrugged. "I dunno."

"Oh." Emma tucked her hands behind her back. "I miss you."

With the toe of his boot, William rubbed a line in the dirt. "Me, too. Is living in town fun?"

Emma's head bobbed. "Miss Adelaide's gonna buy me a doll. See my new hat!" Emma pivoted in front of her brother, sending the ribbons flying, almost losing the bonnet. "Isn't it pretty?"

"Yep." William's gaze drifted from Emma's hat to Adelaide and the longing in his eyes turned to envy.

Adelaide smiled. "Hello, William."

He gave a slow smile. She wanted to scoop him up and take him home, but William wasn't hers and neither was Emma, really.

Ed Drummond, wearing a scowl, came stomping up behind the boy. Adelaide's heart leapt in her chest.

William didn't see him. "Thanks for taking care of—"

A rough hand shoved William, almost causing him to drop the feed sack. "I told you to stow that in the wagon. Obey me, boy!"

"Yes, sir." Head down, William scampered for the wagon.

Adelaide bit her tongue to keep from giving Ed the good lashing he deserved. She didn't dare antagonize the man who held Emma's fate in his hands.

Ed climbed onto the seat, never turning around, leaving William to wrestle with the heavy sack alone. Adelaide hurried to the boy's side and helped him heft the feed onto the back of the wagon. William scrambled up beside it and dragged the sack toward the front when Ed slapped the reins across the horses' backs. The team jerked forward. Losing his balance, William tumbled to the rear of the open wagon.

Emma shrieked.

"Stop!" Adelaide shouted. William grabbed a wooden slat and managed to keep from falling out. As the horses gathered speed, he pulled himself to a sitting position, and held on.

Adelaide released a shaky breath. Though William hadn't been hurt, he could have been—and seriously. Ed had treated him more like a slave than a son and hadn't acknowledged Emma.

Emma returned to Adelaide's side. "He was mean to William."

Adelaide laid a hand on her shoulder. "I know."

Emma's soft blue eyes glistened with tears. "Why?"

Adelaide watched the wagon disappear around the bend. "I don't know." *But I intend to find out.*

"I'm glad he didn't see me." Emma peered up at Adelaide, her eyes luminous. "Do I have to go back there?"

Adelaide bent down and put her arms around Emma. "Don't worry. I'll keep you safe." She held her until Emma noticed a robin on the walk.

"Wait here a minute," Adelaide said, then marched into the feed store and almost bumped into the proprietor standing in the shadows of the doorway. He had to have seen Ed's treatment of the boy. "Excuse me, Mr. Nickels. The man who left here—"

The feed store owner spat a load of tobacco toward a spittoon, hitting the target with ease. "Name's Ed Drummond."

"Did you see how he treated the boy?"

"Nope. Been too busy."

Adelaide only saw one customer inside. She suspected Mr. Nickels of lying and shot him a look she hoped made that clear.

"Mr. Drummond's a good customer, pays promptly," he said, his gaze pinning her. Then he picked up a broom and swept out the entrance, ignoring her.

Adelaide left the store, then reached for Emma's hand and resumed their walk. The way Ed Drummond had talked to Frances that day in the courthouse corridor and his treatment of William now convinced her that the man shouldn't have a child in his care, never mind two. She would see to it Emma and William were safe. But how? *Lord, send me an answer.*

Suddenly she knew what to do. She would go to Charles.

Their shopping finished, Adelaide settled Emma on a bench outside the newspaper office. Her new doll with its open-and-close eyes—a wonder to Emma—would keep her occupied while Adelaide talked to Charles.

Inside the office, Charles's face broke into a wide grin. He closed the distance between them in a rush, as if...*she* mattered.

When have I ever mattered to any man?

"Addie, this is a pleasant surprise." He took her hands in his and gave them a squeeze.

Her concern about Ed Drummond fell away, melted into something warm and soft. She struggled to gather her wits about her, to stick with her reason for coming. Pulling her hands from his grasp, she walked to the window to check on Emma. The little girl's lips moved in a make-believe conversation with her doll.

Adelaide trailed a finger down the glass, then turned to Charles. "I'm concerned about William Grounds's safety."

Charles's brow furrowed. "Why?"

Adelaide took a deep breath, trying to keep anger out of her voice. "I'm alarmed by how Ed treated the boy at the feed store earlier. First, he shoved him, then, while William was stowing a sack in the wagon, Ed drove off, almost causing the boy to tumble out the back."

Charles rubbed his chin. "Perhaps William is causing trouble and Ed is frustrated. Or isn't it possible Ed didn't realize he put the boy in jeopardy?" He smiled. "Not everyone is good with children like you are."

Emma had rebelled a few times. Perhaps William had, too, but that didn't warrant a shove. "There's something else, Charles. Ed completely ignored Emma, like he didn't even see her."

"Maybe he didn't."

"I don't see how he couldn't. He didn't greet me, either."

"Bad manners aren't against the law, Addie."

Why couldn't Charles understand something was amiss? "The boy's afraid of him. I could see it in his eyes."

"Did you see bruises?"

She sighed. "No."

"Was William hobbling?"

"No." She fisted her hands on her hips. "But in my heart, I know Ed Drummond is a cruel man."

"All right, I'll run the incident past the committee. See what they make of it."

Adelaide frowned. "Couldn't you check with someone else in town? Except for you, everyone on that committee is biased."

"They merely followed the Children's Aid Society rules." He exhaled a burst of air. "I'll look into it."

"Thank you." She laid a hand on his forearm, strong and firm, feeling oddly comforted. "Let me know what you find out."

He gave her a reassuring smile. "Of course."

Charles stepped to his desk and sat on the edge. A book clattered to the floor from the teetering pile. While he stooped to retrieve it, Adelaide gathered the pencils scattered on the desk, organizing them in the cup with points down. It wouldn't do for Charles to get graphite embedded in his palm.

She glanced at Charles. A telltale crease marked the middle of his brow, a sure sign of his irritation. Her hands fell away.

"My, but you're a busy bee."

He touched her hand and tugged her to him.

"The incident upset Emma. Something seemed to be going on, something unspoken between the children."

He appeared to focus more on her mouth than the words coming out of it, tempting her to forget what mattered—the children and the issues between them. "Where's Emma now?"

"She's sitting on the bench outside, talking to her

new doll. I didn't want her to overhear our conversation."

"So I have you all to myself." Charles raised a brow and motioned toward the pencils. "Since you're determined to fix things, how about fixing dinner tonight?" He had a twinkle in his eye, daring her to agree.

If he came to supper, she could work on convincing him to investigate Ed Drummond. "All right."

Charles's smile broadened. "Say six-thirty? That gives me time to finish here and still go home to clean up."

"Six-thirty is fine." She walked toward the door. "Do you like pot roast?"

Charles blocked her way by leaning against the frame. "It's my favorite."

She smiled, enjoying the tease. "I can't make it if I don't get home."

With a grin, he stepped aside, giving her room to pass.

"Why, hello, Charles. Oh, hi, Adelaide."

Adelaide turned and almost bumped into Fannie Whitehall, who'd appeared out of nowhere. Or perhaps Adelaide was so besotted she'd failed to notice her. "Hello, Fannie."

Fannie beamed at Charles. "Will you be my guest at our church picnic? It's the second Saturday in June." She clapped her gloved hands together. "Please say yes."

Apparently Fannie had decided not to play possum, her lessons in demureness forgotten. Why hadn't Adelaide thought to ask Charles herself? Because finding an escort for the church picnic was the least of her priorities. At such gatherings, she felt out of place, a solitary oak at the edge of an evergreen forest.

Without children. Without a husband. A woman alone.

Still, knowing Charles could be going with Fannie poked like a misdirected hatpin. Well, he deserved a woman whose mind didn't keep up with her mouth. "Goodbye," Adelaide said.

Fannie took Adelaide by the elbow and walked out a few steps with her. "Was I demure?"

"You were fine." No need to point out that ladies, when issuing an invitation, didn't usually clap. She'd best remember Jesus's command to love her neighbor, instead of having such uncharitable thoughts about Fannie.

Beaming, Fannie rushed back inside, no doubt for Charles's answer. Adelaide gathered up Emma and her doll and left. He might be coming to supper tonight, but she had no claim on the man. Over the meal, they'd share a conversation about William, about her ideas for future columns. Nothing else.

Before they'd crossed the street, Adelaide had started wading through the menu in her mind. She'd add red-skinned potatoes, carrots and onions to the meat. Applesauce she'd canned last fall would be tasty. This simple meal would give her time to make a pie. Oh, she almost forgot. After bragging to Fannie and Charles, she'd have to serve biscuits, careful not to burn the bottoms.

While Emma played with her doll, Adelaide prepared the meal, then mixed the biscuit dough, vowing that with God's help and Charles as her ally, she'd get both children out of the Drummond household permanently.

When she'd finished, Adelaide oversaw Emma's bath, then brushed her hair until it shone and helped her into the new dress she'd made. "You look pretty, sweetheart."

"That's 'cause I look like you."

In the mirror, two blondes with fair skin and blue eyes peered back at them. Heart full, Adelaide hugged Emma. "Thank you. Why don't you read while I get ready?"

After Adelaide bathed, she donned her finest dress, a rose gown with a tight fitting bodice and enormous puffed sleeves that narrowed to hug her forearms. Pulling her hair up into a chignon, she didn't have a single, solitary thought in her brain except soon Charles would be in her home, sitting at her table.

In the kitchen, her belly roiling in anticipation, she set the table. Then she walked into the parlor and fluffed the pillows, picked a piece of lint off the love seat and checked the clock on the shelf.

Below, the bell jingled. "He's here!" Emma called.

"I'll let him in." Adelaide hurried to the top of the stairs and to the door. Seeing Charles through the glass, her mouth went dry. Wearing a dark gray suit and crisp white shirt, he was a beautiful sight. She opened the door and stepped back.

"Evening, Addie." He gave her a dazzling smile, then lifted his nose in the air and sniffed. "Hmm, smells good in here." His gaze skimmed over her. "Looks good, too. That's a pretty dress."

"Thank you." The admiration in his voice warmed her, but what she wanted to know—and dared not ask— was if he had accepted Fannie's invitation to the picnic.

They stood gazing at one another, neither saying a word. The way he studied her, a way no man had ever looked at her before, Adelaide forgot all about Fannie's invitation.

She pivoted on her heel. "If you'll follow me…"

"Gladly," he said.

She heard the shop door close and glanced back. He wore a lazy grin. A thrill snaked through Adelaide, making her glad Emma waited upstairs. Instead of being all soft and starry-eyed, she should remember why she'd agreed to this invitation. It had nothing to do with her and Charles, everything to do with Emma and William's future.

Adelaide led him through the shop. The aroma of pot roast hauled them up the stairs by their noses. "Supper will be ready soon."

Charles smiled. "I'm starved."

Could he see her hands shaking? Why couldn't she feel comfortable entertaining a man?

Emma bounded to them. "Hi, Mr. Graves."

"Hello, Emma."

Adelaide motioned to the love seat in the parlor. "Please, make yourself at home."

He lowered his lanky body onto the dainty furniture, dwarfing the delicate piece. He surely couldn't feel comfortable, yet he looked at home, self-assured, as if he didn't have a care in the world.

He crossed an ankle over his knee, and patted the seat beside him. "Can't you join me, Addie, even for a minute?"

"I... I have things to do. Emma, show Mr. Graves your new doll." The little girl raced to her room. Adelaide fled almost as fast as Emma.

In the kitchen, Adelaide put her hands to her burning cheeks and glanced around, trying to get her bearings. Her gaze fell on the pan next to the stove. Oh, yes, she needed to bake the biscuits. Having Charles here had taken every rational thought from her mind. She popped the pan in the hot oven and then lifted the lid on the roaster. Perfect. Everything would be ready as soon as the biscuits finished baking.

She returned to the parlor and found Charles sitting beside Emma. He held the new doll, looking about as comfortable as a trapeze artist without a net. Adelaide bit her lip to keep from laughing and perched on the chair across from them.

Emma pointed at Charles. "He's the daddy."

"We're just pretending," Charles cut in quickly. If the tone of his words hadn't, the look on his face made it clear Charles had no wish to ever be the daddy.

Adelaide's smile faded until she realized there wasn't a bachelor alive who'd want to be caught playing with dolls. Why did she always look for trouble behind Charles's every word or action? She reminded herself of a hedgehog rolling into a ball to protect its vulnerable underbelly. Not an attractive image.

She could take a lesson from Fannie and gain some of her boldness. As long as she didn't end up with Fannie's giggle.

Or end up hurt like her mother.

Chapter Ten

Adelaide's parlor wasn't overdone with bric-a-brac like most Charles had been in. Her collection of photographs, books and well-placed items made the room cozy and welcoming.

Emma carried her doll to the piano and fiddled with the keys. She chattered while she did, telling her doll about her made-up tune. Dear, sweet Emma, without a care in the world, so unlike Charles at that age.

"I never realized the furniture in here was so small," Addie said, taking a chair across from him. "Maybe that's because Jack wasn't much taller than I."

"Jack?" Charles straightened. "Who's Jack?"

Adelaide waved a hand of dismissal, as if the name meant nothing. "Oh, Jack was a guy who had the notion we should marry."

It bothered Charles to think Adelaide had once had someone in her life. But why wouldn't she? Pretty, industrious, smart and apparently a good cook, if the enticing aromas permeating her home were any indication, Addie would snare a man's attention. "Why didn't you marry Jack?"

She shrugged. "I didn't love him."

Charles leaned forward. "How could you be sure?"

"How much time do you have?"

Charles chortled. "That bad? So what topped the list?"

"Let's see his conversation was limited to the weather and…well, the weather. He dozed off right after supper. He…" She averted her gaze. "I don't mean to be unkind. Jack wasn't a bad person."

Just then, Emma tried to play "Three Blind Mice" and hit so many wrong notes Charles suspected she'd left off a mouse or two.

Addie winced, but shot Emma an encouraging smile, then turned back to him.

"Is that all you had on your list?" he said.

She lowered her voice and leaned a little closer, even though Emma's playing threatened to drown out her words. "He…well, he gave me the willies."

Ridiculously glad, Charles chuckled. "Hmm, the willies. That's definitely *not* a good basis for marriage."

"That's what I thought," Adelaide said. "Mama insisted I had no one to compare him to, and should just grit my teeth and ignore the effect he had on me."

"That could get mighty hard on a woman's teeth."

"What? Oh!" Addie laughed.

Charles thought the sound enchanting. A desire to pull her into his arms crashed through him, but he didn't dare.

Addie jumped to her feet. "Oh, no!"

Charles caught a whiff of something burning. He followed Addie to the kitchen where she lifted a smoking pan from the oven. She tossed it onto the breadboard, dismay written all over her face. "This is terrible."

Turning Addie toward the table, he gently pushed her into a chair then removed his coat. "You sit. I'll handle the rest."

"No, you're my guest."

"This guest knows his way around a kitchen." He removed the biscuits from the pan and cut off the blackened bottoms, biting back an urge to tease her. No need to make her feel worse. Burnt or not, he'd rather be eating Addie's biscuits than Fannie's. Even gladder she hadn't married Jack.

He snuffed the thought. Being around Addie made him question everything upon which he'd carefully built his life.

She made him rethink his doubts about church, his anger at God...questions too painful to examine.

Yet despite all that, he still wanted to be with her.

"At least let me serve before the food gets cold."

He gave her a salute. "Yes, ma'am."

She rose and grabbed a towel to pull the roast from the oven, then began cutting up the meat. She ladled vegetables around the platter and set the dish on the table.

Emma ran into the kitchen. "Is dinner ready? I'm starving!"

"Yes, it is. Go wash up," Adelaide said.

Soon, they assembled at the table, an odd put-together group, not a family, exactly, but still, too close to one for comfort. A bouquet of lilacs in the center teased at his nostrils. Addie's warm, full table held a charm for him he hadn't found at the Becker House or at his own cheerless table.

Addie and Emma folded their hands and bowed their

heads. Charles blinked, then did the same. Addie said a simple prayer.

As they ate, his gaze kept returning to Addie's, but Emma's endless chatter kept conversation between them at a minimum.

At last, Emma asked to be excused. Soon the notes of "Mary Had a Little Lamb"—well most of them—drifted through the air.

"The pot roast was delicious, Addie. Everything was. You're an excellent cook."

"Thank you. My mother taught me."

"Well, you know the old saying—the way to a man's heart is through his stomach." Charles patted his. "You've created quite a path tonight."

Addie stacked her silverware on top of her plate. "I'm not sure there's any truth to that old adage."

"Why?"

Addie ran her thumb down the handle of her spoon. "My father left when I was a baby. Clearly my mother's cooking skills didn't keep him home."

"Maybe his leaving had more to do with who *he* was, than with her cooking."

She nodded, then removed the napkin from her lap, laid it on the table and folded it neatly, smoothing it with her fingers until it looked like it had never been used.

"What's on your mind?" he asked.

She raised her gaze to his. "I feel terrible that my mother jilted your father and caused trouble for you."

"Well, if she hadn't, we'd be brother and sister." He chuckled, and then took her hand. "My father is the one to blame, not your mother. I'm sorry I didn't see that at first."

"I can understand why you'd resent my mother, and

then me. Especially after hearing the contents of your father's will."

"I don't resent you or your mother." Charles joined her at the sink. "My family isn't a topic for good digestion."

His brow furrowed. He didn't want to discuss his past.

Charles touched her hand. "It's hard to talk about."

"You don't have to tell me."

"I couldn't talk about this with anyone but you." He gave her a weak smile. "Unlike your father, mine stayed—all the while beating the tar out of us."

Pain ripped through him, and he flinched.

She touched his arm, tears spilling down her cheeks. "I'm sorry."

He smiled and for a moment, covered her hand with his own. "You and I had rough beginnings, but we survived and our pasts brought us together, in an odd way, with the will."

Charles cleared his throat. He didn't want to think about his father. "Let's not talk about any of that." Just for a moment, he'd wanted to pretend he wasn't a product of his past. "Let's talk about you instead."

"Would you care for coffee?" Adelaide asked, avoiding Charles's probing gaze.

"Please."

She quickly cleared the dishes and then poured two cups from the pot on the stove.

"Your father never contacted you in all those years?" Charles asked.

"My only contact came through his attorney after he died. He left me his money, the little he had."

She wouldn't tell him the reason her parents had married. Still, Adelaide knew she should stop talking so much, but his warm gentle eyes made her want to share her past. "I can't blame my father entirely. Mama was a critical, aloof woman."

Charles's brows knitted. "My father put her on a pedestal."

"She must have changed. I could never please her. I wasn't pretty enough, smart enough. I suspect she resented me." Her lower lip trembled. No one had loved her. And now Charles knew that, too. She covered her mouth with her hand, dropping her gaze to the contents of her cup.

"Aw, Addie, something must have been wrong with your mother's eyesight." He took her chin in his hand, lifting her gaze to his. "You're a talented, intelligent, caring woman."

She soaked up his words, leaning in to the comfort of that hand. "I wasn't asking for a compliment."

"I mean every word." He studied her, his gaze tender. "After your childhood, I'm amazed you want a child."

"Why? I'm not like my mother."

"How can you be sure?" He grew remote, pulling inward.

The question pestered at her. If she ended up alone without a husband, without a child to love, would the disappointment turn her bitter?

Aside from the faraway sound of a barking dog drifting through the open window and the muted one-sided conversation between Emma and her doll, the kitchen grew silent.

Adelaide shook her head. "I could never be like my mother."

Charles raised a skeptical brow. "If pushed far enough, you can't tell what a person will do."

She folded her arms across her chest. "I'm offended you think I could treat a child unkindly."

"I didn't mean to insult you. I'm merely saying we don't know ourselves until we're trapped and desperate." His mouth thinned. "I'm a newspaperman. I've seen mankind's depravity."

"Then you should understand my concern about Ed Drummond."

"You could be reading things that aren't there."

She sighed, refusing to argue with him. "I want to protect those children. *And* hopefully initiate some change, so Emma can grow up in a world where her opinions matter."

"Those are lofty goals." He rolled up his sleeves. "Here, let me do this. You did the cooking. I'll do the cleaning."

She swished around some soap in the pan of hot water, then handed him the dishrag. He scrubbed a plate and sloshed it through the rinse water, handing it to her to dry. For a second, their fingertips touched and the plate almost fell to the floor.

"That was a close one," Charles said with a laugh. "Don't want to break the dishes. I may not be invited back."

Adelaide's heart thumped in her chest. *He wants to spend more time with me.* But wouldn't that risk everything she'd worked to build—a life dependent upon no one but God.

Besides, if God had brought a man into her life, wouldn't he be a church-going man? Or did God want her to bring Charles to worship? If so, she'd failed.

With all these confusing feelings, she knew one thing for certain. If she let herself, she could care about this man.

She excused herself to look in on Emma and found the little girl with her doll in her arms curled on the settee, asleep. Gratitude brought sudden tears to her eyes, but she blinked them away and returned to the kitchen.

Soon side by side, she and Charles chatted about nothing, about everything. Keenly aware of his every move, the rise and fall of his broad chest as he breathed, his large hands slipping over the surface of her plates, the hair on his forearms wet and curling from the water, she couldn't tear her gaze away.

Even wearing a dishtowel tucked into his waistband, every inch of Charles looked male. The evening was a fantasy of what married life could be. Yet he distanced himself every time she got close. Charles didn't want permanence, nor did she.

They scrubbed and dried all the dishes. Charles removed the towel and laid it on the counter. Without thinking, Adelaide picked it up and hung it on a knob to dry.

"Cleaning up after the cleanup man?" He chuckled and she smiled, unperturbed by his teasing. But then his expression grew sober and he put his hands around her waist. "We're a good fit, you and I."

He lifted a hand to her hair. "You're a beautiful woman." He took a step back and rested his forehead on hers. "I'd best be going," he said in a husky voice.

The thought of Charles leaving made her feel lonelier than she'd ever felt in her life. "You can't go," she said, smiling. "I made a cream pie."

He shook his head. "Sounds delicious. But—"

"It's one of my grandmother's recipes," she cut in before he could decline. "Sweet and yummy."

"Ah, Addie, I can't stay." He cupped her face in his palm and kissed her lightly on the temple.

Before she could say anything, he snatched his jacket off the chair. "Thank you again for dinner," he said, and then walked out of the room. She heard his footfalls on the stairs and a second later, the bell echoed his goodbye.

Charles had no interest in a future with her. Had she been thinking she could trust a man? If she was ever going to take a chance on love, it would have to be with a special man who shared her beliefs, shared her trust in God.

A man who wanted to do more than give a child a legal name, the only thing her father had given her.

In the meantime, there would be no trusting these wild feelings. She descended the stairs to lock the door to the shop, locking Charles and all those head-spinning thoughts outside.

The next morning, Adelaide woke with the memory of Charles's presence at her table. She knew the Scripture about being unevenly yoked. Charles had told her he believed in God. Perhaps he refused to go to church because he blamed God for his childhood.

Yawning from a restless night, Adelaide trudged to Emma's room. For once, Emma got out of bed on Adelaide's first call, chock-full of questions about the evening with Charles.

In the kitchen, Adelaide cut Emma a piece of pie for breakfast, hoping the treat would distract her from the subject.

Emma scrambled into her chair. "Did you have fun?"

Adelaide set the plate in front of her. "Yes." *More fun than I care to admit.*

Emma took a bite of pie. "He didn't like the food?"

Adelaide rubbed her temples. "Why do you say that?"

Her gaze darted to the pie, with only one piece cut out of the circle. "'Cause he didn't eat pie."

"Guess he was full." Adelaide took another sip of coffee, wondering why Emma couldn't be a sleepy-head today.

Emma licked her fork clean. "Did you play games?"

"Uh, no."

Emma rested her chin on a palm. "Then what *did* you do?"

Adelaide met her earnest, perplexed eyes. "We talked."

"That's *all?* That sounds boring."

"Grown-ups like to talk." Adelaide rose from her chair and took her cup to the stove. "Better hurry or you'll be late."

After scraping the last bite of pie from the plate and downing her glass of milk, Emma ran to her room, leaving Adelaide alone with the memory of what *had* transpired between her and Charles last night.

They'd shared their pasts and that had forged a deeper bond between them. But then, he hightailed out of here as if the kitchen had caught fire.

Since they'd met, her life had been turned upside down. Now she desired things—a voice, family. Things she couldn't have. Within minutes, she and Charles went from connection to conflict to connection. She'd never felt more alive, nor more miserable. She wouldn't let him keep her off-kilter. Nothing good could come from this silliness, nothing except trouble.

She wouldn't give up trying to have a voice in the community. He'd said good cooking made a path to his heart. Maybe food would forge a path to his brain, too. If she took him a piece of pie from dinner, in between bites she could talk to him about writing a column on an issue important to her. And take back the reins of her life.

Charles took the slice of sugar cream pie from Addie and laid the plate on his desk. The way he'd taken off last night, he'd expected her to be mad, not to be bringing homemade goodies. He admitted he was glad to see her. "Thanks. I'll have that with lunch."

"You're welcome."

"And thanks for dinner, too."

"Even with burned biscuits?" She laughed. "That's my comeuppance for bragging."

"Anytime you want to give those biscuits another try, I'm available."

She smiled and he drank it in like a thirsty man. "You're a glutton for punishment," she said.

"No, I'm merely a glutton." Why was he asking for another invitation? Hadn't he already vowed to stay away? He eyed the pie. "I may have to eat a bite to see if the crust is burned."

"The pie is perfect, as are all of my bribes."

Ah, there was more to this visit than his stomach. "Why are you trying to bribe me?"

"I'm hoping the pie might sweeten your reaction to a proposal." She took a deep breath. "I'd like to express some of my views in the paper."

"On topics besides fashion?"

The lines around her mouth tightened. He'd known her long enough to recognize her annoyance.

"I do hold opinions that have nothing to do with hats."

Addie had a great deal of opinions and many conflicted with his. "I expected as much. You're an intelligent woman."

"I'm not here for a compliment. I want you to take me and my views seriously."

He shoved back from the desk. "What views do you wish to express exactly?"

Eyes shining with the light of an evangelist, she smiled. "I want to write about issues important to women."

He folded his arms across his chest. "Like what?"

She lifted her chin. "Getting the vote, for one."

When Addie tackled a topic, she picked a mountain not a molehill. Thus far, even he'd steered clear of women's suffrage, the kind of subject that lit tempers and canceled papers.

"I don't see how you can work women getting the vote into a fashion column."

Her brow furrowed. "Did I say I wanted to combine the two? I want two spaces in the paper. What I want is a voice."

Why must she get involved with the paper? Wasn't it enough to run her shop and let him handle what was rightfully his? "A voice? *Two* columns?"

"Unless you'd prefer I express my views in editorials."

He parked his arms across his chest. "You can express your views in letters to the editor, like any citizen of Noblesville. But I'm the editor. I write the editorials."

"I own half of the paper. That gives me a right to the editorial page. Along with anything else I'd like half of. Like this desk." She cast a dismayed glance at the towering mess. "At least then there would be a few cleared inches of space."

She'd gone too far. Addie might have integrity, but she wanted too much from him. This was *his* paper. *His* desk.

Well, it might not be totally his, but once the two months were up, it would be. Until then he didn't need her "voice" in his paper or anywhere else. He knew what his readers liked.

"Stick with things you know, Addie."

"What? Birds and fruit on hats?" She glared at him. "Is that all you believe I think about?"

He reached out a hand to her, to still the rough waters between them. "As a businesswoman, you know more than the average wife and mother. Still, with your shop, you have enough to deal with. No reason to waste your time in politics."

She looked as if he'd slapped her. Though he'd only meant to compliment her, too late he realized his wife and mother comment had cut her to the quick. He couldn't take it back without making it worse.

Addie's blue eyes flashed. "No reason? No *reason,* Charles? The selection committee you sat on, a committee comprised of men, denied me a child."

"We were merely following Children's Aid Society rules."

She stood.

"Yes, but who comprises that group? *Men* are making the decisions in the Children's Aid Society, in the entire country."

He put his elbows on the desk and made a steeple with his fingers. Addie's delicate appearance seemed incompatible to her tough-minded opinions. He'd remain calm and she'd see reason. "Men have the best interests of their womenfolk at heart. They aren't trying to harm you."

"Perhaps not. But why must a woman rely on a man to fight for her? Why can't I speak up for what matters to me?" She strode to the window, pivoting back to him. "The committee turned me down. You don't want my editorial input. Well, here's a news story for you, Charles Graves. I am the only one, besides God, who knows what's best for me. I should have the right to make those decisions. So should every woman."

"I'm not trying to—"

She pointed at him, cutting him off. "Do you want to know what's ironic? *Your father* is the first man in my life who opened a door for me. Now you're standing in the middle of that door, arms spread wide, trying to keep me out. Well, I own half of this paper, and I won't be denied a voice in this town."

Charles jerked to his feet, sending his wheeled desk chair rolling into the wall. "My father wasn't opening a door for *you*. He was slamming one in *my* face! This paper is my life. Having the freedom to run it, to see it grow and prosper are all I have. I don't appreciate you trying to take that from me."

Her blue eyes turned stormy. "I'm sorry my ownership of the paper is such a burden, but you're stuck with me. Be glad I have a shop to run so I don't have time to work here, but I won't be an owner in name only. That's not how I'm made."

"Relinquishing control of the paper isn't how I'm made."

"This is my chance to help women, to change their lives for the better, to change this town for the better."

Were her motives as pure as she believed? "Or grind an ax?"

She fisted her hands on her hips. "That's insulting."

He sighed. "I know you have good intentions. But have you thought about how your editorials will affect the paper's circulation and the harmony of this town? You'll be stirring up trouble between men and their wives. You might end up hurting, not helping women."

"That's ridiculous." She held out a hand to him. "Why can't you understand how much I want this?"

Charles strode to her side, determined to make her see the risk she'd be taking. "I've been in this business a long time. I know a thing or two. The town fathers won't take kindly to a rabble-rouser in skirts."

"I don't need a warning, Charles. I need your support."

Why must she borrow trouble the paper couldn't afford? "I can't give it."

"You don't want me to have that voice, do you? You'd prefer a woman to cook and clean, bear children and keep her opinions to herself." She shook her head. "I've always felt like an outsider. My life doesn't fit the dutiful wife and motherhood mold of my friends. You're like every other man I've met. You'd say anything to keep the paper to yourself. Well, I insist, Charles! I need this chance."

"I'm only trying to protect you."

"From what? A paper cut? A spelling error?"

"From yourself." He looked her in the eyes. "Don't you know what this could cost you?"

"You're worried about losing a few subscribers. I'll—"

"Emma."

The name stopped her cold. She looked away, considering his words, and then met his gaze. "I'd rather Emma saw me as a woman who fought for what she believed in, not as a woman too scared to speak her mind."

Charles stepped away, disquiet lying heavy in his soul. He hadn't convinced Addie of anything. "Write the column. I suppose I can't stop you. I hope you're prepared for the consequences."

She met his gaze, her eyes the color of a wind-tossed sea. "All my life I've been paying for the consequences of my mother's actions. It's about time I started earning my own."

Red hair frizzing around her peaches and cream complexion, Fannie gazed across the table at Adelaide with puppy-like eagerness. If only she could toss a bone out the door, maybe her protégée would chase after it. Then Adelaide could go back to her orderly life and run her shop in peace.

That being unlikely, she might as well get on with it. Maybe she could have an impact on Fannie, however small, that would help the girl to be more…well, proper in her pursuit of men. And that help might lead to what Fannie wanted more than a career, more than a voice, more than an identity of her own.

A husband.

Though Adelaide hadn't met with success in that area, she would teach Fannie about fashion and etiquette. When it came to looking for a mate, she'd let the girl fend for herself.

"Let's start with decorum," Adelaide said.

"Decorum, does that mean how I dress?"

"Decorum means proper behavior, the same as demure. *Godey's* says a woman's demeanor is to be reserved. Sedate. Shy." Not the terms she'd use to describe Fannie, but after Adelaide's recent confrontation with Charles, the words didn't fit her, either.

Wrinkling her nose, Fannie rested her chin in her hands. "Demure sounds boring."

Adelaide tended to agree. She'd learned she didn't care much for keeping her mouth shut when a good deal needed to be said. Still, Fannie carried friendliness to an extreme. "Perhaps at first," Adelaide said carefully, "but as a woman gets to know the man, she shares more of her thoughts."

She'd certainly given Charles a piece of her mind. They'd reached the point where they disagreed about everything. Perhaps she needed a few lessons in demureness. Maybe then she could live in the confines of her gender and still be her own woman.

"Carriage is important. A woman of breeding doesn't take a room by storm. She walks with grace and dignity." Adelaide strolled across the room, posture erect, chin level with the floor, eyes straight ahead. She turned to Fannie. "You try."

Fannie lurched to her feet, almost knocking over her chair, then shook in a fit of giggling. She leaned against the table until her laughter subsided, then followed in Adelaide's tracks, her skirts swaying provocatively. "Like this?"

"Ah, a little less movement of the hips."

Fannie's brow puckered. "I thought men liked that."

They did indeed. "You don't want to give the wrong impression."

Fannie stared at her blankly.

"That you're…well…unchaste."

"Oh!" Fannie's mouth gaped open, releasing a nervous laugh.

"Now, try again."

This time Fannie carried herself with a modicum of dignity.

"Much better."

Fannie guffawed.

"You know, Fannie, frequent giggling detracts from a woman's demeanor, especially if she giggles for no reason."

"So I should just smile? You know—the kind of smile that doesn't show my teeth?" Fannie attempted the serene smile, which triggered yet another bout of giggling. "Oh, mercy me, I can't."

Muscles knotted at the base of Adelaide's neck. She'd once possessed patience in abundance, but Fannie's first lesson in deportment had only begun, and already Adelaide struggled to relax her jaw.

Part of the problem stemmed from Adelaide's recent doubt that a woman should have to conform. A man never worried about how he walked or smiled.

Fannie sniggered. "I'm glad I'm not one of those people who giggle so much they get on people's nerves."

By now, Adelaide was grinding her teeth, but Fannie didn't notice.

Instead, she practiced her smile, keeping her lips together. "How's this?" she said, then giggled raucously.

Adelaide rubbed a hand over her eyes. "Fine. Perfect."

Inwardly, she admitted her first attempt to help one of the women of Noblesville had failed miserably. Effecting town-wide change with words had to be easier than helping Fannie learn to walk across a room without swishing her backside like a busy broom.

Chapter Eleven

A week later with the first of her suffrage articles in print Adelaide passed the dry goods store and almost bumped into Lizzie Augsburger coming out with her arms full of packages. Lizzie's green eyes twinkled, as if she had a funny story to tell. "I'm glad I ran into you. Since you've started writing articles, reading the paper is exciting."

Her words warmed Adelaide clear to her toes. "Thank you."

"I don't miss an issue. Your fashion column's such fun. I totally agree with your thoughts on suffrage, too," she said, using a low confidential tone. "Women should have the vote."

"How did your husband react?"

"Your column caused quite a stir." She waved her free hand. "Got George's sap flowing. Why, he threatened to cancel the paper, told me to buy my hats somewhere else, like there's anyplace else to buy quality hats in this town." She chuckled and shifted the bags in her arms. "I kind of enjoyed the show. It's been ages since we've discussed more than, 'Pass the potatoes.'" Lizzie smiled. "You've brought exactly what we need into our house—a touch of controversy."

"Glad I could help. I think."

"Don't worry. We made up. And that was fun, too." She cocked her head. "Maybe next, you should tackle those nasty spittoons. The men in this town miss half the time. A lady has to watch her step."

They said goodbye and Adelaide headed to the bank, suddenly weary. George Augsburger, the most even-keeled man in town, had threatened to cancel the paper. Everywhere she went she got a reaction to her columns. Her words may have enlivened the Augsburger marriage, but they weren't doing much for *her* life.

She'd made no inroads in her quest to become Emma's mother. She'd wired Mr. Fry. In his reply he suggested she leave the matter in the committee's hands. William's teacher told her he was missing school but Superintendent Paul told Charles many of the boys stayed home during spring planting.

Inside the bank, footsteps clicking on the tiled lobby floor and echoing off the pressed-tin ceiling overhead, she walked toward the teller's window to deposit her meager receipts. Business in the shop had slowed. If this continued—

"Miss Crum!"

John Sparks stood at the door to his office, motioning for her. What did the president of the bank need with her? From the expression on his face, she didn't want to know.

She crossed the lobby to meet him.

In the shaft of sunlight filtering in from his office window, Mr. Sparks's bald head gleamed. "This stand you're taking on women's suffrage—can't imagine what you're thinking." Behind his thick glasses, Mr. Sparks blinked in rapid succession. "Well, aren't you going to explain?"

She prayed her answer wouldn't hurt her chances of keeping Emma. "Women are citizens of this country, but without the vote, they can't influence the policies that affect them."

"They have husbands to do that for them."

Did everything come down to a woman's marital status? Adelaide counted to ten. "Not every woman is married."

Mr. Sparks shifted his gaze to the floor. "True." He crossed his arms and rejoined her gaze. "But men study the issues and vote for the good of the entire community, for women and children. No need to clutter ladies' minds with government."

Decked out in her Sunday best, Mildred Rogers, the sheriff's wife, entered the bank, paused a moment, then inched closer. Customers who had finished their business and were leaving the bank, slowed as they passed, then stopped to listen.

Adelaide had come to make a deposit, not stand on a soapbox, but she said, "Women have good minds and are capable of studying issues." A murmur of agreement left Mildred's lips. Adelaide cocked her head. "How does *Mrs*. Sparks feel about it?"

Mr. Sparks's brows rose into what had once been his hairline. "Why, I never asked her."

No surprise there. "Maybe you should." Adelaide smiled. "It never hurts to get a woman's opinion."

A couple men stood listening to the exchange. "Are you that troublemaker from the paper?" the tall one asked.

"Yes, that's her," Mr. Sparks said, wagging his finger. "If women get the vote, the next thing you know, they'll be telling their husbands what to do."

Ah, the core of the controversy. How could she make them understand she upheld the Biblical example of marriage? "Having the right to express their opinions at the polls will merely give women a right to be heard, not a right to silence men."

Mrs. Rogers waved a hand as if asking for permission to speak. "I agree with you there, Adelaide." Mildred shot Mr. Sparks a glare, then moved a step closer. A group of onlookers now circled them, arguing among themselves.

"See all the trouble you're causing? All this talk about women voting puts a knot in my belly." Mr. Sparks rubbed his stomach as if to prove it. "Change. That's what it is. And once that's the law, no telling where it'll lead."

A thin man shot a wad into a nearby spittoon. "Next thing you know, women will be wearing the breeches in the family!"

Adelaide shook her head. "Getting the vote will give women the *same* rights as men. Not more."

"Miss Crum, you're turning this bank into a sideshow." Mr. Sparks shooed the growing group of listeners toward the counter. "The tellers are waiting, folks."

People inched away, looking as if they'd like to leave their ears behind. A few didn't budge, including Mildred, but Mr. Sparks stared them down and they finally left.

Mr. Sparks moved closer to Adelaide, within inches. "With your involvement at the paper, I wonder how you have time to care for Emma," the banker said, his tone sinister.

The threat stomped on Adelaide's lungs and she inhaled sharply. "I write my columns while Emma is in school."

He shook his head. "The controversy's got to affect the little girl. You're molding an impressionable young mind. Classmates are probably teasing her as we speak."

"Are you suggesting the committee would move Emma to spite me? Hasn't she been through enough?"

"I see it as removing Emma before you confuse her." He leaned closer. "If I were you, I'd stick to fashion columns."

Mr. Sparks stepped to his office, giving her one last warning scowl before closing the door with a click.

Motionless, blood pounding in her temples, Adelaide recalled Charles's warning about this very thing. But she'd felt compelled to speak out, to explain the importance of women getting the vote.

Mr. Paul and Mr. Wylie would undoubtedly share Mr. Sparks's view. Would her words cost her Emma? Had she stepped out of God's will for her life?

God, please show me the way.

To get a better view, Charles pushed through the crowd. Only a smoldering shell remained of the Anderson house.

He found owner Matthew Anderson and jotted down names and ages of the family and the cause of the fire— a knocked-over kerosene lamp. Then Charles walked over to speak to Sheriff Rogers. He'd run a story, explaining the Andersons' plight, which should generate donations for the family of six.

Charles's gaze swept the scene one last time. Mrs. Anderson, holding her baby son in her arms, and two young daughters huddled in a circle of sympathetic ladies. Mr. Anderson and his older boy stood apart, staring at the ruins, when Ed Drummond, of all people, approached. Curious, Charles edged closer.

Anderson laid his hand on his young son's shoulder. "I'm mighty grateful we all got out," he said to Drummond.

A shadow crossed Ed's face. "That's all that matters."

"Reckon you know that better than anyone, Ed."

Drummond nodded, cleared his throat and then directed his attention to the boy. "A fire's pretty scary, hey, Tad?"

"Yes, sir." The boy heaved a sigh that seemed to weigh more than his small frame. "My straw-stuffed kitty burned up."

Ed ruffled the young boy's hair. "Soon as I heard about the fire, I started gathering things from the neighbors. I've got clothing and blankets in my wagon." He directed his words to Anderson, but his eyes remained on Tad's soot-stained cheeks. "I remember seeing some toys. Wanna go look?"

A grin spread across the boy's face. "Sure!"

Charles couldn't believe he'd suspected Drummond, a man this kind, even tenderhearted toward a child, of abuse.

At the wagon, Ed turned back to Matthew Anderson. "If your family needs a place to stay, the Phillips family has offered their home."

"The missus and kids are going to her sister's. With chores to do twice a day, I'll stay and sleep in the loft."

Charles's gaze turned to the imposing barn and the livestock now turned out to pasture.

As if on cue, Drummond and Anderson swiveled their heads to the ruins. "The fire department couldn't save the house, but I'm grateful they kept it from spreading to the barn."

Ed clapped a hand on Anderson's shoulder. "As soon as it cools down, fourteen men from church will be out and start raising a new house on that foundation. With that many able-bodied men at work, before you know it, you'll be moving in."

Anderson bowed his head and swiped a hand across his wet eyes. "I appreciate it. More than I can say."

"I'll never forget you did my chores after… Eddie."

"It was the least I could do." Anderson tugged his son to his side. "When I think how close—" He stopped, shook his head.

Charles walked to the lane, mounted Ranger and rode to town, thinking about Drummond. Ed had gathered what the burned-out family needed and would help rebuild the house along with thirteen others from his church. He'd realized a frightened boy needed a stuffed animal to cuddle. The man didn't fit the description of any child beater he'd ever seen.

But then, Charles's father had been a caring man in the community, always joking, likable—and yet, a fraud.

Could Ed be a fake, too? Charles shifted in the saddle. He flicked the reins, refusing to think about Adam Graves.

His mind turned to Addie. To mention Ed's philanthropy would start a disagreement. Were her suspicions the product of her unconscious hope she'd somehow end up with Emma?

He couldn't take the chance on a hunch. If he did anything that led to Ed and Frances losing those children, and he was wrong, he'd hurt an innocent family *and* ruin his credibility.

Still, he wanted Addie to have Emma. She was a different woman than the one he'd first met at the interview. *That* Addie held her emotions inside. This new Addie stood up for what she believed in, laughed easily, but most importantly loved Emma.

When Emma returned to the Drummonds, Addie's heart would break. At the prospect, his stomach clenched.

Adelaide clung to a thread of emotional conclusions, not to the strong rope of cold facts. For her sake, he either had to disprove her theory—or if abuse existed, uncover the truth.

With the paper out this morning, he had some time and would drive out to talk to Tulley. Maybe Ed's neighbor would give new insight. He'd ask Addie to ride along.

Even with the turmoil between them, picturing Adelaide's face in his mind, he longed to have her near.

At the livery, Charles left Ranger in the care of the freckle-faced stable hand, and then loped toward the center of town and crossed the street to Adelaide's shop.

As he entered, two ladies toting hatboxes walked past. He held open the door and they gave him a friendly nod.

"Ladies," he said smiling, and then closed the door after them. He crossed to where Addie stood and soaked up some of the radiance from her face. Was it the sales or could he be the reason for that glow?

"Charles." His name sounded gentler, more refined coming from her lips. "This is a surprise." She fingered a garment on the counter. "I figured you were still angry with me."

How could he ever be mad at anyone with eyes that blue? "And you with me. Considering our dual ownership of the paper, it's bound to happen. As a newsman, I've learned not to take a dispute personally."

"As a woman, I've learned a man can be wrong— without taking it personally." She shot him a triumphant smile.

He chuckled. "I kind of enjoy that temper of yours."

Her eyes widened. "Me? What about you? You—"

"See how easy it is to raise your hackles?"

She let out a laugh. "So you came to pester me?"

"No, ma'am." He stepped closer. "I came to look at you." Her face colored, pretty as a pink rose in bloom. He liked tipping her poise with a few words. "And to hear about Jack."

On the counter, she began ironing the garment's folds with her hands. "I shouldn't have said those things about Jack."

"Oh, but I'm glad you did."

Her chin went up and she shot him a look that would have squelched a weaker man, but Charles merely laughed.

"Don't think you're perfect. You have faults, too."

"Name them."

She examined her nails. "I can't waste my day listing them. You're a smart man. Surely, you can figure them out yourself."

He chuckled, then let his gaze roam her face, memorizing every contour. The high cheek bones, pert nose, slim straight brows. He couldn't let her down. "You looked busy when I came in."

"Those ladies were my first paying customers since my column came out." She sighed. "Still, I've got to start on fall hats. I've decided to ask Laura Larson to help in the shop two days a week so I'll have more time with Emma."

Charles laid a hand on hers and gave it a squeeze. "And for me, I hope."

"All I can concentrate on is keeping that precious little girl." Adelaide pulled her hand from under his.

"That's why I'm here. I have to see Joe Tulley, one of our county commissioners, for an article. His farm edges the Drummond place. If you want to ride along, we'll ask his opinion of Ed."

"I'd love to." Adelaide gave him a dazzling smile. "What do you want to see the commissioner about?"

He blinked. His mind suddenly blank as a new chalkboard. "What?"

"Why are you interviewing Mr. Tulley?"

He cleared his throat. "Ah, Tulley is pushing for upgrading the county roads."

He was reacting as if she were a magnet and he was a pile of iron filings, losing every coherent thought, except ones of her. He rose and walked to the counter to put some distance between them. "I spoke to the committee. They had nothing new to say about Ed, though they all mentioned the tragedy of his son's death."

"Sympathy for the Drummonds' loss colors the committee's judgment. And it doesn't help that Ed's uncle, Roscoe Sullivan, is a respected member of the community."

Maybe she had valid points. Still, he suspected Addie of overreacting, not maliciously, but because she cared.

Deep down, Charles knew Addie would never have permitted a child of hers to be beaten, by anyone, even the child's father. Unlike his mother or hers, Addie had an inner strength, a strength he supposed came from her deep faith in and obedience to God.

For her sake, he'd gather information and see where the facts led, hoping they would point to Ed's unsuitability. But after what he'd seen out at the fire, the gentle way Drummond had treated the Anderson boy, he doubted it. "So far, we have no reason to suspect Ed of abusing William."

He saw disappointment in Addie's eyes, knew how much she counted on discrediting the Drummonds, counted on having Emma permanently.

She returned to her work, but her shoulders drooped.

"A ride in the country will do you good. When can you leave?"

"Emma went home with a friend after school, and she's staying for supper. I can leave at closing time."

He stepped near and caught the scent of her. Crisp and clean, with the faintest hint of honeysuckle. His gaze drifted to those rosy lips. He bent his head... Then realized kissing wasn't appropriate in a place of business. He straightened. "Five-thirty, then."

"Thanks for inviting me," she said a little breathlessly.

He strode to the door, then paused and turned back. "Uh, when, ah, did I say?"

She smiled. "Five-thirty."

"Oh, yeah. I knew that."

Charles said goodbye and then dashed across the

street, back to the world he could control. One where he didn't make a fool of himself because of the way a woman breathed. One where he didn't lose track of what he'd said all because of a woman's smile. Or didn't lose the objectivity he'd prided himself on.

At five-twenty-five, Charles had hitched Ranger to the buggy and pulled up to her shop, a smile of anticipation curved at his mouth. Evidently she'd been watching for him because she immediately stepped onto the walk.

He jumped to the ground, his gaze resting on her face. "Hello again."

"Hello," she answered back.

He stood a moment, merely looking at her. She'd donned a wide-brimmed straw hat with blue ribbons that tied under her chin. Whenever she went out, she wore a different hat. Her stock-in-trade, like the tablet he carried.

Inside that pretty head lived a keen, determined mind, which both fascinated and annoyed him. "You're beautiful."

A blush tinged her cheeks and put a glow on her face even the wide-brimmed hat couldn't hide. "Thank you."

He offered his hand to her, giving it a squeeze. When she returned the pressure, the contact filled him with contentment. Is this how other men felt with the women who cared about them?

He handed her into the buggy, then walked to the other side. She pulled aside her skirts, making room. He climbed in, took the reins and then glanced her way. When he caught her gaze, she lowered her lashes, looking feminine and oh, so alluring.

Seeing her smile, touching her hand, these simple things brought him joy and optimism. He wanted to protect her, to see her have Emma. But no matter how much he longed to be with her, he couldn't marry her.

Not with the blackness inside him.

Flicking the reins over Ranger's back, he forced his gaze to the road, away from Adelaide Crum. He couldn't have her, except for moments like this.

The reminder tamped down his emotions and he resolved to keep the day impersonal. He would focus on *The Ledger* and the state of the county roads. And distance Addie, with her controversial column and her distracting blue eyes, from his mind.

Adelaide laid a gloved hand on his arm and his good intentions faltered. "Thanks for this chance to ask about Ed."

"I want what's best for Emma, too."

They drove out of town, passing a field with shoots of corn cracking the dry soil, then another with winter wheat dancing in the breeze. In an evergreen alongside the road, a cardinal whistled a greeting. Open land pushed to the horizon. Except for the beat of hooves on the road, quiet reigned and a sense of peace settled over him.

Adelaide leaned against the seat and sighed. "I can't remember the last time I went for a ride. I'd forgotten how lovely it is to see nothing but fields."

Empathy rippled through him. Addie had been cooped up much of her adult life, while he'd been free to come and go, riding Ranger into the country whenever he found time.

She removed her hat and held it on her lap. Wisps of hair escaped the knot at her neck and drifted about her face. She pointed to a black horse galloping in the nearby pasture. "Oh, look at him run."

Charles leaned past Adelaide to peek at the sleek stallion. "He's probably tired of those fences and wants to flex his muscles." He found his face very close to hers. Captured by those blue eyes, he couldn't look away.

"It's too bad he's fenced in." She sighed.

He slowed the buggy and with a gentle touch, turned her face toward his. "Do you feel that way sometimes? Boxed in, not by rails but by people's expectations?"

Her eyes widened. "I do," she said softly. "That's why I want a voice at the paper. Do you understand?"

"Why must you work for change? You have nothing to prove."

"I may have nothing to prove, but there are lots of things to *improve*—not just for me, but for all women. With your family situation, you should understand some things need to be changed—like terrorized women, who have nowhere to go."

Charles flicked the reins. Ranger picked up speed. "Neither law, politics nor community expectations kept my mother in that house," he said, his voice gruff. "Her lack of courage did."

"It wasn't only a lack of courage." She laid a gentle hand on his forearm. "She probably had no options."

Her gaze returned to the horse still running around the enclosure. "As a child, did you ever think about running away?"

He nodded. Somewhere along the line this had become about him, not her. "Sure." He exhaled. "But I've learned memories travel with you."

They were both pinned by their pasts. The thought shook him, but he laid it aside to examine later. "Why not learn to ride? On a horse, you can feel that freedom. Feel in control, in tune with the world." He pushed back a wisp of hair that had blown across her cheek. "If you'd like, I can teach you."

She swatted at his hand. "I'll do no such thing."

He shot her a grin. "Too scared?"

"I am not."

"Good. That's what I thought." Then he clicked to Ranger and snapped the reins. He wished he were riding Ranger, with Addie tucked close, his arms encircling her and the wind blowing in their faces. "Once you get used to the size and power of a horse, you might find you enjoy riding as much as I do." He knew how to give her a taste of that freedom. "Here, take the reins." She shook her head, hanging on to the side of the buggy. "I won't let anything happen. Come on, you can do it."

She released her grip and scooted closer, reaching for the leather ribbons.

Charles gave her an encouraging smile. "Good, now flick them." Ranger broke into a trot and Addie gave a little gasp. "Isn't this fun? Feel the freedom, Addie?"

"Oh, yes!" She glanced at him briefly and her eyes shone with delight. As the landscape sped by she laughed.

Memories wafted away on the breeze and for a moment, they both were carefree, released from their pasts.

But up ahead, Charles saw their turn and put out a hand for the reins. "I'll take over now."

"Am I doing it wrong?"

"No, we're here." At his gentle tug, Ranger slowed and turned down the lane. "This is the Tulley farm."

And the return to reality.

Adelaide took in the limbs of huge elms reaching across the lane like a canopy. An occasional burst of sunshine broke through the shade, throwing mottled, swaying patterns upon Charles's face. He had offered to teach her to ride. Even with the exhilaration of the speeding buggy, Adelaide couldn't imagine climbing on a horse, but she'd do it. Not because it meant spending hours with Charles, but because she wanted to come and go as she pleased. For that, she'd risk her neck.

In the Tulley barnyard, Charles brought the horse to a standstill. A black-and-white Border collie barked hello, then ambled over to greet them.

Charles hopped from the buggy, scratched the dog behind the ears and then crossed to her side. Before Adelaide could climb down, he wrapped his hands around her waist and lowered her to the ground.

She wanted to linger in his strong arms, but she had a mission. Giving wide berth to his horse, she started for the house, hoping Mr. Tulley had something tangible against Ed.

An hour later Adelaide's spirits flagged. Mr. Tulley had said only positive things, praising Ed for working his fields while Mr. Tulley's hand healed after losing two fingers to a saw. He'd given example after example of Drummond's willingness to help a neighbor—raising a barn after a tornado, pitching in to harvest crops for an elderly widow.

Charles handed Adelaide into the carriage. "I'm sorry you didn't find what you expected, but after Tulley's assurances, you should feel better about William's safety."

"I've seen Ed Drummond in action. He's not the saint Mr. Tulley made him out to be."

"I'm not saying he's a saint, but there's no evidence

he's a child beater, either," Charles said, climbing in beside her.

As a newsman, Charles would never trust her instincts on this. She had to find evidence.

As they drove up the lane, possibilities scuttled through Adelaide's mind. "If we did a story on the orphans, we'd have an excuse to gather information on the Drummonds."

Charles flicked the reins and they started down the lane. "You're looking for trouble where none exists. Drop it."

"Because you don't want me involved in the paper?"

He scowled. "A newspaper isn't a tool for your agenda."

She folded her arms across her chest. Charles couldn't see trouble if it were marked with a capital *T.* If she could get out to the Drummond farm, she'd do some investigating of her own. "I'd like to learn to ride or maybe practice driving a buggy."

"Really? What made you change your mind?"

"You did."

Charles beamed. "How about starting tomorrow after Emma leaves for school? I'll have you back before time to open."

Her stomach clenched, but she agreed. She'd no longer allow her fear of horses to control her life. Tomorrow she'd learn the skills that would enable her to check on William and Frances and uncover the truth. She could no more ignore Ed Drummond's treatment of William than she could allow Mr. Sparks to scare her from her goal of improving life for women. Since the banker had threatened to take Emma, she'd prayed daily about her desire to work for suffrage and felt in her bones that God had given her this mission, along with the task of protecting the Grounds children. She couldn't allow intimidation to shape her decisions. If she turned her back on others, she couldn't face herself in the mirror each morning.

Charles's piercing eyes scrutinized her. "You're awfully quiet."

Hoping to ease his inspection, she put a hand on Charles's arm. Such a small thing, she supposed, to feel the hard muscle of a man's forearm beneath the fiber of his shirt. But these small touches enthralled her. She forced her mind away from what she could not have. "How did you get into the newspaper business?"

"It's a long story but I'll give you the condensed version. I left home at fifteen and saw a sign in the window of a small weekly newspaper." He grinned. "No one else applied, so I got a job setting type. I slept in the back on a cot, swept the place, did whatever needed doing. In time, my overworked boss asked me to write a news item. One thing led to another." He chuckled. "You could say I fell in love with the smell of ink."

"I'm sure you love more than that."

"I found the urgency of deadlines and being tapped into the pulse of the community, the entire nation, exciting. Since then, my life has revolved around the newspaper business." He frowned. "I'm talking too much."

"I love hearing about your life." Charles had been quite young to be on his own. "So why did you leave home at fifteen?"

He shrugged. "My mother died. Sam had already left. No reason to stick around." He said no more, but she knew by the way he bit off the words that saying more would open wounds.

"With all you've experienced as a boy, why can't you understand my concern about William?"

"My past was hardly the little rough wagon ride that upset you. You have no idea what I went through." He let out a bitter laugh. "Sam and I became experts at lying, could make up a reason for a black eye or cracked rib in two seconds flat."

Her throat closed at his words and she swallowed convulsively. If only someone had helped him. If only she could help him now. "Didn't anyone get suspicious?"

"If they did, they never did anything about it. No one helped us, Addie." He took a deep breath and the sound rattled through him like a speeding train on a mile-high trestle. "No one." Charles met her gaze. The pain in his eyes wrenched her heart. "It's not the same as William, not the same at all."

"My heart aches for you, for the defenseless little boy you were. But isn't your childhood proof we don't know what's happening behind closed doors?"

"Isn't it possible Ed's lack of patience is because he's still grieving for his son?"

Grief didn't give a person the right to shove a defenseless child. "Maybe it's less painful for you to put on blinders."

Dark eyes turned on her. "Maybe you're the one wearing blinders. Admit it—you want Emma. The only way to have her is to prove the Drummonds unfit."

His words stung like nettles in her garden. "I'd never make this up, not even to get Emma."

"You heard Tulley. Ed Drummond is an upstanding citizen."

"So was your father—the minute he walked out the door."

Charles didn't respond.

The buggy closed in around her. She turned away, but found the passing scenery had lost its charm. Her gaze dropped to the spot between Ranger's ears. "I think I went to the wrong man for help."

Charles snapped the reins and the buggy lurched forward. He swung his gaze to her, his eyes cold and distant. "Maybe you did."

Chapter Twelve

At breakfast the next morning, Adelaide couldn't get her mind off the way she and Charles had parted yesterday, couldn't forget his cold, distant eyes. Her suspicions about Ed Drummond had reopened a past he wanted to forget. A past filled with fear and violence. Her eyes misted. No one had cared enough to investigate, wounding him almost as much as the abuse he'd endured at his father's hands.

If she ignored Ed's threat to William's safety, she'd be no different than the bystanders in Charles's world.

Beside her, Emma dawdled at the table with a faraway look in her eyes, not eating, aimlessly stirring her oatmeal.

"Emma, you need to eat or you'll be late to school."

A rap at the kitchen door made Emma jump. The child was skittish. Why?

Adelaide found Sally on the landing wearing a bright blue bonnet on her head, and a dishtowel-covered basket on one arm.

"Good morning! I've brought fresh-baked muffins."

Adelaide flipped back the towel and inhaled the enticing aroma. "Mmm, apple cinnamon." She cocked her head. "You drove all the way into town to bring us muffins?"

"I'd have driven to Minneapolis." Sally chuckled. "Another minute looking at the downcast faces of my men and I'd have pelted them with these muffins!" Sally plopped the basket on the table, then chucked Emma under the chin.

The recipient of Sally's treats before, Adelaide knew the symptoms. "Bad day in the woods for your men?"

Nodding, Sally slipped into a seat. "All four went rabbit hunting yesterday and came home empty-handed."

Adelaide chuckled, and then tipped the basket of muffins. "Look what Mrs. Bender brought, Emma. Want one?"

Emma pushed away her bowl, her face glum. "I'm not hungry."

"She should be sitting in my kitchen," Sally said. "She'd fit right in."

"You usually eat every bite. Are you sick?" Adelaide laid a hand on Emma's forehead, relieved to find it cool.

The child hung her head, looking more like a rag doll than her usual perky self. "No."

Adelaide slid into the chair beside her. "What's wrong?"

"Nothing."

Sally tilted Emma's head up with her fingertips. "I bet she doesn't have her homework done. Or maybe she hates recess. Oh, I know, she wants to stay home and clean. That's it. She wants to scrub the floors, all the windows, even the steps out back."

The slightest smile tugged at Emma's lips. "No."

"Well…maybe she's upset she didn't catch a rabbit." Sally touched Emma's hand. "Is that what's bothering you?"

A glimmer sparked in her eyes. "I wouldn't hurt a bunny."

"Ah, you city girls don't know what you're missing. Rabbit tastes good, like chicken. If my men ever bag any, I'll bring you some fried crisp."

Emma wrinkled her nose. "No, thank you."

Adelaide smoothed Emma's hair. "Something *is* bothering you, sweetie. Can you tell me about it?"

Sally rose. "Well, I'd better get a move on." She flashed Adelaide a look of concern, then slipped out the back.

Soon as Sally closed the door, Emma dropped the spoon and looked up, her eyes swimming with tears. "William."

A chill crept down Adelaide's spine. She drew Emma's hand into her own. "What about William?"

Tears spilled over her lashes and rolled down her cheeks. "I don't know."

Adelaide let go of Emma's hand and began rubbing her back. "You're worried about William?"

Emma nodded, her face contorted in misery. "Uh-huh."

"Tell me, honey, why?" Adelaide continued massaging Emma's back, and waited, every muscle in her body as tense as the small ones under her fingers.

Emma's mouth tightened. She picked up her spoon and began shoveling the oatmeal into her mouth, avoiding the question.

Adelaide laid a hand on Emma's arm to still her frantic eating. "When life gets me down, instead of worrying, I've learned to count my blessings. Before I know it, I feel better."

Taking Emma's smaller hands in her own, Adelaide showed her how to tick off each blessing on her fingers. But even after enumerating Emma's new hat, Adelaide's cookies and a new best friend, the little girl still looked forlorn.

Emma carried the same fears ticking away in Adelaide's gut. The time had come to take action, not tomorrow, not next week. Today.

An hour later, waiting for Laura, Adelaide paced the shop.

The bell jingled over the shop door. "Morning, Adelaide!" Laura shrugged off her shawl and hung it on a peg.

"Good morning. I hate to leave you alone on your first day back, but I have an errand that needs doing. Is it all right if I'm gone all morning?"

"Don't be silly. I'll be fine. Are you going to the ladies' Bible study?"

"Ah…no." Adelaide couldn't lie. "I'll explain later." She gave her friend a quick hug. "Mrs. Brewster is to pick up her alterations today." Adelaide pulled on her gloves, talking fast. "I'll miss a riding lesson with Mr. Graves this morning." Charles might not show up after the way they parted yesterday. "Tell him I'm sorry."

"Are you over your fear of horses?"

"I'm working at it."

"Good for you!" Laura tittered. "Riding lessons are a perfect way to bring you two together. Don't worry about Mr. Graves."

"See you around noon," Adelaide said and left the shop.

Charles wouldn't approve of her plan, but he couldn't

see Ed as a threat to the children. Hopefully, with Ed working in the fields, she could talk to Frances alone.

To get in and out of before Ed came in for the noon meal, she had to hurry. She lengthened her stride, her skirts swirling around her feet. As she neared the café, she passed Mrs. Whitehall tacking up a list of the daily specials.

Mrs. Whitehall's apron was dusted with flour. "Morning, Adelaide."

"Good morning, Geraldine."

"I want to thank you for what you're doing for Fannie. She's practicing her walk, even trying to stifle that giggle of hers."

Reining in her impatience, Adelaide slowed her pace. "Fannie's a lovely girl."

Mrs. Whitehall rosy face broke into a smile. "If you can get away for lunch, I've made apple fritters. The bill's on me. My way of saying thanks."

Adelaide shook her head. "Not today."

At her abrupt reply, Geraldine shot her a probing look.

Adelaide forced a smile. "I'm sorry. Wish I could."

"Well, another time, then," Mrs. Whitehall said, her tone friendly, her suspicion forgotten.

Adelaide promised, and then hurried off. At the thought of driving a buggy alone, a band of nerves tightened around her throat and her touchy stomach somersaulted.

Now, don't go getting jumpy, Adelaide Crum.

In her mind's eye, she pictured Emma and William's innocent young faces. For them, she'd do anything. In the past, she'd been adept at keeping the peace. Since the orphans arrived in town, she'd learned if she wanted to change things, she had to take a stand. Not that she liked looking for trouble, but to protect the children she must.

Ducking into the office of the livery, she found a young man straddling a bench, working something smelly into the contraption the horses wore between their teeth and over their ears. "Good morning." She'd tried to sound confident, but her voice quavered.

"Ma'am." He got to his feet, dropping the equipment and tipped the bill of his cap. Never in her life had Adelaide seen a face with so many freckles.

"I'm, ah, in need of a…conveyance, for the morning."

The young man grinned, displaying a missing tooth. "Well, you're in the right place, ma'am. What do ya need?" He motioned to a hand-chalked sign of the rates hanging on the wall.

She read a list of options. "A buggy will suffice, thank you." Adelaide dug in her purse and paid in advance. They walked into the stable, and the young man left to get the horse.

That had been simple. Now if she could only remember what she knew about driving. She had vivid memories of riding out to the Tulley farm. But most of those memories had nothing to do with driving a buggy.

And everything to do with Charles.

She recalled his strong hands and arms pulling back on the reins to stop the horse, to guide the animal's movements left or right. The memory kicked up her pulse, until she relived his cold demeanor on the ride back into town. She bit her lip. She mustn't think about Charles.

The youth walked toward her, leading a pure white horse.

Fiddlesticks, I might as well advertise my plan in the paper. "Don't you have a less conspicuous one?"

He tugged his cap back off his forehead, revealing a shock of carrot-red hair and scratched his brow. "Conspic, cons… I ain't sure what you're saying, ma'am."

She gave her brightest smile. "I thought a black or brown horse would look nicer with the buggy, more like a matched set."

He shrugged and muttered "women" under his breath, but returned the white horse to its stall. Watching him amble along, as if he had all the time in the world, Adelaide tapped her toe. For one so young, he didn't have a speedy bone in his body.

He crossed to another stall and patted the nose of a dark brown horse, a *big* dark brown horse. "Does Shadow suit?"

The name couldn't be more appropriate. "Much nicer."

Not that she needed to be secretive when she visited the Drummonds—this time. Still, she'd prefer avoiding attention.

While she waited, she roamed the livery. Spotting a rag in the hay, she picked it up and draped it over a rail. If Charles had seen her do that, he'd poke fun at her. Not that she'd mind. She enjoyed his teasing nature, which reminded her of their afternoon in the livery. She plucked a strand of hay from the cloth, thinking of Charles's almost kiss. She might be brave enough to drive a buggy, but falling in love—

She shook herself mentally. She didn't want a man so blinded by his past he couldn't see the present, much less the future.

She strolled down the aisle. Over the half door, Ranger stretched out his neck like he recognized her.

"You want me to rub your nose, don't you, fellow?" She inched forward, grateful for the barrier separating them, and ran her fingers lightly along his broad muzzle. Ranger was a beautiful animal, almost as beautiful as his owner.

If only she could do this investigating with Charles, but he saw things in black and white—the shades of logic—whereas she saw things in hues, colored with emotion and intuition. They were as different as night and day.

She strolled outside and watched the young man hitch Shadow to the buggy, marveling at the horse's patience despite the lad's absurd slowness. If he worked for her, she'd light a fire under him.

"All set, ma'am."

Approaching the animal, Adelaide looked at the beast's wide back and hoped she could show him who was boss. "Thank you." She motioned toward the horse. "Can he be ridden?"

He scratched his head. "Yes, ma'am, but generally, when the horse is pullin', folks sit behind in the buggy."

Adelaide pressed her lips together, holding back a giggle. A giggle that would surely sound like Fannie's. "I meant without the buggy."

He looked relieved. "Yes, ma'am, he sure can!"

The young man gave her a hand. She gathered the reins, hoping she held them correctly. "Is there a brake?"

He blinked. "Not on a buggy, ma'am. Just tie up the horse if you stop somewhere."

"Of course, how silly of me."

He stood looking at her. Realizing he waited for her leave, she said a quick prayer and flicked the reins. The horse took off at a lively clip, throwing Adelaide against the seat. Wiggling upright, she pulled slightly on the reins, and, wonder of wonders, Shadow slowed.

Inconspicuous horse or not, she stayed on the back streets. In the country, she flicked the reins again and Shadow picked up speed. Every bit of her smiled, inside and out, at the thought of doing something this bold, this free, taking control of her worries about Emma and William.

Adelaide knew the Drummonds lived on the next farm beyond the Tulley place, a couple miles down the road. She spent her ride thinking about what she'd say to Frances, and time passed in a blur. A red barn came into view with Drummond, 1882, painted in bold white letters. She tugged on the left rein and drove down the lane to the house.

"Whoa!" she said, and Shadow obeyed. Gathering up her skirts, she climbed down and wrapped the leather around the hitching post, then thanked God for giving her safety. If only her investigation went as well.

She marched to the door and rapped. Through the screen, she caught a glimpse of a shadowy figure. "Frances? It's Adelaide Crum. I'm taking care of Emma."

Frances appeared at the door, looking thinner than Adelaide remembered, gaunt even. Pinned in place, a bib-style, rose-sprigged apron covered Frances's house-dress. Her cotton stockings and rundown shoes befitted a hard-working farmer's wife. A mane of dark hair pulled into a tidy knot framed Frances's face, tanned from working in the garden. "Is she all right?"

"She's fine. May I come in?"

Though she moved slowly with a hint of reluctance, Frances opened the door.

"On such a lovely morning I thought I'd drive out for a visit and catch you up on Emma."

The furrow between Frances's brows eased. "I'd heard Emma was staying with you. I'm glad."

"I love having her with me."

"Is she doing well in school?"

"She's doing much better with her reading. Now math, that's another story." Adelaide smiled and Frances smiled back, sharing the knowledge of Emma's Achilles' heel.

"I'm sorry, I, ah, don't get many visitors. Come in." She followed Frances into the kitchen. Adelaide noticed a slight limp, but, otherwise, nothing appeared out of the ordinary.

"If you'd like a cup of tea, the water's hot."

"Tea would be lovely."

While Frances busied herself with cups and saucers, Adelaide sat on one of the battered Windsor chairs surrounding the gate-leg table and looked around her. The kitchen might be plain, but Frances kept it meticulously clean. "I haven't had the chance to talk to you since your mother's funeral. The service was a lovely tribute to her life."

"Thank you." Frances approached with the tea, and her defeated expression tore at Adelaide's heart.

Was this the look of a woman who shared a home with a violent man? Or the appearance of a woman who'd lost two precious loved ones?

Adelaide added sugar and took a sip. "This is good."

Frances lifted her gaze. "Is Emma happy? Really happy?"

"Very, but she misses William." If she could get the boy home with her, maybe he'd tell what went on in the Drummond house. Adelaide leaned forward. "I've come with a request."

Stirring cream into her coffee, Frances's hand stilled.

"I'd like William to spend the weekend with Emma."

Frances shook her head. "Ed won't allow it."

"Why not?"

"William has chores."

"Surely, it would be all right for one night. I could pick him up after chores Saturday morning and have him back in time to help Sunday afternoon. I'm sure he misses Emma, too."

Frances shifted in her chair. "Won't do any good, but I'll ask," she said with obvious reluctance.

"Thank you." Adelaide took another sip of tea, wondering how to encourage Frances to talk. "Mr. Graves said you'd been feeling poorly. How are you?"

"About the same."

Relief flooded Adelaide's veins. Maybe Frances didn't plan to have Emma back, at least anytime soon. "I noticed your limp."

"My back's been acting up."

"I'm sorry. Are you lifting too much?"

"Aching backs don't mean less work. Washing and ironing needs doing." She folded callused hands in front of her. "I'm not complaining."

Aching backs were common, but Adelaide suspected a more ominous reason for Frances's limp. Not that Frances would confide in her, even if there were. "I'm very sorry about your mother. I know how close you were." Adelaide laid her hand over her schoolmate's. "Sarah acted strong, not the type to...."

Frances pulled her hand away. As she lifted her palm to her lips, her fingers trembled. "I still can't believe it. Ma *was* a strong woman, a survivor. She knew I needed her—" Frances bit her lip. "When Eddie passed, I looked to Ma for strength."

Adelaide noticed Frances didn't mention her husband. "My mother's health failed about the time Eddie died. I've regretted not being able to do much for you."

Frances shrugged "You sent food."

Adelaide laid a hand on Frances's arm, noting its boniness through her sleeve. "I can't imagine that kind of loss."

A long sigh slipped from Frances's lips. "I thought with children in the house, maybe…."

"Maybe what?" Adelaide prodded gently.

"Maybe things would be like they were before."

"But they're not."

Frances shook her head. Tears slipped over her lower lashes. "Losing Eddie nearly killed Ed."

"I can imagine."

But Frances didn't appear to hear, merely looked at a distant spot on the wall. "The morning it happened, I'd gone to Ma's," she said. "Pa had passed a few weeks before, and we were going through his things." She took a breath. "I left Eddie at home with his pa," she said, her voice so hushed Adelaide had to strain to hear. "Eddie's shirttail caught on fire, least-wise, that's what we think. Ed had gone to the outhouse, only for a few minutes, and heard Eddie's screams. He ran to the house, met Eddie coming out, his clothes on fire."

Frances rose from her chair, turning her back to wipe her eyes on the hem of her apron. Tears stung Adelaide's eyes. She couldn't imagine losing a child, especially in such a hideous way. Adelaide stood and gathered her childhood friend in her arms, felt her frailty. How much sorrow could Frances take?

"If only I'd been home." Frances's voice quavered. "And now Ma—I let her down, too."

"You didn't know," Adelaide said gently, holding her tight. "And if she was determined, you couldn't have stopped her."

Frances pulled away, her gaze meeting Adelaide's. "This is a house of death."

Adelaide's pulse skittered. "What are you saying?"

"I can't keep people safe, don't you see?" Frances's voice rose to an eerie pitch.

Adelaide patted Frances's arm, trying to soothe the wild look in her classmate's face. "None of this is your fault. You mustn't blame yourself."

Through the window, a movement caught Adelaide's eye. A man emerged from the woods.

Frances followed Adelaide's gaze, then flinched. "Ed!" Frances swiped at her eyes. "You'd better go."

Adelaide had no intention of going anywhere.

Charles entered Adelaide's shop and found an older woman moving a feather duster over the shelves. Alerted by the bell, she headed his way.

"You must be Mrs. Larson."

"And *you* are Mr. Graves. I knew your father. You look just like him."

Charles pasted a tight smile on his face. "So I've heard."

She offered her plump, dimpled hand. "I've meant to stop at the paper long before this and welcome you to Noblesville. It's a pleasure to meet you at last."

He released her hand. "The pleasure is mine.

Addie—" Heat climbed his neck. How familiar had she become that he'd call her by a nickname in front of a virtual stranger? "Miss Crum speaks highly of you."

Mrs. Larson beamed. "Aw, you've given Adelaide a nickname."

He could see her mind working. He'd best change the subject. "I understand you're helping out at the shop again."

"Yes, I love doing it. Working here gives my daughter a breather. At times, two women in one house can be one too many."

Only half listening to Mrs. Larson, he glanced toward the workroom. Was Addie in there sewing? Making tea? Planning her next editorial? Not that he owed her an apology. Still, he'd disappointed her and that bothered him. "Is Adelaide here?"

"No, she isn't. She had an errand to run."

"I was to give her a riding lesson this morning."

"Yes, she told me." Mrs. Larson smiled and tiny creases danced around her eyes. "Would you join me in a cup of coffee?"

"Sure, but let me get it." *And see if Addie is hiding from me.*

Mrs. Larson laid her palm on her bodice. "How nice."

"Do you use cream or sugar?" he asked, heading to the back.

"Sugar."

He returned with a tray holding two coffee-filled cups, two spoons and napkins alongside a sugar bowl.

"You haven't forgotten a thing. I'm astonished."

"How so?"

"My son-in-law never lifts a finger in the kitchen and

my Bernard, God rest his soul, never served a beverage in the thirty-four years of our marriage."

Charles placed a cup in front of Mrs. Larson. "As a bachelor, I've learned to handle the necessities." He took a seat across from her, then chuckled. "I suspect Addie got cold feet."

"You could be right. I've never known Adelaide to ride." Mrs. Larson leaned toward him, her eyes bright. "You sat on the orphan placement committee."

Charles took a swig of coffee. "She told you about that?"

"Adelaide confides in me, Mr. Graves." She straightened in her chair. "May I confide in you, too?"

Uneasiness settled in his chest. "If you'd like."

She pinned him with her gaze. "Adelaide is a special, giving young woman. Some might even say she's a fix-it kind of woman. Someone could easily take advantage of her."

Not likely. "Addie is a strong, independent woman. She's not about to be taken advantage of, even if someone wanted to, which, let me assure you, I do not."

She nodded, the lines of concern on her face softening. "If I've spoken out of turn, I apologize."

"No need to apologize. I can see you're a good friend."

She eyed him over her cup brim. "As a good friend, I'm also aware of things Adelaide enjoys, like the Black-eyed Susies growing along the roads into town."

The hint couldn't be more obvious. Maybe the daisies would mend the rift between them. Or should he even try? But thinking how pleased she'd be if he showed up with those flowers tempted him. "I appreciate the tip. Anything else I should know?"

Mrs. Larson leaned forward. "Adelaide would scold

me for telling you this," she said, dropping her voice, "but her birthday is in a couple of months, on the twenty-fifth of July."

Charles shifted in his seat. "Is matchmaking a hobby of yours?"

She laughed. "I'm an incurable romantic. I believe love can overcome all obstacles."

This woman lived in a make-believe world. "I have to disagree with you on that point. I've seen that love can't resolve all obstacles, can even die if problems are severe."

She waggled a finger at him. "Perhaps in that case, there hadn't been true love in the first place."

Charles frowned. Perhaps his parents had married for the wrong reasons. Still, how could a man know if he were truly in love? "Yes, well, you could be right. It's impossible to judge."

"No, it isn't impossible. Nothing is impossible." She glanced down at their cups. "My, goodness, I think a refill is in order. I'll be right back."

Charles stared after Mrs. Larson. If only…

He mustn't let this woman override his logic. He knew life held impossible situations, unworkable relationships. Things he wasn't meant to have.

Like Adelaide Crum.

Chapter Thirteen

Frances's hazel eyes went wide with alarm. She took a firm hold on Adelaide's arm, determined to show her out.

"I'm not leaving. I want to ask him about William coming"

"No, don't." She let go of Adelaide's arm. "I'll, ah, I'll go ask him."

Frances scurried to meet her husband, with every step her limp grew more pronounced. As Adelaide watched, Frances gestured toward the house. Ed's face went from calm to angry. He pushed past her, leaving his wife to struggle along behind.

Adelaide braced herself, refusing to give in to the icy fingers of terror snatching at her belly. She sent up a prayer for assistance. A blessed sense of calm settled over her.

Ed clomped up the wooden steps onto the porch and burst through the door, his face contorted into a scowl.

Any man who could harm a child had to be stopped. Adelaide believed Ed Drummond to be such a man. Frances came through the door and joined her husband.

"You want the boy, too, is that it?" he demanded.

"No, I—"

"You've got the girl. You aren't getting the boy. No one's getting another boy of mine."

What was he talking about? He made it sound as if she'd taken Emma from them. "I only want William to spend some time with his sister. She misses him."

Ed shook his head. "Get yourself a husband and have your own children. Stop trying to get mine."

She raised her chin. "Then stop treating them badly."

He stomped closer until he stood over her, the odor of sweat clinging to his clothes. "Who said I hurt children?"

"Are you?"

Crimson dotted his cheeks. "Until I lost—" He swallowed and narrowed his gaze. "I'm doing the best I can. Leave my children and my wife alone."

"I'm only asking William to visit his sister one night." Adelaide marveled at the steadiness of her voice.

"If Emma wants to be with William, she'll come back where she belongs."

"I talked with William's teacher. He's missing school. You're breaking the agreement with the Children's Aid Society."

"Until the crops are in, I need William in the fields." Ed folded his arms across his chest. "I'm teaching him the importance of work and of obedience, like my father taught me." He unfolded his arms and pointed a finger in her direction. "You have no idea who I am. What me and the missus have been through." He tugged Frances close. "I mean to take care of what's mine."

"If any harm comes to William, I'll contact the sheriff."

He shot her a glare, then faced Frances. "You'd better not have asked that meddler here."

Frances shook her head. "She came on her own, Ed. I swear."

"She's not to step foot in this house again."

"I won't let her in. She didn't mean nothing by it."

Ed pushed open the screen door, and then turned to face Adelaide. "Enjoy Emma while you can. I aim to have my family back together." He smiled an odd, secretive smile that didn't reach his eyes, then stalked across the yard.

"You shouldn't have said those things," Frances whispered. "You upset him."

If this visit set the wheels in motion for losing Emma, Adelaide didn't know how she'd bear it. She'd been foolish to run ahead. Why hadn't she prayed about the situation? Adelaide swung around to face Frances. "Tell the sheriff what your husband is like."

Frances looked at her blankly, then sank into a chair, weariness settling on her face. "Give Emma a kiss."

Adelaide bent down beside her and touched her arm. "Come home with me."

She shook her head. "He'd only come after me and blame you for my going. He'll simmer down."

"Please, I can't leave you here."

"Ed needs me. You don't understand what he's been through." She pulled herself to her feet and walked to the sink. First she picked up a knife, then a potato and peeled it. "I've got dinner to fix."

Adelaide couldn't drag Frances out of her home. If Ed was abusing his family, fear or some kind of misguided loyalty would keep her at his side.

"Adelaide."

"Yes."

"You made Ed mad. The more he thinks about it, the madder he'll get. Don't dawdle. Tell Emma William sends his love."

Not looking up, Frances nodded. Though it pained her to do it, Adelaide hurried out the door, leaving her classmate behind.

Clearly Frances blamed herself for the tragedies in her family—perhaps the main reason she wouldn't leave.

Had Ed Drummond been responsible for the death of his only child? Had his wife and mother-in-law known it and been afraid to tell the sheriff? Or perhaps, after tragically losing those they loved, both the Drummonds had lost their minds.

Adelaide untied the reins and climbed into the buggy. She looked back at the small, faded farmhouse, the wood leeched by the sun. "The house of death" Frances had called it, and it looked that way.

Please, God, protect Frances and William.

No one could make her bring Emma back here after her visit today. She'd find a way to get William out of there, too.

As she took up the reins, her hands trembled. What if Ed insisted on Emma's return? Perspiration beaded her forehead. She would do anything to keep Emma and William safe.

Anything.

Slapping the reins on Shadow's back, she drove out of the barnyard, a cloud of dust kicking up behind as the horse clipped along. Her mind drifted to the encounter with Ed. A pheasant flew low in front of the buggy, catching the horse unaware. Before Adelaide could react, Shadow shied and bolted, ripping the reins from her hands. The reins flapped against the horse's back, out of reach. Up ahead she saw a sharp turn.

"Whoa!" But the spooked horse didn't hear. Shadow didn't slow. Adelaide held on with both hands.

Rounding the bend too fast, the right back wheel slid off the road. Adelaide screamed. The buggy tipped dangerously, and then righted, only to slam against a rock. Wood cracked and the buggy lurched, almost throwing her from the seat. The weight of the buggy got the horse's attention and Shadow slowed, coming to a winded halt beneath an elm tree.

Heart pounding, Adelaide scampered down to survey the damage. The wheel tilted outward and the buggy sat at a precarious angle. She peered beneath the buggy. "Oh, no."

Something had broken. This buggy was going nowhere and neither was she.

She looked up and down the road, but saw no one. She didn't dare ask the Drummonds for help. She'd walk to the Tulley farm.

At a distant shout, her head snapped up. In the field next to her, Ed Drummond hurried across his acreage. Before she could move, he broke into a run.

"God, help me."

Remembering Frances's warning, Adelaide raced to the horse and with shaky fingers clawed at the buckles of the thick leather straps on Shadow's back and the front of the buggy. They stuck, then gave way with a jerk. She worked to free the poles holding the lathered horse in place. At last, they fell away.

Holding tight to the leather strap on Shadow's head, as the horse pranced nervously beside her, she glanced over her shoulder. Her heart stuttered in her chest. Ed was getting closer, maybe a hundred yards away.

No time to remove all the pieces of leather. She tugged, yanking the reins free, and then looked again. Ed—fifty yards away and closing the distance fast.

Adelaide ran to the side of the buggy, pulling, coaxing the horse nearer, her fear of the man greater than her fear of the animal. Hanging on to the reins, she scrambled aboard the conveyance and thrust out a leg.

The animal sidestepped away from her rustling skirts. "Please, Shadow, let me get on." Ed ran hard, but Adelaide kept her voice soothing.

As if the horse understood her plight, on her second attempt, Shadow stood motionless. She threw a leg over his back and pulled herself upright. She bunched up the long reins in her hands and held tight to the padded belt encircling the horse's back. Praying Shadow wouldn't get tangled up in all the loose straps hanging from him, she clicked to the horse. He started off slowly. *Too slowly.*

She glanced back. Ed stretched out his arms, ready to grab her. She kicked Shadow's flanks. "Move, Shadow! Move!"

The horse sprang to life beneath her. A death grip on the belt, she slid backward, but hung on, and they galloped up the road as Ed jumped the ditch, shouting obscenities. Over her shoulder, she saw him, fist raised toward her, standing amidst the dust stirred up by Shadow's hooves.

Minutes later, with Ed out of sight, Adelaide slowed the horse, sagged against his neck and thanked God for keeping her safe and for Shadow. The horse had accepted his passenger, dragging gear and all, and hadn't caused her one whit of trouble, a blessing because she had no more heroics left.

She slipped into town by the back streets. A few passersby gawked as she rode past. Back straight, she nodded as if riding bareback through town dragging leather occurred every day.

With the livery in sight, she thought she'd made it without discovery, but then Charles exited the wooden building. He gaped and ran to her, taking hold of Shadow's bridle, bringing the animal to a halt. "Addie, are you all right? What happened?"

She couldn't very well say where she'd been. "I had a problem with the buggy I rented. The wheel broke so I rode the horse back to the livery."

"You rode a *horse? Bareback?*" His normally chiseled jaw hung slack. "Dragging that leather, you could have been hurt."

"Well, I wasn't." It gave her satisfaction to see the amazement in Charles's eyes, and maybe a dash of admiration, too.

He gestured. "Climb down. I'll ride the horse in for you."

Adelaide lifted her chin. "I'm doing fine on my own."

He frowned. "Why were you out in a buggy alone?"

"Don't you have things to do at the paper?"

He took a step back. "You're a stubborn woman, Adelaide Crum," he grumbled as she clicked to the horse and rode past. "And adept at avoiding my questions."

Pretending she hadn't heard, Adelaide rode to the stable door. The freckle-faced lad stopped in his tracks, squinting into the noonday sun. "Sakes alive! What happened?"

"If you'll give me a hand down, young man, I'll explain."

Dropping the water buckets he carried, he ran to her side, probably faster than he'd moved in his entire life. Adelaide slid off the horse, right into his arms. By the time her feet hit the ground, his face matched his carrot-red hair.

Needlelike pain shot through her legs, and they almost buckled beneath her, but she remained on her feet. Peeling off her gloves, Adelaide explained what had happened. "I'm sorry about the buggy. It's out on Conner Road." She smoothed her skirts. "I'll pay for the damages, of course."

"Probably an axle. I'll tell the boss."

Adelaide nodded. "I'll be sure and tell Mr. Lemming how considerate you've been."

Except for a small rip in the seam of her skirt, she looked no worse for her experience. Walking home, every step sent an ache through her backside and up her limbs. Still a tiny thrill of pleasure slid through her. She'd managed to escape Ed Drummond, had ridden a horse—without a saddle, at that—and had even impressed Charles.

When she reached the back of her shop, Adelaide stopped short, her heart pounding in her chest. There on the brick in red capital letters and dripping like blood, someone had painted: YOU'LL PAY FOR THAT MOUTH.

The threat, still damp to the touch, hadn't been there when she left this morning. That meant Ed Drummond could not have penned it. Who had? Who wanted to scare her?

Perhaps someone angry about her stand on suffrage had done this.

Then she remembered Jacob Paul's icy stare when she'd caught him setting that fire a few weeks back. Could it be Jacob, a boy she'd once had in Sunday school?

Inside her shop, Adelaide could barely keep up with Laura's chatter. Normally she loved her friend's chitchat and would want every detail of her visit with Charles, but today she needed time alone, time to think about the meaning of those words in the alley. But most of all on what she should do next about Ed Drummond. What would he have done if he'd caught her? She shivered.

With God's help she'd get William out of that house, maybe Frances, too.

"Adelaide, you look worried to death." Laura's voice cut into her thoughts. "I didn't say *that* much to Mr. Graves."

"What?" Adelaide gave Laura's arm a squeeze. "Oh, I'm sure you didn't. Would you mind staying this afternoon? I forgot some pressing business."

"Is something wrong? You aren't yourself."

"I've let some things slide and now that you're here, I'd like to tend to them. Can you stay?"

"Of course."

"I'll be back in time to pick up Emma from school."

"It's only a few blocks. Why not let her walk alone?"

"No, I couldn't." Adelaide realized too late how sharp her tone had been. "I like to get her myself."

Laura's brow furrowed.

Adelaide patted Laura's arm. "Thanks for looking after things."

Adelaide grabbed her bag and rushed out the front

door, turning right toward the sheriff's office. Dodging a group of men quibbling over who owned the best hunting dog, she hurried to her destination.

By the time she reached the jail, she'd formulated a plan. First, she'd ask the sheriff if there'd been anything suspicious about Eddie Drummond's death. Then she'd wire Mr. Fry, the agent for the Children's Aid Society, and insist he send someone to look into William's safety.

The days when Adelaide stood by and let others determine her future, and the futures of those she cared about, were over.

Resolutely, she turned the handle and stepped inside. Her eyes took a moment to adjust to the dim light. When they did, she blinked in surprise.

Charles. Shooting questions at Sheriff Rogers and scribbling furiously on a notepad. At the sight of him, her pulse skittered.

The door banged shut behind her. At the sound, the men turned around. The middle-aged sheriff's belly rolled over his waistband, but his muscular arms and massive shoulders promised he could handle trouble. Thankfully, in Noblesville, that generally wasn't much. If not for his reporter paraphernalia, Charles, all lean lines and broad-shouldered, could easily pass for a lawman.

Through an open doorway, Adelaide could see two cells. She wrinkled her nose. In the first cell a snoring prisoner, reeking of liquor and vomit, sprawled across a cot. The other cell remained empty, a perfect place for Ed.

Charles greeted her with a frown. "What brings you here?"

She wouldn't tell Charles about her visit to the Drummonds. "I, ah, found something painted on the brick out back of my shop." Adelaide sucked in a breath. "It said, 'You'll pay for that mouth.'"

Charles stepped to her side, his face etched with concern.

The sheriff frowned. "Sounds like someone wants to scare you. Any idea who?"

Adelaide sighed. "I suppose it could be several people. My view on suffrage hasn't been popular."

Charles's mouth tightened as if to stop him from letting out the words, "I told you so."

"Could be the Paul kid getting even with you for reporting his attempt at arson," Sheriff Rogers said.

"I thought of him."

Adelaide glanced at the pad in Charles's hand. The words—Sarah Hartman, murder—leapt off the page. Adelaide swayed on her feet. *Had Ed Drummond killed his mother-in-law?*

Sheriff Rogers pulled out a chair. "Have a seat, Miss Crum, you look peaked."

Adelaide dropped into it.

Charles leaned over her. "Are you all right, Addie?"

Adelaide nodded, but it wasn't true. If Ed had killed Sarah, Frances was alone with a murderer, and William would soon return from school. She had to convince the sheriff and Charles that Ed Drummond had to be the culprit.

"Sheriff, did someone murder Mrs. Hartman?"

"Now what makes you say that?"

"I got a glimpse of Mr. Graves's pad."

Before the sheriff could respond, Charles moved in front of her. "You've had quite the scare today. Why don't you go home and get some rest?"

"Mr. Graves makes a good point." The sheriff patted her hand. "No need to worry your pretty head about such gruesome matters."

Heat climbed Adelaide's neck and she rose to her feet. "Sheriff, my pretty head, as you call it, has a working brain."

"I don't doubt your intelligence, but determining how Mrs. Hartman died is my job."

Before Adelaide could respond, Sheriff Rogers took her elbow and escorted her to the door.

Outside, Adelaide paced in front of the brick structure. They wouldn't listen, yet her future and that of Emma and William depended upon convincing the sheriff who had committed the crime.

She peeked through the front window, could see Charles scribble something on his notepad. If she could only hear—

Slipping around the corner of the building, she headed for the lone barred window. Too high for her to see inside, but she could hear every word and they couldn't see her.

"What made you decide to pursue what you'd originally deemed a suicide, Sheriff?"

Adelaide heard a chair creak. "At the time, I thought it odd to find freshly baked bread in Mrs. Hartman's kitchen. On the table, alongside a cup of tea, was a partially eaten slice. Didn't make sense she'd have a bite to eat, then go out to the barn and hang herself. It looked like someone interrupted her."

"But your search of the premises found nothing to indicate foul play?"

"No—until now. One of the Long boys found this

while digging in the drainage ditch running along the front of the Hartman farm. His father brought it in."

Adelaide wished she could grow two feet taller to see what they were talking about.

"After examining this garrote, I found a gray hair," the sheriff continued.

Remembering Mrs. Hartman's neat gray bun, her gentle smile, Adelaide cringed and sagged against the brick. Just last year, Sarah had bought a pink Easter bonnet from Adelaide.

"Any idea who'd want Mrs. Hartman dead?"

"None. I'll ride out this afternoon and talk to her daughter. See if she has any ideas."

Well, Adelaide certainly had an idea. She pulled away from the building, strode around the corner, took a deep breath and opened the door of the sheriff's office, slamming it behind her.

Sheriff Rogers leapt to his feet. Charles spun to face her.

Adelaide met the sheriff's gaze. "I know who did it."

Charles frowned. "Have you been eavesdropping?"

She pulled herself erect. "What if I have? Didn't you hear what I said? I know who killed Sarah Hartman."

Sheriff Rogers leveled his gaze on her. "All right, you have our attention, Miss Crum. Who killed Sarah Hartman?"

"Ed Drummond. It has to be him."

Sheriff Rogers shoved his chair under the kneehole of the desk and rested his hands on the back. "Why him?"

"I suspect he's been abusing his wife and possibly William, an orphan staying there, and maybe even Emma, William's sister, who's living with me, temporarily."

Sheriff Rogers came around the desk. "Any proof?"

Instead of answering the question, Adelaide asked one of her own. "Did you investigate Eddie Drummond's death?"

Sheriff Rogers rubbed his forehead. "Before you get all fired up, Eddie isn't the first child to die from a stove-related fire. I found nothing suspect about his death. Are you telling me you have information to the contrary?"

"No, but Frances said she wasn't home when it happened and she called her home the 'house of death.'"

Sheriff Rogers grabbed a gun belt from a peg on the wall and strapped it on his hip. "Sounds like the ravings of a highly strung woman who's hiked through hell and back."

"It's more than that. I saw Ed Drummond firsthand. Saw—"

Charles scowled. "You were at the Drummond farm this morning, not running errands."

"What choice did I have? You wouldn't see danger if it hit you over the head."

"What happened at the Drummond house?" the sheriff asked.

She pivoted toward him. "Ed got angry when I asked if William could spend the night with—"

"Did he hurt you?" Charles interrupted.

"No, but he came after me when my buggy hit a rock and broke a wheel."

The sheriff frowned. "Could he have been trying to help?"

"By screaming obscenities? I think not." Adelaide took a deep breath, struggling to slow her speech. She sounded panicky, even to her own ears. "Frances is afraid of him and afraid for me, too. I pleaded with her to come into town, but she refused."

Sheriff Rogers ran a finger over his mustache. "If she were in real danger, surely she'd have done what you suggested."

The sheriff didn't believe her.

Adelaide looked to Charles for help, only to see his seething gaze.

Adelaide paced the room. "Emma couldn't even eat breakfast. I think she knows what's going on, but is afraid to say."

Sheriff Rogers harrumphed as if he didn't put much credence in the actions of a child.

"By going to the home of a man you consider dangerous, you put yourself at risk." Charles thrust a hand through his hair. "Why are you acting foolishly?"

Adelaide heard the anger in his voice and the underlying worry. "I'll do whatever it takes to protect those children." Did she see a flicker of respect in his eyes, even if begrudging? "I had to get evidence. But all I got was a stronger feeling he's an evil man."

"Lots of folks around here think highly of Ed Drummond," the sheriff said. "Can't see why he'd kill his mother-in-law, unless he wanted to get his hands on her property. I'll talk to his wife. See what I can dig up." He turned to Adelaide. "More than likely a drifter killed her, but if you're right, he's dangerous."

Charles took her hand. "Promise you'll stay away—"

Adelaide shook free from his grasp. "I won't stand by and let anything happen to those children."

Charles stepped closer, and his gaze locked with hers. "If you must go out there, let me go with you."

With Charles so close, Adelaide found it impossible to disagree. "I won't go alone."

The sheriff plucked his Stetson from a hall tree near the door. "I'll make a point of seeing the boy."

The tension in her shoulders eased. "Thank you, Sheriff."

Adelaide laid her hand on Charles's arm. "Is the sheriff's investigation of Ed enough reason to take William out of their home?" Adelaide wanted that so badly she couldn't breathe.

The sheriff plopped the hat on his head. "Don't say anything to the committee yet." He turned a stern eye on Adelaide. "If Drummond isn't involved, I wouldn't want to blow this out of proportion. After I get back to town, I'll look into that message on your brick."

Adelaide nodded. Charles took her hand and tucked it in the crook of his arm. They followed Sheriff Rogers from the office.

As she and Charles walked toward her shop, Adelaide's eyes misted. "I can't understand how anyone could kill a sweet woman like Sarah. She never hurt anyone."

"It's anger, uncontrollable anger."

"I can't understand that kind of anger."

"Consider yourself lucky. A man can do unspeakable things to the very people he should love and protect." He lowered his voice. "I've got the scars to prove it."

Adelaide winced for what Charles had endured as a child, a vivid reminder of what William might be going through at the Drummond farm. "Then why won't you believe me about William?"

"I'm a man of evidence, Addie. Show me proof and—"

"The proof is here." She pressed a hand to his chest

right above his heart. "But you never trust your heart, do you?" She pulled her hand away.

"I don't like the idea of finding a man guilty without more hard evidence than we have on Drummond. But whether he killed his wife's mother or not, he's got it in for you, so stay away from him." He exhaled. "With you gallivanting around the countryside, I'll never have a moment's peace."

Adelaide knew one thing for sure. Charles Graves couldn't have it both ways. "You can't tell me how to live my life, Charles, when you're not willing to be a part of it."

With that, she walked away. He made no attempt to stop her.

Chapter Fourteen

That evening Charles stopped at the back of Adelaide's shop. A section of the brick had been painted with black. Addie had wasted no time concealing the threat against her. His chest swelled with admiration for her plucky attitude, though it might get her into deeper trouble.

Whether she wanted him around or not didn't matter. He might not be able to become part of her life, but he sure didn't intend to stand by and let her lose hers.

On the landing, he rapped on the door. Addie opened it, but didn't invite him in. Her face looked carved out of stone, but even with her righteous anger wrapped around her like a hedge, her goodness showed through.

"What are you doing here?"

Not exactly a warm welcome. "I came to apologize."

"Or to see if I have Ranger tied up out back, ready to ride to the Drummond farm?"

He had to protect Adelaide, but he needed to do it without getting her riled up. He chuckled. "No bridles and reins tucked away in that kitchen, as clean as it is. Hmm, smells good, too." He gave her a grin. "Any chance you'd take pity on my growling stomach?"

"Your stomach is not my concern."

"I'll clean up the kitchen afterward."

She tried to hide her amusement, but her mouth twisted up at the corners.

"What's cooking?" he asked.

"If you insist on being nosy, ham and sweet potatoes."

His stomach put in its two cents, reminding him he'd only had half a sandwich at noon. He'd probably find the other half buried in a pile of work on his desk. "If I apologize for trying to tell you what to do, will you toss me a few scraps?"

Grinning, she stepped back to let him in. "Maybe."

She shooed him into the parlor so she could put the finishing touches on dinner. He hoped she believed his excuse for coming. After learning Sarah Hartman had been murdered and now someone wanted Addie silenced, he had no intention of letting her out of his sight. The woman wouldn't take orders unless they came directly from God.

Addie had tried her best to look annoyed, but he could tell she welcomed his company. No matter how brave she tried to appear, Ed Drummond frightened her. Maybe she'd think twice before confronting Ed again.

Emma passed in the hall and saw him. She dashed to his side. "I didn't know you were here!"

"I've been invited to stay for dinner."

She plopped down beside him. "It's my job to set the table. Wanna help?"

"Sure."

Arriving in the kitchen, he filled glasses while Emma laid out the flatware, chattering about her day.

Charles tried to keep out of Addie's way as she hustled about, ignoring him.

Soon they gathered at the table. This time Emma said grace.

"Have you told Emma about your adventure?" Charles asked.

"I've told her I rode a horse. She wants me to teach her."

Charles winked at Addie. "Giving me the boot, Emma?"

Emma's gaze skipped from one to the other, and then a big grin split her face. "I want *both* of you to teach me."

Charles grinned. "You'd make an excellent diplomat."

"What's a diplomat?"

"Someone in government who's a skilled talker, tries to make everyone happy."

"Okay! I like to make people happy. And I like to talk."

Addie touched Emma's cheek. "You make me very happy, sweetheart." She looked at Charles. "It's nice of you to assume Emma might one day hold a position in government. Perhaps my position on suffrage has swayed the editor."

Charles chuckled. When he'd made the comment, he hadn't thought of the implications. He could well imagine Emma getting that choice someday. But, did Addie have to lead the charge?

Toward the end of the meal, the conversation drifted to circulation figures, and Emma caught Charles's eye.

He tapped Addie's hand and pointed at the little girl who had nodded off at the table. "Apparently, we bored her."

Her gaze soft with tenderness, Addie smiled and

rose. Charles scooped Emma in his arms, and followed Addie to the child's room. When he laid Emma down, she opened her eyes. "Do I have to go to bed?" she asked with a yawn.

"You're sleepy," Addie said.

While Addie stayed to oversee Emma's bedtime ritual, Charles returned to the kitchen. As he washed and set the plates to drain, the gentle melody of a lullaby drifted to him.

His mother had sung that same tune to him and Sam. The memories it brought back were bittersweet, tinged with pain and loss, but also with his mother's kisses and gentle touches. The sweet sound of Adelaide's voice carried through him, soothing his spirit. For an instant, he wanted to capture the feeling, to stay with Adelaide and Emma, to promise them ever after.

But the moment passed. He had no reason to think he'd be capable of that kind of love. Everyone who'd loved him had let him down. And he'd do the same.

He returned to the task, scrubbing at the pans. He'd best remember what life had taught him and not let a sentimental song give him hope. Nothing had changed. He must take a solitary path.

A touch on his shoulder made him jump.

"Sorry. I didn't mean to startle you." Addie's gaze scanned the spotless kitchen. "Looks like my timing's perfect."

"I told you—if you cook, I'll clean up." He patted his abdomen. "I got the best part of the deal."

She smiled. Charles reveled in the beauty of that smile.

"Care for a cup of coffee?"

"Sounds good." He dried his hands on a towel. "I

heard you singing. My mother used to sing that song."
He cleared his throat, trying to disguise how much it
had meant to him. "Reminded me of the happy times
she tried to give Sam and me."

She laid a gentle hand alongside his jaw. "I'm glad."

Her touch healed like a balm, releasing some of the
pain of his childhood throbbing anew in him. He covered her hand with his. For an instant, he felt whole,
reborn, but then he dropped her hand and moved away
from her touch.

Adelaide stepped back, giving Charles wide berth.
Once again he'd put up an invisible wall between them,
still running away from what they could have together.
But he wasn't ready, and she wouldn't push him. She
couldn't force love. If it had to be forced, it wasn't love.

Besides, Emma brought enough joy to her life—if
Adelaide got to keep her. For that to happen, she had
to get to the truth.

Had the sheriff learned anything at the Drummond
farm? She wanted to get Charles's thoughts on the murder. "Why do you suppose Ed Drummond killed his
mother-in-law? Do you think he just lost his temper,
killed her in a fit of rage?"

"If he killed her," he said, raising a brow, "he planned
it. A garrote isn't something you just happen to have.
She must have posed a threat, at least in Drummond's
mind."

"Mrs. Hartman? I can't see…" Her hand flew to her
mouth. "Unless she knew Ed beats Frances and threatened to expose him."

He shrugged. "People are murdered for less."

"Your job hasn't made you an admirer of mankind."

"Some would say it's made me callous."

She shook her head. "You may try to be, but you have a kind heart. I see that with Ranger, with Emma, with me." She took another sip of her coffee. "In the short time you've lived here, you've earned the respect of the town fathers."

His brows lifted in surprise. "Why do you say that?"

"Your work with the selection committee, the way the committee agreed with your suggestion to place Emma in my home, Sheriff Rogers's obvious regard."

He smiled. "Placing Emma in your home was an easy decision. I knew you'd take excellent care of any child."

Adelaide reached across the table and put her hand on his arm. "It appears you and I respect one another."

He laid his palm over her hand. "I guess we do."

She pulled out the columns tucked into her purse. "I wrote two columns on women's suffrage."

"Let me see them," he said in a weary tone.

Adelaide handed them over. "I own the paper, too, and I want the first of these to run in the next edition."

Charles glanced at the sheaf in his hand. "Then I don't have much choice, do I?"

"I'd hoped you'd want to support the women in this community, that you'd want to support me."

"I do support you."

In many ways he did, but not in the most vital ones.

He read the pages in his hand and lifted his gaze. "You sound very convincing." He studied her. "You're determined to teach women to be courageous, to expand their sphere of influence, their focus, no matter the cost. Are you sure you're ready to take such a risk?"

That question weighed on her. "Yes, my mind is made up."

"I hope you're prepared for the consequences."

A shrill scream brought them to their feet and sent them racing to Emma's bedroom. Adelaide's heart pounded in her chest. Had Ed gotten into the house?

They found Emma cowering under the covers, quaking. Weak-kneed with relief, Adelaide sank onto the bed and gathered the weeping child in her arms. Charles sat beside them.

"He was here!" Emma wailed.

"Who?" Emma didn't say who lived in her nightmare, but Adelaide never doubted the man's identity. "It's only a dream," she crooned, rocking the little girl on her lap. "You're fine."

Charles put his arms around Adelaide, around them both. Soon Emma quieted and Adelaide sang the lullaby she had earlier. This time Charles joined in, his deep baritone blending with the melody. Emma fell back to sleep.

Nestled in the comfort of Charles's arms, Adelaide let her song trail off to a soft hum, and then looked at Charles. A sense of oneness passed between them. Charles cared for Emma, cared about her, too, or he wouldn't be here this evening.

Filled with contentment, she gently laid the sleeping child on the bed. Pulling up the covers, she kissed Emma's soft cheek. Then she and Charles slipped out of the room.

I can picture us doing that with our own children.

Suddenly, aware he stood behind her, his breath warm against her neck, she turned toward him.

He raised a hand to cradle her chin. The waiting was unbearable, though surely only a few seconds passed while she wondered would he?

And then he lowered his mouth to hers, the feel of his lips gentle and sweet. Her breath caught and she swayed toward him, clinging to his lapels for support. She was taking a huge risk, but her heart refused to listen. His kiss dismissed every coherent thought in her muddled brain. Her eyelids drifted shut, her heart insisting she belonged here.

He pulled away and lifted his palm to her face.

"You pretended to want a meal, but I suspect you came because you were worried. Thank you for watching Emma and me."

"Don't forget to lock up," he said, tucking an arm around her.

They walked downstairs together. At the door he gave her a hug, then slipped out. Leaning against the frame, Adelaide closed her eyes, remembering his scent, the roughness of his jaw under her palm, the timbre of his voice.

Her pulse skipped a beat.

Was it possible? Did Charles love her?

Or was he just as scared as she was by what had happened?

Adelaide woke with a start. Something, some noise had awakened her. Slipping from her bed, she tiptoed to the window and pulled back the curtain. The street was empty. In the moonlight, everything looked peaceful, but a nudge of disquiet sent her to her bedroom door.

She turned the knob, opened it a crack and listened. She didn't hear anything, but she slipped out the door, and padded down the hall. Snuggled under the covers, Emma slept peacefully.

Tension fell from her shoulders as Adelaide headed

back to bed. Whatever she'd heard—a tree branch in a strong gust of wind, perhaps—everything looked in order. She drifted off to sleep.

Chapter Fifteen

The next morning, Adelaide came down the stairs with Emma on her heels, complaining about school.

"You have to go, Emma." Adelaide said automatically. "Did you remember your lunch bucket?"

Emma liked recess and her teacher, but she hadn't yet caught up with her work. Maybe if she—

The thought stuttered to a halt, and so did Adelaide. Emma collided into her back.

"Emma, go back upstairs."

"But—"

"Do as I say."

After making sure Emma obeyed, Adelaide crept down the remainder of the stairway. Seeing no one, she exhaled the breath she'd been holding. Pulse hammering, her gaze darted about the showroom.

Unwound from bolts, pastel ribbons dangled from mirrors and cabinets. Smashed silk flowers and papier-mâché fruit were hurled around the shop. On the floor, fabric lay in twisted heaps. Hats, with crushed crowns and bent brims, settled where they'd been flung.

She moved from behind the counter and stumbled

through the debris, picking up a hat. "Oh, no." The crown had been slit.

The culprit had dumped her desk drawer, along with the bigger drawers holding supplies, but strangely had not tinkered with the cash register. She picked her way to the front of the shop, noting a shattered pane and jagged pieces of glass scattered on the floor. Someone had reached through the opening and unlocked the door. Without thinking, Adelaide turned the lock, though the broken pane made the gesture meaningless.

The noise she'd heard last night must have been breaking glass or perhaps the bell. No, the bell had been torn from its moorings.

A thought slammed into her. A thought so unwelcome she shook her head, trying to shake it loose, but it stuck tighter than flypaper to a shoe.

Only one person could have done this. Ed Drummond.

If I'd come down to investigate, what would have happened then?

He could easily have come up to her living quarters, could have plucked Emma from her bed.

Perspiration broke out on her forehead. Nausea washed over her. She lunged for the back door and deposited her breakfast in the flowerbed, then leaned against the brick, wiping a shaky hand over her mouth.

When her heartbeat slowed, she trudged to the well and primed it, then pumped the handle until water splattered at her feet. She filled her cupped hands with water and rinsed her mouth and face, removing every sign of her weakness.

Dropping to her knees, she turned to the One who controlled the universe. "Thank you, Father, for your protection. Please, let no harm come to Frances, Emma and William. Give me wisdom, Lord, and courage."

Feeling stronger, she rose and dashed inside. She found Emma sitting on her bed, her face pale. "What's wrong, Miss Adelaide?"

"Someone broke the glass in the door last night. Probably boys looking for excitement, but at first it worried me. I'll get it fixed." She patted Emma's knee. "Better hurry or you'll be late."

Avoiding the usual way out, Adelaide led Emma through the kitchen and onto the open-air landing at the top of the back stairs. By keeping up a rush of conversation all the way to school, she avoided any questions from Emma. Before school let out for the day, she'd have order restored.

After settling Emma in her classroom, Adelaide took the teacher aside. Though she doubted Ed would grab Emma in broad daylight in a schoolyard full of children, she asked the teacher to keep a close eye on Emma during recess.

The terror she'd experienced earlier turned to anger. The worst kind of coward, Ed Drummond preyed on women and children. How could Frances stay with him? After the sheriff's visit yesterday, hadn't she suspected Ed of killing her mother?

Adelaide's steps slowed. She hadn't walked in Frances's shoes, hadn't known the fear that could control and subdue the spirit. Like Charles's mother, Frances had few options. She must be terrified for her own life or for the lives of the children.

Down the way, Charles crossed the street, his stride purposeful. On the boardwalk in front of her shop, he stopped.

"What's this?" He pivoted toward her. "Addie, what happened? How did this pane of glass get broken?"

Adelaide pulled the key out of her purse and unlocked the door. "Ed Drummond broke in last night."

"Ed Drummond was here, in your shop?" He followed her inside. "It looks like a cyclone struck. Are you and Emma all right?"

Before she could answer, he pulled her into his arms. The magnitude of what had happened struck full force and she laid her cheek against the rough fabric of his coat.

"He didn't come upstairs?"

Charles believed Ed Drummond had done this.

"No." Relieved to have him here, to share the burden hanging heavy on her, tension eased from her body. "Last night a noise awakened me, but when I checked around upstairs, nothing looked amiss. I didn't come down here."

"Thank God." He picked up one of the damaged hats, poking a finger through the slit in the crown. "This is a warning, Addie." He dropped the hat onto a chair and laid his hands on her shoulders. "The sheriff needs to see this. Will you be okay while I'm gone?"

"Ed Drummond wouldn't bother me in broad daylight. Cowards prefer the dark."

"If he feels cornered, he might do anything. Now stay put until I get back." He gave a lopsided grin. "No cleaning until after the sheriff has investigated."

He'd tried to lighten the mood by teasing her. Adelaide forced the corners of her mouth up. "You'd better hurry, then. I won't be able to resist the urge for long."

Sheriff Rogers poked around and admitted he couldn't find any evidence of who had vandalized the shop, so she and Charles went after the mess like pigs after slop. Well, at least Adelaide tackled the task in an orderly fashion while Charles roamed about the show-room, accomplishing little.

"Addie, is this something worth keeping?"

Adelaide left the pile of bric-a-brac she sorted to look at Charles's latest treasure. He held two pieces of a papier-mâché apple in an open palm, a question in his eyes.

"No, it's damaged beyond repair."

"This apple doesn't tempt you? With a dab of glue—"

She smiled. "No amount of glue will fix that apple."

He tossed it away. "If only Eve had had your strength."

Adelaide giggled. With Charles here, she didn't get much done, but still, she treasured his presence.

A few minutes later, a tickle along her jaw sent a shiver spiraling down her spine. Charles stood over where she sat, sporting a lazy grin and trailing the tip of a feather down her neck. "Maybe if you pressed them in a book?" Charles held out a handful of colorful feathers.

"Their spines are broken. Please, put them in the trash."

"I wouldn't want to toss anything important. I don't see anything wrong with this." He grabbed a long-stemmed silk rose from the pile and held it in his strong white teeth.

Adelaide gave him a playful nudge. "You're hope-less."

Removing the bloom, he hauled her to her feet and slipped it into her chignon. "It looks better here."

Cradling her face in his hands, he brushed his lips across one cheek, then to her mouth with a tender and gentle kiss. He tugged her close, pulling her against his chest. "I worry about you."

"I'll be fine." She prayed God would protect them all.

She glanced at the clock. If she had to keep supervising Charles, she'd never get order restored. "What I really need is to have the glass replaced. Could you do that?"

"Are you sure you don't need me here?"

No matter what he'd said, he looked desperate to leave. "I'll try to manage without you."

He flashed a grin. "I'll be back as soon as I can."

Charles strode for the door and on the threshold met Sheriff Rogers, holding Jacob Paul by the shirt.

"I'm taking Jacob in for questioning," Sheriff Rogers said. "Want to talk to him about a nasty cut on his hand."

Air left Adelaide's lungs. Jacob hated her so much for reporting his arson that he'd destroy her shop?

Jacob's dark eyes sparked with defiance. "I didn't do anything. I cut my hand whittling."

Sheriff Rogers ignored the boy's claim and met Adelaide's gaze. "His father is meeting us at the jail. I'd suggest you come, too, Miss Crum."

Later, inside the jail, the sheriff released Jacob. The boy crossed the room, wearing a scowl on his face, and slumped down in a chair, ignoring his father pacing near the door.

Mr. Paul pointed his finger at Adelaide. "You've accused my son to get even with me."

The sheriff cocked his head. "Why would Miss Crum want to get even with you, Thaddeus?"

"For turning down her request for an orphan, that's why."

Adelaide planted her hands on her hips. "That's absurd."

Sheriff Rogers held up a palm. "Miss Crum didn't accuse your son. I thought of Jacob first thing. You have to admit, Thaddeus, the boy's been in trouble more than out."

Mr. Paul's shoulders stiffened. "That doesn't mean he's done this."

"No," Sheriff Rogers said, "but that ugly cut on his right hand puts him under suspicion."

Jacob shifted in his seat. "I told you, I cut my hand whittling."

The sheriff's eyes narrowed. "Are you left-handed, boy?"

"I'm right-handed but the knife slipped." He smirked. "I never said I was good at it."

Adelaide folded her arms across her middle. "So show us what you're working on."

Jacob gave a cocky grin. "After I cut my hand, I hurled the piece of wood in the river. There's nothing to find."

The sheriff's mouth tightened. "Thaddeus, can you vouch for your son's whereabouts last night between midnight and dawn?"

"He was home sleeping."

Adelaide felt like shaking that smirk off Jacob's face. The boy had no respect for authority.

"Did you sit in his room all night?" the sheriff asked.

"Of course not! This is an outrage. You have no proof my son vandalized that shop."

"Not yet, but that cut puts him under suspicion."

"He explained that." Mr. Paul gestured toward his son. "I'm taking him home."

The sheriff stood over Jacob. "You're free to go, but I'll be watching you."

Father and son headed for the door. As Jacob sauntered past, he brushed against Adelaide's skirts, probably trying to frighten her. Well, he did. After the fire-setting episode, she'd prayed for him. It appeared she had a lot more praying to do. She'd thought Ed Drummond had broken into her shop, but now Jacob appeared to be the most likely culprit.

The heavy door rattled shut. Adelaide met Sheriff Rogers's gaze. "How could you let him go? Surely you don't believe that whittling story."

"I have no proof. I can't arrest him on a hunch or for a bad attitude. I didn't find red paint at the Paul house, but I did find an opened can of red paint in the alley behind the general store." He sighed. "Anyone could have painted that threat or ransacked your shop, Miss Crum. Anyone."

Charles closed his toolbox. He'd replaced the pane in the door. Not that new glass would stop anyone from entering Addie's shop. That insight sank like a stone in his stomach.

Addie came up beside him. "Thank you."

His gaze scanned her face, noting the furrow in her usually smooth brow. What he needed to say would only add to her dismay. "You know, I've been thinking. Printing another article on suffrage is apt to stir up more trouble."

Her gaze, sharp as a well-honed blade, probed into him. "I can't believe my political opinions are behind the vandalism or the threat."

"Until we know what's going on, it might be a good idea to keep your name out of the news."

Her hand motioned around the room. "Jacob is a troubled kid. He vandalized my shop to get even. Or…" Her mouth went dry. "Ed Drummond wants to scare me so that I'll stop investigating his treatment of William. It's ludicrous to think some ordinary citizen could be irate enough to do this."

"Don't be so sure. Suffrage is a hot issue. You're asking for trouble by—"

"I'm asking for nothing, Charles. Except the right to express my opinion so that women like Frances and your mother and, yes, even me, can have some control over their lives."

"I'm not opposed to your position on suffrage. Can't you understand? I'm concerned about your safety."

"You agreed to print my views. Are you breaking your word?"

Why must she make this about them? Didn't she see the danger? He grabbed the toolbox, his jaw as tight as a vise because this stubborn, opinionated woman wouldn't listen to reason.

"Have it your way, Addie," he said, opening the shop door. "You won't listen to me."

Chapter Sixteen

Adelaide gathered another armload of her ruined stock and dumped it into the garbage can, relieved she only had a few more piles to clean up.

The bell jingled, thanks to Charles who had reattached it to the door.

Laura peeked in, carrying a napkin-covered plate. "I heard about your vandalism." Her gaze roamed the shop. "Probably boys running wild," she muttered. "Why, in my day, the boys tore down and reassembled a carriage on Old Man Hiatt's roof." She put the plate on the counter and picked up an unwound spool of ribbon and began winding it.

Clearly, Laura had no idea of the seriousness of the situation. "This wasn't a prank."

Laura tucked the rewound spool into the drawer and turned to Adelaide. "It wasn't? Oh, my. Well, then who did it?"

"The sheriff found no evidence of who did it. I have my suspicions, but for now, I'd better keep them to myself."

Laura's brow furrowed and she looked tempted to

pry, but instead she picked up the plate, peeling back the napkin to reveal the spongy cake beneath. "I brought you a wedge of angel food cake. In a crisis, I turn to sweets." Laura giggled. "Actually, I turn to sweets when good things happen and when nothing happens."

Smiling, Adelaide gave Laura a hug. "Thank you for the cake and for coming. Every time I need you, you're here for me."

"And you for me, dear."

Adelaide could put the gift to good use. "This might soften Charles's resistance."

"Resistance to what?" Laura raised her brows, a gleam in her eyes. "You?"

"More like my words. A couple more columns I've written that he's not exactly eager to print."

"For goodness sakes, Adelaide, you already have a business. You don't need more to do. What you need to concentrate on is that man. Take Mr. Graves the cake and sweeten your relationship." She shook her head. "This vandalism is a sign you need a man to take care of you."

"I can take care of myself. You know that."

Laura sighed. "Would it hurt to pretend you can't?"

Adelaide grabbed a broom and swept the last of the debris into the dustpan. "Why would I do that?"

"A man likes to feel needed." Laura planted her hands on her hips. "All this independence is your mother's fault."

Adelaide straightened. "How?"

"Because of her, you've held in your feelings all those years and now you can't let them go."

Though Adelaide wanted to deny what her friend said, the words resonated inside her. But what did it matter? Letting go of feelings only led to getting them trampled. She dumped the dustpan into the garbage. "I don't let my emotions control me."

"Are those columns about women getting the vote? Lands sake. Don't we ladies have enough to do as it is, without worrying about politics?"

"Don't you want a say in what happens in your life?"

"I'm a widow, I have *all* the say. Even my daughter has started listening to me." She shook her head. "Can you imagine? After all these years, she's decided I might be right about a couple of things." Laura wagged a finger. "You should listen to me, too. Forget politics. Concentrate on finding happiness."

Adelaide's shoulders sagged. Even Laura fought her ideas. "I'd expected the men would need convincing, not the ladies." She laid the broom aside and picked up the plate. "I'll take this to Charles as a thank-you for fixing the broken pane. Will that make you happy?"

Laura nodded. "See, a man can be useful."

"You'd love to see me attached to one, wouldn't you?"

"Yes, dear, I would. Underneath, I think you want it, too."

Adelaide opened her mouth to argue with her, but Laura gave her a hug. "I'm leaving before you start lecturing me on suffrage," Laura said with a wink. "Whether you can vote or take this vandalism in stride, you still need someone to love." Laura sauntered to the door. "Why don't I pick up Emma after school? I'll take her to the café for a glass of lemonade. That will give you more time to…do whatever it is you must."

Even though Laura didn't agree with her, she was supportive, a good friend. "Emma would like that. Thank you."

Adelaide closed the door behind her friend. Laura thought marriage solved every problem, but marriage only meant more trouble. Look at her mother's life, at Charles's parents, the Drummonds. She needed a way to protect Emma and William, not a fairy tale.

She removed her apron and hustled upstairs to wash her face and hands. Later, she checked her appearance in the mirror—not to impress Charles, but to be sure her hat tipped at the proper angle. She folded the column and placed it in her purse, then picked up the slice of cake on her way out.

Crossing the street to *The Ledger,* she resolved to have her way. After all, she owned the paper, too. She wouldn't give up this chance to influence the community.

As she arrived, James left the paper, rushing off to whatever assignment Charles had given him. He seemed like a nice young man, very conscientious. But if he got a chance, he'd probably be telling her what to do, too.

She halted on the boardwalk. There, through the window, stood Fannie, her face aglow, her hand on Charles's arm. A surge of something Adelaide refused to name roared to life in her midsection. As she watched, they broke apart and Charles walked her protégée to the door, laughing at something Fannie said.

Demureness apparently had done its work. Only two lessons and Fannie had Charles pinned to the target.

Adelaide flattened her back against the brick. She didn't want to be caught spying.

Out on the boardwalk, Fannie rose on tiptoe and kissed Charles on the cheek. Casually, as if it were a common occurrence, and then giggled before walking up the street, her skirts swishing like a broom at full speed. Some things never changed.

Adelaide's grip tightened on the plate. She had no rights, no claim on Charles. The concern he'd shown her, the kiss they'd shared, meant nothing. For an instant, the back of her eyes stung. She blinked hard. This had been a difficult day. That's why she felt close to tears. Not because of Fannie and Charles.

Charles started back inside the paper, *her* paper. Then he stopped. "Addie, what a pleasant surprise. I didn't expect you'd have that mess cleaned up for hours." He glanced at his pocket watch. "Oh, the afternoon is nearly over."

"Spending time with a friend has a way of making time fly."

"What?" Then his brain connected with her words. "Oh, you mean Fannie." He studied her and then an annoying grin spread across his face. "You saw that kiss?"

As if Adelaide even cared. She lifted her chin. "You're more than welcome to kiss any woman who'll have you."

"I didn't kiss her. She kissed me—on the cheek." His grin got broader. If he kept it up, she'd be able to shove the plate, cake and all, into that cavern. "Are you suggesting I kiss *you* instead?"

"I'm doing nothing of the kind."

He made a tsk-tsk sound. "My, my, aren't we testy?"

"If you'd had the day I've had, you'd be testy, too."

His expression turned grim. "I'm sorry for teasing you. Come in." He took her free hand and led her into the office.

She should march back home and take the cake with

her, but something stronger than her resolve sent her forward.

At his desk, he eyed the plate in her hands. "So what's under that cloth?"

She cleared a spot and put it on the desk. "It's for you, as a thank-you for repairing the pane of glass." Though now she wanted to take it back. Let Fannie bake him a cake. She hoped he realized the bottom would be charred.

Charles lifted the napkin and leaned over the plate, inhaling. "Angel food cake, prepared by an angel." He gave her a wink. "Even if at the moment, her halo is off-kilter."

Without thinking, Adelaide gave her hat a tug. Some halo, decked out with feathers. "Laura made the cake, not me."

"Did she ask you to bring me a piece? Or was it your idea?"

"Can't you just say thank you? Not everything is a story for the paper!"

He chuckled. "You *are* grumpy, but you're right. Thank you for the cake." He pulled out the chair. "Have a seat. I'll pour you a cup of coffee."

The coffee smelled strong enough to stand a spoon in, exactly what she needed to summon the starch absent from her spine since the break-in. "I'd enjoy a cup."

Adelaide removed her gloves and laid them in her lap. Charles returned with her coffee, looking confident and in control. She wanted to punch him.

"You're fresh as a daisy. I'd never guess what a hard day you've had."

"Are those the same words you said to Fannie?"

He grinned. "Why, Miss Crum, you're jealous."

She dipped her head to sip. "Jealous? Certainly not."

Beaming now, he resembled a bullfrog all puffed up with pride. "Is that so?"

Adelaide lowered her gaze, not daring to look him in the eye. She *was* jealous. And that surprised her. And, worse yet, he knew it. That put her at a disadvantage. "Not at all. As half owner of the paper, I perceived your behavior as…unsuitable for the editor of our newspaper. In public, no less."

She took a second sip of coffee and grimaced. It tasted twice as awful as the first gulp. She jutted out her chin. "I've no interest in who you kiss. Or who kisses you."

His eyes twinkled. "If you're not interested, then I won't tell you why Fannie kissed me."

He played with her like a cat toyed with a mouse. Adelaide let out a gust of frustration. "All right, why? And I'm only asking out of journalistic inquiry, I'll have you know. In case I should decide to write a column on—" she scrambled for something to say "—lip ointments."

He whooped with laughter. "With a tale like that, have you considered writing fiction, Miss Crum?"

"Perhaps I will some day." Here she told one fib after another, trying to pretend Charles meant nothing to her. If she kept this up, God might not think much of her, either.

"I'll give you the scoop. I told Fannie I'm old enough to be her father, figuring that might cool her interest." He grimaced. "I needn't have bothered. James came in and before he left, the two of them were drooling over each other."

Adelaide's coffee splashed up the inside of her mug.

"James and Fannie?" She'd been wrong, as wrong as she could be.

"Grateful for my introduction to James, Fannie gave me a kiss." Then he chuckled. "I never had a woman drop me so quickly, except maybe for you, just now."

Did that imply they had a relationship?

She reached over and set the mug on Charles's desk. "You might have told me right away why Fannie kissed you."

Charles guffawed. "So it's my fault you're mad at me?"

Her claim lacked logic, but she had no other. "Yes, it is."

"Well, you should've asked instead of skulking in the shadows, spying."

"I did not skulk or spy. I… I merely checked my reflection in the glass." She slapped a hand over her mouth to stifle a laugh.

"In that case, will you forgive me?"

"Since you asked nicely, yes, I will."

He took her hand and held it for a long, quiet moment, his large palm, warm and slightly rough against her own. Their gazes locked. Adelaide's breath stopped coming, her heart held its beat. With his other hand, he ran a finger along her jaw, sending shivers down her spine, and then spoiled it by tweaking her nose. No wonder. She probably appeared as desperate as Fannie.

Teddy walked out from the back, carrying an inky piece of equipment. "Boss, can you take a look at this?"

Charles headed over to confer with Teddy. Adelaide rose and crossed to the window. Outside the wide plate glass, the world kept moving. Buggies, wagons, people…

But in this office, a different commotion brewed,

one inside her. She pressed her palms to her hot cheeks, and then drew in a breath that sank to the bottom of her stomach to war with the other conflicts between her and Charles. Yet even with all that troubled her, she had to face the truth.

She wanted Charles.

How did she get into such a mess? Whenever he came near, he kept her heart drumming double time. Why? Besides driving her crazy with his untidy desk, he didn't want her interference in the paper, even when she had every right. And he was pushy and opinionated and stubborn.

And yet…this man helped Mary and her boys. He'd stood up to the committee and had brought her Emma.

In short, though he didn't appear to know it, he gave of himself. And she knew he cared about her. She looked at him, so strong, dependable. He gave her a feeling of comfort, of safety. For a woman used to relying on herself, that was…nice.

Well, sometimes. Something she could get used to, though she knew she shouldn't.

And yes, she liked his kisses. But she could do without them. After all, he wanted her to behave as he thought she should, not how she needed to be. He tried to keep her out of his dream, out of everything important. And he couldn't commit to anything but the newspaper, making it his life.

No, she didn't need a man.

And now she must convince him to continue publishing her suffrage articles. To light a spark that would help other women have the power and voice she, and the generations before her, had lacked. And yet…

A sigh slipped from her lips. She stepped to Charles's

chair and ran a hand over his coat. She fingered his pencils, the things he'd touched; somehow dearer than mere objects should be because they'd been in his hands.

Earlier when Adelaide had seen Fannie out front, the young girl glowed, had a spring to her step. Just being in the reporter's presence had left her changed. Adelaide understood that change, all too well. Caring brought happiness but also recklessness, a tendency to forget what was important.

A moment later, Charles pulled up a chair beside her. He gave her a smile. "You've had a tough day. How about I take you and Emma on a picnic? I want to talk to you about something."

Chapter Seventeen

Adelaide watched Emma clamber over the rocks by the river, delighting in every flower, every bug she came across. Scattered clouds moved slowly across the pale blue sky. What an idyllic spot for their picnic.

Adelaide leaned back, letting the sun warm her face. "When have you seen a more beautiful spring?"

Charles moved closer. With gentle fingers, he turned her face toward his. "All I can see is how beautiful you are."

"Thank you." Her heart leapt at his words.

His gaze locked with hers. "You and I are a lot alike. We're both afraid of feeling too much. Of getting hurt."

"That's because we've been hurt by the people who were supposed to love us."

He plucked a blade of grass. "Except for you and Mary, I've known few truly good people in my life."

"Not even your mother?"

He draped an arm over his bent knee, his gaze focused on some distant point. "Ma said and did things to protect us, to keep the peace as best she could. If that meant stretching the truth or bending her principles, well, she did." He turned to her. "I'm not blaming her, you understand. She lived scared."

Adelaide nodded.

"Now Pa, well, he wore his values like a Sunday suit, shrugging them off when he walked in the door." He cleared his throat. "We'd try to please him, but we never could." Sudden moisture filled Charles's eyes and he blinked it away. "Eventually Ma quit trying. That's when things got really ugly." He raised his gaze. "No one in my life has been like you."

"I'm far from perfect, Charles."

"To me you are." His voice grew gruff. "I don't want to bring you any harm."

"How could you harm me?"

He took her hands and studied her face. "In countless ways." His eyes filled with misery, something close to despair.

She shook her head. Charles would never hurt her intentionally. "No matter what you say, I believe in you. It's your relationship with God that divides us. Even our dispute about writing my column pales in comparison."

Charles released her hands. "I believe in God."

She leaned toward him. "Then why won't you attend church?"

His gaze wandered the grassy bank, watching Emma chase a butterfly. He cleared his throat. "Church has been your haven. My father used Scripture as an excuse to beat us. Attending church was a farce, a pretense to dupe the community into believing we were a happy family."

"That doesn't mean you can't worship now."

He waved a hand to indicate the green grass, tall leafed-out trees, the gurgling water winding through the river. "I feel closer to God right here than I would in church."

"When you stay away from church, you separate yourself from the teachings, the chance to serve and praise God."

Charles rose. "God can't want me there, knowing the resentment I harbor. Knowing the man I am."

What did he mean? She reached a hand to him, but Charles moved out of her grasp. "What are you trying to tell me?"

"I'm a man who can't trust." He stepped farther away, jamming his hands into his pockets. "Even myself."

Adelaide scrambled to her feet. "Why not?"

His head drooped. "I told you. I'm not good like you."

"We're all sinners, Charles. I see the decency in you."

He shook his head. "You see what you want to see."

"You don't have to be perfect before you can come to God. He'll give you the strength to overcome your past."

"I can't. I want to, but I can't." He pulled her close. "I'm sorry." Taking her chin in his free hand, his voice turned rough with emotion. "I know that's not what you want to hear."

It wasn't, but she could see the conflict in his eyes. "Trusting is a choice, a decision. People might disappoint you, but God won't."

"Don't you see? He's already disappointed me." Charles pulled away. "I have to work this out on my own."

"Until you're able to make peace with God, you'll never heal from the past."

Without Adelaide noticing, clouds had gathered. The rising wind warned of an approaching storm.

"I hope—"

He stopped her with a raised palm. "Let's take a walk."

They strolled along the bank. Emma scampered over to show a toad she'd found, then dashed off in search of more discoveries.

Adelaide turned her gaze on the man, who, regardless of her intention, had taken up residence in her heart. Perhaps in time, he'd see how God walked through every day, held the present and every tomorrow in His hands.

As much as Adelaide wanted to convince Charles to come to church, she understood his hesitancy. She'd continue to pray for healing from his past.

They came to a large rock along the riverbank. Charles sat and pulled her down beside him. He drew in a breath and turned to face her, capturing her hands in his. "I have something to ask you, something important." His grip on hers tightened. "Hear me out before you answer. I'm hoping your answer will be yes."

Say yes? She blinked. "Yes or no about what?"

"This has to do with us, with our future. From you, I've learned to speak up about what's important to me."

What did he mean? Her mind ran through the possible questions he could ask and arrived at one.

Did Charles intend to propose?

She'd known him for such a short time. Huge issues between them needed to be resolved. Still, marriage to Charles…

Her heart tripped in her chest. "What do you want to ask me?"

His gaze met hers and he drew in a breath. "Will you—" he hesitated "—sell me your half of *The Ledger?*"

The words slammed into Adelaide's head. *Ledger. Sell.* She jerked her hands out of his grasp. Her supper formed a lump in her stomach. "*That's* what you wanted to ask me?"

"You can still write your fashion column—"

"You want *full* ownership?" A strangled laugh escaped her lips and she rose to her feet. "You'll be so generous as to *let* me write a fashion column?"

Charles only cared about regaining control of the paper. He didn't want to share that part of his life with her. Any part of his life, really. "What a fool I've been." Every inch of her hurt. Tears sprang to her eyes but she willed them away. Pride was all she had, pride and Emma and God who strengthened her.

Back straight and shoulders set, she signaled to Emma. "Time to go home!"

"Addie, wait, I'm only trying to protect you. Can't we—"

"No, Charles, we can't. Not now, not later."

A rumble of thunder sounded in the distance. Emma raced over, interrupting Charles's efforts to argue his point.

"Do we have to go?" Emma whined.

"Yes, it's going to storm." Adelaide took Emma's hand and the three of them walked to the area where they'd picnicked. "We'll come again. Just you and me," she promised Emma.

Pain twisted in her heart until Adelaide could barely breathe. Had she been thinking she could trust a man? That she could risk her heart? Whenever she did, she paid the penalty.

Once again a man wanted to silence her. Even knowing its importance to her, Charles wanted full ownership of the paper, asking her to sacrifice the opportunity to express her views. Well, she couldn't make him love her, but she could hang on to ownership of the paper.

She straightened her shoulders. She would survive without Charles, as she had survived when her mother had kept her at arm's length. The days might be drabber, might not hold the promise they once had, but she would not think about that now.

Emma skipped ahead picking a few dandelions along the path home.

Charles touched her arm. "Please, you don't understand why I want to do this."

Wheeling around, she said, "You know what, Charles? I might buy *you* out. As for this..." She swept a palm over the blanket. "You made a mess of our picnic. Now you can clean it up."

Her heart heavy with loss of something, someone she'd never really had, Adelaide sat sewing in the workroom, grateful for Emma's sweet voice in the showroom as she played with her doll. Thankfully the little girl was blissfully unaware of the impasse between Adelaide and Charles.

Adelaide heard a crash, breaking glass and then Emma's shrill scream. Barely able to breathe, she scrambled to her feet and ran. She found Emma cowering on the floor with shards of glass only two feet away.

Adelaide scooped up the trembling child, doll and all, into her own trembling arms and darted to the corner, away from the window to check for cuts or bruises. "Are you okay?"

Against her shoulder, Emma nodded. "Someone broke the window. I'm scared."

"Of course you are," Adelaide said, rubbing Emma's small tense back.

Carrying the child, Adelaide picked her way through the glass to the frame of the shop window that now had a gaping hole in jagged edges of glass and peered into the street. She saw no one suspicious.

Edging away from the window, the toe of her shoe hit something solid. A rock. A piece of paper had been tied to it with a knotted string.

Hot fury distorted Adelaide's vision and she swayed on her feet. If that rock had hit Emma in the temple, the impact could have killed her. With Emma clinging to her, Adelaide knelt and picked up the stone, the weight of it heavy in her hand.

"Emma, would you like a cookie?" Adelaide asked, forcing a note of cheer into her voice.

The little girl raised her head and nodded. "Can I have two? One cookie for me and one for my dolly?"

"Two it will be."

Later, while Emma sat across from her, nibbling on the treat, with the sweet scent of vanilla and cinnamon from Emma's cookie filling her nostrils and a sickening wad of fear filling her gut, Adelaide removed the string, and unfolded the slip of paper. Barely discernable, the words appeared to be printed by someone using his left hand. It read: You're going to pay for the trouble you're causing.

Adelaide shivered and tears welled in her eyes. She bit her lip, determined not to frighten Emma more. Had Jacob done this? Or Ed Drummond? Or someone else? Her heart stuttered in her chest. Her actions had put Emma's life at risk.

Weeks before her life had been simple with a future

of loneliness spread out before her. She'd taken action, sought change. And now even her home, once a haven, had become a dangerous place. She'd have to go for the sheriff—again.

If only she could turn to Charles…

No. Every fiber of her being yearned to lean into the comfort of his arms, but Adelaide would not run to Charles. She might not know who threatened her bodily harm, but she knew without a doubt if she didn't stay away from Charles Graves, her heart would be broken.

Charles might as well give up his job. Instead of doing any of the hundreds of things that needed doing, he'd spent the morning staring out the window. All because of Adelaide Crum.

Days before, she'd marched off, leaving him indeed, with quite a mess. And she hadn't even given him a chance to explain.

By offering to buy her out, he'd been trying to protect her from herself, from the damage her views brought into her life. Against his better judgment, he'd published her third suffrage article. But that hadn't mended the rift between them.

Addie was right across the street, a wide thoroughfare, but nothing compared to the gulf separating them now. He'd seen the broken glass in her store window, and Sheriff Rogers had told him about the rock-throwing incident. His eyes stung. She'd hired a handyman to replace the glass rather than coming to him for help. For comfort. But that didn't matter. He only cared about her safety.

"Afternoon, Charles."

Charles jerked up his head to see Roscoe Sullivan standing near his desk.

"Hello, Roscoe." Charles took in the wide smile on Roscoe's narrow face. "You look like life's treating you well."

"It is, and that's a fact. Even my rheumatism's eased."

"Glad to hear it."

Roscoe plopped down in the opposite chair, the chair Charles now kept tidy thanks to Addie. She wanted to straighten more than his office. She wanted to straighten him out, too—a job, too big even for Addie.

"I miss the energy of this place, even if I almost ran it into the ground." Roscoe glanced out the window. "Say, I've been wondering, who broke the window in the millinery shop?"

Charles shifted in his chair. "I don't like to say this, Roscoe, but your nephew is one of the suspects."

"That's ridiculous! Where did you get such an idea?"

In dangerous territory, Charles knew to tread with care. "I saw Ed in town that day. And he has a beef with Miss Crum."

"So do a lot of people. That suffrage column of hers has the whole town in an uproar. *She's* the cause of any problem my nephew might have with her." Roscoe jumped up and paced in front of the desk. "From what I heard, she wants Emma *and* William and will go to any length to get them. Even as far as breaking Frances's and Ed's hearts to steal those youngsters away."

Roscoe stopped in front of Charles's desk and leaned on his palms, his face inches away. "She's obviously got you in her clutches. You'd better stop seeing her, Charles. The fact you're courting her gives her status in the community."

Now that Addie wasn't even speaking to him, the irony of Roscoe's words twisted in his chest. "See here, Roscoe, Miss Crum had the respect of the town long before I came."

"That's before she went off her rocker with these obsessions with children and voting."

Charles let out a gust. "She's saner than anyone I know."

"It's your fault. You've given her too much leeway at the paper. Appears to me you're on *her* side."

Even though he questioned the wisdom of her column, he *was* on Addie's side. "Miss Crum is half owner of *The Ledger.* She has a right to run what she wants in the paper."

"I'm going to talk to John Sparks. Emma should be back where she belongs."

Charles's throat tightened. "You need to reconsider that. If Ed did vandalize Miss Crum's shop or threw that rock, he has a serious problem. The children might not be safe wi—"

"What are you saying? That my nephew could hurt a child? Knowing what he went through losing Eddie." He pointed a finger under Charles's nose. "Mark my words. I have considerable influence in this town. If either you or Miss Crum harms my nephew's family, I'll do whatever I can to ruin that shop of hers and this paper. You can bank on it!"

Roscoe pivoted and strode to the door, slamming it behind him, setting the glass dancing in its frame. Charles tugged his fingers through his hair. Roscoe had the clout to ruin their reputations and their businesses.

Since owning the paper, Charles had taken charge of his life, his destiny. Now, thanks to his father's malicious will, he didn't own it outright. Addie's column added fuel to the fire of opposition Roscoe resolved to light. But somehow the paper no longer mattered to him.

He leaned forward, dropped his head in his hands and closed his eyes. And saw the sweet face of Addie. A face filled with joy at receiving Emma, then fear when her shop had been vandalized, and later determination.

His stomach knotted. How far would the evildoer terrorizing Addie go? Where would this end?

That night, restless and unable to sleep, Adelaide climbed the stairs to the attic, hoping to take her mind off the rising hostility and the fear it planted in her mind.

In her hand, she held a lantern, and in her heart, a determination to find a clue to her mother's relationship with Charles's father. Crossing the attic floor near the eaves, she stepped on a squeaky plank. She didn't want to risk waking Emma, but first thing tomorrow morning, she'd nail that board into submission. How many nails would she need?

She knelt on the floor and noticed that the board had no nails. Her heart tripped. She sped to the toolbox at the top of the stairs, removed a screwdriver, then knelt and pried off the loose board.

Underneath the plank, she found a packet of envelopes tied with a thin red string. Butterflies fluttered in her stomach. Could this be what she sought?

She slid the first envelope out and opened it. Her gaze flew first to the salutation, then to the date, September 8, 1866, and then down the page to the signature, Calvin Crum. The father she never knew.

As she read, phrases jumped off the page and hooked her heart. "…not a man to settle down." "…better off without me." "…free you to marry the love of your life."

With only this letter, her father had deserted them, without a doubt breaking her mother's heart. No, not breaking—hardening it. She'd only been a few weeks old when her father left. Tears slid down Adelaide's cheeks and plopped onto the page. She suddenly understood her mother's bitterness, her loss of joy, her distrust of men, distrust that she drummed into Adelaide.

She read on to where her father referred to the love of her mother's life—it had to be Adam Graves.

With shaky hands, she pulled out the next letter from a smaller envelope, addressed in a tight, wobbly script. Not from her father. From someone else.

Adelaide scanned the page and the signature at the bottom. "This is from him," she whispered.

For a moment, Adelaide wanted to put it back under the narrow red string, to not know these things about her mother. But the past had intruded into her life and she couldn't turn back. She read the words from thirty years ago.

January 6, 1866

Dearest Constance,
From childhood on, I expected we would marry. That you could betray me this way, become pregnant with another man's child, is more than I can bear. Though my hand shakes with anger as I write this, I love you still. I will never recover from this blow, but I will attempt to put you out of my mind. I cannot fathom how I will succeed.

Always,
Adam

The paper quivered in her trembling hand, then fell to her lap. This letter must have arrived mere days before her parents' wedding. Had her mother loved Adam? Had she wanted to cancel the nuptials? Or had she married the man she loved?

Adam, with his claim of undying love, hadn't offered marriage. This letter was a rebuke, not a solution to her dilemma. Beneath his declaration of love lay a veiled cruelty.

How had this letter affected her mother? Or her father, if he found it?

Adelaide sighed. Had they argued over Adam? Or worse, had her father left to clear the way for Mama to have the man he thought she loved? Maybe in here...

Adelaide opened the last letter.

October 22, 1867

Dearest Love,

I cannot tell you how exhilarated I was to get your letter. And how devastated. To hear you love me as much as I love you brought untold happiness. Your declaration that you'd never stopped loving me and had made a huge mistake heals the wound that your infatuation with Calvin Crum ripped in my soul.

To know you're divorced and free to marry, now that it's too late, is the vilest irony, the worst of nightmares. For you see, I married a woman I met in Cincinnati and she's already expecting my child. My heart will be with you always, but I can't shirk my duty and leave Beulah to raise the child alone.

If only I could. For in every way she is a disappointment. I feel cheated, enraged at this cruel twist of fate. I cannot stop thinking of you, as you once were, the lovely innocent girl of my dreams. No one will ever fill your place in my heart.

> With undying devotion,
> Adam

And there, in Adam Graves's stifled scrawl, were some of the answers she'd been seeking and even more questions. Imagining the pain these letters must have brought her mother, tears flowed down her face. If Adam wanted to stay with his wife, why had he held on to his feelings for her mother?

She stared again at the yellowed sheet, willing it to provide more answers. But it held the same words as before.

Adelaide wiped her eyes, then folded the letter and laid it in her lap. She couldn't comprehend how her mother and Adam had such a great love for each other, but couldn't love their own flesh and blood.

Whatever Adam had felt, it hadn't been love. Not the kind of love spoken of in the Bible. As they'd read the passage on love, Pastor Foley had explained to the congregation that charity meant the same as love. The words paraded through her mind. Love is patient, love is kind, not easily angered, keeps no record of wrong. Always protects, always trusts, always hopes, always perseveres.

If only she and Charles had grown up in loving homes.

She choked back a sob. The last shred of hope of finding something that would truly explain her mother's indifference drifted like dust to the attic floor. In her unhappiness, her mother had distanced herself, had wasted years, losing opportunity after opportunity to love her daughter.

Replacing the letters in their envelopes, Adelaide slipped them under the string, and then returned the packet to its resting place.

She remained motionless in the attic thinking about what might have been if her mother had seen past her infatuation and realized Calvin Crum wasn't a staying kind of man.

How ironic that Adam Graves couldn't let go.

Or had her mother been the lucky one? If she'd married Adam, would she have suffered as Beulah had? Or had discontent with the way his life had turned out led to such bitterness that Adam had taken it out on his family?

A mouse darted past, his tail flicking as he scooted under a chair and into the dark depths of a corner. Adelaide roused.

Her days had been filled with one shock after another, first the vandalism, then Charles's request to sell him the paper when she'd thought he wanted to propose, then the rock shattering her window and her peace of mind and now these letters from the two men who had ruined her mother's life.

Life wasn't easy, and as Charles once said, was often unfair, but with God's help, she'd survive. Though tonight, she had no idea how.

Adelaide opened the shop as usual, but so weary she feared her bones might collapse beneath her. She'd been up half the night, thinking about the letters, missing Charles. Unable to sleep, she'd stewed about Ed or

Jacob coming after her and the shop's lack of business. She sighed, ashamed when she needed it most, she'd been unable to release her worries to God.

Against her will, she crossed to the window to check for any sign of Charles. Leaning her face against the frame, she ached to have him near. Somehow, she'd find a way to go on without him. Inside she felt hollow, as if a space had been vacated that no one else could fill.

The bell jingled. Forcing a smile to her face, Adelaide crossed to the door to greet her customer. "Mrs. Hawkins, I'm glad you stopped in. I have your alterations done."

Her face pink and moist from the heat of the warm spring day, the buxom matron nodded. "I'd hoped you did."

Adelaide led her to the counter and pulled the wrapped garment from underneath, then handed Mrs. Hawkins the bill. "While you're here, would you like to look for a hat? I've repaired the damaged ones from the break-in. They're a bargain."

Digging in her purse, Mrs. Hawkins shook her head. "If I came home with one of your hats, Leroy would pitch a fit. Roscoe Sullivan told him you and the new editor blame Ed Drummond for the trouble you're having. Leroy's worked up." She slapped the cash to pay her bill on the counter and the coins bounced to the floor. "He and Ed are hunting buddies."

Adelaide bent to retrieve the coins. Did Charles now suspect Ed rather than Jacob or some disgruntled citizen?

Mrs. Hawkins's hands fluttered in front of her like a bird on its first flight. "Where on earth did you get the notion ladies should vote?"

"You don't think women should have the right to express their opinions?"

"Not when it causes me trouble."

"I'm sorry—"

"You should be! I need a new hat and now I have to order it out of the catalogue, without getting to try it on first. Too bad you didn't think of anyone but yourself." Mrs. Hawkins grabbed the bundle and headed for the door.

Adelaide watched her customer's retreating back, biting her lip, squelching a desire to weep. Exhaustion—that must be the reason for her reaction.

Why had she tried to bring about change for herself and the women of Noblesville when all that mattered were Emma and William? And now after her columns, no one respected her suspicions about Ed Drummond's treatment of the children.

She wouldn't write another article on suffrage until she'd gotten William out of that house. Change for women wouldn't come overnight. But harm to the children could. How could she ensure their safety?

Three days had passed since Charles had spoken with Addie, but she never left his thoughts. Determined to protect her, at night he'd watch her window until her light went out, then he'd patrol the streets. When the sun rose in the eastern sky, he'd give up his watch. He didn't bother going home to sleep, but bunked on a cot in the back, tossing and turning until Teddy arrived and the smell of brewing coffee dragged him out of bed.

Across the way, he saw Adelaide and Emma chatting with Mary and his nephews. Obviously, Addie didn't miss him. Nor had she thanked him for printing her third column or criticized him for placing it on the back page. Instead, since their argument, she'd gone on with her life while he'd become a man of stone, unable to function at work, unable to smile, unable to sleep. What had happened to the stoic newsman he'd been? He hardly knew himself.

Remembering the way she laughed, her scent, the essence of Addie, left him longing to talk to her. He left the window and walked to his desk.

Teddy glanced his way. "You're up and down so much, you're making me dizzy. Why don't you go over there?"

"Where?" Charles said feigning ignorance.

Teddy chuckled. "To Miss Crum's hat shop, where else. You've been watching the place all week. Wouldn't it be easier just to go over there?"

Charles dropped into his desk chair. "I'm the last person Miss Crum wants to see."

Teddy took a seat across from him. "You two have a spat?"

Charles leaned back, focusing his gaze on the ceiling. "You could say that."

"Women have a way of squeezing an apology out of us men sooner or later. Tell her you're sorry. Take her a new apron or something." A rumble sounded from Teddy's stomach. He dropped his foot to the floor and unfolded his body from the chair. "I'm heading home to dinner. My advice is to take her flowers and if you're really in trouble, a nice brooch, too."

But Charles knew flowers and trinkets wouldn't solve this mess. He'd destroyed Addie's feelings for him. He wondered why he cared. She represented everything he'd run from most of his life—family, God, marriage. So why did he feel like he'd lost a part of himself? The good part.

When the door to the paper opened, he scowled. Teddy better not have returned to pester him.

Mary poked her head in the door. "Are you busy?"

"No, come in." Seeing his sister-in-law's happy face took the frown off his. "Where are my nephews?"

"They're out front in the wagon nibbling on some of Adelaide's cookies. I decided I could afford a luxury so I bought one of her hats." Mary spun around in front of him, letting him admire it from all angles. "Do you like it?"

"Very much. It suits you." Charles stared at the hat that had lain in Addie's capable hands. For some unknown reason, he brushed a hand along the silky rose hugging the brim.

"Why thank you, kind sir," Mary said with a laugh.

A lump rose in Charles's throat. "How is she?"

"Pretty good, considering you tossed her out of your life like yesterday's news."

"I did not. She tossed *me* out of *her* life."

"Well, if she did, she must have her reasons. She looks almost as miserable as you."

Addie looked miserable? Not when he'd seen her across the way. Did she miss him? Or was she frightened and unable to sleep? Charles circled the room, his gaze never leaving the millinery shop. He hadn't worried like this since his childhood, when he'd listen for his father's footsteps.

Could he protect Addie any better than he'd been able to protect Ma and Sam?

He stopped beside the window and hit his palm against its frame. "If I could only be sure she'll be safe. It's driving me crazy. I watch her place all night."

"You what?"

"With everything that's happened over there, I'm keeping an eye out for trouble."

Mary stepped to his side and straightened his collar. "No wonder you look dreadful." Studying him, she tapped a finger against her lower lip. "Sounds to me like you're in love."

He groaned.

"There are easier ways to protect her." She cocked her head. "You could marry her."

And open her to heartache? Never.

She flashed him one of those knowing woman smiles. "Then she'd be safe. *And* probably get to keep Emma." She gave him a hug. "And you'd both own the paper. Marriage would take care of all your problems."

He studied the floor. "I can't do that."

Mary folded her arms. "The trouble with you, Charles Graves, is you're in love and won't admit it, even to yourself."

He jerked his head up. Everyone talked about love as if it were the simplest thing in the world. He knew better. "I'm not even sure I know what the word means."

"What you want is a guarantee. There's no guarantee with love. No guarantees for anything worth having. Like my boys out there." Charles's gaze settled on Michael and Philip perched on the wagon seat. "I'm both mother and father to them—doing the best I can. I suppose they could grow up and break my heart. But maybe, just maybe, they'll make me proud."

Her voice cracked with emotion. She swiped at damp eyes. "Well, I'd best be going." She gave him a kiss on the cheek. "My advice, Charles Graves—don't let a woman like Adelaide Crum slip through your fingers."

Chapter Eighteen

On Sunday, Charles stood outside the imposing edifice of the First Christian Church. He tugged at the tie choking his neck, buttoned and then rebuttoned his jacket and adjusted his hat. Through the open windows of the church, a song drifted on the cool morning breeze. A long time ago, he'd sung the familiar tune.

Bowing his head, he let the song "What a Friend We Have in Jesus" flow through him, the words soaking into his parched soul. The song promised peace—if he prayed. But he couldn't. Not since his childhood prayers had gone unanswered, destroying something between him and God. Charles swallowed past the lump in his throat. If only he could find that serenity, serenity that had been missing most of his life. Maybe inside the church he'd find the answer, find his way back to God, to that promise of peace.

He tried to lift his foot, to climb the steps leading into the house of worship, but he couldn't move. Sweat beaded his forehead, and the lump swelled in his throat until he felt he'd suffocate. He bent over and dragged oxygen into his lungs.

A cloud passed between him and the sun, covering him in shadow. A sudden chill streaked down his spine.

He couldn't move. Couldn't pray, couldn't worship. Too much stood between him and God.

Listening to the sermon and singing praises, a blessed peace stole over Adelaide, along with the conviction that whatever happened in her life, God sat on the throne, controlled the universe and would take care of William and Emma. If only Charles would attend services, he might find a measure of peace.

She and Emma rose for the benediction and afterward followed the parishioners into the aisle. At the door, they shook hands with Pastor Foley then walked down the steps.

"Adelaide, wait up!"

Recognizing that voice, Adelaide led Emma to one side as Fannie emerged with James. The couple moved toward them and Adelaide noticed Fannie walked with grace. Why, she looked like a lady right out of *Godey's*. Pleased some of her lessons had taken root, Adelaide smiled.

Fannie tugged James forward. "Adelaide, have you met James Cooper?"

"Yes, I have. We've run into each other a time or two."

James's eyes twinkled. "She means that literally, too. I almost plowed her down one morning."

She wanted to ask James about Charles, but didn't. "No damage done." Adelaide grinned. "This is Emma Grounds."

The couple greeted Emma. Then Fannie smiled. "I read your articles. They were wonderful." Adelaide's face must have revealed her surprise because Fannie giggled. "Since I've met James, I'm reading the paper."

"Unfortunately, not everyone agrees with you," Adelaide said.

"Really? Well, it makes perfect sense to me. We ladies are people, aren't we?"

Emma touched Fannie's hand. "I'm a people, and someday I'm going to be a dip...dip...lomat. Mr. Graves told me so."

James lightly tugged at the ribbons on Emma's hat. "Well, if women get the vote, and I hope they do, you'd be my first choice for a diplomat, Emma."

Fannie smiled adoringly into James's face and he beamed back, looking equally besotted. "Wasn't the service uplifting? Did you hear James singing? He has the most beautiful voice."

"Fannie thinks I'm a great singer because she can barely carry a tune."

Fannie giggled. "That's true."

James sighed, love softening his normally probing gaze. "Don't you adore her giggle, Miss Crum?"

Before giving an answer, Adelaide gave Emma permission to join a group of children playing nearby. "Fannie is Fannie," she said, hoping that would suffice.

"That's exactly what I like about her. There's no pretense with Fannie."

The young woman leaned close. "I guess I won't need more of your lessons, Adelaide. James likes me just the way I am."

James accepted Fannie, giggle and all. Adelaide's composure faltered. Had she done the same for Charles?

Having lived without her mother's approval, she should have understood the need for true acceptance.

Taking Fannie's hands, Adelaide gave them a squeeze. "Thank you."

The young woman's eyes widened. "For what?"

"For teaching the teacher a thing or two," she said softly.

A puzzled expression took over Fannie's cheery face, and she giggled again. "Me? Teach you?"

Adelaide nodded, suddenly unable to speak. Why hadn't she seen the truth earlier? "You've taught me more than you know."

Later, as the young couple ambled over to talk to friends, Adelaide pondered the lesson they'd unknowingly taught. When you love someone, you accept them for who they are.

She'd criticized some things about Charles that didn't matter a whit and had judged him for far more than a messy desk.

She, of all people, should understand how a painful childhood could damage a person. Charles had suffered at the hand of a church-going hypocrite. She should have had more compassion for his refusal to attend church. Maybe if they'd read Scriptures and prayed together, or if she'd asked Pastor Foley for suggestions, she could have found a way to help him.

When you love, truly love a person, you help rather than censure. Perhaps her mother had influenced her more than she realized. She hoped it wasn't too late to change.

Thursday afternoon, Emma ran across the school-yard, the pigtails Adelaide had carefully braided that morning flying out behind her and unraveling around her face. Adelaide scooped the little girl into her arms. Hand in hand, they started for home.

Adelaide squeezed Emma's hand. "How was your day?"

"Billy said his papa didn't like what you wrote in the paper. He said you're dumb. What did you write?"

"An essay on why women should be allowed to vote."

"What's dumb about that?"

"Nothing. Some people don't like women to make decisions."

"Like Tad won't let us girls pick teams at recess?"

"Sort of like that."

"Well, it's not fair." Emma thrust out her lower lip.

Adelaide patted the little girl's shoulder, Charles's words, *Life often isn't fair, Addie,* tumbling in her mind.

Adelaide stopped and bent down, hoping to make Emma understand. "I agree, sweetheart. Everyone in this great country should have a say in who makes the rules."

"Can I make some of *our* rules?" Emma asked, her blue eyes shining with mischief, the unfairness of her life forgotten.

Adelaide laughed and tugged Emma toward her for a hug. "We'll have to see about that."

Emma grinned and they walked on. Adelaide had started to say Emma could make some rules if she had the wisdom. But men used a woman's perceived lack of wisdom as their objection for suffrage, putting women on the level of children.

Her mind on suffrage, Adelaide almost bumped into Frances Drummond huddling in front of the pharmacy, her gaze riveted on Emma and filled with longing.

Emma's brow furrowed in concern. "Where's William?"

Frances stroked Emma's cheek. "He's at the mill with Ed."

Before Emma could say more, Adelaide touched her shoulder. "Would you run back to school and get your McGuffey's reader? I'd like you to read from it tonight."

"Sure."

"I'll wait for you here."

Emma gave Frances a smile. "I'm a good reader," she said, then dashed off toward the school.

With Emma out of earshot, Adelaide turned back to Frances, who looked even thinner and paler than the last time she'd seen her. A faded bruise marked her left cheek.

Frances took a shaky breath. "You and Emma love each other. I saw it in both of your eyes." Her voice sounded thick, as if tears ran down the back of her throat. "I want to talk to the committee."

Adelaide's heart thumped in her chest, hope galloping through her. "Why?"

Frances's eyes misted. "To tell them about… Ed's abuse. Get William out of harm's way."

Realizing this decision cost Frances dearly, Adelaide clasped her hands together to keep from giving her a hug.

"You're a good mother. I want you to have both children."

Unable to speak, Adelaide covered her mouth, holding back her tears—tears of joy for her, tears of sorrow for Frances.

"Those articles you wrote in the paper are the reason I'm speaking up."

Adelaide could barely comprehend that her words had given Frances such courage. "Would you like me to go with you?"

"I'd be obliged." Frances dashed away the tears sliding down her cheeks. "Could we meet in the early afternoon? Ed doesn't come in from the fields until dark so I should be able to leave without him knowing."

"How about two o'clock tomorrow afternoon in the courthouse?"

Frances nodded.

"I'll take care of it."

"Thank you."

"For what?" a gravelly voice demanded.

Adelaide's heart skipped a beat. She swung around to encounter the glowering face of Ed Drummond. How long had he been listening? How much had he heard?

"For...helping Emma with her math," Frances stammered, resting a tentative hand on his arm. "Where's William?"

"He'd better be waiting in the wagon like I told him." Ed shrugged off his wife's touch and pivoted to Adelaide. "You're quite the rabble-rouser, aren't you? Now you're trying to turn husbands and wives against each other with your radical ideas."

Ed lowered his head and placed his mouth close to Adelaide's ear. "You aren't as smart as you think you are, missy," he whispered, his breath warm on her neck, raising the fine hairs at her nape. "Leave us alone, and let me take care of my family like God intended."

How dare he liken his treatment of Frances to God's design?

Ed's lip curled into a snarl. "And stay away from the sheriff, you hear? I won't warn you twice."

Fear slithered down Adelaide's spine and coiled in the pit of her stomach.

Ed took his wife's elbow and stalked off. Adelaide watched the Drummonds enter the law office two doors down, and then expelled the breath she'd been holding.

She scanned the street. Long fingers of terror closed a stranglehold on her throat. *Where's Emma? She should be back by now. Had Ed gotten Emma before he joined them?*

Adelaide set off for the school, holding up her skirts and running fast, begging Heaven for Emma's protection. Soon her breath came in hitches and pain gored her right side. Up ahead, she spotted Emma, swinging along and singing at the top of her lungs. Dropping to her knees, Adelaide thanked God for the precious little girl's safety.

Emma saw her and sprinted to her side. "Miss Weaver asked me to wash the slates." Emma beamed with pride and then held up a tan book. "I got my reader."

Rising to her knees, Adelaide draped an arm around Emma's shoulders and inhaled the scent of soap, chalk, damp skin. She'd never smelled anything sweeter in her life. "That's wonderful, honey. You're a big helper."

"Where's Mrs. Drummond?"

"She had an appointment and couldn't wait. Would you like to help me sew a hem this afternoon?"

"Can I thread my own needle?"

Adelaide smiled at the eagerness in Emma's voice. "Yes, and you can thread mine, too. If you'd like, you can thread every needle in my sewing box."

Emma beamed. "I love you, Miss Adelaide."

Adelaide blinked and tears welled in her eyes. Emma's mouth formed a perfect O and her blue eyes grew round with surprise.

"I love you, too." Adelaide gathered Emma close. "So very much."

Emma squeezed Adelaide with all the might in her small body. For a moment they remained motionless in each other's arms, their declarations settling around them, as satisfying as manna from Heaven.

Adelaide played Emma's words over in her mind. For the first time in her life, someone had declared feelings of love. How had she been granted this most wonderful of gifts? What had she ever done to deserve it?

Nothing. Nothing at all.

God had given her Emma, plain and simple. No one was going to take away that precious gift. *No one.*

Later that afternoon, with Laura taking care of the shop and supervising Emma's homework, Adelaide had gone to the paper to ask Charles to arrange a committee meeting, but he wasn't there. Teddy had pointed her toward the livery.

As she stood outside the stable doors, Adelaide watched Charles brush Ranger's coat. Stepping closer, she noticed lines, usually faint around Charles's eyes, now deep and grooved. Dark smudges beneath his lashes revealed his fatigue.

Well, she was tired, too. Tired of waiting for trouble. Tired of handling that trouble alone. Tired of missing Charles.

If only she could move into his strong arms, have them close around her, and for a while, let him take her burdens. But she had no time for games, not when Ed Drummond held William in his clutches.

She straightened her spine. "Charles."

He jerked up his head. "Addie!"

She steeled herself against the joy she heard in his voice. As much as she loved him, he didn't love her. "I need a favor."

He hurried around the horse, his gaze skimming over her, as if making sure she wasn't a dream. "Anything."

"Better hear me out before you make any promises."

Her words slowed his steps. "I'm listening."

"Frances Drummond wants to meet with the committee. To expose Ed's abuse so she can get William out of there." For a moment, too emotional to continue, Adelaide laid a palm over her trembling lips. "She spoke up because…of my columns," she said, her words tinged with wonder.

He nodded. "You're making things happen, bringing change."

"She wants me to have both the children permanently."

"That's wonderful!"

He reached out and drew her into a hug. The scent of his skin, the hard plane of his chest and the heat from his body filled her senses—as familiar as coming home.

She lifted her face and met his gaze, wanting his kiss with a hunger that left her reeling.

But then the smile in his eyes slipped away. He released her and took a step back. "What are the chances the committee will allow you to have them, merely because Frances says so?"

"What she wants should count for something."

Charles's brow furrowed and he studied the floor, obviously hesitant to speak his mind. "You're still a single woman."

His words held the pain of a slap. Again, a man—or the lack of one—made the decisions in her life. "Being a single woman isn't comparable to abuse. Surely the committee would rather I have those children than Ed. The committee only has to talk to Emma to see she's happy with me."

"Things aren't always that simple, that fair."

"No, but I'm not letting that stop me. You know more than anyone how I feel about Emma."

"You're a great mother." He shook his head. "But I need to warn you—that doesn't mean the committee won't find another home for Emma and William, one with two parents. You need to prepare for the possibility."

Behind them Ranger stamped his foot and Adelaide barely resisted doing the same. "Prepare to lose those children? Never! I'm through with my life—my future—being dictated by men." She stepped toward him. "With or without your support, I intend to fight for Emma and William."

He raised a hand then let it fall. "You could be hurt."

She and Charles had spent their lives captives of their pasts, afraid to take a risk. "I may get hurt but at least I'll be living." She bit her lip to keep from crying and poked his chest with her finger. "Too bad you won't do the same."

"You don't understand. I miss you, but—"

"The problem with you—there's always a 'but' in the way."

He flinched, but she didn't care. Clearly he wasn't going to fight for the two of them.

"When should I schedule the meeting?"

"Two o'clock tomorrow afternoon at the courthouse. Tell them Mrs. Drummond has something important to say."

His gaze locked with hers. "I'll take care of it."

"Thank you." She moved toward the door, her reason for being there finished. But her feet dragged and her mind nagged at her, telling her to go toward Charles, toward the man who stood with his arms at his sides. She paused.

Put them around me, Charles. Take a risk.

But he didn't. Instead he walked back to his horse. Anger churned within her, but remembering the lesson Fannie and James had taught her, she tamped it down. When you love someone, you never give up on that person. This might be her best chance to talk to Charles about trust and forgiveness. About God.

She pivoted to where Charles stood. "God loves you. Do you have any idea how much you matter to Him?"

Head down, he leaned against Ranger, quiet and tall, a silhouette against the open door at the other end of the livery.

At last, he lifted his gaze, his pain-filled eyes bleak. "Then why did He allow me to be beaten, Addie?" he said, his voice cracking. "I prayed and prayed God would stop my father. He didn't."

Tears sprang to her eyes. How did she answer that? Would Charles ever understand on this earth? And what of her own lonely childhood? They'd both paid a price for something they didn't do. But she truly believed God had a plan for their lives.

"Charles, I'm not sure why God allowed you to suffer. Maybe we'll never know. But could it be we're the people we are today because of our childhoods? That you and I survived and are stronger for what we experienced?"

Please God, help me say this right.

"Maybe you went through that nightmare so you could help others—if you'd let God use you."

Charles took a step back. "God wouldn't use me. He isn't close to me like He is to you."

What did Charles mean? She wasn't getting through to him. "God hasn't moved. Let Him into your heart."

Then the thought came—lifting a huge weight from her shoulders. Only God had the authority to bring Charles to Him. She'd do all she could, but in the end, saving Charles remained in God's hands.

Still, before she left, something else needed saying. "Open the Bible. All you need is in there."

He grimaced, his face etched with years of hurt and struggle, as easy to read as *The Ledger*. "You make it sound simple." He picked up the brush, running it along Ranger's side.

"It *is* simple. Let Him in."

He turned to her, his gaze forlorn, ripping at Adelaide's heart. "Which door do I open, Addie? All of mine were nailed shut a long time ago."

Her eyes misted. "You said you believe in God."

"Yes, but unlike you, I don't believe He gets involved with people's lives. If He did, He'd never tolerate my father, or the Ed Drummonds in this world." Charles's mouth thinned. "From what I've seen, evil goes unchecked and the innocent suffer."

How could she get through the wall he'd built? "Your past and the newspaper business have skewed your view of mankind. Good people outnumber the bad."

Down the way, a horse neighed and Ranger nodded his head as if he understood. God had created the animal world with care and purpose. How much more He cherished human beings fashioned in His image. Yet God demanded obedience.

"I can't say what He'll do with your father, with

the evildoers of this world, but His Word promises He will judge."

Charles's eyes glittered. Were those tears? "I'm sure that's true," he said softly, returning to his brushing.

She wanted to touch him, to hug him to her like she did Emma, but she kept her distance, afraid she'd be rebuffed. "You're thinking about your father. Well, I've been thinking about him, too. Wondering why he left such a will. Maybe, before he died, he repented."

Charles snorted. "Why would you think that?"

"Couldn't the will be his way of bringing us together? Trying to give us the life he and my mother never had." She took a breath. "Maybe Adam *wasn't* trying to hurt you."

"You have it all figured out, but it's all conjecture. There's no proof he repented. No evidence of that at all."

As usual, Charles wanted tangible evidence, but weren't a man's actions proof of change? "You believe your father gave me half of the paper to hurt you, but think about it," Adelaide said. "If he'd wanted to hurt you, he could have sold the entire paper right out from under you or left it all to Mary." She held his gaze. "With the two-month time frame, he gave us a chance *and* a way out. Isn't it possible he regretted what he'd done to his family?"

"What if he did? It doesn't change anything, except maybe he got to die in peace," he said, his tone bitter.

"Oh, Charles, if your father truly repented, then he'd have enormous remorse." She sighed. "I'm heartsick he used my mother as an excuse to hurt you and your family. I wish I could undo that, but I can't." She took a deep breath. "Any more than I can change the fact my mother couldn't love life, couldn't love me...or maybe she just couldn't show it." Trying to make him understand, her voice rose, filled with earnestness. "We aren't responsible for their choices. You'll never forget what your father did, but you can forgive."

"Forgive *him?*" Charles hurled the grooming brush across the livery and it thudded against a post, falling into a pile of straw. "I can't."

"With God's help, you *can* forgive. You can do anything."

"Did it ever occur to you God might not want to help me? God knows me better than you do, Addie. I'm not His man."

Charles had said something like this before. "Why do you say that?"

He turned his back to her. "God can't approve of a man like me. There are things you don't know. Things I can't tell you."

She laid a palm on the back of his head, letting her fingers settle into his thick hair. "You can tell me anything. Anything, Charles."

He didn't speak, didn't even look at her. She'd done her best. She had nothing left to say. Her hand fell away and her throat constricted. She could barely get out, "I'm leaving now."

Charles touched her hand, halting her. "I'll be there tomorrow with the committee. I want you to have Emma and William. You know that, don't you?"

"I know." She pressed a hand to her chest. "Until you let God in and learn to forgive, you won't be able to move beyond your past."

"Can't we at least—"

"No!" She started for the door. "Nothing has changed between us, Charles. Nothing at all."

Chapter Nineteen

In the uneasy silence the ticking pendulum of the clock echoed off the courtroom walls. Dwarfed by the imposing two-story coffered ceiling, Adelaide struggled to keep her composure. Across from her, Charles leaned against the witness stand. The rest of the committee sat at the prosecutor's table, staring at her, their eyes hard and suspicious.

The courtroom, the only room available for their meeting, had seemed a fitting place to mete out justice to Ed Drummond, but instead, Adelaide appeared to be the one on trial.

Her gaze darted to the cased walnut clock, its hands pointing to half past two. With each tick, her anxiety grew until her breathing grew rapid and shallow, bringing an odd tingling to her limbs.

Where was Frances?

Mr. Paul's pocket watch clicked shut. "Miss Crum, I don't know what game you're playing, but I, for one, am tired of it."

These men were angry, ready to pounce. "It's not

a game, Mr. Paul. Mrs. Drummond wants to disclose Ed's abuse of her and William."

Mr. Paul scowled. "So you say, but I don't see her."

"Something must have detained Frances," Adelaide said, trying to delay. "I'm sure she'll arrive shortly."

Despite her words, Adelaide wasn't sure of anything and shot another glance at the timepiece. But clock watching didn't make Frances materialize. Had Frances lost her courage and changed her mind? Had Ed learned of her plan and stopped her?

Adelaide closed her eyes and prayed harder for Frances's arrival, her foot jiggling in rhythm to the ticking clock.

Charles folded his arms over his chest. "Mrs. Drummond isn't that late. We'll wait."

Mr. Sparks scowled at Charles. "Graves, you've let this woman use *The Ledger* to spread her rebellion and disrupt the harmony of our little town. And now she claims the wife of one of our upstanding citizens is going to condemn her own husband." He snorted. "She's using this committee—"

"She's doing nothing of the kind." Charles's gaze traveled around the group. "Gentlemen, let's not take chances with a child's life. Until we're assured of William's safety, the boy should be removed from the Drummond home."

Grateful to Charles for standing up to the others, Adelaide gave him a wan smile.

Mr. Wylie shook his head. "Without Mrs. Drummond's testimony, there's no reason to disrupt William's life."

"Frances said she would be here," Adelaide spoke up. "Her husband must have caught on—"

"And what, killed her?" Mr. Wylie leaned his chin on fisted hands, hunching his powerful shoulders, his tone scathing. "My, my, Miss Crum, you do have an active imagination."

Bile rose in Adelaide's throat, leaving behind the acrid taste of fear. "Oh, I hope not."

"You'd better hope he *has*. Because, as things stand now, we won't let Emma remain with you, a woman who'd accuse an innocent man to serve her own purposes."

Adelaide felt the blood drain from her face and the room dipped slightly. Take Emma? *Oh, God, help me.*

Charles crossed to the table, crimson coloring his neck. "Miss Crum doesn't lie. If she says Mrs. Drummond asked her to set up this meeting, then it's true."

Mr. Sparks's eyes narrowed. "Spoken like a suitor, Graves."

Adelaide gasped and clutched her seat for support. "It's not like that."

Mr. Sparks tapped a pencil on the table in front of him like a gavel. "Perhaps not, but from what Roscoe Sullivan has told this committee, and from what I've seen with my own eyes, you two are, shall I say, *very* friendly? One could even say wantonly."

"Mr. Graves has been seen leaving your shop after hours, Miss Crum," Mr. Paul said, rising from the prosecutor's table. He strolled past her, speaking with eloquence as if addressing a jury. "Surely, women's hats aren't the draw."

Charles stepped in front of Mr. Paul. "You owe the lady an apology, Paul. Miss Crum is a woman of virtue. I won't allow you to imply otherwise."

No apology came from Thaddeus Paul's narrowed lips, but he scuttled back to the table.

How could Mr. Paul, who'd known her most of her life, believe her a loose woman? Had the times she'd questioned the committee and her suffrage views fueled this reaction? Or was he retaliating for her reporting Jacob to the sheriff?

Adelaide rose. "I can't believe you'd imply I'm lying and Mr. Graves is in cahoots with me." She took a deep calming breath. "When all you need to do is ask Sheriff Rogers to ride out to the Drummond farm and make sure Frances and William are safe."

"The sheriff doesn't have time to snoop into the lives of decent citizens, any more than we do. We have businesses and farms to run." Mr. Wylie turned to Charles. "Well, unless *you* have time for such foolishness, Graves. From what I hear, the paper is losing subscribers."

Adelaide's gaze flew to Charles and read the truth of Mr. Wylie's words in his face. Hadn't she heard the same from others in town? Her own shop suffered for a lack of business thanks to her attempt to make change in a town that viewed change as anarchy.

Mr. Wylie spoke a few whispered words to Mr. Sparks and Mr. Paul. The men nodded and folded their hands. Mr. Wylie rose. "The committee has decided how to proceed."

Charles frowned. "I wasn't consulted."

Mr. Sparks kept his gaze on Adelaide, ignoring Charles. "We feel Miss Crum isn't the proper influence on a young girl."

Charles threw up his hands. "That's ridiculous!"

"Emma will be returned to the Drummond home today," Mr. Sparks continued.

Adelaide's knees buckled and she dropped into the

nearest chair, fighting for control. *God, help me keep Emma safe.* "Emma is afraid of Ed Drummond. Leave her with me until the sheriff investigates."

Mr. Sparks settled onto the edge of the table. "You knew putting Emma in your care was a temporary solution."

Memories of Emma's nightmares stomped through Adelaide's mind. To remove the child from her home would be cruel. These weren't cruel men, not really. They just didn't see the truth.

"Please, don't take Emma to the Drummonds'. Leave her with me until you find her a new home."

"The Drummonds are her guardians," Mr. Paul said. "*If* Mrs. Drummond supports your story, then we'll relocate the children."

Emma would be yanked from her arms and thrust into the terror-filled world of Charles's childhood and she couldn't find the words to stop it. "Frances won't admit her husband's abuse in front of him. She's afraid of Ed."

Charles laid a steadying hand on her shoulder. The others took note of his touch, their faces set in lines of disapproval at the small act of kindness.

"Miss Crum is right. Mrs. Drummond won't speak openly in front of her husband. Don't risk leaving the children there."

Mr. Wylie sighed. "I can't believe Ed would hurt anyone. I've known him for years."

Charles pivoted to Mr. Wylie. "My father was a churchgoer, who battered, bruised and broke the bones of his wife and two sons," he said, his voice hoarse with emotion. "No one realized it, or if they did, they closed their eyes. Please believe me in this. You don't know what goes on behind closed doors."

The pain of the admission plain on his face, Charles stood silent. No one spoke. Adelaide wanted to soothe what his openness had cost him, but she didn't dare, not with the suspicions the committee had already voiced.

"Talk to Sheriff Rogers. But whatever you do, don't take Emma to the Drummonds," Charles said in a pleading tone.

Mr. Paul cleared his throat. "All right, we'll talk to the sheriff and bring the Drummonds in here for a meeting. See what they have to say. But let me make it clear, Miss Crum. Emma will no longer be staying with you."

Adelaide stiffened. "What gives you the right to make that decision?"

"We're the local arm of the Children's Aid's Society. Once this is settled, we'll be in contact with Mr. Fry."

"At the distribution, Mr. Fry said the children could refuse to go with anyone they didn't trust. Emma won't go back willingly. If you won't let her stay with me, then put her with Laura Larson's family. Emma will feel safe there."

"We'll take that into consideration," Mr. Wylie said, "though we only have your word that Emma doesn't want to return to the Drummonds and her brother."

"Ask Emma where she wants to go. Ask her!"

"We'll talk to the child, when we pick her up from school."

Tears spilled down her cheeks. "Please, let me get her so I can tell her goodbye. Prepare her," she begged. "I won't cause any trouble."

"Goodbyes will only upset the child." Mr. Sparks

thrust his hands into his pockets. "We're acting in Emma's best interest."

Charles scowled. "This is a travesty! You think you know what's best for a little girl you've barely met? Until you've gotten to the bottom of this, leave her with Miss Crum. As a member of the committee, I—"

"You are no longer a member of the committee, Charles."

"What are you saying?"

"You've lost your objectivity where—" Mr. Sparks's gaze moved to Adelaide "—Emma is concerned."

The banker turned to Adelaide. "Don't attempt to see or take Emma out of school. In your emotional state, you'll frighten her."

Mr. Paul leaned toward her, his gaze issuing a sharp warning. "If you refuse to abide by our decision, you will force us to place Emma in another community."

Adelaide gasped. If they did that, she'd never see Emma again. With a shaky hand, Adelaide wiped her eyes.

"The matter is settled," Mr. Wylie said. "Meeting adjourned."

With no hope of changing their minds, Adelaide watched the men walk to the door, each step stomping on her heart until the intensity of the pain all but crushed her.

She looked at the defense table. She and Charles should have sat there. They'd been accused of lying and worse. Three men had proclaimed themselves judge and jury, grabbing the power of the bench, giving no thought on how the verdict would frighten an innocent child. Neither had they acted swiftly to protect a wife and child from abuse.

Through the window, against the overcast sky, tree

branches danced in the rising wind. In the distance, she heard the rumble of thunder. A storm brewed, and Emma didn't have an umbrella…

A sob pushed against her throat. If these men had their way, she wouldn't see Emma again. Wouldn't hold that precious child in her arms, wouldn't share the love they'd just learned to speak. If these men had their way, she'd never teach Emma a new song on the piano or help her stitch silk flowers on a hat. If these men had their way, she didn't know how she'd survive.

Tears spilled down her face and onto the fabric of her dress, marring the silk with the dark stain of loss.

Charles came up beside where she sat and handed her a handkerchief.

"You warned me, Charles," she said, wiping her eyes. "The suffrage articles cost me Emma. I didn't believe my neighbors would let politics destroy their sense of fairness."

He gave her shoulder a squeeze. "It's not over yet, Addie." He tugged her to her feet and enfolded her in his arms.

She pulled away from him. "It's ironic when we're no longer seeing each other that gossip is flying through town like tumbleweeds in a windstorm."

The clock tolled the hour. Adelaide's ice-cold hands twisted. "I'm afraid something awful has happened to Frances," she said, her voice trembling. "I've got to check on her."

Charles lifted her chin and his gaze bored into hers. "Addie, no matter what, don't go to the Drummond farm."

She squared her shoulders, ready to disagree.

"Please," he added, softly. "Until we see what Ed is up to, stay with Laura."

Shaking her head, Adelaide walked to the rail. "I won't put Laura's family in the midst of this. I can take care of myself."

He came after her and brushed away a tendril of hair that had escaped her chignon. "Adelaide Crum, you are the most stubborn woman I've ever known." A smile softened his words.

Oh, Charles, I've missed that smile.

But she only said, "I've had to be."

"So you have." He touched her cheek. "I miss you."

Why did he keep touching her? Didn't he know his smallest contact triggered a longing that increased her pain? And she'd reached her limit? "But that doesn't change anything, does it?"

His hand fell away. "Let me see you."

"Knowing there's no point, there's no future for us?" Her heart squeezed in her chest, aware her next words would bring another loss. First Emma and now Charles, the two people she loved most in the world. "No, I won't see you."

Charles's dark eyes clouded, with regret or with yearning? Adelaide didn't know. She was tired of struggling to understand. If God meant them to be together, then He would have to work it out. She had nothing else to give.

He stepped closer and took her gloved hand, then rubbed it with his. "Can we call a truce? Concentrate on keeping you and the children safe without tying anything more to it."

She shrugged, as if she didn't care. She could pretend with the best of them. "I believe Ed Drummond finally has you worried. Now that it's too late, you're trying to put a tiny bandage on a gaping wound."

His brow furrowed. "I don't understand."

"They're taking Emma away from me, Charles! Why? Because I'm single. Isn't that what it comes down to? And all you can worry about is that Ed Drummond will hurt me, but you've hurt me more than he ever could!"

Before he could respond, Adelaide walked out of the courtroom, away from Charles, from his inability to change. But in her heart, she knew her being single wasn't the only reason they'd taken Emma. The columns she'd written had made matters worse, not only for her and Emma, but for Frances, too.

Adelaide would never forgive herself if Frances had paid a price for her need to speak out.

Alone in the courtroom, Charles stood with his back to the judge's bench. Lightning flashed and rain beat against the windowpanes. Outside a storm raged, but nothing like the storm inside him. He'd let Adelaide and Emma down, when they needed him most. But if Addie truly knew him, she'd never agree to take his name.

Deep in the abyss of his mind, a memory clawed its way to the surface and demanded a hearing. This time Charles couldn't stop it. He didn't even try.

Recalling that night, a lifetime ago, held him captive; a dark and inexcusable deed kept him in a prison without bars.

He'd come home from his after-school job to find his father beating his mother for the hundredth time. Except this time, Pa wasn't slurring his words or swaying on his feet.

This time, Pa was stone-cold sober.

Ma cowered on the floor, begging him to stop, apologizing for some pitiful infraction of Pa's ever-changing rules.

Inside him something as thin as a twig gave way, something that had held tenuous control over the rage, rage that had been building and building and building for years.

He hurled himself at his pa, swinging fists, grabbing Pa's throat, not seeing, not thinking, only wanting him to stop.

He hadn't heard Ma begging him to release his hold. Hadn't been aware of Pa's hands grasping at his arms, first strong, then…weaker and weaker.

He heard nothing but all those years of screams. All those nights he stood by, a helpless child, weeping and wondering when his turn would come.

If Sam hadn't returned and pulled him off in time, Charles knew without a doubt he would have killed his father that night. A sob escaped his throat. What kind of man wouldn't stop even after his father had gone limp under his squeezing hands?

The answer was clear—a man *like* his father, a man with a deadly temper, a man with whom God could have no relationship.

He could never marry Addie. Never be a father to Emma or William. Never enter God's house and taint it with his presence.

He slid to the floor. "Oh, God. Help me."

But once again, Heaven remained silent.

Charles buried his face in his arms and wept.

That evening, Charles trekked from Laura's house toward Addie's shop. The afternoon rain had stopped, leaving a light, clean scent to the air, in sharp contrast to his dismal mood.

Roscoe had all but shut down Addie's business because of what he'd called that spinster's meddling and now, thanks to the committee, Addie had lost Emma. Though all those worries weighed on him, Charles's main concern was keeping Addie safe.

Mercifully, the committee had decided to keep Emma in town—for now—which guaranteed Addie wouldn't ride out to the Drummond house. Tomorrow, Wylie, Sparks and Paul would meet with the Drummonds. If, as he suspected, Frances had been harmed, then the committee would finally be roused out of its complacency.

In some ways, he couldn't blame the others. Until recently, he hadn't seen Ed Drummond as a dangerous man.

With the key Addie had given him earlier, Charles unlocked the door to her shop. She sat at the small table in the center of the showroom facing the door. When he entered, her head snapped up. But then seeing him, she bowed over an open Bible, reading the Scriptures while running a finger along the pink ribbon on a small straw bonnet she held in her hand. Emma's hat.

His gut knotted in anger. The committee had taken Emma, unconcerned about Addie's suffering. He'd hurt her, too, more times than he wanted to remember. But through it all, she prayed, read her Bible, trusted in God.

Addie had once told him God had given her Emma. Well, if He had, He'd also taken the little girl away.

Charles walked to the table. She looked up with dry eyes, crisscrossed with tiny veins of red, evidence she'd been crying. He had news he hoped would bring a smile, though without Emma, he knew Addie's heart had broken.

He cleared his throat. "I checked on Emma."

"How is she?"

"Baking cookies with Laura and looking happy. She asked me to tell you, she's saving you some cookies."

Her eyes glistened. "I want to slip over there to see her, but the committee could be watching the house."

"I wouldn't put it past them." He fingered the brim of his hat. "Late this afternoon, I rode out to the Drummond place. Ed blocked the door and claimed Frances was lying down with a headache. It would have taken a fistfight to get past him. With William there, I couldn't risk that." Before she could ask, he said, "William looked fine. One good thing—we know Ed's at home, at least around five o'clock."

"Did the sheriff go with you?"

"He's been on County business all day, something about tax rolls. Right now, he's over at the Reilly saloon, stopping a fistfight. He'll be watching your place tonight, too."

Her face a mask of misery, Addie fingered the pages of the Bible. He wanted to pull her into his arms, hold her and comfort her.

But she'd made it clear she no longer wanted that from him.

Want it or not, she needed it. He took her hand. "Come here," he said softly and tugged her to her feet. She burrowed into his arms, rocking him back on his heels.

"Emma's fine. I know how you miss her. But until we see what Drummond will do, it's good she's not here."

She pulled back and lifted a questioning gaze.

"I don't want to alarm you, but I don't believe for a minute Frances had a headache, unless Ed gave it to her."

"I'm afraid for Frances and William."

"I know," he crooned, tightening his grip. "Maybe once the committee talks to Frances, they'll let you keep Emma."

Addie pulled away. "You don't really believe that, do you?"

He couldn't meet her gaze.

She kissed his cheek. "Thank you for not agreeing. You're a good man."

His throat tightened. He knew he wasn't a good man, but he treasured her words. "I'll check upstairs."

She nodded, then walked to the counter and picked up a partially finished hat.

Charles climbed the steps for the last time and walked into each room where shadowed memories paraded through his mind. Memories of meals shared in this kitchen. Of Emma plunking at the piano in the parlor while he'd teased Addie about her Jack-induced willies. Here, in Emma's room, of him and Addie soothing her nightmare with a lullaby.

He stepped to Addie's room, the one room he'd never seen. Neat as a pin, like the rest, his gaze roamed over the ruffled curtains at the window, the brush and comb set on the dresser, the white bowl and pitcher on the washstand. Eyes stinging, he fingered the feathered bird atop the hat that lay on the seat of a rocker, recalling their banter on the first day she'd worn it.

In the hall, he took one last look at the rooms that had made him feel more at home than any place he'd ever been.

Knowing he wouldn't be back slowed his step, but only for a moment. He had a job to do. He headed down the stairs.

Addie sat where he'd left her. With a thimble, she pushed a shiny needle through two layers of heavy felt joining the brim and crown of a hat.

He stopped, frozen by the image of her, absorbing her profile, the tilt of her neck, the sense of her inner strength he admired. But *that* strength would be no match for Ed Drummond.

He thought of losing her, thought of his world without Addie in it, and his heart tripped in his chest. How could he survive? What kind of place would this town be without Addie?

He reached the bottom, walked to the back and checked the door and window, then returned to the showroom. "Whether you like it or not, I'm standing watch down here tonight."

"I've told you that's not an option. People will talk."

"Let them!"

"Hasn't enough damage been done by gossip?"

Tentacles of guilt clutched at Charles's throat. If he hadn't told Roscoe he suspected Ed had vandalized Addie's shop, would the committee have taken Emma? If he had refused to publish her essays, would she be in this mess?

He kissed her forehead. "You won't answer the door to anyone? Not even me?"

She looked up and gave a feeble grin. "Especially not you."

"Good."

Her brow furrowed. "Why not you?"

"If somehow Drummond overpowered me, he could

use me to get to you. Promise, you won't let anyone in, not me, not anyone."

She nodded.

"Really, Addie?"

"Yes, I promise."

Sudden tears welled in his eyes. He made a big production of digging in his pocket for her key and then handed it to her. "Walk me to the door and lock it behind me."

Her face pale and drawn, Addie rose, a woman he couldn't marry but a woman he would protect, at all costs.

At the door, she touched his arm. "Be careful," she said softly, her gaze traveling his features. "I'm praying for you."

Her concern for him ripped at his shaky composure and he could only nod. He slipped out and waited until he heard the click of the lock behind him.

He checked the street and alley. Seeing nothing unusual, he crossed to *The Ledger* and let himself in, tracking mud on the wooden floor. If Addie saw this, she'd scold him for not wiping his feet. If only all they had to concern themselves with was a little dirt.

Earlier, Sheriff Rogers had been called away to the saloon, disrupting their speculation about whether Drummond would come after Addie tonight. Charles hadn't laid eyes on Rogers since.

He'd tried to pray for her safety, but his childhood had taught him he couldn't count on God.

It was up to him and him alone to protect Addie.

In the back room, he squatted before the steel safe, and rotated the dial, four right, two left, six right, counting the clicks with each turn until he heard the lock open. Inside, he found what he sought and pulled away the soft cloth. In the glow from the gaslight, the pistol's barrel gleamed.

He fingered the smooth ivory-inlaid butt, surprisingly beautiful for an instrument of death.

Convinced every man needed a gun to protect what was his, Sam had given it to him for his birthday a few years back. Charles had never fired it at anything more than a target.

Yet, tonight, the next night—some night—that would change. Ed would come after Addie. And Charles would be waiting.

Grabbing a box of ammunition and his gun belt, he picked up the handgun and closed the six-inch-thick door, giving the dial a twirl. He walked to the cot and sat. He opened the chamber of his gun and inserted the first bullet, then another, until he'd filled each slot. Slipping the gun into its holster, he rose and buckled the belt, shoving it down on his hips.

With his right hand hanging loose over the holster, Charles whipped out the gun, aiming at a spot on the wall about the height of Ed Drummond's heart. If forced to use the gun, he hoped the target practice in Cincinnati wouldn't fail him.

Charles lowered the gaslight, walked out of the room, through the dark office, to the main door. In the doorway, he scanned the deserted street. A horse, tied to a hitching post down the way, nickered, eager to return to a comfortable stall. In front of Addie's shop, a cat promenaded down the walk, then sprang at something Charles couldn't see. Music from the honky-tonk piano drifted on the night air. How odd to find everything

looking normal when at any moment this peaceful scene
might erupt in violence.

Addie's shop was dark. Overhead he spotted the light
in her bedroom. He hoped she could sleep. If only he'd
overruled her and stayed below in the shop. But that
wasn't Addie's way.

Dear, sweet Addie with her adherence to her impec-
cable morals and a stubborn streak as wide as the Ohio
River in spring. She had spunk, hope and a heart the
size of Texas—and wonder of wonders, faith in him.

Tonight he wouldn't let her down. And tomorrow,
well, if they got that far, he'd help her get the children.
He needed her back in his life, had missed her every
moment of every day since they'd been apart. He hadn't
realized what a hollow man he'd been before he'd met
her. How much she'd brought to his life, until he'd lost it.

He slipped across the street, moved toward the
back of her building, his gaze darting from shadow
to shadow, alert to any sound, searching for trouble.
Searching for Drummond.

He saw no one, yet he couldn't shake a sense of evil,
heavy and thick. He positioned himself between her
building and the next. From here, he could see both
front and back of her shop.

He waited, his emotions galloping between hot fear
and cold dread, yet certain that if he had to, tonight he
could kill.

Chapter Twenty

Minutes stretched into hours. The sheriff had yet to appear. Charles ran a hand across his face, the rough stubble scratching against his palm, more tired than he'd ever been in his life. Each eyelid seemed to weigh a pound. With a fist, he rubbed his eyes, gritty from lack of sleep. He was running out of steam. If he didn't get some coffee soon, he would be asleep on his feet. At the paper, a pot of coffee brewed so long ago it could wake the dead, sat on the stove.

He took another look around before heading across the street to *The Ledger*. He'd be gone for two minutes. Nothing could happen to Addie in that length of time.

Adelaide jerked awake. Her heartbeat pounded at her temples, echoed in her ears while she held her breath, listening. An odor smacked her in the stomach.

Pungent, sickly sweet. Kerosene.

Silently, she slipped out of bed, shoved her arms into the sleeves of her wrapper, and then edged toward the door. Easing it ajar, she peered into the dark hall. The smell seared her nostrils, slithered down her throat.

Then from below came a noise. Mind-numbing panic seized her limbs and she couldn't move.

Ed's in the shop. God, help me. He's going to burn it down around me.

A faint creak from downstairs caused the tiny hairs on her neck to stand up. Another creak.

He's coming. He's coming up the stairs.

For me.

Adrenaline shot through her body. Ed Drummond wouldn't burn her alive, wouldn't beat her senseless without a fight.

Holding her breath, Adelaide slid through the narrow opening on soundless feet. Then she pressed her back to the wall and glided down the ebony shadowed hall, avoiding the small table ahead, the rug farther down that liked to catch her toes. In the shadows, she could make out the doorway to the parlor. If she could reach the kitchen, she'd escape down the back stairs to the yard. From there she could run to safety. To Charles.

She thanked God for the darkness of the hall, and her navy wrapper that concealed a white nightdress, a sure beacon for Ed.

Down the hall, a door squeaked. Emma's room. Thank God, Emma slept at Laura's.

Heart pounding so loudly in her ears that Ed must surely hear it, Adelaide clamped a hand to her mouth, stifling an urge to scream. She heard heavy breathing now. He was closer. He would be in her room next, and when he saw her empty bed, he'd realize he had no need to move quietly.

And he'd come running.

Yet, Adelaide slipped along the wall, not daring to make any sudden moves that might draw his eye.

At last, she reached the kitchen and felt for the butcher knife she kept near the sink. She grabbed the fat handle. Then the sound of furniture crashing, loud cursing, stilled her hand. Feet pounded through the hall. And then, a second later, she heard "You're dead, missy!"

Move, Adelaide. Move!

Holding the knife, she raced for the back door. Her free hand shot out and grasped the knob. She yanked, but the door didn't budge. With shaking fingers, she fumbled with the bolt and, finally getting it to turn, flung open the door and sprinted onto the back landing.

Fresh air burst into her lungs. Before she could finish the breath, he jerked it out of her. Her collar was held firmly in Ed's grasp, yanking her back. To him.

"Got ya now!"

Screaming, Adelaide spun, wiggled out of her wrapper and plunged down the stairs. The knife slipped from her hands, clattering down the steps. Heavy work boots clomped down after her. She jumped from the last few steps to the ground and ran. Expletives exploded behind her.

She tore blindly across the yard. Her lungs burned, her muscles shrieked, her heart thundered, each step a prayer.

She slammed into something solid and familiar. *Charles.*

"Addie!" Charles shoved her behind him seconds before Ed threw himself at him. The men tumbled to the ground. Thudding fists and shouted curses pierced the night air.

They rolled, a tangle of arms and legs, pounding flesh against bone. Ed was heavier and filled with the lethal power of hate. Charles would surely die. Their grunts and groans scrambled her mind.

"Lord God in Heaven, save Charles!"

Struggling to think, her heart pumped wildly in her chest. And then she knew. *The knife, find the knife.*

She sprinted to the stairs and scampered up, searching in the faint moonlight. Where? Where had she dropped it? She retraced her steps. "Please, God, please, help me!"

And then, at the bottom of the steps, she spotted a glint of steel. She scuttled down and snatched the knife, then ran across the lawn, slipping on the wet grass, to where the men raged and warred.

On their feet now, they jabbed and ducked, swerved and confronted in some macabre dance while Charles struggled to reach the gun on his hip. Charles had a gun?

Ed's hand whipped out, grabbed Charles's throat, then squeezed, laughing while Charles's fingers clawed at Ed's hands, eyes popping, body jerking, struggling against the monster.

Ed twisted position, tightening his grip. Charles was flailing, Ed rejoicing.

She wouldn't let Charles die.

Adelaide circled them, looking for an opening, a position at Ed's back, praying for accuracy. She took a great gulp of air, trying to ease her breathing. *Steady.* If either of them moved, she'd miss, or worse—hit Charles.

The moon slid from behind a cloud, washing light over the men. Adelaide raised the knife high above her, poised, aiming for Ed's back. Ed swore and threw up an arm. Before she could strike, Charles pivoted, lifted his knee and caught Ed in the groin. Ed crumpled to the ground, rolling, moaning, cursing.

Charles raced to Adelaide's side.

Charles's throat throbbed, his eyes stung. Shoulders heaving, he pulled Addie to him. Each gasping breath burned his lungs, tore at his ribs. He shoved words from his mouth. "Are…you…all right?"

"Yes! Are you?"

Dragging in air, he nodded. Gently, he pried her fingers from the death grip she had on the knife and then dropped the weapon at their feet. Covering the blade with the heel of a boot, he gathered her into his arms and pulled her close. "Thank God…you're…safe."

A movement. Drummond crouched, ready to spring. Charles shoved Addie away and in an instant, grabbed Ed's outstretched arm, pulling it up and back behind him with a jerk. Ed screamed in pain and crumpled face-first onto the ground.

Whipping his gun from the holster, Charles stood over him, cocked the gun and raised the barrel until he'd leveled the sights with Ed's head.

Writhing on the ground, Ed twisted around and saw the barrel. He threw up his hands. "Don't shoot! Have mercy!"

Charles curled his finger around the trigger. One shot. That's all it would take to rid the town—the world—of this demon. His finger tensed. The slightest pressure and Ed would die.

A bead of sweat slipped down Charles's palm. Blood hammered his temples. Rage distorted his eyesight. A voice pounded in his head. Kill him. Kill him. *Kill him.*

From deep inside, another voice echoed in his skull.

*Then you're no different than he is, no different than
your father.*

Charles shook his head, clearing his vision. Drummond had shown no mercy to Addie, or Sarah, or Frances.

But Charles wasn't God—he wasn't anyone's personal judge and jury. He relaxed his finger. The gun dropped into place in his holster. He couldn't shoot Drummond, an unarmed man, no matter how much he deserved killing. Unless he had no other choice, Charles didn't have it in him to take a life. But Ed would pay for his crimes. Charles would see to that.

Sheriff Rogers, gun drawn, ran from the shadows. "What happened here?"

Charles grabbed Ed's collar, pulling him to his feet. "Drummond tried to kill Adelaide, Sheriff."

"He attacked me!" Ed screamed, twisting in Charles's grip.

The click of the sheriff's gun being cocked issued its own warning. "That's enough out of you, Drummond. Raise 'em." In the sights of the sheriff's gun, Ed's hands shot skyward. "Charles, check him for a weapon."

Charles moved behind Drummond. The odor of kerosene filled his nostrils. Like a match under dry kindling, the stench of Drummond's intentions sparked a fury inside him. "You coward! You were going to burn her out."

"She had it coming! Turning a man's wife against him, sticking her nose into my business—"

"Like Sarah?" Sheriff Rogers asked.

"I never killed Sarah." Drummond twisted around to face the sheriff. "You ain't got proof I did."

Charles ran his hands over Drummond's shirt and

down to the man's pockets. Inside the right rear pocket his fingers closed around something, something that pulsated in Charles's gut with the force of a sledge-hammer.

In the moonlight with a balmy breeze lending a benign feel to the night air, a ghoulish sight hung from Charles's outstretched hand.

A garrote.

Adelaide gasped. Rogers handed his pistol to Charles and cuffed Drummond's hands behind his back. Charles tossed the cord to the sheriff.

"You're mighty fond of them things, Drummond. Planning on killing Miss Crum with this? Then incinerating the place to make it look like an accident?"

"That busybody wants to take all I have—the orphans, my reputation, my wife. Can't you see? I couldn't let her do that."

"Tell it to a judge and jury." The sheriff pocketed the garrote, muttering under his breath. Then he retrieved his gun and aimed it at Drummond. "Better get this scum to the jail before I'm tempted to wipe my boots with him."

He turned to Charles and Adelaide. "I took a brawler with a broken hand over to the doc's a moment ago." He jerked his head toward Ed. "His missus is there. She's taken quite a beating."

Addie slumped against Charles. "How bad is she?"

"Doc isn't sure she'll make it."

Addie moaned. "What about William?"

"William brought her in. Somehow he got Frances in the wagon. He's fine." Sheriff Rogers jerked up Drummond's head by his hair and shoved his face close. "Real tough guy, aren't you, Drummond, going after children and womenfolk?"

"If Frances had stayed home where she belonged, my boy wouldn't be dead."

Adelaide jerked out of Charles's arms and moved toward Ed. "How dare you blame Frances for Eddie's death. It was an accident." She gasped. "Or was it? Could you have set fire to your own son?"

Ed's staggered. "Kill...my boy? Don't you see? My boy's death killed me." Ed's body shook with sobs.

"How could you beat Frances, the woman who bore that child?"

Ed's lip curled. "She was planning to leave. Take my boy and move in with Sarah. I kept my family together...the only way I knew how. Frances always fought everything I said, everything I did. And you..." He pointed to Addie. "You egged her on."

"I've heard all I can stomach." Pulling Drummond along by the arm, the sheriff strode out of the yard, calling over his shoulder. "I'll need your statements. Tomorrow's soon enough."

Relief flooded Charles, then bone-numbing fatigue. He tugged Addie close. Drummond would be in jail where he belonged. He couldn't harm Addie or Emma or William ever again.

"I could have lost you," he murmured in her ear, his voice raspy. The magnitude of that possibility careened through him like a barbed arrow, hitting bone, marrow and muscle and lodging near his heart.

He breathed in the scent of her hair hanging loose about her shoulders, breathed in her goodness, the goodness he'd been in search of his entire life. Addie cared for him more than he deserved. She fought for what she believed in. And she believed in him.

Adelaide could hear Charles moving around the apartment, methodically opening the windows, releasing the stench of kerosene. Taking charge. On any other day, she would have helped, but her muscles had turned to jelly.

Charles returned to the kitchen, intent on making tea. He fumbled around in the cupboard, muttering under his breath.

"It's in the left door of the cabinet, in front."

"Thanks."

A few minutes later he handed her a steaming cup of tea. "Drink up. It'll help get rid of the shakes."

Adelaide took the cup, grasping its warmth like a lifeline. Her hand trembled and drops of the liquid splashed across her fingers, but she drank deeply, easing the chill that facing death had seeped into her bones.

"Will you be all right for a minute?" he asked.

She nodded.

"I want to open the back door of the shop." He gave her shoulder a squeeze, and then took the stairs at a run.

Adelaide put the cup on the table and leaned against the chair. Icy fingers gripped her heart. If Charles hadn't overpowered Ed, could she have stabbed him? From somewhere deep inside came the certainty that in self-defense or to save Charles, she could have killed—or died trying.

Closing her eyes, she thanked God she'd never have to know. She asked the Almighty to be with Doc Lawrence, to help him ease Frances's pain and save her life, if it wasn't too late.

What a hard life Frances had endured. First losing her only child, then the murder of her mother, now this severe beating.

Charles returned to the kitchen and paused in the doorway. Even battered and bruised, he looked solid, trustworthy, in control. Charles, the man she loved. His smile dazzled her. His voice soothed her. Tension slipped off her shoulders and her breathing slowed— all because Charles stood nearby.

"I found an empty can of kerosene near the back—" He glanced at her and stopped.

Without warning, a deluge of tears flowed down her face. Charles dropped to his knees at her feet and took her hand in his. "What is it?"

"I feel responsible for what happened to Frances." She covered her mouth with a fist. "When she asked to talk to the committee, I should've insisted she stay in town with me." Her voice broke. "Instead, I thought only of myself."

"You weren't thinking of yourself—you were thinking of William." He rose, tugging her with him, drawing her into the comfort of his arms. "Ed would have gotten to Frances, no matter what you did, or what the sheriff tried to do. The man's deranged." He leaned back, cupped her chin with his hand. "Frances did what she did for William, not for you."

With the pads of his thumbs, he gently brushed the tears away and then kissed her cheeks, the tip of her nose and each eyelid. His words and the touch of his lips brought healing, a blessed release from self-blame.

"My brave Addie."

"Brave?" Her voice shook. "Me?"

"You're the bravest woman I know. I saw you with

that knife, ready to enter the fray. I've never been so scared."

She shivered. "He was trying to…to kill you."

Charles pulled her tight against him. A moan tore from his throat. "Oh, Addie, I could have lost you."

She loved Charles for his courage, for the risks he'd taken to protect her. For being a loving man, though he didn't believe that yet. She started to say she loved him, but then bit back the words. She wouldn't say them just because they'd shared this terrifying night.

Charles stepped back and met her gaze. "We're alive, Addie. We've survived Ed, and we'll survive the trouble in this town. Marry me. I'll see that you get Emma and William. I'll give you everything you ever wanted—a home, a family."

She heard the sweet words and wanted to say yes. He had been in her heart since the first day she'd walked across the street after placing that ad. Her feelings for him had grown until she couldn't imagine life without him. But she couldn't marry him, not without the three little words he did not say.

If she forced his hand, perhaps he would. "What about love?"

A shuttered look came over his face. "I want to, but, I don't know what love is. Something's missing…inside. But—"

Her heart plunged. "No buts, Charles." She couldn't marry him and relegate herself to a life half-full. "I won't settle for less than love."

Tears collected in his eyes. "I can't survive being separated from you. Please say that's enough."

"I wish it were." She sighed. "No, Charles, I won't

marry you." The finality of her words struck like a bolt of lightning, searing her heart.

"If we're married, we might be able to have Emma and William. That's the only way you'll get the children. Don't you see that?"

His words stung and she moved past him. "That's probably true. But what kind of a marriage would that be for me? For you? For the children?" Her heart lurched into her throat. "You're afraid to love. You can't even speak the word. You can't forgive God for your past, can't worship. You're stuck back there, Charles. Well, I'm looking to the future."

He flinched. "Addie... I don't know what to say."

She met his gaze, tried to see what truths were hidden in the depths of those dark pools. "You make your living with words and now you can't speak the words that will open your heart to me."

"I'm not like you."

"People can change. I have. Before I asked for one of the orphans, before I expressed my views in the paper, I didn't speak up on issues that mattered to me. And you know what? I like the new me. You may not realize how much you've helped me change. Whether you meant to or not."

"You've always been strong."

"I get my strength from God, from His word, from worshipping in His house. I can't marry a man who won't trust God and I won't settle for a loveless marriage, even for a child." Her voice broke. "E-even for Emma." She squared her shoulders. "I won't end up like my mother."

"I wouldn't leave like your father did." He took her

hand. "If you'll marry me, I'll be committed to our marriage."

"I believe you. You'd stick by me. You'd fill a seat at the table, take care of the hundreds of details a husband would. And day by day I would die in tiny increments, waiting for the words that might never come."

"What do you want from me?"

As if he didn't know. "I want *more* than a commitment. I had that much with my mother." She softened her voice. "I want your *love,* Charles. I've spent a lifetime without it. I know now what it's like to feel it. And you…you still don't understand how important love is." She bit her lip, determined not to cry, and pushed him away. "Please—go."

He hesitated, took a step forward.

"You don't have to worry about me anymore."

He stood, looking bereft, but saying none of the things that would have changed her mind.

She lifted a palm to his cheek, seeking one last touch. "You deserve a lot more than you think. One day, I hope you'll believe that and find peace."

Her hand fell away. "You know the way out."

Addie deserved love and Charles didn't have it to give. He left by the back stairs, too tired to move with any speed. Every muscle in his body ached, and his brain was numb with fatigue.

But he still had enough presence of mind to go to *The Ledger* by an indirect route, in case some night owl would see him and spread the story, hurting Addie.

As if he hadn't hurt her enough. She'd asked only one thing of him—to love her.

She had no idea what she asked.

His mother had loved his father and look where that had gotten her—years of demeaning treatment and pain. He'd even loved his father once, always hoping Adam Graves would change, but he never did, and Charles's love had withered and died. Replaced with fiery hot anger at his father and, yes, at himself, for being unable to handle the situation he called his family.

Everyone he'd ever loved had hurt him or let him down, even Sam, getting himself killed in a barroom brawl. He believed Addie was different. But what if he didn't have that kind of giving love in him? What if his capacity to love had been destroyed in the place he'd once called home?

Charles entered *The Ledger*'s office. His steps, hesitant, unsure. He walked like an old man, probably from the beating he'd taken and given. The printing press sat silent, the energy gone from the room, along with the appeal of the place.

In the back, he knelt before the safe and removed the bullets in the cylinder, then laid the gun and belt inside, shut the door and twirled the lock.

He might have saved Addie from Drummond, but he'd let her down tonight. Just as the selection committee had let down the Grounds children.

Well, there was one thing he *could* do for Addie, for Emma and William. Tonight. He headed out the door.

Chapter Twenty-One

❧

Within minutes Charles had dragged John Sparks and Thaddeus Paul from their beds. Morris Wylie lived too far out to get tonight, but if he needed to, in the morning Charles would be knocking on his door, too.

Once he explained the evening's events, the two men agreed to accompany him to Frances's bedside.

At Doc Lawrence's they found William looking dazed, sitting in the outer office. Mary sat nearby, calm and competent as always, doing what she could to comfort the boy.

Charles gave her a weak smile.

Mary gasped. "What happened to you?"

He looked at William. "I'll tell you later."

Mary nodded, studying first Charles and then the somber faces of his companions.

"How's Frances?" Charles asked.

"About the same. Daddy wrapped her ribs, set her arm and stitched her up." Mary lowered her voice. "He's not sure about her organs."

"Is she conscious?" Mr. Sparks asked.

"Yes, amazingly, she is." She looked at the boy and

smiled. "I've been telling William, Frances is a strong woman."

Sparks and Paul went inside to see Frances. Charles lagged behind. He hoped Frances had the strength to tell the men what they needed to know. He couldn't do anything in there. But maybe, like Addie once said, he could help the boy.

Head down, William drooped in the chair, the slump of his shoulders telling Charles plenty. His hair and clothes were disheveled and stained, probably from Frances's blood. Hands clasped tight in his lap, he didn't look injured, at least not on the outside.

Charles sat on his haunches and laid a hand on the boy's shoulder. William flinched. Charles should have known better than to touch him. "I'm Charles Graves, William, a friend of Emma and Miss Crum."

Frightened eyes turned to him and then darted away. William seemed to shrink into himself, trying to be invisible.

Charles's heart tumbled. He knew the signs. Charles removed his hand, giving the boy some distance. "I've been in a bit of a fight, but I'm fine. And Mr. Drummond is in jail."

William turned solemn eyes on him. "He is?"

"Yes. And that's where he's staying." Charles patted his stomach. "I'm starving. Are you hungry?"

William shook his head.

"How about some milk? I bet Doc even has a cookie or two." Charles put out a hand. "Come on. Let's raid the icebox."

William hesitated, his gaze sliding from Mary, to the closed surgery door and then to Charles. His gaze caught, held there and then he rose and stepped beside Charles.

Mary blinked damp eyes. "I'll check on Frances."

Charles and William walked down the hall to Doc's kitchen. Dishes, glasses, half-full cups of cold coffee covered every surface. Addie would have a heyday in here. Nice to know another bachelor in town would fail Addie's neatness test.

Charles found two clean glasses in a cabinet and filled them with milk. Then pulled out a chair for William at the small drop-leaf table and sat beside him. For the second time today, Charles had no idea what to say.

If only he could find the right words, the words he would have wanted, needed to hear as a boy. "I'm sorry about Mrs. Drummond. She's a good woman."

Turning his glass in his boy-size hands, William nodded.

"It took courage to get her to the doc's."

William's lips pressed in a tight line, but he kept his eyes averted. Still, Charles could see tears well up in pools, though not a single one dropped onto his tanned cheeks.

Charles pushed his untouched glass aside and leaned his chin on his hands. "I know what it's like, William."

The boy didn't look at him, didn't speak.

"I know the fear, the anger. What it's like to try to keep the peace…and fail."

"How?" he said softly, head down, spirit wounded.

"I grew up in a home with a pa like Ed Drummond."

William's head snapped up. Charles waited, letting the words connect them, seeing the moment the boy understood.

"I remember how the hair on my neck would rise,

how my gut would knot." Charles swallowed against the old familiar lump in his throat. "How I wanted to run, but knew running would only make it worse. It was the same for you, wasn't it?"

Slowly, William nodded.

Charles lifted William's chin with a palm. "I want you to know something else."

The boy's tear-filled eyes, the color of the sea on a cloudy day, met his.

"It wasn't your doing. *None* of it was your fault, William. You were never the reason for what was said or done. *Never.*"

Charles said *never* again and again until a sob tore from William's throat. The tears spilled over now, slipping down William's cheeks in little rivulets, leaving trails on his dirty face. As he wept, William's breath came in gulping hitches.

Charles rose and knelt before the boy, pausing only a second, and then pulled William tight to his chest. For a moment, William held himself stiff, his heart knocking against Charles's torso, and then he burrowed into Charles's arms.

"I was afraid."

"I know. I know." Charles clutched the boy and swayed to the rhythm of remembered pain that branded the mind and spirit.

"I didn't know how to make him stop," William spoke into Charles's shirt.

Old feelings of inadequacy and helplessness roared through him. "Stopping Ed wasn't a job for a boy. It was a man's job."

"I… I always made him angry."

Ah, familiar words from his past. "Ed Drummond's

sick. Sick in the head and in the heart. Like my pa. His anger had nothing to do with what you did or didn't do. It was *him*." Charles shifted William in his arms and caught his gaze, then repeated, "It was *him*."

William's gaze tumbled away from Charles. "I hate him."

"I know about hate." All too well. Hate lived in him still, gnawing at him, dumping the past on his every today. As surely as he held William, hate held Charles in its clutches.

Suddenly, he knew what else needed to be said to the boy, to himself, the boy he used to be. "When we can, you and I need to forgive. Hating eats us up inside, keeps us from trusting all the good people." Good people like Addie.

The harsh lines in William's face eased, leaving his expression solemn, but perplexed.

He ran his hand through the boy's silky strands. "Forgiving won't be easy."

Though Addie had told him he should, until that moment, Charles hadn't truly comprehended the importance of forgiving. He had to forgive his mother for staying, and then his father for inflicting wounds that might have mended on the outside, but underneath festered still. Until he could forgive, he'd be stuck, unable to move beyond his past.

And so would William.

"What Ed did was wrong, bad," Charles said, "You'll never forget, but you can forgive him because he's ill." His words an echo of what Addie had tried to tell him about his own father.

William swiped at his eyes. "Why's he sick?"

"That's a tough one. I don't know." Would he ever know? Did it even matter?

"Will I...will I be sick like him?"

Charles remembered that first day at the schoolhouse, how William had taken Emma's hand and comforted her. This very night, the boy had rescued Frances instead of running. Everyone started out in life with the capacity for good and evil. Some people, like William, served good, while others, like Ed Drummond, served evil.

"No. You're going to be your own man. You can choose what kind of man that will be."

As William clung to him, tears ran down Charles's cheeks. Together they wept for two innocent boys, for William and for the boy Charles had once been. They'd both faced an enemy far bigger than them.

"You're a good boy," Charles crooned, cradling William in his arms. "A good boy."

The words resonated in Charles's head. *He* had been a good boy, no matter how much he'd heard otherwise. He and William had both done the best they could. And they both could choose a new future.

Not only must he forgive his family, Charles knew he must make things right between him and God. Because he knew without a doubt God had saved him—then and now.

Charles turned his gaze upward.

God, I'm hoping You can forgive me for my anger at You, for questioning Your will.

Forgive me for trying to kill my father, for holding on to bitterness, for not worshipping.

Help me make a fresh start. A fresh start with You.

The dark oppressive load slid from Charles's shoulders and in its place came a long-awaited sense of peace. It filled him with surging hope, warm acceptance, calming certainty. And then, he knew without a doubt. He, Charles Graves, a man who didn't deserve it—

God loved, truly loved him.

God had heard. God had answered. God had forgiven.

Charles awakened to someone calling his name. He groaned. His entire body throbbed, his throat burned. Then it hit him.

Last night before stumbling into the closest bed, the sagging cot at *The Ledger,* he'd battled Ed Drummond, proposed marriage to Addie and spoken with God.

No ordinary evening.

The rest struck him full force, like an uppercut to his aching jaw. Addie had turned down his proposal. Was it too late to make up for causing her nothing but pain?

And if so, what would he do without her? No other woman measured up to Addie. The most amazing thing of all—*she* loved *him.*

A spark of understanding exploded in him. His pulse tripped and his heart raced in his chest. With every speck of his being, he grasped the truth. He loved her, too.

I'm in love with Addie.

"Charles?"

Clutching his ribs, Charles rose with a groan from the cot and staggered to the door. Roscoe Sullivan took one look at him and blanched. "Charles? You okay?"

"Yeah." Charles crumpled into his desk chair and sucked in his breath. That hurt. Everything hurt, as if he'd been run over by a wagon and three teams of horses. "What time is it?"

"Almost nine-thirty."

Addie would be awake, getting ready for church. He'd get cleaned up, then make amends. He started to rise. "I'm sorry I can't talk now, Roscoe."

"Wait!" His gaze took in Charles's face, the bruises on his neck. "Ed did that. Those are *his* fingerprints."

All the fear and anger Charles had stowed during Addie's narrow escape slammed into his lungs. "Yes. Your nephew broke into Addie's home and tried to kill her."

"I know." Roscoe dropped into a chair, his head drooping between his shoulders. His face looked haggard, as if he'd aged ten years. "Is Miss Crum all right?"

Charles pulled back from his anger, realizing Roscoe had also suffered. "Yes, just shook up. Ed splashed kerosene all over the shop. He planned to set it on fire after he'd…" Charles couldn't finish, couldn't bear to consider what would've happened if he hadn't gotten back.

"Thank God she wasn't harmed. I should have seen… what Ed had become. I should have known Frances couldn't be that clumsy." Roscoe's voice quavered and his eyes filled with tears. He swiped them away with the back of his hand and took a shaky breath. "I've been over at Doc's. Frances made it through the night, but she's got a lot of healing to do."

"I hope she makes it." Frances had shown a passel of courage and, thanks to her husband, had endured more pain than a human being should. "I can imagine how tough this is for you, Roscoe. I'm sorry."

"No, I'm the one who's sorry. If only I'd listened to you, somehow I could have stopped this madness." A faraway look came into Roscoe's eyes. His lip trembled.

"Ed was the cutest little tyke. I used to take him fishing. We'd sit on the bank along White River and he'd chatter like a magpie. I'd say, 'Little less talking and a little more fishing, boy.'" As he spoke, Roscoe mopped at his tears with his bandanna. "Eddie's death must've made him snap."

Roscoe stuffed his handkerchief into his pocket. "I came to tell you something else. Frances asked the committee to give custody of William and Emma to Miss Crum. The committee agreed." He gave a wan smile. "Those poor kids have been through enough. Staying with Miss Crum will give them stability. I figured you'd like to tell her."

Charles could well imagine the look of pure joy the news would put on Addie's face. Soon as he could get Roscoe out of here, he intended to put another look of joy on her face. That is, if she'd have him.

"I'll try to undo the damage I did to the paper and her reputation." Roscoe hauled himself to his feet. "I'm headed over to the jail to see Ed. I despise what he's done, but I'm all he has."

Charles walked Roscoe to the door. He clamped a hand on the older man's shoulder. "I'm sorry." The words sounded hollow, but he couldn't find better ones.

Roscoe left and Charles's gaze swept over the printing press, the narrow drawers of type and reams of newsprint. Because of his father, he'd come to this town, fulfilled his dream of ownership. How strange Adam Graves had done that for him after all those years of misery.

Stranger still, by making Addie a co-owner of the paper, Adam had put Charles and Addie together. Addie had been right. His father had reached out to him from the grave. And this time he had thought of someone besides himself.

Charles checked the clock. Nine forty-five. If he hoped to win Addie, he'd have to make sure she didn't doubt his love. She might even make him eat a little crow. He grinned. If so, he deserved a huge helping. And he knew just where he'd find her this bright Sunday morning.

He hadn't shaved, had fought and slept in his rumpled clothes, but he had to do this. Now.

He half ran, half stumbled the three blocks down Ninth Street and skidded to a stop outside the First Christian Church. Worshippers, shocked looks on their faces, parted like the Red Sea to let him pass. Snatches of conversation told him people had heard about last night.

A man Charles didn't know but recognized clapped him on the back. Another hollered, "Good work, Graves!" A third shook his hand. "I'll be taking the paper again, especially if you keep Miss Crum's column."

But he paid no attention. Instead he searched the crowd. Then, he spotted her at the top of the steps, talking to the pastor. Addie. A vision in a blue dress and hat—no birds on this one, he thought with a chuckle, just a simple rose festooned ribbon encircling the crown. Hands resting on Emma's and William's shoulders, her face radiated serenity. His heart lurched in his chest.

"Mr. Graves!" Emma yelled, catching sight of him.

He waved at her, searching for another welcome.

Addie's gaze traveled the assemblage, a puzzled expression on her face. He hurried closer, until he stood at the bottom of the steps. He held his breath, waiting…

and then her lips curved in a smile, filling him with a sense of rightness.

Oh, how he loved this woman. Her goodness, the hope she'd steadfastly clung to, her strength. He would spend his life trying to live up to her faith in him.

"Miss Adelaide Crum!" Charles called up to her, quieting the crowd. "I'd like the honor of attending church with you and Emma and William."

She extended a hand toward him but he held up his palm. "Before we go in, I have something to say."

Adelaide took in Charles's battered, smiling face and her insides went liquid with hope. Around her, puffy white clouds drifted across the sky, and a flash of red disappeared into a nearby evergreen. A gentle breeze tickled her nape as the cardinal added his song to the song in her heart.

Charles laid a palm on his chest. "I'm in love with you!" he shouted up at her.

Adelaide's heart leapt at the words she'd been waiting for all her life, the words she needed to hear from Charles.

"I want to share our dreams, bring up these children and grow old together." He released a shaking breath. "I've been able to forgive. I've asked God to forgive me. And though I have no idea why, He has! I'll be thanking Him this morning—in church—for His love and for yours, that is, if it's still available."

Tears sprang in Adelaide's eyes. At last, Charles realized God loved him. He wanted to worship in church. He loved her.

She wished for the words that would change her life, yet waited to see if the editor in him could string together words strong enough to rope her in. Not that it would take much, she decided with an inward grin.

"Oh, and one more thing." He paused. Her heart beat a hundred times in that moment. "Will you marry me?"

She folded her arms across her middle, a tease on her lips. "Not unless you ask me proper."

Charles took the steps two at a time. At her feet, he went down on one knee, raising an arm in a beseeching manner, triggering a few chuckles from the men and dreamy sighs from the ladies.

Adelaide had to hold herself tight to keep from throwing her arms around his neck. Waiting, every moment slowed to a crawl.

"Adelaide Crum, will you do me the great honor of becoming my wife?"

"Yes!" she cried, the word bursting from her lips. "Yes, Charles, I'll marry you!"

A cheer rose up from the congregation and Emma danced around Adelaide's skirts as the reality sank in—she and Charles would spend the rest of their lives together. After years of loneliness, God had given her the desires of her heart.

When the hubbub subsided, Charles's gaze sought the children's. "Emma, William, is it all right with you?"

At Adelaide's side, William's face lit up like a Roman candle. Emma threw her arms around Charles's neck and hugged him with all her might, until she squeaked.

Over the little girl's head, Charles gaze sought Adelaide's with an intensity that promised he'd be there today, tomorrow and always, that they'd be a family, a real family. Slowly, he rose, scooping up Emma, never taking his eyes off Adelaide.

He pulled William close, then took her hand, his

grip firm, and faced the minister. "I've been away a long time, Pastor. Do you suppose God will remember my name?"

Pastor Foley smiled, his hazel eyes crinkling. "Not only your name, but the exact number of hairs on your head."

Charles nodded. "He's probably been tempted plenty of times to pull out a hank."

The pastor chuckled. "Good thing God doesn't work that way or we'd all be bald."

Smiling, Charles tugged Addie close. "It looks like we're going to need your services."

Pastor Foley gave an approving nod. "Whenever you say."

"I hear July twenty-fifth is a special woman's birthday."

"How did you know?" Adelaide asked.

"I told him!" Laura threw her arms around Adelaide and then lowered her voice. "Thank God you're both all right! My knees ache from praying!"

Pastor Foley pulled out his pocket watch, and flipped it open. "Well, I'd better get this service underway." He smiled. "See you inside."

Parishioners flowed past, heading into the church, stopping long enough to give them congratulations. The men slapped Charles on the back and the women hugged Adelaide, some with tears welling in their eyes.

Mr. Paul came up beside them, the tufts of hair on his head swaying in the breeze. "With a strong woman like Miss Crum, you're going to have your hands full, Graves."

"I wouldn't have it any other way."

"A woman like that keeps a man from making some

serious mistakes." His gaze met Adelaide's. "Like the ones I've made. I'm sorry, Miss Crum."

This whole town needed a lesson in forgiveness, starting here. Adelaide laid a hand on his arm. "You're forgiven," she said then watched him enter the building.

Everyone in town, well, at least, the membership of the First Christian Church, appeared happy for them.

Roscoe Sullivan climbed the steps last, slowly, as if he didn't have the strength to go on. He stopped before Adelaide, his gaze downcast. "I'm sorry for the trouble I caused you."

Mr. Sullivan had tried to turn the town against her, but if she couldn't forgive him, would she be any different than her mother? He had been taken in by his nephew, as had most of the town. Adelaide gave him a smile. "I accept your apology and hope you'll visit William and Emma. They could use a grandfather."

For a moment Roscoe stood speechless. "I—I'm grateful for your clemency."

"It took me a while to learn to forgive, Mr. Sullivan," Adelaide admitted, glancing in the direction of the cemetery. "But forgiving feels awfully good."

As the bell tolled, announcing the start of the service, everyone had entered the church. "Alone at last," Charles said, bending down and giving her a tender kiss. "Despite the bird in your hat, I love you, Adelaide Crum."

Adelaide gave him a playful punch on the arm. "Despite the mess on your desk, I love you, Charles Graves."

The first hymn drowned out their laughter.

Charles's expression grew serious and he hauled her to him. "I love you," he said, his voice husky with emotion.

She'd never tire of hearing those words from his lips.

She would hear his voice today, tomorrow and all the tomorrows after that, confident she had found the person God intended for her, for them both.

"You know, Charles, it's like my heart was an orphan...and it's found a home. In you."

"Oh, Addie, I'm going to spend the rest of my life showing you how wonderful home can be."

His words were a promise for all the days to come.

* * * * *

*Widowed father Boothe Powers needs a wife in order
to retain custody of his son. Emma Spencer was sure
to see the practicality of such an arrangement.
Emma's heart yearns for marriage and children.
But she has her own secret anguish…*

**Read on for a sneak preview of
The Path to Her Heart by Linda Ford**

"We don't even like each other. Why would you want to
marry me?" At the untruthfulness of her words, heat left a
spot on Emma's cheeks. She'd tried to tell herself otherwise,
but she liked Boothe. Might even admit she'd grown slightly
fond of him. Okay. Truth time. She might even be a little
attracted to him. Had been since her first glimpse.

"I like you just fine."

"I'm a nurse. Have you forgotten?"

He hesitated. "Well, as nurses go, you seem to be a good
one."

She snorted in a most unladylike fashion. "I'm thrilled
to hear that."

"Surely we could work around that."

"I think not. Can you imagine how we'd disagree if I
thought one of us or—" Her cheeks burned. She'd been
about to say *one of our children*, but she couldn't say it
aloud. "If I thought someone needed medical attention?"

"I'm desperate."

"Well, thanks. I guess." Just what she'd always dreamed
of—the last pick of someone who was desperate.

"Wait. Listen to what I have to say." He pulled a battered envelope from his back pocket.

Nothing he said would change the fact they were as unsuited for each other as cat and mouse, yet she hesitated, wanting—hoping—for something to persuade her otherwise.

He waved her toward a pew and she cautiously took a seat. "This is a letter from a lawyer back in Lincoln informing me that my brother-in-law and his wife intend to adopt Jessie."

She gasped. "How can that be?"

He looked bleak. "I needed help after Alyse died and Vera offered. Only then she wanted to keep Jessie."

Emma pressed her palm to his shoulder. "Surely they don't have a chance?"

He slowly brought his gaze toward her. At the look of despair in his eyes, her throat pinched closed.

"I went to see the lawyer in town and he says the courts favor people who have money and their own home, but especially both a father and mother. My best chance is to get married."

She settled back, affronted to be no more than a means to an end, and yet, would her dreams and hopes never leave her alone? "And I was the only person you could think of?"

He shrugged. "You're fond of Jessie."

A burning mix of sympathy and annoyance shot through her. She withdrew her hand from his shoulder even though she ached to comfort him. She sat up straight, folded her hands together in her lap and forced the words from her mouth. "Yes, I'm fond of Jessie but I can't marry—not you or anyone."

Don't miss
The Parson's Christmas Gift & The Path to Her Heart
by Kerri Mountain and Linda Ford,
available December 2018.

www.LoveInspired.com

LIHEXP00672

SPECIAL EXCERPT FROM

Love Inspired®

*With her family in danger of being separated,
could marriage to a newcomer in town
keep them together for the holidays?*

Read on for a sneak preview of
An Amish Wife for Christmas *by Patricia Davids,
available in November 2018 from Love Inspired!*

"I've got trouble, Clarabelle."

The cow didn't answer her. Bethany pitched a forkful of hay to the family's placid brown-and-white Guernsey. "The bishop has decided to send Ivan to Bird-in-Hand to live with Onkel Harvey. It's not right. It's not fair. I can't bear the idea of sending my little brother away. We belong together."

Clarabelle munched a mouthful of hay as she regarded Bethany with soulful deep brown eyes.

"Advice is what I need, Clarabelle. The bishop said Ivan could stay if I had a husband. Someone to discipline and guide the boy. Any idea where I can get a husband before Christmas?"

"I doubt your cow has the answers you seek, but if she does I have a few questions for her about my own problems," a man said.

Bethany spun around. A stranger stood in the open barn door. He wore a black Amish hat pulled low on his forehead and a dark blue woolen coat with the collar turned up against the cold.

The mirth sparkling in his eyes sent a flush of heat to her cheeks. How humiliating. To be caught talking to a cow about matrimonial prospects made her look ridiculous.

She struggled to hide her embarrassment. "It's rude to eavesdrop on a private conversation."

"I'm not sure talking to a cow qualifies as a private conversation, but I am sorry to intrude."

He didn't look sorry. He looked like he was struggling not to laugh at her.

"I'm Michael Shetler."

She considered not giving him her name. The less he knew to repeat the better.

"I am Bethany Martin," she admitted, hoping she wasn't making a mistake.

"Nice to meet you, Bethany. Once I've had a rest I'll step outside if you want to finish your private conversation." He winked. One corner of his mouth twitched, revealing a dimple in his cheek.

"I'm glad I could supply you with some amusement today."

"It's been a long time since I've had something to smile about."

Don't miss
An Amish Wife for Christmas *by Patricia Davids,*
available November 2018 wherever
Love Inspired® *books and ebooks are sold.*

www.LoveInspired.com